THE INDIAN STOOD
NAKED IN THE SUNLIGHT

The blond girl lay on the rocks below, as bare as he.

He stepped forward, stood looking down at her. He towered above her. Her head fell back, her eyes met his, and she trembled. His long arm encircled her waist and he pulled her to him in a slow, burning kiss that made her bare knees buckle, her body melt against his.

"Tonatiuh," she murmured breathlessly as his blazing eyes touched her breasts with such fire she could feel the heat.

"Amy, you're beautiful," he said. She felt a stirring low in her belly, the feeling that his hands as well as his eyes were caressing her, touching her where she'd never been touched before.

Also by Nan Ryan from Dell:

SAVAGE HEAT

CLOUDCASTLE

SILKEN BONDAGE

SUN GOD

NAN RYAN

A DELL BOOK

For
Maggie Lichota
My patient and professional editor

Why are we always saying good-bye
to somebody we like . . .

James Jones
From Here to Eternity

Published by
Dell Publishing
a division of
Bantam Doubleday Dell Publishing Group, Inc.
666 Fifth Avenue
New York, New York 10103

ISBN: 0-440-20603-0

Printed in the United States of America

Published simultaneously in Canada

October 1990

10 9 8 7 6 5 4 3 2 1

OPM

PART ONE

1

The Indian stood naked in the sunlight.

His name was Tonatiuh—Sun God in the language of his mother's people, the imperial Aztecs. The name fit him. Standing there on the rocky banks of the Puesta del Sol River, his tall, wet body glistening in the bright desert sunshine, Tonatiuh appeared to be a young god.

Around his neck, a heavy gold chain supported a gold medallion, his only adornment. The exquisite Sun Stone, resting on his smooth bronzed chest, glittered and flashed with the slightest movement of his lithe body.

Tonatiuh's bronzed face was as smooth and beautiful and innocent as a young child's. His luminous black eyes were warm and friendly, his nose straight, the curving nostrils suggesting a passionate nature. His lips, wide and perfectly formed, were the sensuous lips of his Castilian father, Don Ramon Rafael Quintano.

Tonatiuh threw back his head and shook his heavy raven hair, feeling the rivulets of water slide down his backbone and over his buttocks.

Rubbing his long, black eyelashes that clung damply together, he dropped agilely to the rocks, stretched out, and allowed the sun to dry the beads of moisture from his chest and belly and long legs. A slim arm bent and draped across his closed eyes, Tonatiuh lay perfectly still, loving the feel of the hot sun touching his bare body.

He smiled with lazy contentment. This particular secluded bend in the Puesta del Sol was to him a jealously guarded haven. No one else knew of it. It was his own secret sanctuary. A place he had shown no one, would show no one. Here the river meandered down a sloping waterfall, the cascade spilling into a freeform lagoonlike pool. And, miraculously, from the barren rocky banks sprang lush greenery to shade the splashing falls and the clear water below. And, high above, where he now lay, a huge jutting rock overhang was the perfect place to meditate quietly or to doze in the burning Texas sun.

On this hot June morning, young Tonatiuh had no time for meditation or dozing. He tilted his forearm back from his eyes and glanced up at the glaring sun. It would soon be directly overhead. And, when it had reached its zenith, he was to be waiting, with the Sullivans' fanciest carriage, at Orilla's private railroad spur for the arrival of the noon train from San Antonio.

Amy Sullivan, the *patrón*'s only daughter, would be on that westbound train. She was returning home today after five years away in New Orleans at some fancy girl's finishing school. The homecoming was all her father and his father and the servants and the hands had talked of for weeks. A big celebration party was planned for this evening, and already stay-over visitors filled the many guest rooms of Orilla's sprawling hacienda.

The blistering sun suddenly went behind a cloud. A dark shadow fell across the smooth boulder where Tonatiuh lay. He rolled to a sitting position. His black eyes turned somber as a fragment of a forgotten dream suddenly came back.

She had appeared to him again. Her long, black hair falling down her back, her strange, ceremonial robes flowing about her slender body. She had stood at the foot of his bed and shown him a set of numbers.

A five and three sixes: 5,6,6,6. No. No, it was 6,6,5,6. Nothing more. Just those numbers. Then she had disappeared with the dream.

A hawk circled overhead in the cloud-darkened sky. Tonatiuh felt a chill skip up his naked spine. Involuntarily he shuddered, suddenly feeling uneasy.

The hawk winged away. The cloud drifted past. The blazing sun came out again to warm Tonatiuh's troubled soul as well as his chilled body. The dream and the numbers had flown with the hawk, and the corners of Tonatiuh's black eyes crinkled with a smile.

He draped his forearms atop his bent knees as his thoughts returned to Amy Sullivan. He recalled a plain-looking child—skinny, frecklefaced, and blond. Feet always bare and dirty, knees and elbows constantly skinned.

Little Amy. She was the only one who called him Tonatiuh. Even his father called him Luiz. Walter Sullivan, the *patrón,* and all the ranch-

hands called him Luiz. The servants called him
Luiz, and even the people in the village.

He was Luiz Quintano to everyone except the
beautiful Aztec princess who had named him
Tonatiuh. And to little Amy.

Tonatiuh suddenly shot to his feet. He went up
on his toes, stood poised for a minute, then came
back down on his heels. He clasped his hands behind his head, thrust his pelvis forward, expanded
his chest, and sucked in his belly. He inhaled
deeply of the dry, desert air, his face lifted to that
fiery God for whom he had been named.

Sighing, he bent and picked up the tiny scrap of
well-tanned, supple leather that served as a
breechcloth. When his groin was covered and the
thong tied securely atop his right hip bone, Tonatiuh gave a low, soft whistle and his favorite stallion came prancing toward him.

On a slow-moving train steadily snaking its way
west across the endless emptiness of southwest
Texas, a beautiful young girl was smiling. Unbothered by the heat and the dust and the mile
after mile of monotonous scenery, Amy Sullivan
was aglow with excitement.

Five years!

Five long years since she had seen this magnificent land of flowering cactus and swirling dust
storms and relentless heat and blazing sun and
starry nights. Leaning up to the train's open window, Amy inhaled deeply, catching the familiar
scent of the creosote bushes.

She yipped with joy when a couple of rugged
vaqueros, laughing and shouting in Spanish, galloped alongside the train, twirling lariats high

over their heads, making as if they would lasso the steam-driven locomotive.

Amy joyfully swept her new straw bonnet off her head and waved it wildly to the laughing cowboys. She felt her heart race with exhilaration when they reined in close enough for her to make out the distinctive SBARQ brand on the rumps of their horses.

Orilla vaqueros!

She called to the riders. "It's me! Amy. Amy Sullivan. I've come home!"

The expert horsemen yanked up on their reins, making their mounts rear their forelegs high in the air as they swept the sombreros from their dark heads in a welcoming salute. Amy responded to their gallantry by clapping and blowing kisses and watching until the pair finally pulled up, wheeled about, and turned back.

Still smiling, Amy sighed contentedly and leaned back. Already the train was traveling across Orilla land! She was back on the ranch. Within the hour she would be home. Would it have changed much? No, she happily answered herself. Her big, good-hearted daddy would still spoil her unmercifully. And her two older brothers would still resent it. And Don Ramon Quintano would still tell exciting stories of the Aztec princess who had been his wife. And his son, Tonatiuh, would ignore her. Just as always.

Amy continued to smile. She wouldn't mind. She had been a bit of a brat before she'd gone to New Orleans, and she couldn't blame Tonatiuh for not wanting her tagging after him constantly. What twelve-year-old boy would want an eleven-year-old girl trailing him?

Amy tried to imagine how Tonatiuh would look at seventeen. It had been so long since she had seen him. There were times when she could not recall his face. Would she recognize him? Would he recognize her?

The slackening train made Amy sit up straight. It was slowing and she knew that the moment had finally come. In seconds she would be stepping out onto the platform to be greeted by her daddy. She was already up out of her seat when the sound of the brakes screeching to a halt made her put her hands over her ears. The train stopped with such a sudden jolt, she pitched forward against the empty seat.

Her heart thundering, Amy stepped out into the aisle and hurried forward, so anxious she nervously sprang up and down in place while the conductor threw open the train door. A big smiling porter jumped out and placed a small wooden stoop down for Amy to step on.

Taking her hand, the porter announced needlessly, "Orilla, Miss Sullivan. You is home."

Amy never answered. She couldn't.

While the grinning porter piled valises and trunks and hatboxes on the wooden platform behind her, Amy Sullivan stood in the hot Texas sunlight on Orilla's private railroad spur staring at the silent man who had come alone to meet her.

He was tall and slim and awesomely handsome. He wore a pair of snug, buff-hued trousers that clung to his lean flanks and long legs. A collarless pullover shirt of pale-yellow chambray, open at the throat, stretched across wide shoulders. He held a dark sombrero in his hands before him, his tanned fingers loosely clutching the wide brim.

His blue-black hair gleamed in the noonday sunlight and his eyes, almost as black as his hair, held a warm light that was frighteningly compelling.

Tonatiuh.

Remaining totally motionless, Luiz Quintano stared with unblinking intensity. He had expected a child, but a very grown-up young woman stood before him. Tall and slender and excitingly beautiful. Beneath a small hat of rose straw, gleaming golden hair was arranged in an attractive mass of silky ringlets that framed her lovely oval face. Her eyes were as blue as the clear Texas skies and her mouth, full and moist, held a hint of restrained humor at the corners. Her lissome body was pleasingly draped in a stylish suit of rose linen, its narrow lapels lying across a surprisingly full bosom.

Amy.

The train chugged away and left them.

And still the pair stood as they were, staring at each other, the very air around them crackling with a strange, unexplained tension.

It was Amy who finally broke the spell.

"Will you take me home, Tonatiuh?" she said, and smiled prettily at him.

He took a step toward her. His voice was low and soft when he answered, "Only if that's where you want to go."

Flustered, Amy nodded.

He came even closer, so close she could see the powerful pulse throbbing in his smooth bronzed throat and the hot light in his beautiful black eyes. He smiled then, an endearing, boyish smile.

And he said, "Welcome home, Amy. We've missed you."

2

―――
―――

"I hope," said Luiz, putting his hands to Amy's slender waist and carefully lifting her up onto the front seat of gleaming black landau, "you're not disappointed that the *patrón* did not come to meet you." He climbed up beside her and turned to look directly into her eyes.

"Do I look disappointed?" Amy said boldly, feeling as if her cheeks were afire.

Luiz's dark eyes dilated. He swallowed hard. "You do not. You look . . . you look . . ." He stopped speaking, tore his eyes from hers, and hastily unwrapped the long leather reins from around the brake handle.

She touched his shoulder. "Go on. How do I look? Tell me."

"Very beautiful," he said, not looking at her, and Amy could have sworn his handsome olive face was suffused with high color.

Tingling with a wonderful excitement that had little to do with being home, Amy smiled and managed a sweet, sincere thank you. Luiz spoke softly to the matched bays and the carriage rolled away, its wheels churning up fine dust to hang suspended in the still, dry air.

Amy, clasping her hands in her lap, stole covert

glances at the classic male profile beneath the dark sombrero. As she studied the heavily lashed eyes, the high slanting cheekbones, the full, perfectly shaped lips, she found herself wondering jealously if there was already a woman in Tonatiuh's life. Or perhaps women.

"There's a homecoming fiesta for you tonight," Luiz said, turning to catch her frowning. "What is wrong?" he asked.

Amy shook her head. "Nothing. Not a thing. You will be at my party, won't you?"

"If you want me there," Luiz said, and then he smiled at her. A flashing, sensual smile that managed to communicate fully the message that he knew very well she wanted him to be there. And that he wanted to be there just as badly.

"I want you," Amy said, purposely pausing, then adding, with an appealing coy smile of her own, "at my party."

And she thrilled at the flash of dark fire that leapt into his ebony eyes.

His blue eyes aglow, his blond head lowered, a man sat behind a large pine desk in the upstairs library of Orilla's thick-walled, salmon-hued adobe hacienda. Before him, a worn brown leather journal was open, and stacks of cash were scattered around on the desk's smooth surface. The man's forefinger was skimming down long columns of black figures filling the leather journal's white pages. The neat rows of sums brought a pleased smile to the blond man's wide lips.

Across the spacious room, lounging lazily on a long rawhide couch, was another blond man, slightly younger and larger. A half-full tumbler of

Kentucky bourbon in his hand, booted feet stretched out before him, he too was smiling.

The Sullivan brothers, Baron behind the desk, Lucas on the couch, were taking full advantage of their sister's homecoming. Amy's long-awaited return had caused quite a stir at Orilla. The flurry of activity suited the brothers fine. With so many distinguished guests arriving at the ranch, everyone in residence was pressed into service. From the youngest Mexican boys who saw to the carriages and horses to the old retired black house cook whose barbecue was famous across Texas, everyone at Orilla was busy.

Walter, the elder Sullivan, and Don Ramon Quintano, joint owners of Orilla, had graciously hosted an early-afternoon riding party of visiting dignitaries, an illustrious group that included the governor of Texas and the governor of the state of Chihuahua. The all-male contingent was—at this very hour—inspecting the huge Orilla spread with its large herds of cattle and horses.

Walter Sullivan had strongly suggested that his grown sons go along; Baron had declined for them both. Prior commitments, he had told his father without apology. Some other time, Dad.

Baron had hardly waited until the last mounted rider passed beneath Orillas' tall white ranch gates before he turned, grinned at his younger brother, and said, "How about it, Lucas? Ready to go up and have a look at the stingy old bastard's bank books?"

"What are we waiting for?" said Lucas, picking up a glass and a stoppered decanter of whiskey.

As the visiting gentlemen guests galloped across the desert rangelands, and their ladies rested in cool, dim Orilla guest rooms, and the servants cleaned and cooked and decorated for the evening's party, Baron sat behind his father's desk and counted the stacks of cash and pored over the accounting books he had removed from the wall safe behind the life-sized portrait of his long-dead mother.

"Jesus, Lucas, we're gonna be a couple of rich sons a bitches one of these days." Baron's blue eyes twinkled with joy as he opened bankbooks and saw huge accounts in El Paso del Norte, San Antonio, Pecos, and in the village's little bank, the Ranchers Bank of Sundown, Texas.

Nodding, Lucas, took a long pull of whiskey. "How much, Baron? How much we gonna be worth?"

"Millions," said his brother. "If Don Ramon is still alive when Dad dies, we'll offer him some cash, buy him out."

Lucas swallowed another drink of whiskey. "I don't know. That little Spaniard is one smart fellow. I'm not so sure. . . ."

"Well, I am," Baron cut him off. "When the time comes, I'll make it very clear to the *don* that he and that pretty-boy Indian son of his are no longer welcome on Orilla. By the time I'm through explaining it, he'll be more than willing to take Luiz and some cash and disappear."

Lucas grinned, then asked, "Think we'll be able to get our hands on Amy's share?"

Baron rose from the chair. He too was grinning. "I've already started working on that."

"You have? How? She's still just a kid. You can't—"

"She's a grown woman and it's time she started

thinking about marriage." Baron gathered up the cash, the account journals, and the bankbooks and carried them to the wall safe. Over his shoulder he said, "And I've got the perfect husband in mind."

Lucas chuckled loudly. He knew Baron was talking about their close friend, Tyler Parnell. Tyler liked a good time, same as they did, and the three of them had spent many a rip-roaring night together at the saloons and bordellos on both sides of the border.

"It'd sure be fun to have old Tyler for a brother-in-law. Only trouble is, he don't have no money or land or nothing."

"Exactly," said Baron, giving the safe's combination a spin with his forefinger, replacing his mother's portrait, and turning to face his brother. "The prospect of a life of ease here on Orilla should make Tyler Parnell perfectly willing to take our sister for his blushing bride."

"Well, I guess he might, but how are we gonna make Amy say yes to him?"

Baron shrugged. "Women seem to find Tyler attractive. I've invited him here tonight in hopes he and Amy will discover each other."

Lucas chuckled. "Amy'll have to be a derned sight prettier than when she left Texas or there ain't gonna be no man discover her."

"That's true. But there'll be plenty of men who'd like to get their hands on Orilla," Baron reminded him.

"Lord, I hadn't thought of that. Somebody might up and marry our homely little sister just to get part of our ranch."

"Bull's eye, brother." Baron circled the desk and leaned back against its edge. "Tyler Parnell has to marry Amy. I can easily control him. Amy will naturally sign her land over to her new husband, and I step in and relieve him of it. Long as Tyler's got enough money for a drink of whiskey and a pretty Mexican gal, he'll be content."

"Me and him both," Lucas said, and laughed.

Baron simply smiled.

His hat pulled low, his blue eyes squinting against the glare of invasive sunlight, Walter Sullivan sat his favorite piebald gelding on an elevated spit of land. Gesturing with a sunburned hand, he proudly pointed out to his mounted guests the huge herd of longhorns grazing on the tobosa grass-covered flats below.

Walter Sullivan and his piebald gelding were as rugged as the rough land. Sullivan's broad, craggy face with its permanent squint lines at the corners of the eyes, deeply furrowed brow, sun-darkened cheeks, and heavily cut chin resembled the stark desert topography. An aging, solid-hewn, tough, and moral man, Sullivan possessed a rustic grace, just like the untamed land.

The big piebald gelding Sullivan sat astride was cut from the same resilient cloth as his master. A deep-chested, fleet-footed animal, the gelding was brave, intelligent, and possessed amazing stamina. His eight-year-old body showed the marks of his harsh environment, just as his master's. The SBARQ brand on his rump was not the only badge the gelding proudly wore. Half his right ear had been lost to a striking panther. A deep, long-healed wound on his withers was gratis a renegade Apache's flaming arrow. His fetlocks were badly scarred from countless punctures of the tall, spined leaves of the lechuguilla, a cactus found only in the harsh Chihuahuan desert.

Man and horse were well suited to the region. Both loved it, both had been raised on it, both would die here.

And both took what life handed out with no complaint.

Orilla's co-owner, the still-handsome, silver-haired Don Ramon Rafael Quintano, was just as resilient, just as uncomplaining as his Texas partner. A soft-spoken, slow-to-anger man, the *don* had worked alongside Sullivan under many punishing Texas suns, but at fifty he looked remarkably much as he had at age thirty when he was the dashing young grandee who had won the heart of an exotic sixteen-year-old Aztec princess. His fair Castilian face was unlined and smooth, his body slender and wiry, his manner one of calm assurance.

The *don* loved Orilla. There was, in fact, only one thing on earth he loved more. His only son, Luiz. He was extremely proud of the strong and beautiful young man who was intelligent and respectful and industrious. The *don* was ever grateful that when his days on earth were done, the legacy of the Orilla would pass to his son.

Each time Don Ramon sat his blood bay stallion and quietly looked out over the far-reaching expanse of rangelands from beneath his big sombrero, his Spanish heart swelled with pride. Half of everything, as far as the eye could see and well beyond, belonged to him. And to his son. And his son's son.

* * *

When the landau reached the tall white ranch gates of Orilla, Amy asked Luiz to pull up for just one moment.

The enchanted Indian gladly complied. He smiled indulgently when, as soon as the carriage had halted, Amy stood up, plucked off her straw bonnet, and threw her arms out in a wide encompassing gesture. She tipped her blond head back and looked up at the high beamed archway above.

Hanging suspended from the sturdy crossbar—and gleaming brilliantly in the sunshine—two-foot-tall, hammered silver letters spelled Orilla.

Amy, laughing happily, reached up as if to touch the letters. Her raised fingertips were a good eight to ten feet beneath them, even standing as she was in the landau.

"You are going to fall and get hurt, Amy," said Luiz, and reached up to put a steadying hand to her waist.

Amy turned within his firm grasp, lowered her eyes, and smiled down at him. "No, I won't. You won't let me." Slowly she eased back down to the carriage seat, her hands atop his, her expression one of complete trust. "You'd never allow me to get hurt." She gazed into his fathomless black eyes. "Would you, Tonatiuh?"

"Never," he said with fierce determination. His hands tightened possessively on her waist. The sudden, surprising strength in the lean, grasping fingers caused Amy to gasp with startled pleasure. And she experienced a heady sensation of unnamed delight when Luiz, still clinging forcefully to her waist, urged her closer, so close his face was mere inches from her own.

His taut features softened. He smiled and said softly, "Never, Amy."

3

Atop a natural rise, at the end of a long drive lined with Texas sabel palms sat Orilla's sprawling hacienda, its leaded-glass windows winking like precious jewels in the afternoon sunlight. Completed in the summer of 1841, the imposing mansion with its eighteen-inch-thick salmon colored adobe walls, red-tiled roof, and polished brick floors was the finest dwelling for a hundred miles in any direction.

Built in the shape of a giant horseshoe, the house was designed to ensure the total privacy of two separate families. And so it was that in the hacienda's main section, there was not one but two spacious sitting rooms, or *salas,* and two long dining halls.

Identical wings, stretching back toward the stables and outbuildings, boasted gigantic master suites as well as ten guest bedrooms each. The Sullivans occupied the west wing of the southern-facing hacienda, the Quintanos the east.

Every major room on the lower floor, including an enormous oak-floored ballroom, opened onto a beautiful courtyard where the natural plants of the high desert were lovingly nurtured by brown-skinned gardeners. Myriad cactuses bloomed profusely almost year round, brightening the days with their vivid splashes of purple and yellow and red. And sweetening the warm, romantic nights with their subtle, intoxicating bouquet. Settees of painted iron lace were scattered in among the yucca, esperanza, and tall century plants.

An even dozen servants cared for the house and gardens. Seventy-five cowboys and vaqueros worked the big spread, living year-round on the ranch. Huge whitewashed barns stabled a hundred horses and another four hundred grazed the various horse pastures of Orilla. Great herds of longhorns—thirty-two thousand at last tally—foraged the chino and tobosa grasses of the flats and the blue stem and side-oats gamma of the distant mountain slopes.

Approaching the enormous adobe structure rising from the barren, treeless land, Amy was struck anew by just how much she had missed Texas and Orilla. Silently vowing that she would never again leave, she took a moment to commit everything to memory, passionately certain that today was one of the most important days of her entire life.

She wanted to remember it all, every tiny detail. The heat of the sun on her face. The sight of the huge hacienda framed by the clear blue sky. The expression in Tonatiuh's jet eyes when she stepped off the train. The strength of his hands on her waist.

What was the date? The fifth . . . no, no. The sixth . . . the sixth day of June. June the sixth, 1856.

Five-year-old Manuel Ortega, standing watch on the shaded front patio, spotted the landau coming up the drive. The excited son of Orilla's head cook flew inside shouting, *"Madre, madre*, the *señorita* is here! She is here!"

Everyone dropped what he was doing to rush outdoors. Baron and Lucas Sullivan, lolling idly in the downstairs sitting room, looked at each other, rose, and unhurriedly made their way to the stone patio. The landau's wheels crunched to a stop on the circular graveled drive. Luiz quickly jumped down, tossed the reins to a waiting stable boy, and raced around to lift Amy from the carriage.

When he set her on her feet, she flashed him a broad smile, grabbed his hand, and excitedly drew him along with her into the yard and up the front walk.

When the pair stepped onto the shaded patio, Amy dropped Luiz's hand. He stopped, came no farther. Smiling, he stood there at the edge of the stone porch, watching while she ran to her brothers. The servants, beaming and chattering in rapid Spanish, stood a respectful distance away while the Sullivan brothers greeted their sister.

"It's so wonderful to be home!" Amy exclaimed, giving Baron's cheek a quick kiss, then turning to Lucas. "Did you two miss me?"

"Little Amy?" Lucas was incredulous. "That really you?"

Hardly believing his eyes, Baron Sullivan purposely hid his surprise. "Of course it's our own little Amy," he said, smiling easily. "She hasn't changed all that much." Looking over Amy's head at the silent Indian youth, he gestured dismissively. "That's all for now, Luiz. Pedrico and Armond can see to the luggage. You must have something to do."

Luiz nodded, annoyed that he had been so rudely excused. He was not surprised. He had never been a friend of the Sullivan brothers. They refused to recognize him as an equal, delighted in acting as if he were one of the servants. But they treated him this way only when the *patrón* and his father were absent.

As he started backing away, Amy whirled about, hurried to him, and touched his forearm, saying softly "Until tonight?"

"Yes. Tonight." With eyes only for Amy, Luiz Quintano did not notice the look of hatred that came into Baron Sullivan's frosty blue eyes.

She felt radiant.

Her gown was white lace. A wide ruffle around the low-cut neckline displayed creamy shoulders, a smooth slender back, and the swell of her high, full bosom. A shimmering sash of pale-pink taffeta emphasized her small waist, its streamers flowing to the floor. Her full skirts were a series of wide, lacy ruffles, held out by a stiff horsehair petticoat. Her dancing slippers were of soft white kid, her stockings sheer white silk. Her golden hair was parted in the middle, pulled back on one side and secured with a dainty pearl clip. A vivid pink blossom was tucked behind her small left ear.

She was alone in her bedroom.

Magdelena and Rosa had helped her dress and then graciously departed, declaring repeatedly that she was *muy bonita*. She hoped it was so. She wanted to be very pretty on this special night. She wanted Tonatiuh to fully realize that she was no longer a child. She was a woman.

A knock on her bedroom door made Amy forget she was a woman.

"Daddy!" she shouted excitedly, and flew across the room to throw open the door.

Walter Sullivan, dressed in his finest, stood in the hallway gaping down at the daughter he'd not seen in five years. The big man looked dazed. He stared at Amy as if she were a stranger.

"Daddy, Daddy," Amy cried joyfully, and threw her arms around his neck. "I missed you so much!"

His big, work-roughened hands slowly came up and clasped her waist lightly as if she were a china doll and might easily break. But his astonished blue eyes closed with pleasure when the affectionate young woman rained kisses over his sun-wrinkled cheek.

"Sweetheart," he managed at last, setting her gently back. "I never dreamed . . . you're so . . . my God, Amy, you're all grown up."

"Yes! Isn't it wonderful?" She took one of his hands in both of hers and tugged him inside. "Spend a few minutes with me, Daddy, before we go downstairs?" Her luminous blue eyes held an almost pleading expression.

"Why sure, honey. Sure," he said, still shaking his graying head in wonder. Amy guided the aging rancher directly to the peach velvet chaise, urged him to sit, and quickly dropped to a low footstool in front of him. For the next ten minutes, while the downstairs rooms filled with party guests and music played by a mariachi band wafted up to them, father and daughter got reacquainted.

Walter Sullivan was sorry he hadn't been there

to meet her train. His role as host to the visiting
guests had made it impossible. She understood
fully, she assured him. He inquired as to the
health of his sister, Amy's Aunt Meg. Amy told
him that Aunt Meg was fine, but that she had wept
sorrowfully when Amy had kissed her good-bye.

Amy told her daddy of her friends at the finishing school, of the subjects she had studied, of all
the sights she had seen in New Orleans.

Finally, smiling, her father had to raise a big
hand and break into her excited revelations, re-
minding Amy that they had guests waiting downstairs and that the party was for her.

Up she shot from the foot stool. "Yes! How do I
look? Do I look all right?

The big rancher rose and took her hand. "So
pretty it scares your old daddy." He kissed her
forehead and ushered her out of the room.

Amy swept into the crowded ballroom on his
arm at shortly after nine, feeling confident and
excited.

She was vaguely aware of the turning of heads
and the heightened whispering that their entrance caused. While she smiled and nodded and
graciously accepted welcome-homes and compliments, her anxious eyes flicked over the crowd.

It was not until her father was turning her about
on the polished dance floor that she spotted him.

He stood alone and apart, at the back of the
ballroom by one of two tall carved doors thrown
open to the courtyard. He wore a formal charro
suit of midnight black and a shirt of fine white silk.
At his throat was a carefully tied scarf of flaming
crimson, the daring splash of color picked up by
the red blossom in his lapel. His jet-black hair was

neatly brushed back off his high forehead and his ebony eyes glittered in the candlelight from the wall sconce above his left shoulder.

Those glittering black eyes were locked on her.

". . . and couldn't believe my eyes," said Walter Sullivan, speaking to his distracted daughter.

With difficulty, Amy tore her gaze from Luiz. "I'm sorry, Daddy. What did you say?"

Walter Sullivan smiled down at her. "Honey, I was just saying that I still can't get over the change in you. When I knocked on your door expecting to see my little Amy, and found you there instead, it was just about too much for this old heart."

"Excuse me, Dad." Lucas Sullivan, already tipsy at this early hour, stood smiling at them. Beside him was a tall, richly dressed, broad-shouldered man with casually combed brown hair, twinkling hazel eyes, and heavy lips that were widening into a smile. "Amy, I'd like you to meet Tyler Parnell." He clamped a hand on Tyler's back. "Ty, my lovely sister, Miss Amy Sullivan."

"May I?" said Tyler Parnell, and not waiting for a reply, deftly took Amy in his arms and danced her away.

Walter Sullivan turned angry eyes on his younger son. "I don't want that man around Amy, do you understand me?"

"Why not, Dad? Tyler Parnell is one of the few eligible bachelors in Sundown."

Walter Sullivan snorted. "Parnell is a worthless lazy drunk and not fit to be in the same room with my only daughter!" Irritably he glanced around. "And where's Baron? It doesn't look right for my son to be late like this."

Lucas grinned. "I expect him down any minute. He told me there was something he had to take care of, Dad."

Walter Sullivan's blue eyes snapped with annoyance. "You sure he didn't say he had a woman he had to take care of?" Scowling, he turned and made his way from the crowded dance floor.

His sons were a bitter disappointment to Walter Sullivan. Neither had married. Neither were hard workers. Neither had any principles. Lucas never got far from a bottle and Baron never got far from a woman. Fearful that one or the other or both would shame him before his illustrious guests, Sullivan went in search of his firstborn. If he knew Baron, he was out in the moonlight somewhere with somebody's daughter, sweetheart, or wife.

"We can't, not here. Not like this."

"The safest place in the world."

"Baron, there's a house full of people. We'll be caught." Mrs. Boyd J. Calahan turned her face away to evade his kiss. "You should have come this afternoon while Boyd was out riding. Like you promised."

"I wanted to, darlin', but I was tied up." Baron took her chin in his hand, turned her face back to his, and kissed her.

The pair stood in an upstairs guest room where, only five minutes earlier, state senator Boyd Calahan had left his wife to finish dressing, admonishing her to hurry. No sooner had the senator descended the stairs than Baron, still wearing casual attire, had entered from the balcony.

"Well, you missed your chance." Martha

Calahan swept his hand away from her breast and pouted.

"You don't mean that," Baron murmured, peeling the low bodice down and freeing her left breast. He lowered his head to trail kisses down her bare shoulder.

"I most certainly do," said Mrs. Calahan, thrilling to the touch of his heated lips on her tingling flesh. "I want you to go and leave me alone."

Baron lifted his head. His icy blue eyes looked accusingly into hers. His hands fell away and he shrugged. "Very well. Perhaps the next time you visit Orilla." He turned and started for the door.

"Well . . . wait . . . I—" The chemise-clad Mrs. Calahan ran across the bedroom, darting in front of him to press her back against the door. She favored him with a sensual smile and, reaching up to toy with his open shirt collar, said, "You don't have to give up so easily."

Baron brushed her hand away. "Mrs. Calahan," he said coldly, "I have no time for games. We both should be downstairs. And since you insist on playing the coy little tease, that is exactly where I'm going."

"Baron, no!" Martha Calahan threw her arms around his neck and pressed her voluptuous body to his. The forty-six-year-old senator's wife was extremely flattered that a handsome young man sixteen years her junior desired her. While she was devoted to her rich and powerful husband, she did so enjoy the stolen moments of ecstasy with this passionate blond Adonis. "Please. Make love to me. It's been so long. Six months since you were in San Antone."

Baron finally smiled. His hands sliding around

her waist and down over her firm bottom, he said, "Now, that's better." His fingers tightened under her rounded buttocks. He lifted her up and carried her to the bed. "Finish undressing," he ordered, and began unbuttoning his shirt. In seconds they were both naked and Baron was pressing her down on the bed.

"You're just terrible," she murmured huskily when he pushed her legs wide apart. "If you had the slightest bit of respect for me, you wouldn't insist on making love with my husband right downstairs."

"But my dear Martha, that's not true. I respect you deeply," Baron whispered, and slid swiftly into her. "Very deeply."

"Oh, yes . . . yes. . . . Deeply, darling," Senator Calahan's wife sighed.

He was miserable.

More miserable than he had ever been in his life.

Luiz Quintano had not moved from his spot beside the door, and his fierce black eyes had not left the ivory-skinned young woman in the white lace dress.

Amy was again, for the third time this evening, in the arms of the suave, unscrupulous Tyler Parnell. Parnell was holding her very close and whispering in her ear.

For the first time in his seventeen years, Luiz Quintano experienced the agony and frustration of jealousy. His stomach burned and his heart squeezed painfully in his chest.

His fingers ached to touch her white skin. His arms tingled with longing to hold her. But he wouldn't be holding her, he wouldn't be touching her. He didn't know how to dance.

Cursing himself for being an awkward, unsophisticated fool, Luiz could stand it no longer. He whirled on his bootheel and hurried outdoors, feeling as if he were going to be ill. Out in the courtyard he tore at the choking red scarf and undid the top button of his silk shirt.

"Too warm for you inside?" Don Ramon, elegantly dressed, stepped out of the shadow, a long cigar in his hand, his white teeth flashing in the moonlight.

Luiz stuffed his hands deep into his trouser pockets and hanging his unhappy head, nodded. He was in no mood to talk, even to his father.

"Walk with me," invited Don Ramon. "We'll enjoy the night air together."

The pair strolled along wide promenade paths through the fragrant garden. Don Ramon spoke in a low, level voice, his son reluctantly listening. "Señorita Amy has only returned today, Luis. Everyone is eager to enjoy her company. She, in turn, must be charming and gracious to her guests. When the others have gone, there will be plenty of time." The elder Quintano halted and looked up at his tall son. "To be her friend. That is what you wish, is it not?" His heavy brows lifted questioningly.

"Yes," said Luiz. "I want us to be friends."

Don Ramon again smiled and touched his son's cheek. "And that you will be. Good friends. Now, come, let's go back inside. You've not yet eaten. Nor have I."

Don Ramon tossed his cigar away and the two Quintanos returned to the house. Atop a long linen-draped buffet table, on huge silver platters, was an array of foods to dazzle the eyes and tempt the palate. Giant cured hams and large roasts of beef. Turkey and duck, oysters and shrimp. Imported smoked fish, pâté, and caviar. Puddings and ices and fresh fruit in cream.

But Luiz had no appetite. To please his father, he filled a china plate. But when only minutes later he handed it to a servant, the food had hardly been touched. Excusing himself, he wandered away. Back into the ballroom. Back to his post beside the door.

Amy was miserable.

More miserable than she had ever been in her life.

The evening was totally ruined. Luiz had not asked her to dance. While she had dizzily spun about the floor in almost every pair of male arms, including the governor's, she had not been held by the only pair she really wanted around her.

Her bare shoulders ached to feel his dark fingers touching them. Her whole body tingled with longing to have him hold her. Trapped once more in the uncomfortably close embrace of Tyler Parnell, Amy glanced plaintively at Luiz, and was stung by the coldness she saw in his expressive black eyes. He looked distant and unreachable, as if the thought of dancing with her so bored him, he simply refused.

Amy sighed unhappily.

Nothing had changed. Five years had passed and everything was the same. Tonatiuh still regarded her as a worrisome child. It hurt badly. Especially when only this afternoon she had been so certain he had seen her in a totally new light. She had thought . . . hoped . . .

"I've a fine idea, Amy," Tyler Parnell whispered, his lips so close they were touching her ear.

She pulled back a little. "Which is?"

His arms remaining firmly around her, he said, "I'll grab a glass of champagne and we'll take a stroll in the moonlight."

"No," she said quickly. She looked again at Luiz and promptly changed her mind. She gave Tyler Parnell one of her most flirtatious smiles and said, "Yes. Let's do."

Seconds later the pair walked outside, Parnell's arm possessively around Amy's waist, a glass of chilled champagne in his hand. From across the large ballroom, Walter Sullivan saw the couple leave. His big hand tightened on his liquor glass and his blue eyes clouded with concern.

Baron Sullivan, on the opposite side of the room, stood easily charming a circle of enraptured females. He also noticed Tyler and Amy's departure, and his blue eyes shone with satisfaction.

But most telling of all were the tortured dark eyes of a heartbroken young Indian.

4

At noon the next day, everybody said that old Esau's barbecued beef was the most tender and the tastiest he had ever cooked. Accepting the compliments with beaming pleasure, the black man straightened his shoulders and held his white head high with pride.

Even the ladies returned for seconds of the spicy, succulent beef, shading their fair faces with dainty parasols and cheerfully exclaiming that they would never be able to get into their fancy ball gowns come evening. The big, brawny men came back to the steaming barbecue pit again and again, unbothered by the broiling sun or the fit of their clothes.

Amy Sullivan, exhibiting the fine manners she had learned in New Orleans, pretended a pleasure she did not feel, an appetite she did not have. Knowing how much her good-hearted father wanted her homecoming to be perfect in every way, Amy, holding a plate of beef and potato salad on her lap, ate sparingly and laughed and gossiped with the girls and ladies on the big shaded east patio.

But Esau's beef was tasteless to the disappointed young woman. She had hardly slept and she felt tired and out of sorts. She wished desperately that she could snap her fingers and all the guests would magically disappear. Or that she could set her plate aside and flee to the cool privacy of her room.

It had been just more than twenty-four hours since she had stepped down from the train. And in those twenty-four hours she had been unable to forget, even for a moment, the sweep of Tonatiuh's thick, dark eyelashes, the curve of his full, smooth lips, the touch of his warm hand.

Amy's restless gaze once again did a slow, thorough sweep of the rolling lawn beyond the patio. Her father, standing directly in front of Esau's smoking barbecue pit, was holding court with the governor, Senator Calahan, and a neighboring rancher, young Doug Crawford. A few feet away, lounging indolently against the stone wishing well, Lucas and Tyler Parnell were sipping bourbon. Tyler kept casting lascivious looks in her direction. A shiver of distaste skipping up her spine, Amy quickly looked away. After last night's stroll in the courtyard, she hoped she never again found herself alone with Mr. Tyler Parnell.

A deep male voice suddenly blending with all the feminine ones drew Amy's attention to the far end of the patio. Baron, in a blue cotton pullover shirt open halfway down his chest and a pair of tight buckskins, was crouched on his heels between two seated, smiling women. One was the plain, unmarried daughter of a merchant, the other the pretty eastern-bred bride of Sundown's bank president. Both were obviously charmed.

Amy shook her head and continued her search but failed to find the one face she most wanted to see. She spotted Tonatiuh's father, Don Ramon, graciously escorting someone's elderly mother toward the hacienda from the lower lawn. The frail old woman was clinging tenaciously to his bent arm and Don Ramon was gallantly accommodating his steps to the slowness of hers.

"Will you excuse me, please," Amy said, setting her plate aside and rising to her feet. She went to meet the approaching pair.

"May I be of help?" she asked sweetly.

"Ah, Amy, how thoughtful you are," Don Ramon said as Amy fell into step and gently took the old woman's free arm. "It's Amy Sullivan, Mrs. Cassidy," he said. "You remember Amy."

The old woman's watery eyes blinked up at Amy and Amy read the confusion there. "Who? Who'd he say you was?"

Amy smiled. "Why, Grandma Cassidy, it's me. Amy. Walter Sullivan's daughter."

Grandma Cassidy frowned. "Walter's daughter? Walter have a daughter? I thought Walter had boys."

Don Ramon exchanged glances with Amy over Grandma's gray head. They got the old woman into the big house and Amy, asking that Don Ramon please wait, took the aged guest to her room, helped her into bed, and pulled the drapes against the sun. Grandma Cassidy was snoring by the time Amy tiptoed out.

Don Ramon was waiting in his walnut-paneled study. Hands clasped behind him, he stood before a tall bookshelf lined with leather-bound volumes. He turned and smiled when Amy entered. "You are a sweet and considerate young lady, Amy."

"No," she said, truthfully, "I'm not. I only

wanted to speak with you." She lifted her skirts of pale-yellow cotton and anxiously crossed to him. "Where is he, Don Ramon? Why isn't he here at the barbecue?"

Don Ramon continued to smile easily. He shrugged and said, "Luiz was not feeling well this morning. He asked that he might be excused. I told him he could be."

"He's sick? Why didn't you say so! May I go up and check on him? He might need something." She turned to leave. Don Ramon caught her, gently drawing her back.

"You misunderstand. Luiz is not ill. He went for a ride. He will return soon. Do not trouble yourself."

"A ride? Where? Where did he go?"

"I did not ask. He did not say."

Amy sighed. "I wish . . . I wish. . . . Oh, Don Ramon, I don't know what I wish!" And the forlorn expression that came into her lovely blue eyes was identical to the one he had seen the night before in the dark eyes of his son. She turned and walked away, dejected, and the sensitive Don Ramon, looking after her, wished he could help, but knew that he could not.

The *don,* continuing to smile, stayed on in the quiet study. He sat down in his favorite easy chair, thinking of Luiz and Amy. He was afraid a fullblown romance was about to blossom between them. All the signs were there.

His smile disappeared and he sighed wearily. While he would be pleased if one day the two should marry, how would the *patrón* feel about such a union? Although Walter Sullivan seemed genuinely fond of Luiz, he might be bitterly opposed to having a mixed-blood son-in-law.

They were both so young and so innocent. They knew nothing of life and its treachery. He hoped they would wait until they were both more mature to choose a life's mate. Luiz was only seventeen, and Amy had just turned sixteen.

The *don*'s green eyes closed and he grinned sheepishly. Ah, what hypocrites are we who have grown old.

Happy memories arose as his thoughts turned back twenty years to another party, another June, another sixteen-year-old beauty.

He had not wanted to go that evening. Had strongly considered sending his regrets. But as a late June dusk settled over Mexico City, Don Ramon Rafael Quintano, dressed in evening clothes, stepped down from a gleaming carriage before the Chapultepec Palace.

In his white-gloved hand, the *don* held a gold-engraved invitation. After presenting it to the presiding butler, he was ushered down a long corridor and to the wide landing directly above a gigantic marble-floored ballroom.

More than one feminine heart pounded as the slim, handsome Spaniard stood, arrogantly scrutinizing the glittering crowd. But his was the heart that pounded the heaviest when his green-eyed gaze came to rest on the most beautiful young girl in the room.

She was tall and slender and her straight, coal-black hair reached to well below her waist. She wore a long emerald-green wrap-around robe trimmed in bands of gold and tied up on one shoulder in the Aztec fashion. Golden armlets caressed her bare, slender arms. A heavy gold chain around her throat supported a large gold disk that rested in the valley between her breasts. On her slender wrists were bracelets of gold and jade, and on her feet were sandals encrusted with precious gems.

As if she were a mystical witch commanding that he come to her at once, Don Ramon Quintano descended the marble steps and walked straight toward the exotic young beauty. Her black, almond-shaped eyes held a strange, almost frightening light, and her ruby lips were so darkly red they appeared to be stained with wild berries.

When he reached her, Don Ramon realized that he was trembling. His host, Presidente Antonio Lopez de Santa Anna, standing beside the unusual beauty, made the introductions.

Don Ramon looked into the dark hypnotic eyes of the young Aztec goddess, Xochiquetzal, a hereditary princess and direct descendant of the first Xochiquetzal.

Don Ramon, an educated man, knew exactly what the name meant. Precious Flower. The personification of beauty and love, goddess of the flowers. Never had he known anyone whose name fit so perfectly.

He immediately loved and desired her. And he was sure, by the look in those awesome black eyes, that she desired him as well. The prospect of waiting for weeks, even months before he could possess her brought instant suffering to the romantic Latin.

But the goddess Xochiquetzal was not like the other sheltered young women present in the palace that night. She did as she pleased. She answered to no one. She followed no rigid restrictions of protocol or custom.

And so, shocking her hosts, she calmly took Don Ramon's hand and silently led him away. Out in the garden, the sixteen-year-old goddess turned to the smitten Spaniard, put her slender arms around his neck, and lifted her beautiful face for his kiss.

He kissed her and when their heated lips finally separated, she said, "I have seen your arrival in the stars. And in the smoking mirror as well. We are to marry, this much I know. But—" she sighed —"I cannot promise we will be together always." Those black eyes flashed at him as her slender body molded itself to his.

"Does it matter?" he managed huskily. "I want you forever or for as long as you will be mine. Marry me tomorrow, *mi querida.*"

"No," she said with calm authority. "It must be tonight. The old *padre* awaits in the palace chapel. Come."

While hundreds of guests danced on in Chapultepec's ballroom, Don Ramon Rafael Quintano and the Aztec goddess, Xochiquetzal, were married in a quiet ceremony in the palace chapel. Afterward, Xochiquetzal ushered her bridegroom up the marble stairs to a large, luxurious bedchamber.

There, in the bright Mexican moonlight that streamed in through the tall palace windows, the bride unselfconsciously took off the gold-trimmed emerald gown, her bracelets of gold and jade, her golden armlets, and the jewel-encrusted sandals.

Naked save for the gold medallion, she lifted

the heavy gold disk and told the bridegroom, "This, my husband, is an exact likeness of the magnificent Stone of the Sun that once adorned the Great Temple of Huitzilopochtli in the central square of Tenochtitlán. The face you see in the center represents the Sun God."

Don Ramon nodded but remained silent.

"The four lesser gods around the Sun God are the gods of earth, wind, fire, and water." She allowed the gleaming disk to fall back to her breasts. "Our son will be called Tonatiuh in tribute to the Sun God."

She stood naked and beautiful, so surprisingly bold her jealous bridegroom suddenly suffered a new kind of pain. His heated eyes admiring her bare loveliness, he wondered at her virtue. But then she smiled and came to him. She took her husband's hands in hers. She turned them up and kissed both palms. Then she placed one on her bare left breast. The other she drew down between her legs.

"Yours are the only hands that have ever touched me, Ramon. We Aztecs are a moral people. I am a virgin. Just as your coming was foretold in the stars, so it was ordered by the gods that I come to you untouched. I have never even kissed a man. Will you teach me how to love you?"

Her happy husband drew her protectively into his close embrace. "*Sí,* my precious flower. I will teach you. My own, my love."

The next day the newlyweds fled the hot, steamy city. For the remaining long, lovely months of summer, the pair honeymooned in seclusion on Mexico's emerald coast. When autumn came, Don Ramon took his bride far, far north to live on a small Spanish land grant, a wedding gift from his family.

Don Ramon built his bride a small adobe home and took her to visit their nearest neighbors, a big light-haired Texan, Walter Sullivan, his wife, Beth, and Sullivan's younger sister, Meg.

The Sullivans were friendly and made the Quintanos welcome.

For a time the Quintanos were happy, even in that lonely, desolate land. But the living was not easy. Don Ramon had little luck on his small rancho in that barren place. Don Ramon's bride, the lovely Xochiquetzal, could not even coax maize to grow in such parched soil, much less the flowers and greenery that she loved.

Worse, the goddess failed to become pregnant, and she wept bitter tears each disappointing month. A year passed, then two. Three.

One blistering August day in 1838, Don Ramon returned to their modest home at the end of a tiring day to find his beautiful wife aglow with happiness. She told him that he was going to be a father in the spring. They drank Madeira from silver goblets and made love as the sun went down.

At sunset on April 17, 1839, Xochiquetzal went into labor. Her frightened husband said he would ride at once for the doctor. She stopped him. She would need no physician. He pleaded to at least summon Señora and Señorita Sullivan. No. She wanted no intruders sharing the experience. He, her husband, would deliver their child.

Terrified, Ramon nodded, lighted the lamps, and prepared himself for the longest night of his life. His fearless goddess did not share his dread.

As if she were off on some lovely holiday, she smiled and hummed and tidied up the adobe.

At midnight she stripped off all her clothes, save for the golden Stone of the Sun. She leisurely bathed by candlelight. Naked, she climbed onto the clean, white bed, sat with her back propped against the pillows, drew her parted knees up, and placed her bare feet flat on the mattress.

When the tearing pains began to come regularly, she threw her arms up behind her, gripped the round cylinders of the heavy brass bedstead, and made not one sound.

While Don Ramon pressed cooling cloths to his wife's pain-contorted face, her throat, her limp dark hair, Xochiquetzal calmly called on the ancient gods in the native Nahuatl tongue. Her frightened husband did not understand the language of the Aztecs, and more than once he wondered if she were offering up prayers in preparation for her death.

The toil of childbirth stretched on into the wee hours of the morning. Don Ramon was beside himself with worry. He watched the black eyes of his beloved dim with the intense pain, saw rivers of perspiration wash over her full breasts, her enormous belly, her long, spread legs.

The April sun came up and still Xochiquetzal sat upon her bed of agony, unable to expel the child within. Noon, and still she struggled, weak but unconquered. Feeling that God must surely be punishing him for some past forgotten sin, Don Ramon was certain that his wife and his unborn child were going to die.

The afternoon heat grew unbearable inside the close bedroom. Don Ramon's damp shirt and trousers clung to his slim, hard body, perspiration dripped from his thick hair into his green eyes. He stayed on at her bedside, loving the suffering woman more than he loved his own life, silently vowing that when she drew her last painful breath, he would join her in death. Her eyes already were closing. The hour was close at hand.

The sun had begun its slide toward the western horizon. The hot, dry air began to cool. Xochiquetzal's black eyes opened. To her husband's shock, she smiled at him. Her face was suddenly serene. The light from the setting sun turned her bare, gleaming body a pale orange hue.

Pushing with the last ounce of strength in her pain-weakened body, she said triumphantly, "The time is now."

And so it was.

Tonatiuh was born just as the sun said good-bye to earth. While the healthy infant squalled out his rude introduction to the world, his tired, happy mother fell into instant sleep, and his relieved father cried unashamedly with joy and thanksgiving.

When the baby was but four months old, Don Ramon came home one sweltering August noon to find both wife and child missing. He rode straight to Walter Sullivan's place, supposing that his goddess had grown lonely and was visiting the two Sullivan women.

But a Mexican servant met him at the door and told him that *Señora* Sullivan had just learned she was to have a baby in the spring. The señora and the *señorita* had left that morning. They had gone to New Orleans. They would remain there until the baby came.

Don Ramon turned away. Frantic, he went in search of his wife and child, riding across dry washes and cactus-dotted plateaus and baked desert flats.

It was sundown when he saw something glittering brilliantly atop a basalt mesa. He anxiously spurred his winded mount up the rough tableland.

Tonatiuh, squalling his head off, sunburned and hungry, lay atop the barren mesa. He was naked. Fastened around his neck was the heavy gold chain. Atop his bare belly lay the gold Sun Stone. Beneath his dark head was a sheet of folded, strange-looking paper.

Ramon picked up his unhappy son, cradled him in one bent arm, and lifted the paper. A fine tissuelike paper, made from the bark of a fig tree, Ramon recognized it as the kind used by the Aztecs more than five hundred years before.

Slowly, carefully, he unfolded the fine paper and began to read.

Ramon

"Ramon."

"What?" Don Ramon blinked in surprise, then smiled. "I am sorry," he said, rising. "I . . . my mind was in the past."

Walter Sullivan grinned at him from the doorway. "A nice place to visit, but we can't live there, *amigo.* Come, the regulars are in the card room."

5

It was said that Pedrico could see more with one eye than most people could with two.

The one-eyed Pedrico Valdez had been an Orilla houseboy since before Amy was born. She'd heard whispers from the servants of how the quiet, slender man had lost his left eye.

When he was little more than a boy and living alone in Paso del Norte, he had become bewitched by a pretty cantina singer. All his money went to buy presents for the red-lipped, dark-eyed woman. He wanted to marry the lovely Angelica, his angel. She laughed and kissed him and promised to say yes just as soon as he turned twenty.

But, alas, his Angelica was no angel, and one hot moonlit night a handsome stranger rode into the border town, walked into the cantina, and stole Angelica's fickle heart.

Angelica's jealous boy lover, Pedrico, challenged the love thief. A fight ensued. The stranger pulled a knife. Pedrico was unarmed. He lost his eye and his love and was left for dead in an alley.

Walter Sullivan found him, took him to a doctor, then brought him out to Orilla to recuperate. Pedrico had been there ever since. The eye he had kept had never again settled on a woman, although more than one pretty Orilla housemaid had found the slender man with the black eye-patch and quiet manner appealing.

His wounded heart still belonged to Angelica.

His fierce loyalty belonged to the *patrón*.

Now, on this warm June morning, Pedrico, a linen-draped breakfast tray balanced atop his spread fingers, knocked gently on Amy's closed bedroom door. He spoke the magic words he knew she was longing to hear. "Señorita Amy, wake up. All the guests have gone."

He waited, his lips lifted in a smile beneath a thin black mustache.

In seconds the heavy carved door flew open and a sleepy-eyed young girl blinked at him. "Are you sure, Pedrico?"

Nodding, he stepped past her into the bedroom. After placing the tray on a polished drum table at the room's center, he marched over and drew the heavy drapery, allowing bright morning sunshine to flood the room.

"Senator and Mrs. Calahan departed at sunrise," he announced with a smile. "There are no longer any visitors at Orilla."

"Thank the good Lord," said Amy, tying the satin ribbons at the throat of her robe and climbing atop the rumpled bed where she sat cross-legged. "Finally some time to myself!"

Pedrico, pouring coffee from a gleaming silver server, nodded and said, "Does this mean you do not wish to be disturbed?" He crossed to her, a fragile cup of steaming black coffee in his white gloved hand.

"It most certainly does," she said, reaching for

the coffee. Sensing something and catching a definite twinkle in his eye, she asked, "What's going on here? There's something you're not telling me."

Pedrico grinned. "An impatient young man awaits downstairs, but if you'd rather not. . . ." He shrugged.

"Who?"

"Luiz Quintano."

Amy shoved the coffee cup back at him. "Tonatiuh is here? Now?" Her eyes gone wide with excitement, she bounded off the bed. "Pedrico, you devil! Why didn't you say so!"

"I am saying so now, Señorita Amy. Luiz has come to see if you might wish to go for a ride this morning. What shall I tell him?"

"You tell him yes!" she said, her quick mind racing ahead, choosing what she would wear, settling on a beautiful pale-yellow chamois riding skirt, split up the middle, and an expensive, never-before-worn yellow silk blouse. She *had* to look her best. "Of course I want to go riding with Tonatiuh."

"I thought so," said Pedrico, winking his one eye at her. "He is waiting on the east patio."

Luiz Quintano nervously paced the wide stone-floored patio, his palms perspiring, his stomach tied in knots. He had risen with the sun, so anxious for a chance to see Amy alone he had been unable to sleep.

Before going to bed, he had carefully laid out the clothes he would wear today, choosing what he hoped made him look older, more like a man.

But when he had dressed at dawn, somehow he had looked all wrong, foolish.

In disgust, he had changed. Then changed again. When his big, dark-paneled bedroom was littered with discarded clothes, he had finally put back on the very ones he had so carefully laid out the night before.

Now, jittery, doubtful, he wished he had worn something less conspicuous. He should have thrown on a pair of worn buckskins and an old shirt. Now Amy would think he was vain. Or worse, believe he was trying to show off for her benefit. That is, if she came down at all. Which she might not.

She might simply laugh and tell Pedrico that the last thing on earth she wanted to do was to go riding with a boring seventeen-year-old Indian.

Luiz gritted his even white teeth.

Before his eyes rose the hated visions: Amy swallowed up in the suave Tyler Parnell's arms, spinning dizzily about on the dance floor. Amy laughing and tossing her blond head as Parnell whispered in her ear. Amy, on Parnell's arm, sweeping right past him and out into the moonlit gardens.

Luiz's dark eyes closed in frustration.

Amy Sullivan wouldn't come downstairs to go riding with him this morning! He was a pitiful fool to have come here thinking she would. He was making a spectacle of himself. And everyone would know. Pedrico would tell all the others. He would become an object of ridicule at Orilla.

His eyes flicked open.

He couldn't let that happen. He *wouldn't* let it happen. Anxious to be gone from the scene of his impending shame, Luiz whirled about and strode hurriedly across the stone patio toward the tall, dense hedge at its edge.

Emitting a sigh of relief when he had disappeared through the opening in the tall hedge, he had gone only a few steps when he heard her calling his name.

"Tonatiuh, I'm sorry I'm so late, but I—" Amy, stepping out onto the patio, stopped and looked about, puzzled. "Tonatiuh?"

A movement at the back hedge drew her attention. She looked up as Luiz stepped into the opening in the dense green shrubbery. Framed by the tall hedge, he stood, unmoving, feet apart, looking directly at her. Speechless, she stared back at him.

He wore a long-sleeved shirt of sky-blue cotton and dark-brown trousers that covered all but the toes of his polished cowboy boots. Rows of silver buttons ran up the side seams of the tight pants, and around his slim waist was an elaborately intaglioed western belt. On his hands were gloves of soft velvety chamois and at his throat was a bandanna of a deep chocolate hue.

Blue-black hair glinting in the sunlight, jet eyes locked on her, he quietly said her name.

Amy.

Nothing more. Not good morning, Amy. Not it's nice to see you. Only Amy. But the way he said it filled her with the same strange excitement she'd felt the day he met her train.

He started toward her and Amy felt her knees turn to water. He approached her, the clanking of his big roweled Mexican spurs in rhythm with her quickening heartbeat. When he stood directly before her, she caught the flicker of doubt in the depths of his beautiful black eyes.

"I . . . I . . . thought you might like to go for a ride," he said, a tiny muscle jerking involuntarily at the corner of his mouth. "But if you don't, why, I can . . ."

"Please," she broke in, lifting her hand, longing to touch him, not daring to do so. "Take me. I want to ride with you, Tonatiuh."

He smiled then. It was a smile so unexpected, so warm and dazzling that she caught her breath. She blinked happily when his gloved fingers took hold of her upper arm and he quickly ushered her across the patio toward the opening in the hedge.

"I saddled a couple of horses," he said, still smiling broadly, then added, "just in case."

Amy smiled too, and looking up at his bronzed face, she wondered how he could have possibly doubted that she would want to go riding with him. But she said nothing. Happy, excited, she allowed the tall lanky young man to hurry her across the rolling back lawn and out the gate to where a couple of mounts stood saddled and waiting.

"I chose the black mare for you, but if you'd rather have the—"

"I want her," Amy said, her appreciative eyes on a shimmering black with white stocking feet and a white star on her face. "She's beautiful, Tonatiuh."

He beamed with pride and pleasure. He placed his hands on Amy's waist to lift her up into the silver-trimmed, black leather saddle. He looped the long reins over the black's neck and handed them to her. When she was astride the mare he stood smiling up at Amy, his gloved hand idly toying with the stirrup.

"Think you remember how to ride?" he teased, feeling lighthearted for the first time in a week.

"Catch me if you can" was Amy's challenging answer. She wheeled the responsive black around, touched her spurless bootheels to its flanks, and the mare shot away.

Luiz stood there for a moment, watching the beautiful girl ride away from him, her wild golden hair streaming out behind her, the sound of her laughter filling him with a new kind of happiness that was so wonderful it scared him.

Grabbing up the reins of a huge iron-gray stallion, Luiz swung up into the saddle, touched his spurs to the big beast, and raced swiftly after the laughing gilt-haired girl.

The gray stallion easily overtook the black mare. An expert horseman, Luiz had been placed in the saddle alone by the time he was two. Since the age of twelve he had been training fine Orilla horses, and the *patrón* said he was the most accomplished *jinete* on the ranch. Luiz took great pride in his position and was pleased that the older, more experienced Orilla horsemen embraced him as their equal.

Moving up alongside Amy, Luiz reined in, slowing his iron gray to the smaller black's easy gait. He shot Amy a smile, then wordlessly the pair rode knee to knee away from the Orilla's many adobe buildings. Across the sandy soil they loped, heading northeast to where the ground sloped gently upward.

Far away on the distant horizon, a series of ridges rose, turning into green foothills, and finally blending into the hazy blue Guadelupe Mountains surmounted by the rising spire of the El Capitán peak. The air, clear as glass, made the distant string of mountains seem deceptively close.

The sun hot on their faces and the wind stinging their eyes, they galloped headlong across open deserts, unbothered by the blazing heat of summer. Farther and farther they rode, the only sound that of their horses' hooves striking the baked ground.

Feeling as if she would never be tired again, Amy wondered how long it would take them to ride all the way to the mountains. She turned in the saddle to shout the question to Luiz, but he motioned for her to pull up. Amy nodded and slowed the black.

They had traveled quite a distance. The Orilla headquarters were far behind. They had reached an elevation several hundred feet higher than where the hacienda sat on the desert floor. A stand of cottonwoods close by on their left told Amy they were near the river.

Luiz confirmed it when, after they came to a halt and the horses were stomping and blowing, he stood in the stirrups, pointed to the northeast, and said, "I'd like to show you my own special bend in the river. No one else knows about it."

Pleased that he would consider sharing a secret with her, Amy said, "I promise I'll never tell anyone."

"I believe you," he said with such conviction Amy was even more pleased.

"It's still a good four miles upriver, Amy. If

you'd rather wait until some day when it's cooler, we can."

"I don't want to wait. I want you to take me there now."

They followed the twisting streambed, climbing as they went, and when they reached their destination, Luiz dropped his reins and lithely dismounted. He lifted Amy down from the black's back and set her on her feet. He watched her, amused by the look of bewilderment on her face. He knew she was disappointed. She was eyeing the thick clump of tall willows before them, her forehead knitted. She turned her head and caught the faint sound of rushing water, and gave him a questioning look.

Like an excited child, Luiz said, "Close your eyes."

Amy happily obeyed. He took her hand in his and eagerly led her through the tall willows and cottonwoods. Inside the ring of willows, he drew her around in front of him. He carefully positioned her on the edge of a smooth, flat rock, choosing a cool and shady spot beside the clear lagoonlike pool.

When Amy stood directly in front of him, he turned her slightly so that when she opened her eyes, she would be looking directly at the splashing waterfall.

He took a deep breath and said, "Now, Amy."

She opened her eyes and stared. And couldn't believe what she saw before her. They were standing in a lush shaded bend in the river. A deep, clear pool below them was being constantly fed by a cascading waterfall above. Emerald-green grass grew on the river's banks, along with an array of wildflowers and climbing vines.

It seemed impossible that such a tropical paradise existed in the middle of the stark Chihuahuan desert.

Her eyes wide with wonder, she turned to Luiz. "I must be dreaming. We can't really be standing here in the cool shade below a waterfall."

"But we are," he assured her. "The pool is so deep I can dive into it from atop that big boulder." He pointed to a large jutting overhang of rock beside the rushing falls.

"You swim here?"

"All the time."

"I envy you," Amy said wistfully. She sat down on the grassy banks and hugged her knees.

Luiz quickly dropped down beside her. "You needn't. You can swim here." He paused, then added, "With me."

Amy's head snapped around. She looked into his dark, expressive eyes and wondered suddenly why he was being so kind and attentive after the shabby way he had treated her all week.

"Why have you ignored me the whole time our guests were here?" she now demanded haughtily. "You never danced with me once! You hurt my feelings."

A pained expression came over his bronzed face. He looked out across the placid river, then he swallowed hard and told her the truth. "I do not know how to dance."

"You don't know . . . That's the reason you . . . ?"

"Yes!" he exploded, and his tortured gaze swung back to her face. "I do not know how to dance! I am awkward and clumsy and I . . . I . . ." Amy's sudden burst of laughter made him stop speaking. Quick anger flared in his black eyes. "Is it so funny to you?"

"Yes. Yes, it is. Can't you see that it's funny?"

"I cannot." He glared at her.

Continuing to laugh, Amy touched his tense face with gentle fingertips. "Tonatiuh, do you honestly think I cared if you knew how to dance?"

Skeptical, he said, "Well, didn't you?"

"No! I don't care if you never learn to dance! It makes no difference." Impulsively she grabbed up one of his gloved hands and, holding it in both of her own, affectionately pressed it to her cheek. "I thought you didn't want to dance with me. Can't you see, I thought it was me."

"Well, it wasn't. It was me." His glum face began to soften, but he couldn't help adding defiantly, "I am not Tyler Parnell."

"I know," she said, "and I'm so glad. So very glad." She released his hand, but her warm blue eyes stayed on his face.

Luiz remained unconvinced. "I'll bet if he had you here right now, he'd . . . he'd . . . kiss you."

Amy looked him straight in the eye. "No, he would not. I wouldn't let him, just as I didn't let him when we walked in the garden." She smiled, and then said very softly, "But I would let you kiss me, Tonatiuh." Her fair face growing pink, she added shyly, "If you wanted to."

His face swiftly reddened. "I do want to. I want very much to kiss you, but . . . but . . ." He sighed. "Like dancing, I don't know how to do that either. I've never kissed a girl."

"I'm glad," Amy said, and meant it. "Nobody has ever kissed me. We can learn together." She lifted trusting eyes to his. "Can't we?"

Luiz grinned boyishly. "Yes," he said, "we can."

His heart galloping in his chest, he slowly peeled off his chamois gloves and dropped them to the ground. When he turned more fully toward her, Amy held her breath. His lean brown hands came up to gently frame her face.

Amy had no idea what she was supposed to do with her hands, so she wrapped her fingers loosely around his wrists.

His dark eyes held hers for a moment, then dropped to her mouth. Under his intense scrutiny, Amy's lips began to tremble and she felt as if her lungs were going to explode.

But then he smiled understandingly at her and said in low, gentle voice, "Breathe, my sweetheart."

Nodding, Amy gratefully exhaled, and they both laughed. When finally they had quieted, Luiz's laughing black eyes turned somber, then warm. He tilted Amy's chin up, lowered his bronzed face, and kissed her.

It was an innocent kiss. Two shy, eager pairs of lips tentatively meeting, fleetingly touching, then quickly withdrawing. But the brief chaste kiss was sweetly exciting to the naive young pair.

Awed by the wonder of it, Luiz said, feeling powerful and protective and possessive, "It is not enough that I'm the first to kiss you, Amy."

"It's not?" She stared wide-eyed at him.

His big, dark eyes flashed with ardent intensity and he said in carefully modulated, slightly accented English, "I must be the last as well."

Amy quickly opened her mouth to assure him he would be. But his warm lips covered hers in another tender kiss and she simply sighed, secure in the knowledge he knew, without her telling him, that he would be.

Her first. Her last. Her only.

6

The thick-walled hacienda sat baking in the July heat, all its shutters closed against the broiling sun, giving it the appearance of a big, somnolent monster with dozens of eyes, all tightly shut.

Inside all was silent, save for the striking of the tall cased clock in the downstairs hallway. Two P.M. Siesta time. The siesta, adopted from their neighbors to the south, was a custom enthusiastically embraced by the people dwelling in the deserts of far southwest Texas.

At Orilla, in the hottest part of the day, family and servants alike retired to their dim, shuttered bedrooms, sleep the only weapon against the awesome afternoon heat.

One member of the Orilla household had long ago discovered a better way to battle the dry, hot Texas afternoons. Baron Sullivan fought the fierce heat with a heat of his own. Nobody enjoyed siesta time more than Baron.

It had been back in the summer of '41—the year his mother had died and they had moved into the newly built hacienda—that an entire staff of new servants was hired. Magdelena Torrez, a widow of twenty-eight, and her tiny four-year-old daughter, Rosa, had come from the village. Magdelena was to be Orilla's upstairs maid.

Baron had noticed Magdelena right away. Fascinated with the way her large, soft breasts swayed and bounced beneath the cotton blouse she wore, he wondered how she would look without it. And he wondered how he could find out.

The answer came to him one hot August afternoon while he lay wide awake in his dim bedroom, bored and restless. He suddenly began to smile. He rose from his bed, crossed to the door, and stepped out into the hall. He looked cautiously about, saw no one, and headed straight for his father's room. He opened the heavy carved door, stepped inside, and saw his bare-chested father flat on his back and sound asleep. Baron went directly to the tall mahogany bureau and pulled out the top drawer. There in the very back in the corner was a small, blue velvet–covered box.

Baron flipped the box open and took from its satin bed the glittering diamond pendant that Walter Sullivan had given his bride on their wedding day. Baron palmed the pendant, closed the box, and put it back in its place. Within seconds of entering his father's room, he was back outside.

He silently descended the stairs and went to the back of the house toward the servant quarters. He stopped before Magdelena Torrez's door. He listened for a moment, heard nothing, opened the door, and went inside.

Blinking in the dim light, he saw, across the room, on a double bed by the window, Magdelena and her tiny daughter, Rosa, sleeping peacefully. He stared, smiling. His pretty Magdelena wore only a cotton camisole and a ruffled petticoat. A strap of the camisole had slipped over her shoulder and the satiny brown swell of her full breast was a tempting sight.

Almost as tempting as the glimpse of a smooth, firm thigh revealed by the twisted, high-rising petticoat.

Baron reluctantly tore his gaze from the voluptuous woman. He moved to the small pine chest of drawers, looked about, and saw on its top Magdelena's sewing box. He opened the box and placed the diamond pendant inside. He hurried back to his room and sprawled out on his bed, smiling dreamily to himself.

It would be, he knew, the last monotonous siesta he would ever have to endure.

Baron rose at midmorning the next day. He knew that the others had finished their breakfast hours ago and departed. When he started downstairs, he purposely yanked a button off his shirt. With the button in hand, he went in search of Magdelena Torrez.

He found her in the *sala*, dusting. She didn't hear him approach, so he was treated to the sight of her rounded bottom rising in the air as she bent to flick the feather duster across a low windowsill.

Startled when he said her name, Magdelena quickly straightened, turned, and smiled.

"Oh, Señor Baron," she said, nodding to him, "you will have to eat your breakfast alone. The others, they are gone." She shrugged apologetically.

"Doesn't matter," said Baron. "Actually, it's you I was looking for." He showed her the mother-of-pearl button. "Could you possibly sew this on for me? This is one of my favorite shirts."

"Oh, *sí, sí,*" she said, nodding happily, "I do it right now."

"You're awfully nice, Magdelena," said Baron.

Embarrassed, she took the button and stepped past him. He followed her from the room and down the hall. Magdelena stopped before her door.

She said, "I will be right out."

But Baron trailed the woman right inside her bedroom. When he closed the door behind them, Magdelena's dark eyes blinked. Hurriedly she moved toward the chest where she kept her sewing box. Baron was right behind her. He stood smiling at her while she nervously opened the box's lid to look for a spool of thread.

"Why, Magdelena, what . . . what is this?"

Baron reached inside her sewing box and brought out the glittering diamond. Lacing the delicate chain through his fingers, he allowed the gleaming bauble to swing back and forth before Magdelena's stunned face.

"I—I . . . do not know," she said, her wide eyes locked on the swinging diamond.

Baron's eyes were on it too. Then they shifted to Magdelena's face. "This is my mother's! You stole my dead mother's diamond pendant." His expression became one of hurt disbelief. "How could you, Magdelena? After all we've done for you."

"No!" she said, shaking her dark head. "I—I . . . do not know how the diamond got there. I would never. . . . I am innocent, Señor Baron. You must believe me, you must!"

"I don't," he said. "I don't believe you and neither will Dad."

"*Madre de Dios.*" She gasped. "He has to believe me. *Por favor,* Baron. I never do such a terrible thing."

"Then what is my mother's necklace doing in your sewing box. Answer me that."

"I—I do not know. Help me, oh *Dios,* please help me."

As if talking out loud to himself, Baron said, "This is awful. In Texas thieves go to prison. I just don't. . . ."

"Prison!" she cried. "No, no. My little Rosa. What will happen to my baby? I beg you, do not tell the *patrón.* I cannot lose this home. Is the only one I have, the only one my little Rosa have. Would you let her go hungry again?"

"Would you?" he said, and his tone softened.

"No." She sobbed. "No, tell me what to do, help me, please."

Maybe I *can* help you, Magdelena."

A glimmer of hope surged through her. "Yes?" she said, grabbing his arm. "Oh, Señor Baron, I would be so grateful, I do anything to pay you back."

The very words he had wanted to hear. He knew he had her. Magdelena Torrez had come to the Orilla destitute. Uneducated, with no family, she'd been left widowed and homeless by a penniless drunken peón.

Baron smiled down at the worried woman. "Anything, sweet Magdelena?"

"Anything," she said, not caring what he might ask of her, so long as her baby Rosa had a home and food.

"I'll take care of this for you," Baron told her. "I'll put it back where you got it and no one will ever be the wiser. It will be our secret."

"Gracias, gracias," she said, terrified the *patrón* would never believe that she had no idea how his dead wife's diamond necklace had turned up in her sewing box. "You are so kind, Señor Baron."

That very afternoon, as the house fell into the slumberous quiet of siesta, a very uneasy Magdelena Torrez silently climbed the stairs and stood just outside Baron's door.

Without knocking, Magdelena opened the door, stepped quickly inside, and closed it behind her. Heart in her throat, she leaned back against it. Across the spacious room, lolling indolently on his bed, lay Baron Sullivan.

His chest and feet were bare. He wore only a pair of dark trousers that rode low on his naked belly. Arms folded beneath his head, he turned slowly and smiled at her.

"Come here, Magdelena."

She shook her head back and forth and remained where she was.

He chuckled and rolled off the bed. He crossed to her, holding out his hand. When she took it, he pulled her slowly to him. His arms went around her and Baron knew he'd found heaven. The feel of her big, soft breasts, her belly, and her strong thighs pressing against his body was incredibly exciting.

Immediately the thought struck him that she would feel even better when he got her undressed. He raised his hands and pushed her blouse down off her shoulders.

"Please," she said miserably, "this is wrong, Señor Baron. You are just a boy. Sixteen years old, a *niño* still. A baby."

"Make me a man, Magdelena," he said huskily.

When she still continued to struggle, he added, "I want to be your man. And for the sake of your little Rosa, you will be my woman."

In moments she was naked in his bed. She had been there, every afternoon, for the next dozen years. At first she had been a reluctant lover. But soon the shame of their affair was overshadowed by a stronger emotion. Love.

Magdelena had fallen in love with him and in so doing had been more than eager to please him. He liked that. He liked Magdelena. She was pretty, passionate, and available. His own live-in love slave, ready to satisfy his every hunger.

They had shared some very good years, so it was a hard thing to do when the time came to end it. He'd allowed the affair to continue long past her exciting him. Finally he had had no choice.

The end came one September afternoon in '53. Sated, he lay in the heat, his eyes sliding over Magdelena, bare, and perspiring beside him. She had changed since that first afternoon. Once she had been voluptuous, now she was overweight. Her olive face had been unlined and pretty, now wrinkles were visible even in the dim light. Her black glossy hair had threads of silver running through it.

Baron yawned, stretched, and said, "Go, Magdelena. And don't come back."

Her head shot up. She looked at him with hurt, questioning eyes. "Not come back? But why, *querido?*"

"Why?" he mocked, reaching out and cupping a heavy, sagging breast in his hand. "Look at yourself." He ran a forefinger accusingly over her large, dark nipple. "You are fat."

"I will lose weight," she said hopefully. "I fix myself up for you, *querido.* You will see, I will—"

"It won't work. You're too old for me. How old are you, Mag? Forty-five? Fifty?"

"You know I just turn forty last month!"

"All the same, that's too old. Good God, woman, I'm just twenty-eight." Again he yawned. "Go, darlin', I'm tired, I want a nap."

Magdelena silently rose and dressed, her heart obviously breaking. He was grateful she was the kind of woman who would wait until she was in her room alone to weep. Good old Mag. She had more class than most women.

Now, lying alone in his room on this steamy July afternoon, he fondly recalled the good times they had shared. He would probably have missed Magdelena, if he hadn't found someone to take her place the same week he had sent her away.

The door opened, drawing Baron from his pleasant reveries. A smiling young woman stepped inside, closing the door behind her. She stood at the room's center, provocatively shedding her clothes while Baron watched.

She came to the bed naked, leaned over, brushed a kiss to his belly, then stretched out beside him. While her hand swept enticingly down his chest, his heated gaze slid over her small, firm breasts, her flat stomach, her strong thighs.

Immediately aroused, he pushed her legs apart and moved between them. And enjoyed again, just as he had on that first afternoon, a pleasing tightness as he slid into her.

She excited him greatly. His release was quick in coming. After he'd climaxed, he collapsed atop her, the only sound in the stillness that of his labored breathing.

When his breath was no longer short, he heard the sound of horses' hooves striking hard-packed earth.

Curious, he slid from his lover and walked to the room's back window. He saw a pair of riders galloping toward the northeast. One was atop a coal-black mare, the other astride a gray stallion. One was a girl with long blond hair, the other a boy with hair of midnight black.

His eyes narrowed with disgust, Baron Sullivan stood naked at the window, watching until Amy and Luiz disappeared over the slope of the horizon. He came back to the bed and stood at its foot, his arms crossed over his chest.

"My baby sister's gone for a ride with Quintano." He frowned. "Again."

The woman in the bed pushed herself up on an elbow. "Darling, they are full of energy. Of course they do not wish to spend the lovely summer afternoons asleep," she said.

"Yes, well, I can well imagine how they do spend them."

"Baron, no! Such a thing to say."

"Don't you 'Baron, no' me." He uncrossed his arms and circled the bed. "I know damned well that dark-skinned Aztec is getting between my sister's lily-white legs."

The girl in bed shook her dark head and patted the mattress. Baron dropped down beside her. She leaned over and playfully bit his shoulder. "Is it so different from you getting between mine?"

"Very different," he said. "I ought to kill the bastard."

"Mmmmm." She kissed his throat. Her face moved lower and she brushed kisses to his bare chest. "My mother would want to kill you if she knew about us."

Baron stroked her hair. "No, she wouldn't. Your mother likes me." He urged her down on the bed. "Magdelena has always liked me." He kissed her. "And I like you."

"I *love* you," she said. "I love you, Baron."

"Ah, that's sweet, little Rosa." She touched him with warm hands and he sighed. "Yes. Oh, yes, Rosa, Rosa. My own little Rosa."

7

As Baron Sullivan watched disapprovingly from his bedroom window that hot July afternoon, the youthful riders galloped across the sun-baked land, headlong into the shimmering waves of heat rising from the desert floor. Laughing and calling to each other, they were filled with the sweet anticipation of an afternoon spent splashing in the cold waters of their hidden Puesta del Sol River lagoon.

Still, as anxious as the pair was to reach their private shaded paradise, they simultaneously pulled up on their mounts the minute they had topped and ridden over the rising sandstone ridge that separated them from Orilla.

Showing off a bit, Luiz gave his iron gray a spoken command and the mighty stallion reared up on his hind legs, his nostrils flaring, his unshod hooves pawing at the air. Luiz released the long reins, slipped backward out of the saddle, and, clinging to the gray's long flowing tail, slid down over the beast's hindquarters until he was seated squarely on the ground. Then he turned the tail loose, scrambled between the gray's hind legs, and moved up under his belly. Shooting to his feet, he stood, arms crossed, beneath the rearing, whinnying stallion.

Still in the saddle, Amy sat motionless atop her black mare. She watched with a mixture of horror and admiration. She was so relieved when Luiz stepped unhurriedly away only a split second before the powerful stallion's hooves came back down to earth, she chastised him even as she applauded the impressive feat.

"Tonatiuh, I wish you wouldn't do things like that. It scares me," Amy said, her blue eyes troubled.

Grinning, he walked up to her, plucked her out of the saddle, and slowly lowered her to the ground directly before him. With his tall lanky body, he urged her back against the motionless mare. He looked down into Amy's worried, upturned face and said, "Old Malpais would never hurt me." He lowered his dark head and brushed a teasing kiss to her lips. "Would *you?*"

Inhaling deeply, her senses were assailed with the scent of his sun-heated skin, his clean raven hair. "Never," she murmured, then leaned her head back against the smoothness of the saddle and raised her hands to grip his trim waist. "I'd never hurt you, Tonatiuh."

He smiled. "Nor I you."

He stopped smiling and gazed at her with an unwavering, dark-eyed intensity that both thrilled and frightened her. His hand leisurely moved up to her shirt front. Long, tanned fingers slowly gathered up a handful of the white cotton yoke and he gently urged her up on her toes as he stepped in closer.

His mouth hovering barely an inch above hers,

the heavy gold chain glittering around his brown throat, he said, "May I?"

Wanting him to kiss her just as badly as he wanted to, Amy nervously put out the tip of her tongue, licked her dry lips, and said, "Yes, oh yes."

She sighed with pleasure when his warm, smooth lips gently settled on hers. When his fingers tightened on her blouse and his tongue swept tantalizingly along the seam of her lips, Amy sighed more deeply. Her eyes closed and her lips parted for him. His tongue quickly penetrated and did amazing things to the sensitive insides of her mouth.

Amy's pulse raced. Her heart pounded. The long, open-mouthed kiss continued and became as blazing hot as the July heat. His fingers continued to clutch her blouse, pulling the fabric tight over her breasts. His knee slipped between hers and his steel-hard thigh pressed intimately against her in a way she knew must be wrong, because it felt so right.

Kissing him hungrily, a crazy thought flashed through Amy's mind. Tonatiuh truly was a Sun God. Her Sun God. A Sun God that burned her with his brilliance, set her afire with his incandescent heat. A dangerous solar deity that caused the blood to boil in her veins and a fierce fever to seize her heat-weakened body.

The passionate young pair were quickly learning about kissing. Their lingering, lustful embraces now bore little resemblance to the timid, experimental caress they had shared that first day at the river. In just six weeks their kisses had graduated in intensity until there were times when, sweet as the kisses were, they were not enough.

Times when Amy was left shaken and yearning, Luiz tortured and suffering.

At last Luiz lifted his dark head. His chest rose and fell rapidly. His throat gleamed with perspiration beneath his open-collared shirt. His black eyes were heavy-lidded with desire.

Amy, just as unnerved, locked her hands behind his waist and swallowed with effort, feeling dangerously weak.

Luiz laid his forehead against Amy's and said, "I think we'd better ride on to the water." His fingers finally released their grip on her shirt front.

"I hope I can make it," she answered breathlessly, her eyes shut.

He raised his head, smiled, and kissed her closed eyelids. "I'll get you there, sweetheart," he said. He gently drew her arms from around him and held her upright by her belt while he bent and scooped up the mare's trailing reins.

Then he picked Amy up and carried her to his waiting stallion. He lifted her astride and climbed up behind her. Quickly he tied the mare's reins to his saddle's rigging ring and they got underway, the riderless mare docilely following the big stallion over the barren tablelands.

"Feeling better now?" Luiz said against Amy's tousled hair.

Enclosed in his arms, Amy curled her fingers around the saddlehorn and leaned her head against his left shoulder. Sighing, she said, "Much better, thank you. When I'm with you I always feel good. And safe, so safe." Smiling, she glanced up at him.

"Safe?" he repeated. "Ah, *querido,* I am not sure about that. You are so beautiful, so tempting.

My father says, *'La mujer es como el vidrio, siempre esta en peligro.'* 'A woman is like glass, always in danger.' "

Amy laughed. "Even if that were true, I would only break if you dropped me abruptly. Or threw me away. You wouldn't do that, would you?"

He laughed. Then sobered and said, "Amy, if the time comes when one of us is to be tossed away and forgotten, it will be me."

Amy's hands automatically came back to clutch at the hard-trousered thighs cradling her own. "No! Don't talk like that. I could never give you up. Could never forget you."

He smiled, pleased, wanting to believe her. While she turned and rained reassuring kisses over his cheek, he laughed and imagined, not for the first time, how wonderful it would be when they were married, living here together on the wild, beautiful land they loved, the land that would belong to them.

He was surely the luckiest person ever born. The two most precious things life had to offer would one day be his.

Amy.

And Orilla.

When the sweethearts reached the tall stand of willows guarding their river redoubt, they laughed and raced to see who could get undressed first and into the cold, clear water.

Rolled up behind the cantle on Amy's black mare were the cut-off knee-length buckskins and the heavy denim shirt that she had used for swimming those first few weeks she was home.

Now they remained where they were.

On a hot afternoon a couple of weeks ago, Luiz

had turned to Amy as she started to disappear into the privacy of the willows and said, "Would it offend you if I stopped wearing a shirt and these heavy trousers when we swim?" He plucked at the sides of his hot, heavy pants.

Wondering what he had on underneath, she had shaken her head. Swiftly he had whipped off his shirt, unbuttoned the heavy trousers, and sent them to the ground. He kicked them aside and stood there, smiling at her, wearing nothing but a skimpy suede breechcloth.

It was the first time Amy had seen him without his shirt, much less without his trousers. Holding her own folded bathing attire in her arms, she stared openly at him. It seemed gloriously strange that his chest and legs were as bronzed as his face.

She had seen her father hurriedly wash up in the kitchen on occasion. While his face and throat and his heavily muscled arms were sun darkened, his chest, where a shirt always covered him, was pale. Tonatiuh, unlike her father, had no hair on his chest. It was smooth and hairless and beautiful. He was long waisted. His gleaming torso tapered into corded ribs and a flat, hard belly. His legs were long, the thigh bones strong-looking beneath the coppery skin. The briefness of his breechcloth afforded revealing glimpses of his firm bronzed buttocks.

Like the innocent she was, Amy blushed, realizing that what most fascinated her was that part of his anatomy which was barely concealed beneath the skimpy loincloth. She felt her face go crimson when her eyes fell on a tiny string of leather tied atop his bare hip. It struck her that with one quick jerk of that loosely tied knot, Tonatiuh would be totally naked.

Her embarrassed gaze flew up to his face.

Stammering, she said, "I . . . ah . . . I'll go put . . . my—"

"Don't," he said, and took a step toward her. "You're wearing underwear, aren't you?"

"Certainly!"

"Then why not swim in it? When you get out, the sun will dry it within minutes."

She stood there for a moment, looking at him, undecided. It was hard to think clearly with a tall, bronzed, near-naked Sun God standing there before her.

"Yes, I suppose I could do that."

Luiz smiled, reached out and touched her cheek. I'll go on and get into the water while you undress."

She nodded. "All right."

But he didn't move. Stayed right where he was. Amy dropped the clothes she held and turned away from him. Her hands shook a little as she unbuttoned her blouse and slipped her arms out of the sleeves. She bent and pulled off her boots and stockings, then straightened.

Still undecided, she stood there feeling his eyes on her back, wondering if she should put her blouse right back on. Her hands went to the buttons of her trousers. They were easier to unbutton than to button, and then she was left with nothing more to do than to take them off.

She put her thumbs into the sides of the waistband, wiggled her firm little derriere from side to side several times, and twisted free of the trousers. When they slipped down over her hips to her knees, she bent forward, pushed them to the ground, and stepped free of them.

And didn't realize just how much her companion, watching every move she made, had enjoyed the performance.

Slowly Amy turned around and the grin that was playing at Luiz's lips began to fade. Amy stood there facing him in a lace-and-ribbon–trimmed cotton chemise and underdrawers, with the cutest little smile of shyness he'd ever seen on her lovely face. The chemise's straps were narrow, its bodice was very low, revealing delicate ivory shoulders and a swanlike throat and slender arms. The fabric pulled tightly across her high, full bosom, the lace perfectly positioned to hide the crests of her breasts.

The narrow sash of her underdrawers was tied securely at her small waist and filmy lace, at midthigh, decorated the hem of the underwear—a provocative little garment far more daring than anything he could have imagined. Her naked legs were long and pale and her thighs were so firm and perfectly formed he felt his throat grow dry.

"I—I . . . think we'd better get into the water, don't you?" she said.

"The sooner the better," he admitted.

Now on this oppressively hot July afternoon, they stripped down to their underwear and eagerly climbed the steep, vine-covered rocky trail up to the huge flat boulder overhang beside the rushing falls. In seconds they stood there in the fierce sunlight, high above the cold, deep pool.

Luiz waited while Amy wound her loose, golden hair into a thick rope and pinned it haphazardly atop her head. When she'd finished, she squinted up at him and said, "Ready at last. Shall we dive? Want me to go first?"

"I have a better idea," he said, and knelt down on the smooth rock. "Climb on my back, we'll go down together."

"Yes!" Amy quickly agreed. After stepping around behind him, she promptly wrapped her arms around his neck, her legs around his back. Luiz's arms came up under her knees and he rose to his feet, shifting her high upon his back. While Amy laughed he moved to the rock's edge. He positioned himself directly on the rim, his bare toes hanging over.

"Hold on tight," he cautioned, and stepped off the ledge.

Amy screamed all the way down. They hit the cold, smooth water and went straight down, almost to the pool's rocky bottom. Amy clung tightly to Luiz's neck, her legs locking around his waist. He scissored his feet and shot to the surface, pulled her around in front of him, kissed her wet, laughing lips, then threw her over backward.

For a time they played happily in the cold, invigorating stream, racing across its width, water fighting out in the middle, doing acrobatics below the surface. When Amy came up coughing and choking after an endurance test of breath-holding underwater, a worried Luiz gathered her up in his arms, swam to the banks, and carried her out of the water.

"You all right?" he asked anxiously as he gently sat her down on a blanket spread on the shaded grass.

"F-fine . . . fine," she managed between

coughs, and smiled appreciatively as he helpfully patted her back.

But soon the coughs ceased and the back pats changed to caresses. Then the kisses began and in moments the afternoon's refreshing swimming excursion turned into the stirring, sensual exploration that could only lead to growing frustration.

Or to fulfillment.

8

Her neat, upswept hair was still a light golden
hue. Not a single strand of gray marred its shimmering blondness. Her tall, willowy frame was as
slim as when she was a girl. Her pale, oval face was
remarkably unlined, the skin as dewy fresh and
flawless as when she had been a vain young Texas
beauty.

Only the eyes gave her away.

A respected New Orleans spinster, Miss Margaret Ann Sullivan was still considered a handsome
woman. Her eyes had not faded from the vivid
blue they had always been. But in their indigo
depths was that telling expression; a knowledge of
life gained solely from living it, a quiet sadness
that comes only with the passing of years, the loss
of youthful dreams. The silent acceptance of one
who has quietly settled with life.

Margaret Sullivan had lived, since age twenty-
five, in comfortable loneliness in a luxurious,
two-story white mansion on tree-lined St. Charles
Avenue in the Crescent City's enchanting Garden
district.

The immaculate house belonged to her. Her
older brother, Walter, had generously bought it
for her the year she left Texas, the summer of

1839 when she was twenty-four years old. Now she had passed her forty-first birthday and all those years had been spent in this white, iron-lace-trimmed house.

She had never been back to Texas.

For more than a decade Margaret Sullivan had held a research position in the genealogy department of the university library at nearby Tulane. Not that she needed money. Walter Sullivan was a very wealthy man and saw to it that his only sister was well taken care of.

Margaret spent her days at the library, where she enjoyed her work. She loved the absorbing research and the bright young students and the pleasant three-block walk to the vine-covered university.

She loved having a reason to get out of bed each morning.

At the stroke of three every afternoon, Margaret Sullivan put on her hat and gloves, unfurled her parasol, and walked home. And always, as she ascended the steps to the wrap-around gallery, she offered up a silent prayer that when she walked into the foyer, she would see a letter lying in the silver calling card basket atop the hall table.

If she saw no letter, she proceeded directly up the stairs to her room, changed her clothes, and came back down. She went into the sunny drawing room where the curtains were of purest white lace-embroidered and oyster damask, the fine gray carpet was Brussels, and the oyster fireplace imported Carrera marble. She sat down on the silk-covered couch to wait.

Within minutes her housekeeper, Stella, entered bearing a gleaming silver tea service. When

Stella had placed the tray on the table before Margaret, the aging black woman shrugged sturdy shoulders and said apologetically, "No letter today, Miss Meg."

Margaret smiled. "Perhaps tomorrow."

"Yessum, tomorrow." Then Stella would add sorrowfully, "Sho is quiet 'round here since Miss Amy gone back to Texas. Yes, suh, mighty quiet. Too quiet, if you ask me." Muttering, she would go back to her kitchen while Margaret leisurely sipped her tea.

A letter was waiting one sweltering day in July when she reached home, weak from the three-block walk in the humid Louisiana heat. Her eyes fell on the square white envelope with the small, neat handwriting and immediately she felt revived.

Smiling, she took off her gloves and hat, dropped them carelessly on the table, and snatched up the letter. Like a young, excited girl, she flopped down on the second step of the carpeted staircase and eagerly ripped open the envelope.

Auntie Meg,

Is it as hot in New Orleans as it is on Orilla? I hope not, because I'm sure the kind of summer we are having would kill all your beautiful begonias.

Oh, Auntie, it seems ages since I left New Orleans. So much has happened! Can you keep a secret? I know you can, and you must! For a while at least.

Remember me telling you about how Tonatiuh always ignored me and acted as though he was much older than I, when in fact there is only a year's difference between us?

Well, all that's changed. And *he* has changed! He's a man now and so handsome it takes your breath away.

Aunt Meg, we're in love! Isn't it wonderful? I've never been so happy before, but *please* don't tell Daddy. You know Daddy, he would say we're too young and don't know what we want. But we do. We want each other.

I've told no one and neither has Tonatiuh. Everyone here thinks we are just friends and that's best for now.

I must close. Pedrico is leaving for Sundown and I want him to post this for me. Besides, it is almost time for Tonatiuh and me to ride up to Sunset River. We go there every afternoon to swim.

I miss you so much! Come home to Texas and Orilla where you belong!

> Your loving niece,
> Amy

Smiling, Margaret lowered the letter. Carefully she refolded it and placed it back in its envelope. She climbed the stairs to her bedroom, crossed the deep-rose rug to the set of white louvered doors giving onto the small back balcony. She pulled the doors open and drew a deep breath of the heavy, moist air.

She turned and placed the letter atop her rosewood writing desk, then picked it up again. She sat down, took out the letter and read it, then read it once more. She stopped smiling.

Pressing the letter to her breasts, her blue eyes clouded with worry. Should she immediately write Walter and warn him to keep a closer eye on Amy? No. It wouldn't be fair to Amy to reveal the secret she had shared. Besides, it was probably nothing more than a girlish infatuation born of the long separation between the two children.

And, should it prove to be a serious, lasting relationship, it might be the best thing. From what Walter said, there was no finer man than Don Ramon Quintano, no better-mannered, harder-working boy than Luiz.

Margaret Sullivan hoped she was doing the right thing in keeping quiet. Amy's happiness was all that mattered. God knew she did not want Amy's life to turn out like her own.

Cold, solitary Christmas Eves while everyone gathered with their families. Sultry summer nights alone in a bed meant for two. Bleak Sunday afternoons that stretched on endlessly. Sudden tropical storms blowing up out in the Gulf, and where were the sheltering arms to protect her?

Alone. Always alone. Eating, sleeping, laughing, crying.

Margaret Sullivan had grown used to it, and she didn't mind anymore. But she wanted better for Amy. Amy must have all the happiness she herself had missed. A full, rewarding life that a woman could not hope for without a husband. Her own faithful, loving husband.

Only hours after Baron Sullivan had seen Amy and Luiz ride away from the ranch that July afternoon, he went in search of his father. He found Walter Sullivan in the upstairs library behind his pine desk. He was not alone. Don Ramon sat across from him. Baron stiffened when he saw the *don* sitting calmly smoking a long brown cigar as he looked over an Orilla account book. It had never sat well with Baron that Orilla was co-owned by the Spaniard. He'd heard the story, many times, of how the *don* had come to his father with the proposition: "I divert my water, you share your land."

Baron thought Walter Sullivan had gotten the short end of the deal. He should have claimed Quintano's water and kept all the land. It rankled Baron that the green-eyed Spaniard and his half-breed Indian son considered themselves his equal. As far as he was concerned, they were not and would never be.

Walter Sullivan looked up when his oldest son entered the library. "Yes? What is it, Baron?"

Baron crossed the room. "Dad, I need to talk to you."

"What's on your mind?"

Baron glanced at the Don. "A family matter, Dad."

The Don politely rose. *"Con permiso . . ."*

"No, no, sit down, Ramon." Walter gestured. "You just got here." He said to Baron, "We'll be finished here within the hour."

"Well, this can't wait an hour," replied Baron. He cast another glance of annoyance at the *don.* Then: "Maybe it's just as well you're here, Quintano. What I have to say concerns you as well as Dad."

Walter Sullivan looked puzzled. "Then say it."

"Luiz and Amy are slipping off together while we're all asleep during siesta. I've seen them more than once. I saw them leave the ranch this afternoon."

Walter Sullivan leaned way back in his chair and crossed his arms over his chest. His heavily cut chin jutted out and his fair face flushed with anger. "Nobody's slipping around, except maybe you. My God, it's summertime. The kids ride up to Puesta del Sol to wade in the water."

Incensed, Baron looked from his father to the *don*. "You mean you know about it? You let her go?"

"What the hell's the matter with you, boy? Of course I let her go. Any reasons why I shouldn't?"

"Yes, there is. What do you think those two *really* do up there all alone?"

"I just got through telling you. They pull off their boots and—"

"You can bet their boots are not all they pull off. Better put a stop to it now or your precious daughter is going to be ruined." He added, sneering slightly, "If it's not too late already."

Walter Sullivan's arms came unfolded and he rose to his feet. "You ever say anything like that again, I'll order you off this ranch, so help me! I'll cut you off without an acre of Orilla! Not only are you slurring your sister, you're saying the *don*'s son isn't trustworthy. I won't have it, you hear me? You owe him an apology, goddamn it."

Don Ramon waved a brown hand dismissively. "It is not necessary."

Walter, furious, shook his head. "Why, Amy and Luiz are a couple of the sweetest kids that ever lived, and I never worry about them for a minute." He stepped around the desk and faced his son. "You say anything to either one of those children and you'll answer to me. Understand?"

Baron nodded, his eyes an icy blue. "Sure, Dad. I understand."

"Now get on out of here and stop trying to cause trouble for everybody." He scowled after his son's departing back, then returned to his chair and dropped wearily into it.

He heaved a deep, heavy sigh and said, "I apologize for Baron's unforgivable rudeness." He closed his eyes, then opened them. "It's my fault, I spoiled my boys when I should have made them work hard. I should have raised them the way you did Luiz."

"*Amigo*, who is to say what is right? If I raise my son wisely, perhaps it is because we come from a country that has known poverty. A poor country where a man has to work really hard to survive, where people have given their lives for a tiny piece of land."

Sullivan nodded. "Well, I commend you. You're a rich, powerful man, but your son never treats the help as if he is above them. He works hard, unlike my two lazy offspring."

Pleased, Don Ramon smiled and reminisced, "If you recall, Luiz had an unhealthy amount of arrogance when he was a child. Then came that day he wanted the valuable stud I bought in Kentucky. He demanded that I give it to him. So I did. And a dozen other horses as well. I told him he had to feed them, water them, exercise them, do everything for them." The *don* laughed, fondly recalling how hard the boy had had to work. "Not everyone fully appreciates how unglamorous it is to shovel out stalls. It certainly keeps you from thinking you're the most important thing in the world."

Walter grinned. "Well, you can be proud of the boy."

Don Ramon gave no reply. He drew another cigar from his breast pocket and for a time the two friends sat in silence. When the *don* spoke, his tone was guarded. "Walter, as you said to Baron, Luiz and Amy are just children. But suppose when they are older they start to care about each other? Fall in love?"

"Old friend, isn't that really what we'd both like to see happen? To have them marry? For my grandchildren to be your grandchildren? To know that Orilla will kept together?"

The *don* felt his heart fill with gladness. He said, "It is my fondest wish."

"Mine as well. So long as it's several years down the road. Why, they're just kids." He laughed heartily. "Still wading in the river like when they were babies."

9

The Indian stood naked in the sunlight.

The blond girl lay on the rocks below, as bare as he.

Luiz Quintano stood unmoving atop the high basalt overhang by the falls of Puesta del Sol. The spray from the rushing cascade peppered his noble dark head and slim bronzed body. Beads of water clung to the long, thick lashes of his unblinking jet-black eyes. Eyes that were locked on the beautiful naked white girl below.

Amy Sullivan lay motionless on a smooth flat rock beside the cold, clear river. Her bed of stone was completely shaded by the tall cottonwoods and silvery willows. Her pale, bare body was sheltered from the blazing desert sun's fierce rays. She lay there beside the placid stream, her slender legs stretched full length, the palms of her hands flat against the rock. Her unbound blond hair was fanned out appealingly around her head. Her lush, dark lashes were half lowered over her vivid blue eyes. Eyes that were fastened on the handsome naked Indian above.

It was nearing summer's end.

The waning days of a scorching September would soon give way to the slightly cooler ones of

October. Since that June day when Amy had stepped down from the train to see Luiz waiting, they had had eyes only for each other. Had lost sleep thinking of one another. Had fought against what both knew would happen one day.

Today was that day.

They had reached the river and immediately begun undressing. But Luiz, after shedding only his shirt and boots, had stopped. His hands fell to his sides and he silently watched while Amy wriggled out of her tight trousers. When she wore only her lace-trimmed underthings and stood twisting her heavy hair into a golden rope, she frowned at him and said, "What are you waiting for? Take off your pants."

He didn't do it.

He continued to look at her in a very penetrating way. Amy's cheeks flushed. The palms of her hands began to perspire. The air she breathed was charged with excitement and expectation.

Luiz stepped forward and stood looking down at her. All six feet of him, towering and lanky. Her head fell back, her eyes met his, and she trembled. His long arm encircled her waist and he pulled her to him. He kissed her as he'd never kissed her before, a slow burning, totally commanding kiss that caused her bare knees to buckle, her body to melt against his.

When at last his lips left hers and he lifted his head, Amy's cheek rested against his bare chest. For a moment his hand cradled her head, then swept down the side of her throat to her shoulder. He pushed the delicate strap of her chemise down and curled long, tanned fingers inside the garment's low, lacy bodice. Amy's head came up off his chest. She moved back a half step and looked into his eyes.

"Let me look at you, Amy," he said, his voice surprisingly soft and low. "All of you. That's all I ask."

She couldn't speak. She nodded her head as his gentle hand swept the chemise's bodice down and away from her left breast. She heard his sharp intake of air and saw the muscles in his bronzed throat move with his nervous swallowing.

"Tonatiuh," she murmured breathlessly as he swiftly lowered the lace-trimmed chemise to her waist.

His blazing black eyes touched her bared breasts with such fire she could feel the heat. Her nipples instantly responded. The soft, satiny crests immediately tightened and stood out in twin peaks of sensation.

"Amy, you are beautiful," he said, and she could tell by the change in his voice that he was awed by the sight of her. His admiration made her feel gloriously happy. When his hands went to the narrow sash of her underpants, she never even considered stopping him. She gave a little startled cry of surprise when, overpowered by a need to inspect all her feminine charms, Luiz impulsively yanked her underwear down over her flared hips.

Amy shuddered instinctively. She was totally naked now, her underthings nothing more than discarded wisps of useless cotton and lace encircling her bare feet. She flinched when Luiz agilely dropped into a crouching position before her.

"Step out of these," he commanded softly, and she nervously obeyed. He picked up her underthings, held them tightly in his hand as if afraid she might change her mind and put them back on before he'd had the chance to examine her lovingly.

Expecting him to come to his feet, Amy felt her bare belly quiver when he remained as he was, crouching there before her, his hot eyes lingering unashamedly on the triangle of blond curls between her thighs. Just as when he'd looked at her breasts, Amy felt a stirring low in her belly, a contracting of tight muscles, the feeling that his hands as well as his eyes were caressing her, touching her where she'd never been touched before.

"*Dios,*" he muttered huskily, "*Dios, querido.*"

Amy held her breath when he abruptly dropped her lacy underwear. His hands came up to clasp the curve of her hips. Forcefully he pulled her to him and pressed his hot cheek against her bare stomach. She knew his eyes were closed because she felt the restless flutter of his long lashes against her sensitive flesh.

"Amy, my Amy," he whispered, his breath a hot flame upon her fluttering belly.

As quickly as he had laid his cheek against her, he lifted it, released her hips and rose to his feet. Staring hungrily at her, he drew her to him and kissed her.

Amy could tell by his violent heartbeat against her naked breasts that he was excited, but she was far too naive to realize just how excited. As his mouth ground into hers and he crushed her to his hard body, she felt a sudden dizziness and warmth, a new kind of hunger and restlessness.

His smooth, warm chest felt wonderful pressed so tightly to hers. The shimmering gold Sun Stone, caught between their bodies, felt like a disk of hot molten lead against her breast. The hard finish of his trousers was mildly abrasive to her bare thighs and stomach and, strangely, that too felt very good.

Luiz suddenly tore his flaming lips from hers. Amy blinked in confusion when he forcefully set her back from him. She said his name and followed after him when he wheeled around and stalked hurriedly away.

"Stay where you are," he said over his shoulder, and Amy, perplexed, stopped. She watched, puzzled, as he agilely climbed the vine-tangled path leading up to the falls. Dazed, short of breath, she dropped down to the flat rocks, wondering what she had done wrong, what was bothering him.

She lost sight of him for a time, but kept her anxious eyes raised to the huge jutting boulder high above. And gave a small little sigh of relief when he emerged through the watery mist of the falls.

He had discarded his trousers. He stepped to the rim of the rock and looked silently down at her as if in deep thought. Finally he moved his bare feet slightly apart. He took a deep, slow breath. And, with his black eyes holding hers, he gave a yank to the leather string tied atop his hip, and his loincloth fell away.

Amy felt all the air leave her body. Shocked, she stared unblinkingly at the tall, naked Indian. She had never seen a man totally nude. She'd heard schoolgirls whisper about men's hairy, ugly bodies and how they planned only to let their husbands make love to them in the darkness of the night. There was nothing ugly about Tonatiuh. He stood there in the midday radiance and she felt the heart inside her swell with pride. He was beautiful. Every dark gleaming inch of him. Don Ramon had said, proudly, that in the Aztec culture, Tonatiuh was a *philli,* descended from nobles. It was easy to believe. He looked fierce and proud and noble.

Slowly Amy lay back on the smooth rock. She fanned her hair out around her head, stretched her legs, and placed her hands, palms flat, on the level apron of stone. She waited. Young though she was, she somehow knew that her Aztec Indian Sun God was communing with the ancient spirits. Sensed that he was lost in some strange meditation ceremony that was a prelude to their lovemaking.

Tonatiuh was going to make love to her here in this shady glade. She was unafraid. She sighed, feeling wonderfully happy and strangely relaxed. Her eyes never left the raven-haired, naked Sun God whose water-beaded body was coiled tightly, his fire intentionally leashed.

He went up on his toes, raised his arms high over his head, looked directly up into the burning sun, stayed like that for interminable minutes. Then dove gracefully into the pool. Underwater he swam directly to the rocky banks where Amy waited. With his strong arms he easily pulled himself up, rose to his feet, and took the three long strides to where she lay.

He stood just above, rivulets of water coursing down his gleaming copper body.

He lifted his arms and swept his wet, dark hair back off his face, then fell to his knees beside her. While she watched, rapt, he pressed his hands to his temples, then folded them over his heart, then lowered them to cup his groin.

"My head, my heart, my love. All belong to you."

Touched, she solemnly nodded. His hands left his body, moved to clasp her temples.

Understanding completely, she said softly, "Yes, Tonatiuh, all my thoughts are yours." His hands moved to cover her heart. "Yes," she said, "oh, yes." He sat back on his heels and with one hand atop the other, he gently cupped the blond curls between her pale thighs. "Y-yes—yes," she managed, her breath short, "it is yours. All my love belongs to you."

While one of his hands left her, the other remained and slipped more fully between her legs. His fingers touched her briefly with a fiery intimacy before he stretched out beside her, took her in his arms, and, holding her very close, said, "Amy, I stood above and asked the sun and the ancient spirits for some sign, some vision to show me it is right for me to touch you. To make love to you today." His arms tightened around her. "It was withheld from me, so I can only assume that I should leave you untouched." He drew a ragged breath "But I cannot. And even if the time is not right, I know that you are my *tonali*. My fate. My destiny. It was written in the stars a millennium ago. Since it is so, why must I wait to be inside your body?"

Amy, pressed against the lean, naked strength of him, said with trusting devotion, "There is no reason, Tonatiuh. I belong to you."

"Sweet love," he murmured, and urged her over onto her back once more. He yanked the heavy gold medallion up and slid it over his shoulder to fall on his back so that it wouldn't hurt Amy. He lay on his stomach beside her, his torso partially covering hers. Anxious, and more afraid than he'd ever been in his life, he began kissing her. And as he kissed her, his hand cupped her warm, firm breast, his fingertips gently plucking at its crest.

Luiz was as pure and as unschooled in the ways of love as was Amy. Terrified that he would hurt her, yet wanting her so much he felt he couldn't wait another second, he continued to kiss and caress her, hoping he would somehow know when she was as ready as he.

Amy clung tightly to him, on fire from his kisses, devastatingly stirred by the touch of his gentle hands on her tingling flesh and by the heavy, hardness pulsing against her belly.

When Luiz lifted his head and gazed down at her, Amy murmured breathlessly, "Tonatiuh, I don't know exactly what I am supposed to do. You'll have to show me."

A muscle danced in his jaw. He said, "We learned to kiss. We will learn to make love together."

He kissed her again and his hand swept down over her stomach and went between her legs. He gently pressed his middle finger to her sensitive flesh. And felt a fiery wetness. He dipped his fingertip into that wetness and slowly spread it upward. Amy winced with the pleasure of it and her back arched.

Eyes sliding closed, she said, "Tonatiuh, may I touch you the way you're touching me?"

Surprised but pleased, he answered, "Nothing would make me happier."

She smiled dreamily, rolled up to a sitting position, and urged him down onto his back. Her eyes wide with wonder, she shyly reached out with both hands and wrapped them tentatively around his powerful erection. Awed and awkward, she clasped him as if he might break. And blinked with delighted surprise when he stirred involuntarily in her hands.

While she could have been content to play and explore all afternoon, Luiz was terrified that any second he would explode in shuddering release. Teeth clenched, heart pounding, he lay there for only scant seconds, in sweet agony, before he pushed her hands away and anxiously sought his place between her legs.

He thrust into her and felt the tightness and the tearing and saw the look of pain that came into her eyes. But he couldn't stop. He had no notion how to control his out-of-control body. He pumped wildly into her, the pleasure so intense he moaned with ecstasy. In seconds it was over.

For a time they lay entwined, Luiz murmuring words of love and apology, anxiously assuring her that he'd never hurt her again. Promising he would learn to become a better lover. Amy, kissing his worried bronzed face, consoled him and swore that she loved him so much that being in his arms was ecstasy.

Luiz carried her to the river and bathed her with such loving tenderness, Amy derived far more joy from the bath than she had from the actual act of love.

Sweeter still was when they got out of the water

and Luiz lifted her in his arms and carried her all the way up the trail to the rock overhang beside the falls. They stretched out to let the sun dry their bodies. Peacefully they lay in each other's arms as the sun began its slide toward the western horizon.

Sighing, Amy placed her hand atop the gold medallion resting on Luiz's smooth chest and murmured lazily, "Tonatiuh."

"Yes?"

"Tell me more about the Sun Stone."

10

He smiled, kissed her forehead, and his hand covered hers atop the glittering gold medallion. Sighing deeply, his smooth bronzed face changed subtly. His classic features took on a dreamy, trancelike appearance as legends and images and voices from the past came forth to rule his consciousness.

"The gold disk I wear represents the huge Sun Stone that rests in the old temple in Mexico City. The stone depicts the Aztec cosmos—our gods, our cultural rites—and the calendar by which my people calculated time. In the very center is the face of Tonatiuh, our Sun God, from whom I take my name." He fell silent. His breathing became very heavy, almost as if he were asleep.

Amy's fingers tightened on the medallion and she said softly, "Go on, please."

"Mexico City was *our* city. The Aztecs'. Our patron god, Huitzilopochtli, led his people out of the distant northern land of Aztlan and into Mexico. He promised his followers a place that would be theirs. They would know where to build their city because they would see an eagle perched on a great cactus devouring a serpent. Huitzilopochtli led them onto an island and they found the eagle on the cactus. They settled there and called their city Tenochtitlán—Place of the Cactus."

Luiz's eyes moved rapidly beneath his closed lids, as one who is sleeping deeply.

"They built their pyramids of the sun and of the moon. They had their religion, their art, their poetry. Their riches. They bothered no one. Then my father's people came from Spain. Moctezuma, the supreme emperor of the Aztec, believed that the Spaniards were white gods come out of the sea. So he allowed Cortez and his conquerors to march unopposed right into his beautiful city and seize it."

Amy was looking at Luiz's face. His eyes were still closed, but his face had gone rigid.

"The Spaniards took our most beautiful women for their own. But not from my Aztec ancestors. Their bloodline remained pure until my mother married my father. I am the first *mestizo*—mixed blood—in either my father's or my mother's family."

"Yes, I know," said Amy softly. "Don Ramon said it was meant to be—that your mother told him so."

The tenseness left Luiz's face. "This is true. My mother's *tonali*— her fate—was to have a son by a pure-blooded Spaniard." A smile began to play Luiz's lips. "She gave him a great deal more than me."

Amy smiled too. This was her favorite part of the story. The part where the wild and beautiful hereditary Aztec princess left her infant son alone atop a basalt mesa.

Without prompting, Luiz began to speak of that

day when the goddess Xochiquetzal had left husband and son and returned to her people.

"It was the first August of my life," said Luiz, his voice low and soft. "It was nearing noon and I was asleep. My mother awakened me. It was hot, very hot. She gave me a cooling bath and when she had finished, she did not dry me off or put any clothes on me.

"Instead, she carried me outdoors and, holding me in one arm, she climbed up on the bare back of my father's favorite stallion and rode away from our little adobe home. When we had gone many miles across the parched deserts, my mother guided the stallion to the top of a flat mesa. She dismounted, walked to the very center of the black basalt tableland, and lay me down.

"She sat on her heels beside me.

"For a long time my beautiful mother stared down at me with those dark, exotic eyes. Then she kissed me, and I felt the wetness of her tears against my face. She said, 'My son, I love you. But I can no longer stay. I am going back to my people, but I leave something in my place.'

"She took the gold Sun Stone medallion from around her throat, held it to her lips, and kissed it. Then she struck the rock with the heavy gold disk and, looking into my eyes, she said in the Nahuatl tongue, 'From this barren rock will flow a cold, clear life-giving body of water. I give to you, my little Tonatiuh, the water and the Sun Stone. The water to make you rich. The Sun Stone to protect you from evil.'

"She placed the medallion on my stomach and fastened the heavy chain around my neck. She held out her hand to me and I clasped her little

finger in my fist. She smiled and said, 'Ask your
father to forgive his restless princess. Tell him the
prophecy is complete. The time has come for me
to go.'

"Then she rose and left me there, naked and
alone."

Luiz fell silent, smiling.

Amy, easing up on an elbow, studied his handsome face. Leaning close, she softly kissed his
closed eyelids and said, "Tonatiuh, I have, of
course, heard the story from Don Ramon. But
. . . you were only a infant, just four months old.
How could you possibly know how your mother
looked? What she said when she left you?"

Luiz's eyes opened. His smile fled and he looked
intensely at Amy. "Don't ask me how I know. But
I know. I can't explain it. But I know exactly what
happened and everything my mother said that
day. I still remember how she looked."

Amy stared at him. Nodding, she said, "I believe
you." She lifted the gold medallion and held it in
the palm of her hand. "Your mother told you the
Sun Stone would protect you from evil?"

"Yes."

Amy pressed her lips to the gleaming disk.
"Then be careful that you never lose it."

"I will," Luiz said. He grinned suddenly and
rolled up into a sitting position. "And I'll be careful not to lose you as well. Which means we'd
better be getting back to Orilla before they start
to wonder." He took the medallion from her,
leaned down, and kissed her. Her arms went
around his neck.

"Yes. I promised we'd be home by sundown,"
she said.

"Then we'd better get our pants on."

Laughing, they hurried back down the trail to put on their clothes. Soon they were dressed, but Amy asked Luiz to give her a minute to brush out her tangled hair. She rummaged around in her reticule for her hairbrush, became frustrated when she couldn't find it, sat down on her heels and poured out the reticule's contents.

"Here you are," she said aloud, and snatched up the gold-backed hairbrush.

"Want me to do it?" Luiz asked, and crouched down facing her.

"No. It won't take a minute, but thanks." She drew the brush vigorously through her hair. "You can gather up the stuff I poured out if you want to help."

Smiling, he nodded, and went about placing the spilled contents back inside the small purse. His eyes fell on a small item that made the smile leave his face.

A ticket. A blood-red ticket with black numbers.

Luiz picked up the ticket, blinked, and read the numbers on it: 6 6 5 6.

His hand began to shake slightly. "Amy, what is this?" He held it up to her.

Hairbrush posed in midstroke, she glanced at the ticket. "What? Oh, that. It's my railroad baggage ticket from the day I came home from New Orleans." She went back to brushing her hair.

Luiz, feeling as if he were suddenly suffocating, gripped the ticket with its damning numbers tightly in his palm. Unsteadily he rose to his feet. A sudden breeze rustled the leaves of the cottonwoods and the setting sun plummeted below the distant hills. A sudden chill seemed to slice through the heat of the late afternoon.

An inexplicable fear gripped Luiz. The foreboding dream. The half-remembered warning. The quartet of numbers. 6,6,5,6. Now he knew. Amy had come home on June 6, 1856. 6,6,5,6. Amy was the danger.

His danger.

"No!" Luiz choked out. He reached down and yanked Amy to her feet, kissing her with all the love and fear in his wildly beating heart.

"Tonatiuh, what is it?" she asked anxiously when at last he tore his lips from hers.

He shook his dark head, pressed her close, and Amy felt the trembling of his tall, spare body against her.

His doubts became her own and she gripped his shirt front, closed her eyes tightly, and said, "You're not sorry we made love, are you?"

"No, sweetheart," he said, fighting to regain his composure. "And I never want you to be sorry either."

She pulled back to look at him. "Why would I be?"

He stared into her trusting blue eyes. Loving her as he did, he carefully concealed his growing apprehension.

"No reason," he said, and grinned at her. His hand slipped down over the curve of her bottom and he gave it a playful little slap. Then he laughed and added, "But we'll both be sorry if we don't get home."

The crumpled red ticket with the bold black numbers dropped from his open fingers, fluttered to the ground, and blew away.

* * *

That same evening after dinner, Baron Sullivan found his brother Lucas on the west patio. Alone in the moonlight, Lucas sprawled lazily on a padded settee, his long legs stretched out before him. His booted feet rested atop the low adobe fence that bordered the patio. On his face was a half smile. In his hand was a tumbler of Kentucky bourbon.

Lucas was well on his way to becoming drunk.

Baron sighed and joined his brother. Taking the tumbler of whiskey from Lucas, he set it aside.

"We need to talk, Lucas."

"Can't we talk while I drink?" was Lucas's reply.

"No." Baron dropped down onto the settee. "I want you to listen to me. We've got big trouble."

"Big trouble? Well, all the more reason I'll need a drink," Lucas said, grinning.

"Forget your damned whiskey! I overheard the old man and the Spaniard talking this afternoon. Know what they're planning?"

Lucas frowned and shook his head.

"A marriage between Amy and the uppity half-breed."

"We can't let that happen. I ain't gonna have no Indian for a brother-in-law."

"You are if we don't work fast. Ride into town. Drag Tyler Parnell out of whichever whorehouse he's in and get him out here to the ranch. I'll see to it Amy comes down and entertains him."

"How you gonna do that? She don't even like Tyler much."

"Leave that to me. Now get going and don't come back without him."

"Whatever you say." Lucas rose from the settee and reached for his tumbler of whiskey. Baron beat him to it. He tossed the bourbon over the low adobe enclosure and set the empty glass down.

"Little brother, you see to it Tyler hangs around Amy long enough to get her pregnant and I promise you can have all the whiskey you want for the rest of your life."

Lucas grinned, stepped over the fence, and headed for the corral. Baron returned to the house, climbed the stairs, knocked on Amy's door, and entered without waiting for a response.

Amy, fresh from a bath and wearing only her nightgown, gasped and reached for a robe. "What do you want? I was about to go to bed."

Baron walked right past her into the large dressing room. He took down a frilly pink frock, came back into the bedroom, and tossed it across Amy's bed.

"Put this on. You look real sweet in pink."

Amy narrowed her eyes. "Don't be ridiculous. I'm tired and I'm going to bed."

"It's not yet ten o'clock. Why, I wonder, are you so tired?" Baron started to grin. "I've got an idea I know the real reason, baby sister."

Amy's face flushed hot. "You know nothing."

Baron gave her a smug look. "Don't I? You and the son of that crazed old Aztec woman slipping off every afternoon where nobody can find you. Honey, you might fool Dad, but not me." He moved a half step closer. "You're letting that half-breed get to you."

Amy turned quickly away and tried her best to sound indignant. "I don't know what you're talking about."

Baron chuckled. "Honey, your secret is safe with me. You came back from New Orleans all grown into a woman and I don't blame you for wanting a little loving. But your dark-skinned Sun God is just a boy. You need a man. A man like Tyler Parnell."

Amy whirled back around to face Baron. "Get out my room!"

Baron's evil smile remained in place. "Tyler likes you, Amy. He's coming out here to see you tonight."

"I have no intention of seeing Tyler Parnell tonight or any other night! I can't stand him."

"Better learn to like him, honey. If you don't, I'll have to tell Dad about you and pretty boy."

Amy was trapped. She knew Baron. He would do it. And if he did, she and Tonatiuh would be in serious trouble. Their fathers would keep them apart. Worse, they might punish Tonatiuh.

"I—I'll give Tyler Parnell an hour this evening. No more," Amy said.

"Ty will be flattered," said Baron, failing to mention that this was to be only the first of such Friday evenings she would be expected to spend with Tyler Parnell.

It was a miserable hour for Amy and a triumphant one for Baron. When Amy at last said good night to her unwanted guest, Baron emerged to invite Tyler Parnell to call on Amy again the next Friday evening. Parnell was more than eager. Baron was not worried about his father's keen dislike of Tyler Parnell. An early riser, Walter Sullivan retired to his room each night at ten.

Amy thought about telling Tonatiuh of her predicament but decided against it. There had always been bad blood between him and her brothers. They hated Tonatiuh, especially Baron. She was afraid for Tonatiuh. If he intervened on her behalf, it would cause him serious trouble.

So she kept to herself the fact that each Friday evening she was required to spend an hour alone with the twenty-nine-year-old Tyler Parnell. It would be temporary. She would purposely behave so coldly toward Parnell he would soon lose interest.

In each other's arms every afternoon at the Puesta del Sol hideaway, it was easy for the young lovers to forget that anyone else existed. For them, no one did. After their first total intimacy, the healthy young pair made love every day. They were wildly in love and gloriously happy and never dreamed that as the hot, hot days of an Indian summer gave way to the clear, beautiful ones of autumn, their innocence was not all that was slipping away.

Youth and trust and happiness was dying as well.

The beginning of the end came one cool October night after the most wonderful day they had ever had. Luiz, lying awake in his bed that night, thinking of Amy, grew restless. Rising, he pulled on his pants and went for a walk.

Circling the big hacienda, he strolled toward the west patio. The Sullivan's patio. And there he saw Amy in the moonlight with Tyler Parnell. Heartsick, he turned numbly away, returned to his room, and paced the floor in agony.

Still, all would have been made right had the pair been allowed one more afternoon together.

Amy would have told him the truth, that Baron was blackmailing her. That she cared nothing for Tyler Parnell.

But she never got the chance.

11

"Domino!"

Pedrico Valdez, his one eye twinkling, grinned at the surprised man across the pine desk. "Domino, *patrón*," he said again, and triumphantly crossed his arms over his chest.

Shaking his graying head, Walter Sullivan couldn't believe it. Each night for over a decade, he and Pedrico Valdez had played a two-handed game of dominos. In all those years he had never been caught with this many bones left in his hand.

"You finally got me, Pedrico," he said, smiling broadly, two unplayed ivory dominos held loosely in his cupped palm.

"Yes!" said the pleased houseboy. "How much, *patrón?* Lots of count, I hope."

He lifted the pen from its inkwell and leaned over the white tally sheet, eager to write down the score. He waited. Walter Sullivan said nothing. Pedrico looked up questioningly and saw an expression of horror on the big rancher's florid face.

"Dios, patrón!" He dropped the pen. "What is it?"

Pedrico jumped up from his chair so quickly it toppled over backward. Terrified, he circled the desk, anxiously asking what was wrong. But Walter Sullivan could not speak. He clutched frantically at his chest and his face contorted with pain.

Making gasping, wheezing sounds of agony, the big rancher's eyes rolled back in his head and he slumped forward in his chair, dead of a heart attack. Clutched tightly in his big fist were the two unplayed ivories.

The 6-6 and the 5-6.

While a punishing Texas sun beat down with a vengeance, Amy stood between her brothers in Orilla's small, well-tended graveyard. Directly before her was the heavy bronze coffin bearing the body of her father.

A black-robed *padre* conducted the service in Latin while vaqueros and cowboys and the townsfolk of Sundown tearfully paid their last respects.

Feeling strangely cold in the midmorning heat, Amy was in a daze of grief. She couldn't believe that a man as vigorous and alive as her daddy could be gone so suddenly.

The brief service ended.

Amy stepped forward.

She stooped, picked up a handful of the dry Texas soil her father had loved so dearly, and slowly sprinkled it over the bronze coffin. She lifted the black veil from her face, leaned down, pressed her lips to the casket, and said soundlessly, "Rest well, Daddy. Orilla is in good hands."

Throughout that long, hot afternoon callers filled the many downstairs rooms of the salmon-colored hacienda. Magdelena and Rosa and Pedrico passed among them, bearing silver trays of cooling drinks. In both dining halls, long buffet tables were spread with an array of foods to feed the lingering guests.

Amy graciously served as hostess, standing between her brothers, shaking hands, accepting condolences. But her blue eyes kept sweeping the crowd in search of Luiz. She finally spotted the gleaming blue-black hair, the dark, handsome face. But Luiz was not looking her way.

Inwardly sighing, she turned back to greet Douglas Crawford, the big, strapping, red-haired neighboring rancher and his pregnant wife, Shirley. She thanked the young couple for coming and accepted their expressions of sympathy.

Late that afternoon, Amy released a gentle sigh of relief as Pedrico closed the door after the last of the departing mourners. Fleeing at once to the sanctuary of her room, Amy stripped her hot, black dress away, bathed her prickled skin in cooling water, slipped on a fresh chemise, underpants, and lacy petticoat, then sagged tiredly to the bed.

Her head throbbing, her eyes scratchy, she stretched out to rest. In her depression she longed desperately for Luiz to hold her, to comfort her. To love her.

"Tomorrow," she said softly in the gloom, "tomorrow we will ride to the river."

But there would be no tomorrow for Amy and Luiz.

In his father's library down the hall, a revengeful Baron Sullivan stood at a tall front window. He watched an Orilla buckboard roll down the long drive, kicking up dust in its wake. Pedrico was driving. Magdelena and Rosa were seated beside him.

Baron had sent the trio into Sundown to distribute baskets of food left over from the wake. He didn't want them underfoot.

He had a score to settle.

Baron shrugged out of his dark funeral coat, yanked off his tie, opened his stiff white collar, and rolled up his sleeves. He instructed Lucas to bring him a piece of strong rope and the coiled black bullwhip he kept hidden under his bed.

While Lucas hurried to do his brother's bidding, Baron took down his father's worn gunbelt from the cedar coat tree. He eased from the holster the engraved Rogers and Spencer six-shooter. He loaded the long-barreled pistol and stuck it in the waistband of his dark trousers.

Lucas returned and Baron casually looped the coiled black bullwhip and rope over his left shoulder. He looked at his brother.

"No time like the present," he said, his icy blue eyes determined. "Let's go down and have our little talk with the half-breed."

Lucas fully approved. Tipsy, he nodded eagerly. "Looks like you've got something in mind for the boy lover."

Baron, crossing the room, said over his shoulder, "Yes, I have. An invitation to leave Orilla." He headed for the staircase. "But first I want to hear him confess to his transgressions."

Luiz was outside on the deserted east patio.

His discarded black suit jacket tossed over the back of an iron lace chair, white dress shirt half open down his dark chest, he lay on a padded yellow chaise. Stretched out on his back, hands folded beneath his head, he brooded alone in the late October sunlight. Melancholy and confused, he desperately longed for an opportunity to talk with Amy.

It was Monday and they'd not been together since Friday afternoon. Friday night he had seen her with Tyler Parnell. Had she betrayed him?

A movement in his side vision caused Luiz's dark head to snap around. With the quickness of a cat he was up off the chaise facing the approaching Sullivan brothers. He knew by the look in Baron's cold blue eyes that he was in danger.

His tall body tensed, black eyes flashing with unease, he said, "What do you want?"

It was a short conversation.

Drawing the engraved sidearm and pointing it directly at Luiz's chest, Baron said, "Your immediate and lasting absence from Orilla."

From that moment everything happened so fast there was no time for talk. Lucas sprang quickly forward and pushed Luiz toward the patio's low gate with such force, Luiz lost his footing. He stumbled against a white iron lace table, upsetting it and its contents. A crystal water pitcher and glasses crashed to the rough brick floor, shattering.

Landing amid the broken glass, Luiz suffered cuts to the palms of his hands and his forehead.

He never felt it.

Angered, he shot to his feet with the agility of an acrobat and came at Lucas, fists raised, ignoring the gun pointed at him. He managed to tag Lucas squarely on the chin, but it was much like a pesky insect stinging a grizzly bear. Incensed, Lucas slammed a beefy fist into Luiz's left jaw and sent him sprawling again.

Luiz felt the white-hot pain explode inside his head. Stunned, he was struggling to his feet as Don Ramon, hearing the commotion, came rushing out of the hacienda.

The *don* saw Luiz knocked backward by Lucas's punishing blow, saw Baron holding the leveled gun, saw the coiled black bullwhip and rope slung over his shoulder. Fear gripped him and he pleaded with the vindictive brothers to spare his only son.

For his trouble he was backhanded by Lucas. Blood spurted from the *don*'s split lip. He reeled backward, but stayed upright by sheer force of will. Facing down the loaded pistol, he turned to Baron. Clutching at his shirt front, he begged for rationality.

Baron wasn't listening.

He grabbed the *don*'s arm and carelessly flung him halfway across the brick patio. Don Ramon crashed into the overturned table. His head struck the table's sharp iron edge and he slumped to the brick patio floor. Luiz, forgetting his own pain, hurried to his fallen father.

Bright blood oozed from the *don*'s silver hair and his green eyes stared sightlessly. Frantically Luiz felt for a pulse in his father's throat. There was none.

Don Ramon Rafael Quintano was dead.

Stunned and immobile for only an instant, Luiz was totally enraged by his father's senseless, brutal murder. His smooth olive face a mask of fury, Luiz leapt up.

He did not come at Lucas, but at Baron. Like a dangerous animal loosed from its cage, he attacked with such speed and lethal strength, Baron was too numbed with fear to fire the pistol. Clasped in a viselike bear hug, the gun hung useless at his side. Baron felt the breath being squeezed from his body. He was certain this maddened Indian was going to kill him before Lucas could pull him off.

"Goddamn you to hell!" Baron snarled, gasping for breath, when at last his brother was able to drag Luiz away.

Lucas had a hard time subduing Luiz. Finally he was able to pin the infuriated youth back against his big solid frame with one muscular forearm crushing Luiz's throat. With his other hand, he twisted Luiz's left arm behind his back.

Still unnerved from his unexpected brush with death, Baron glared angrily at the restrained half-breed. He moved up close and said in a low, cold voice, "You'll pay for that." To his brother he said, "Let's get him down to the ranch gates."

Lucas and Baron forced Luiz from the patio and out to the front drive. The pair dragged the struggling Indian down Orilla's long palm-lined drive to the tall white ranch gates rising skyward in the blood-red rays of a dying Texas sun.

When the trio stood just below the white gates, Lucas held Luiz while Baron uncoiled the rope and tossed one end up over the archway's high supporting beam, then slowly fed enough slack so that the rope dangled down within reach.

Lucas drew Luiz's hands in front of him and tied his wrists securely with the rope. Then he yanked Luiz's trussed hands high above his head, pulling the rope so taut the young man felt his arms would be jerked from their sockets.

Baron allowed the coiled black bullwhip to slide

down from his shoulder. After shoving the gun back into his trousers, he smiled evilly, uncoiled the whip, and began to flick it slowly, making the long whip snap loudly in the air before Luiz.

With Luiz's hands secured and stretched high over his head, Lucas tore the white shirt from his back, not stopping until it lay in shreds on the gravel drive and Luiz was bare to the waist, the sun turning his smooth bronzed flesh the color of brick.

Baron, purposely trailing the bullwhip's tip in the dust, eyed the gleaming gold Sun Stone medallion resting on Luiz's chest. He wrapped his fingers around the circular disk and gave it a vicious yank. The chain snapped and fell away from Luiz's throat.

For a moment Baron held the gleaming gold medallion in the palm of his hand. Staring down at it, he sneered, knowing that the superstitious half-breed believed the medallion was an Aztec amulet against evil and danger. He opened his fingers and let it fall to the ground at their feet. Smiling, he ground it into the dust with his bootheel.

A demonic gleam in his blue eyes, Baron said, "Lucas and I don't take too kindly to the notion of a barbarian redskin sleeping with our little sister. What have you got to say for yourself, half-breed?"

No answer.

Luiz didn't make a sound.

Baron wasted no more time. He moved around Luiz, stepped off exactly eight paces, then turned. Standing directly behind the trussed young man, he lifted the black bullwhip high in the air.

And brought it singing down on Luiz's bare back.

Luiz's tautly stretched body recoiled from the agonizing blow and his eyes closed briefly from the stinging pain. A wide white welt appeared on the coppery skin and within seconds tiny beads of bright-red blood rose to dot the wound.

His back felt as if it were afire. The rope chafed the tender flesh of his wrists and the muscles of his cruelly stretched arms pulled painfully. His left jaw throbbed from Lucas's blow and was already swollen and discolored. But most of all, his heart hurt.

Still he remained mute.

The brothers goaded Luiz.

Baron came up close behind him. He blew cooling air on the burning abrasion and said they didn't really want to hurt him. Told him they would cut him down if he would tell them—in explicit detail—exactly what he and Amy had been up to all those long, hot afternoons.

Was little Amy beautiful naked? Did she claw his back and cry out? Had he shown her all the ways of making love? Was he able to satisfy her?

If he told them everything they'd let him go.

Luiz Quintano was a gentleman.

He'd allow the Sullivan brothers to kill him before he would say one word about Amy. His white teeth clenched, Luiz stared impassively into the flaming red sun, refusing to respond to their vulgar taunts. Not so much as a flicker of an eyelash disturbed the expressionless mask of his handsome face.

For his stoicism, he received more lashes. Baron raised the long black bullwhip twice more and brought it down on Luiz's back. They jeered him, called him Sun God and Tonatiuh, and asked where was that mystical Aztec power now when he needed it.

Just before applying one final lash of the whip, Baron stepped up behind Luiz, clasped a handful of his thick blue-black hair, jerked his head back, and said coldly, "Maybe this will teach you not to be sticking your stiff Indian cock into high-class white girls."

12

Luiz held his dark head proudly erect, his slim, battered body rigid. His black eyes remained flat and expressionless. He stared fixedly at the flaming western horizon beyond the cool, blue distant mountains and wordlessly called to the spirits of his ancestors, the brave sun-worshipping Aztec.

The Sullivan brothers were not pleased with Luiz's lack of reaction. Baron, especially, was disappointed. His hatred of the quiet *mestizo* was intense, and he had hoped to bring the proud mixed blood to his knees. To hear him beg for mercy.

Frustrated that nothing of the kind had occurred, the resourceful Baron quickly came up with new plan. One guaranteed to produce a response.

Smiling, he stepped in front of Luiz and said, "Don't go anywhere, old Sun God. We'll be right back." He tauntingly hung the evil black bullwhip around Luiz's neck, then turned and walked away, motioning for Lucas to follow. Baron had decided to bring their sister down to witness her lover's pain and humiliation.

The brothers hurried back up the long drive, went inside the hacienda, climbed the stairs, and

burst into Amy's room. She awoke with a start to
see Baron crossing the sun-reddened room. The
chill she had felt earlier returned. Nervously she
sat up.

"What is it, Baron?" she said, her breath short.
"What's happened?"

"You're coming with us," he answered, offering
no further explanation.

The wispy hair at the nape of her neck standing
on end, Amy threw her legs over the edge of the
bed and got up. "All right," she said evenly, "soon
as I get dressed, I'll—"

"Dress later," he said with firm authority.
"Somebody wants to see you."

"Who? I thought everyone had gone." She
looked down at herself. "I can't see anyone without my clothes." With dread, she wondered if
Baron meant Tyler Parnell was downstairs.

Dread turned to fear when her brothers
dragged her from the house. Oblivious to the
driveway pebbles bruising her bare, tender feet,
Amy was overcome with a blinding, choking terror. She knew instinctively that they had Tonatiuh. That they meant to harm him. Why were
they taking her to Tonatiuh when all they had
ever wanted was to keep them apart?

Amy winced when she saw, framed against the
flaming red sky, the proud, beautiful youth she
loved hanging helpless and hurt from Orilla's tall
white ranch gates.

When she was close enough to see the bleeding
stripes zigzagging his bronzed back, her first impulse was to scream and run to him, to fling her
arms around his dear neck and promise she'd save

him from further harm. But she wisely checked herself.

She had always known that her brothers hated Tonatiuh, but she had had no idea how much. Had never dreamed they were capable of committing such a despicable act as this. She fought to keep her wits about her, knowing it was not yet over, that they might kill Tonatiuh if she intervened.

They led her around to face Luiz. Immediately she saw that the protective Sun Stone was missing from his dark throat.

"Why, Baron?" was all she said. Keeping rigid control over her emotions, her blue eyes remained dry of tears as they met Luiz's. He looked at her. And for the first time his obsidian eyes flickered with deep emotion, a fact well noted by the observant Baron.

"Why have you done this to him?" Amy asked, longing to reach up and wipe the blood from Tonatiuh's scraped forehead, to brush a bead of perspiration from his dark eyelash.

"We Sullivans protect our women and our land. We won't hold still for a half-breed putting his filthy hands on either," said Baron. Closely watching his sister's face as she looked at Luiz, he asked, "Do you love this uppity redskin?"

It was a loaded question and Amy knew it. If she admitted she loved Tonatiuh, they would send him away forever, perhaps even kill him. If she didn't admit it, the consequences might be the same. Amy thought fast. If Baron believed that Tonatiuh actually had no hold on her heart, he would surely feel less threatened. And less vindictive. She looked squarely at Baron.

"No," she said evenly, "I don't." Her gaze returned to Luiz. "The Indian meant nothing to me." She shrugged bare shoulders. She smiled and flippantly added, "I was only amusing myself with the savage Sun God."

Baron carefully studied her face. Her expression gave nothing away; she appeared completely placid. His gaze shifted to Luiz. He looked stricken, as if Amy's callous words had caused far greater pain than any meted out by the whip. Baron grinned, reached up, withdrew the bullwhip from around Luiz's neck, and held it out to his sister.

"Prove it."

The lump in her tight throat was choking her. Her rapidly beating heart was not supplying enough oxygen. But Amy serenely nodded, took the whip, and stepped around the trussed Luiz. On weak, leaden legs she took several steps, stopped, and turned, the lacy white petticoat swirling about her bare legs.

And smiling as if she were thoroughly enjoying herself, she lifted the deadly bull whip high and brought it cracking down sharply across Luiz's bloodied, bronzed back.

And felt a bolt of pain sheer right through her heart when his beloved body jerked reflexively to the punishing blow. Her face remained composed. She was most convincing. So convincing she was certain that Tonatiuh would hate her for the rest of his days on earth.

Better his hate than his death.

The brothers laughed and applauded their sister's mettle. Coming to her, Baron relieved her of the heavy whip, gave her an affectionate hug, and said, "Honey, I've misjudged you. I thought

maybe you cared about the dirty half-breed." He
shook his blond head. "Hell, I can understand
physical hunger." He laughed heartily. "So you
tumbled in the hay a few times with the savage.
No harm done. I've been guilty of amusing myself
with the Mexican servants."

"My favorite whores are Mexicans and Indians," offered Lucas, grinning.

"No, sir, we're not blaming you, Amy," Baron
assured her. "I don't know though." His smile disappeared. "I think we ought to kill this arrogant
redskin for daring to touch our pale, pretty little
sister."

Amy's pulses pounded. She felt as if she might
faint. She had to do something and fast.

"I have a better idea," she said, sauntering back
around to face the prisoner.

Her petticoat brushing the gravel beneath her
bare feet, she stood in front of Luiz, hoping for the
chance to send him a message with her eyes. She
never got it. Baron was right at her elbow.

Devilishly taunting the miserable captive, Amy
stooped, picked up the gold medallion from the
dirt, and looked at it with mocking disdain. She
considered shoving it deep into Luiz's pants
pocket. Instead she handed it to Baron.

Stepping closer to Luiz, she provocatively
rolled an ivory shoulder, allowing the delicate
strap of her chemise to slide teasingly down her
arm. She gave her head a haughty toss, causing
her long unbound hair to spill around her shoulders, the dying sun behind her making a fiery red-
gold halo of the shiny tresses.

She put out the tip of her tongue, licked her lips
wetly, and said, "Send the soft, spoiled half white,

half Indian back where he belongs." She lifted her chin and looked straight into the tortured black eyes.

"Where's that, Amy, honey?" asked Baron.

"Across the border into old Mexico for a life-time of loneliness and poverty among his own kind!"

With her cold, biting words, the fiery sun disappeared. A warm red afterglow lingered to bathe the dark face, the smooth chest of her proud Aztec sweetheart.

Feeling a sob threatening to erupt from her tight throat, Amy turned swiftly away. She knew that she would see Tonatiuh as he was now—coppery skin tinted pink, black eyes gone dead—in her haunted dreams forever.

While unshed tears stung her eyes, Amy started back up the long drive, stopping when she had gone but a few steps. Turning, she called nonchalantly, "Baron, make sure that ugly Sun Stone goes with the Indian."

"We'll dispose of both in the deserts of Mexico tonight," he responded. "Now you go on and make yourself pretty. Tyler'll be coming to see you after a while."

As twilight descended, Amy stood at the upstairs landing before the huge window and watched three horseman gallop away from the ranch, heading south. Silhouetted against the violet western sky, Tonatiuh, his hands tied to the horn, turned abruptly in the saddle and glanced back at Orilla.

That's when they came.

The hot, gushing tears she could no longer hold back. Tonelessly murmuring his name, Amy fell to her knees and wept bitterly, her slender shoulders shaking with her misery.

Pedrico, returning from Sundown, found her hovering in the gloom. Sobbing hysterically, she told him all that had happened. At once he shouted for Magdelena and Rosa, and he told the heartbroken Amy he would go after Luiz.

She clutched at his arm. "I don't know where they took him. I only know they mean to dump him somewhere in Mexico."

His one eye gleaming with fierce determination, Pedrico said, "I will find the boy."

"Please," she cried, "tell him I'm sorry, that I didn't mean it. Dear God, I didn't mean it!"

Magdelena, putting her arms around the heartsick young girl, said to Pedrico, "And if you don't find him?"

"Then I will never return to Orilla."

It was past midnight when finally they pulled up on their winded, lathered mounts. They had crossed the Rio Grande south of Esperanza and continued riding until they were deep into the vast, lonely Chihuahuan desert of northern Mexico.

"Far enough," Baron said, standing in the stirrups, looking out over the hard, lonely country.

Not bothering to dismount, Lucas reached over and untied Luiz's hands from the saddlehorn, but left them bound together. Grinning, he roughly shoved Luiz off the horse, saying as he did so *Adiós,* Sun God."

Luiz instinctively put out his tied hands in an attempt to break the fall, but one booted foot snagged briefly in the stirrup, and he landed on his back in a cluster of prickly pears. A hundred tiny needles pricked his raw, lashed flesh.

With effort, he rolled away, lay there on his belly, bound hands out before him, waiting, wondering if they would kill him. Not caring if they did.

"Death is the penalty for touching our sister," said Baron. "You'll be buzzard bait by morning."

He reached in his pocket, drew out the Sun Stone, and tossed it carelessly to the ground. The heavy disk landed several yards away from Luiz.

The Sullivans rode away at once, taking with them the spare mount, leaving Luiz Quintano alone without food and water in an empty, dry wilderness of scattered mesquite trees and creosote shrubs and wild, hungry animals.

His face and hands were skinned from the shattered glass of the ranch patio. His jaw was discolored and badly swollen from Lucas's powerful fist. His bare, dirty back was shredded by the stinging bullwhip's lashes and stuck by the prickly pears. His heart was broken beyond repair. In physical and mental pain, the wretched young half-breed lay on the hard desert floor under a full Mexican moon.

Allowing his emotions to surface at last, he felt hot tears spring to his eyes and wash down his dusty cheeks. He cried like the frightened child he was, and as he wept, he crawled awkwardly on his bare stomach, his bound hands before him, toward the solace of the gold Sun Stone winking at him in the moonlight.

Every inch he crawled was pure agony. He was stiff and he hurt all over. His vision was blurred with his tears. His throat was dry and parched. In the night silence he could hear his own labored breathing. And a coyote yapping far off in the distance.

He continued to inch his way forward until, with a muffled groan of relief, his trembling fingers touched the glittering gold medallion.

He gave a weak shout of triumph as his long fingers curled securely around it. Tightly, as if his life and the afterlife beyond depended on it, he squeezed the symbolic Sun Stone.

Above him, bright twinkling stars filled the night sky. The full white moon climbed higher in the heavens. A lone nighthawk swooped gracefully upward, the moonlight silvering its outstretched blue-black wings.

Luiz saw neither the stars or the moon or the wheeling nighthawk. Salty tears drying in dirty tracks on his battered face, his slender, hurting body gave a tiny shudder of deep, consuming weariness.

And he passed out.

13

As young Luiz's trembling brown hands wrapped themselves around the Sun Stone, a sleeping woman, hundreds of miles sway, felt those lean fingers close tightly around her heart.

That fierce gripping of her heart immediately awakened her. The woman sat up and clutched her bare left breast. Beside her, the lethal weaponry she kept ever at hand—a huge, slumbering, snowy white mountain lion—stirred, raised his ferocious head, and stared at her, his yellow eyes gleaming.

The woman pushed her long, raven-black hair from her dark eyes and looked warily about. All was as it should be. She was alone in her comfortable chambers. The wall torches that continuously illuminated the high mountain cavern burned brightly, casting the usual patterns of shadow and light upon the stalactites and stalagmites.

All was quiet save for the low, inquisitive growl of the great cat. The woman silenced him with a raised hand. Then she kicked off the soft, luxurious bed covers of fur and rose to her feet. Naked, she crossed the spacious rock chamber of her private quarters. The albino lion remained where he was, watching.

From a large, low wooden trunk the woman removed a flowing robe of soft white wool. She pulled the warm white robe down over her head, pushed her arms through the long, loose sleeves, and allowed the supple garment to settle over her slender curves and whisper down to her small bare feet.

She raised her long-nailed fingers up to free her thick, black hair from the robe. The dark tresses fell down her back to just below her waist. Not bothering to put on slippers, the white-robed woman moved across the huge chamber toward a tunnel. The big cat rose and followed.

Through the dim, winding tunnel the woman and the lion proceeded until they reached a much larger, now-deserted chamber where the ceiling of the cavern had been blackened from ancient fires built there by long-departed ancestors. At the room's center, a low, smoldering fire burned even now.

Woman and cat moved purposefully toward the burning cedar chips. The woman raised her slender hands. She clapped them together three times in quick succession, the sound echoing throughout the vast, silent chamber.

Within seconds half a dozen sleepy-eyed men, wearing brief white loinclothes and carrying an array of weapons, appeared. They stood mute in a semicircle, all eyes fixed on her.

In a voice calm and low, she gave them their instructions.

She told them to build up the fire until the chamber glowed with bright light and fierce heat. To bring from the chamber's vault her talismatic black necklace. To fetch a handful of the amaranth seeds favored in Aztec rites, seeds the Spanish had outlawed. To light the hundreds of brown candles lining the rough stone walls of the chamber. To burn the dozens of sticks of incense resting in earthen plates. To get a large vessel of *pulque* so that she might drink enough of the liquor made from the milky juice of the maguey cactus to see what others could not.

At this last instruction, the tall, muscular warriors exchanged no skeptical glances, felt no apprehension despite the knowledge that *pulque* was "a whirlwind, a cyclone that covered everything with evil" and that only old people were allowed to drink as much as they wished.

The laws and taboos that restricted the behavior of others did not apply to the raven-haired, white-robed woman. A rite of some sort was to take place in the high mountain cave that night, and the woman's loyal followers did not question her orders. They simply carried them out.

One hour after the woman had been pulled from her sleep by the hand gripping her heart, she lay lounging before a fire so large and hot it caused perspiration to drench her slender body, the long white robe to stick to her heated flesh. The white lion lay close beside her, shooting flames of the fire reflected in the depths of his huge yellow eyes.

From a golden goblet the woman drank thirstily of the forbidden *pulque,* nibbled on the amaranth seeds, and idly fingered the black necklace at her throat while a thick, blue haze of incense sweetened the stifling hot air of the chamber.

The half-dozen warriors did not join her at the fire. They kept their places a discreet distance away as if standing at military attention, not so much as raising a hand to wipe the sweat dripping into their eyes.

The woman suddenly sat up straight.

Her black eyes widened and she stared into the leaping flames. She saw within them a young, dying boy alone under a full desert moon. With a vividness that mere mortals could not begin to imagine, the woman saw the injured youth lying unconscious, his bare back bloodied, his jaw swollen and purple, his skinned fingers clutching the gold medallion.

And her heart.

Tears sprang to her eyes. Tears of anger. But tears of joy as well. He needed her. For the first time in all these years, her beautiful son needed her. She would bring him here to be with her. She would shelter him in this high mountain cave in Mexico.

She would not let him die.

The woman tossed away the gold goblet of *pulque* and dropped a handful of amaranth seeds back into the golden dish. She rose to her feet, unbothered by the heavy white robe clinging to her wet body.

Speaking softly, but with authority, she issued specific orders to her apostles.

They swiftly obeyed, not caring that the woman was known as *La Extranjera*—Strange Lady. They knew her by another name.

The goddess Xochiquetzal.

Pedrico Valdez's lathered buckskin stallion, sensing his rider's sudden urgency, stretched out into a thundering gallop.

It was nearing sunrise and the pair had been riding all night. Both were winded and tired. And determined.

Now as the one-eyed Orilla houseboy spotted something black lying near a huge Spanish dagger plant, he felt his pulse race. That emotion was telegraphed to his responsive steed and the weary stallion labored to transport his master quickly forward.

Pedrico dropped the reins and dismounted a few feet from the suspicious black object. His breath short, he fell to his knees and lifted the pair of men's black trousers, the knees torn and ripped, the wrinkled, dirty fabric soiled with dried blood.

He shook his head no.

The bloodstained pants could belong to anyone. This was Mexico, a long way from Orilla. The trousers couldn't be Luiz's.

Pedrico had almost convinced himself it was so until he saw, beneath the giant dagger, a pair of gleaming black cowboy boots. One sat upright. The other lay on its side in the sand. A small silver adornment on the boot glittered in the light of the rapidly rising sun.

Then he knew.

Pedrico dropped the torn black pants and reached for the boot. He lifted it, muttering "No, no, no" as he saw upon the boot's pull strap, inlaid in silver, the SBARQ brand. Only the proud young Luiz Quintano owned such a pair of boots.

Clutching the boot to his chest, Pedrico rose. He stood looking all around him, fearing that any second his eyes would fall on the murdered boy's body. He saw nothing. He stooped, picked up the matching boot, and carefully secured them behind his cantle.

Pedrico Valdez remounted his waiting stallion. He sat in the saddle and looked out over the forbidding stillness of a brutal land already growing hot though the sun had barely risen. Miserably he wondered where in this hard, dried-out land of fierce suns he would find the remains of the handsome young Aztec.

Pulling the wide brim of his sombrero low over his one eye, Pedrico headed south.

When Meg Sullivan entered the foyer of her New Orleans home one chill Saturday afternoon in early November and her eyes fell immediately upon the letter in the silver calling-card basket, she was genuinely reluctant to open it. It was the third message she had received from Amy in as many weeks.

The first—the telegram telling of Walter Sullivan's death—had been an unexpected blow from which she had still not recovered. Not a week later a short letter had arrived from Amy saying that Don Ramon had been killed in an accident and his son, Luiz, had disappeared.

Meg reached out a gloved hand and picked up the small blue envelope. She sat down on the stairs and opened it. Her hands shook a little as she unfolded the neatly written letter.

> Dearest Aunt Meg,
> After all the tragedies, I finally have good news. I'm getting married. In less than a week—on Saturday night, November the 8th—I'll become the bride of Tyler Parnell.

I wish more than anything that you could be here to share in our happiness. We plan to make our home out here on Orilla; isn't that wonderful?

Love,
Amy

Meg Sullivan slowly lowered the letter. She closed her eyes and sadly shook her head. It didn't take much of Meg's intuitive common sense to know that the one person she loved most in all the world was concealing a broken heart behind brave words.

She opened her eyes and sighed wearily.

Today was Saturday, November 8. The wedding day. Too late even to send a wire asking Amy to wait, to reconsider her hasty decision.

Her temples suddenly pounding, Meg Sullivan rose and climbed the stairs, her dreams for Amy's lasting happiness forever gone.

In Sundown, Texas, on that warm November Saturday night, Miss Amy Sullivan, exquisitely beautiful in a gown of white antique satin, walked down the aisle of the Catholic church on the arm of her brother, Baron. In a candlelight ceremony that lasted less than ten minutes, she took the name of a beaming Tyler Parnell.

Tyler Parnell was the happiest of grooms. He now had everything he wanted. A pretty, naive young wife who happened to be one of the richest women in all of Texas. He would live the rest of his life in splendid ease at Orilla with nothing more required of him than to keep little Amy pregnant, happy, and submissive.

Smiling as his blond bride stood at his side facing the robed *padre,* Tyler Parnell was confident he'd have little trouble fulfilling his end of the bargain. It had been amazingly easy to persuade her to marry him. Even Baron was pleasantly surprised that she had agreed so readily.

When he had asked Amy only a week ago, she was the one who had suggested they not wait, that they be married right away. He foresaw no problem in having her sign over her portion of the vast land she'd inherited.

Land that was worth a fortune.

Or had been.
Until then.
On that same November evening an elegantly robed, exotically beautiful black-haired woman came out of her comfortable quarters deep inside a high mountain cave. With a huge white mountain lion at her side, she walked through the strong, cold winds that pressed her robes to her slender frame and sent her waist-length black hair flying wildly about her head.

Undaunted, she climbed to where the high mountain mists enveloped her, kissing her face with its chill dampness and swirling around her like great clouds of smoke so thick it couldn't be penetrated by the human eye.

But this woman could see through it.

Could see well past the tumble of basalt rocks and steep volcanic mountains and pinnacles of sandstone and sheets of solid granite. Could see across towering mountain ranges and verdant valleys and parched deserts.

Could see all the way to far-off Texas and to a cold, clear river. A river fed by deep artesian wells beneath tons and tons of stone. A swiftly flowing river that had changed an arid wasteland into a verdant rangeland.

Had made men rich.

Staring unblinkingly through the mystical mists, the angered goddess Xochiquetzal drew her delicate brows together.

And the river ceased to run.

PART TWO

14

Amy Sullivan Parnell was lonely.

Achingly lonely. Had been all day. Ever since early morning when she had stood on Orilla's railroad spur and watched her only child wave madly from the train's window as the locomotive's heavy wheels began to turn on the steel tracks.

With Juana as her chaperone, her adorable, energetic nine-year-old Linda was off to New Orleans for her first-ever visit—without her protective mother—to Auntie Meg's. Now, at mid-afternoon, Amy wandered aimlessly about the big, empty hacienda, wishing she had never allowed Linda to go. How was she to survive the long, lonely summer without her precious baby?

Hating the silence that surrounded her, Amy went into the kitchen looking for company. Magdelena was there alone, kneading dough. She looked up when Amy entered. Her dark eyes snapped with indignation and Amy realized immediately that she'd find little camaraderie here. Magdelena gave the floured bread dough a vicious pounding. Amy knew the reason.

"Magdelena," said Amy, "do I really deserve the *mal de ojo*— the evil eye?"

"*Sí,*" answered the stocky, gray-haired woman. "*Sí,* you do! A pretty young child traveling alone across the world! Is not safe or—"

"Mag, she's not alone, Juana is with her," Amy interrupted. "And it's not across the world, it's just across Texas and the gulf to Louisiana."

"Hmmmp! Too far for a nine-year-old! Only a *niña*. A baby. Go off without her mama to stay all summer."

"Linda wanted to go 'without her mama.' She was excited to be spending the summer alone with her Auntie Meg. And Aunt Meg is thrilled to have her."

"Sure! She thrilled. What about us? What we supposed to do around here without Linda?" Magdelena put her flour-dusted hands on her broad hips and glared at Amy.

Amy smiled and gently accused, "You, Mag, are as bad as I am. You're not concerned about Linda's safety. You're thinking only of us."

Magdelena made a sour face, then finally nodded. "Is true." She sighed heavily. "I am lonely already and she gone only a few hours." Tears sprang into her dark eyes.

Amy crossed to her. "There, there," she soothed, knowing it was not just Linda whom Magdelena missed. It had been five years since her daughter Rosa's death and still Magdelena felt the pain as strongly as if it had happened yesterday. Putting her arms around the heavyset middle-aged woman, Amy said, "Why don't you go take a refreshing bath and I'll get one of the vaqueros to drive you into Sundown for a nice long visit with Mary and the new baby."

Amy knew that would lift Magdelena's spirits. Magdelena had been fond of the quiet Mary Gonzales when Mary had been a servant at Orilla. Now Mary was a married woman with three small boys and a three-week-old baby girl and Magdelena was crazy about the little ones.

Sniffing, Magdelena said, "And what about the evening meal? Who will fix it?"

Amy gave her an affectionate squeeze and released her. "Who will eat it is a better question. I'm not the least bit hungry."

"You have to eat! I will not allow—"

"Mag, go see Mary and the kids. I'll be fine."

"You sure? I be glad to stay here with you and—"

Amy shook her head. "I'm going for a ride. See if I can't tire myself out so I'll be able to sleep tonight." She turned and started from the room. "I'll tell Fernando to bring the buckboard around for you in half an hour. Will you be ready?"

Finally Magdelena smiled. "I will be ready."

Amy smiled back at her. "Have a lovely time, stay as long as you please, and I'll see you tomorrow."

Less than an hour later Amy, astride the faithful old sorrel gelding Rojo, loped across the parched rangeland, heading northeast. Her worn sombrero pulled low against the afternoon sun, she watched dust devils dance across the deserted, barren plain where once longhorn cattle, thousands of them, had grazed and grown fat on meadows of tobosa grass.

Amy laid her heels to Rojo's flanks and the responsive creature went into a full gallop. The speed felt good to Amy. The desert, though bone dry and dusty, was not yet oppressive with the blazing heat of summer. The April winds that stung her cheeks and caused her eyes to water were cool and pleasant, not the harsh furnacelike blasts that would make riding disagreeable come June and July.

Momentarily forgetting everything save the immediate pleasure of riding a great mount across the stark emptiness, Amy smiled and lifted her face to the sun. She could feel the beating of old Rojo's powerful heart between her knees, the pull and surge of his muscles as he galloped swiftly across the burned-up, savagely beautiful land.

On and on they thundered, and Amy hardly realized when they'd reached the Puesta del Sol, since no stand of rustling cottonwoods, no silvery willows rose on its rocky banks to meet the clear blue skies. The cottonwoods, the willows, all the lush green shrubbery had wilted and died a long time ago.

Amy pulled up on the reins and Rojo came to a swift, dust-flinging halt, snorting and blowing as she slid down off his bare back. Allowing the reins to fall to the ground, she walked around in front of the big beast, patted his muzzle, and apologized for there being no cool, clean water for him to drink.

Rojo shook his head about and whinnied loudly as if he knew exactly what she was saying. She smiled, pressed her cheek to his shiny forehead, then turned and started down the rocky banks of the Sunset River.

When she reached a smooth, flat boulder di-

rectly beside the dry riverbed, Amy sat down.
After removing her sombrero, she slapped it
down beside her and lifted her heavy blond hair
up off her neck. She looked out at the wide, water-
less river before her and felt a deep sadness.

She could remember a time when cold, clear
water rushed down the winding stream. A time
when hundreds of thousands of gallons of clean,
life-giving water flowed down the twisting turning Puesta del Sol. A time when a continuous waterfall spilled with great ferocity from the jutting
rocks above.

Amy took off her boots and stockings. She
pulled her hot skirts up to her thighs and wrapped
her arms around her knees. She shook her head
and sighed.

The rocks over her head were bone dry. The flat
riverbed was only sunbaked clods of clay left from
the last spring rain. It was nothing but mud that
had dried and broken into pieces and curled up
around the edges.

Staring at the seared dry wash, Amy decided
the once-beautiful river looked much like she felt.

Inert. Used up. Shriveled. Lifeless.

Despite the fact her twenty-sixth birthday was
still more than a month away, Amy knew that the
best was behind her.

The best had been so beautiful. But so brief. So
very brief it had almost faded entirely away. Like
a glorious dream, vivid upon awakening, then
growing ever dimmer until it is completely lost.

Ten years.

Ten years and try as she might, there were
times that Amy could not recall exactly how Tonatiuh looked. Certainly she remembered that he

was tall and slim and masculinely beautiful, but as the years passed, the face she had loved so much had become shadowy, no longer clear in her memory.

Maybe it was just as well. Perhaps by the time she turned thirty-six, she wouldn't be able to remember Tonatiuh's boyishly handsome face at all. Amy drew a long breath. So much had happened in the ten years since she had seen him.

The hasty wedding to Tyler Parnell less than a month after Tonatiuh had been cast into the Mexican desert. The waiting for Pedrico Valdez to return with news of Tonatiuh, waiting that had stretched on into hopelessness. Pedrico had never returned and she had been forced to face the sad facts.

Tonatiuh was dead.

The empty marriage to Tyler Parnell. Within weeks of the wedding, he was away more nights than he was home and she didn't have to wonder what he was doing. She was aware, when she walked down the streets of Sundown, that friends and neighbors were whispering that Tyler's young bride had failed to make him happy. No one seemed to wonder, or care, if he made her happy.

It was during that first miserable year that the river Puesta del Sol had mysteriously dried up. Almost overnight the rushing, flowing stream had turned into a dark, stagnant pond where swarms of gnats danced on its torpid surface. Within weeks even the standing puddles were gone and bewildered longhorns stood in the dry creekbed, pawing at the sand, searching futilely for a drink of water.

By the time Linda was born, thousands of cattle had died from thirst and dozens of Orilla vaqueros had left the big, troubled spread. And Tyler Parnell was starting to doubt his decision to marry her. Amy knew—had known from the beginning —that he, like her, had had a hidden purpose in marrying. He wanted to get his hands on a portion of Orilla. With the ranch's value plummeting daily, Tyler felt he had made a bad bargain.

He used the ranch's dilemma as a further excuse for excessive drinking and womanizing. On the warm May evening when Amy went into labor with Linda, Tyler was not at home. He was drunk. And he was with another woman. Since both Sullivan brothers were off merrymaking with their neglectful brother-in-law, Magdelena sent one of the cowhands to Doug Crawford's bordering ranch.

Big Doug Crawford went for the doctor and sent the Orilla cowpoke in search of Tyler Parnell. Crawford and Dr. Haney reached Orilla in plenty of time, but it was dawn before Tyler arrived.

Linda, a perfect six-pound girl with light downy hair and a round face, came into the world shortly after 3 A.M. Doug Crawford, pacing the corridor beyond Amy's door, was the first male other than the doctor to see the crying newborn in the arms of her exhausted mother.

The weeks that followed were happy ones for Amy. The child was a magical little person whose every gurgle filled her astonished mother with pleasure. Shirley Crawford came often to visit, bringing her own six-month-old baby girl. The two young mothers had much in common, but not when it came to husbands. While Tyler paid little attention to wife or child, the red-haired Doug Crawford worshipped his pretty wife and their daughter. And Shirley openly adored the gentle, hard-working rancher.

Orilla continued to decline as years of drought plagued the desert southwest. Baron and Lucas and Tyler, once such close friends, began to bicker, to blame each other for what had happened to the ruined ranch. Not one of the spoiled, lazy trio ever considered helping out, and it was up to Amy to make the decisions, to oversee the workers, to run Orilla.

Baron was the first to leave. In the fall of '60 he packed up and headed for the gold mines of California, and the way Rosa moped around after his departure, it was evident that the pair had been lovers. When, not three months after he'd gone, Baron sent for Rosa, the overjoyed young woman ignored her mother's tearful pleadings and went to join the man she loved.

It was that same autumn that the string of tragedies that had begun with the death of Walter Sullivan continued. Shirley Crawford and her young daughter were killed by renegade Apaches within sight of their small adobe ranchhouse. Doug Crawford had not been at home that fateful Saturday morning. He was in the village of Sundown buying a doll for his daughter.

It was little Nell's fourth birthday.

The next spring the War Between the States broke out, and a lost, heartbroken Doug Crawford joined the Confederate Army. Lucas went down to Mexico, and Magdelena received a letter from Rosa in California saying she wanted to come home but had no money. Baron, Rosa admitted to her mother, had sent for her to use her for his own gain. He had forced her into prostitution. Magdelena, distraught, tearfully showed the letter to Amy. Amy sent Rosa the money to come home, but the young woman never made it. After weeks of waiting and watching, a brief letter arrived from Baron stating that his "poor, darling Rosa" had become sick and had died.

He did not mention the fact that the once-pretty Mexican girl had died of the disease common to prostitutes. But her mother blamed Baron for her baby's death all the same.

The calculating Tyler Parnell, waiting to see which side had the better chance of victory, enlisted in the Union Army in the spring of '62 and perished a year later at the siege of Gettysburg. Around that same time, heavily decorated Confederate war hero big Doug Crawford was sent home to Texas to recuperate from wounds sustained in battle.

Amy and Magdelena visited Doug daily, taking food to the sickly man. Many afternoons Amy would stay on after Magdelena returned to Orilla. She'd read to the big, lonely man and listen attentively as he reminisced about the war, the loneliness, the past. By the time he was fit enough to return to action, Amy could see in his eyes that he had fallen in love with her. When Doug Crawford shyly asked if she would wait for him, she agreed.

Letters came from him gratefully professing that she had given him a reason to live again after he thought there was none. He wanted her to be his wife when the war was over, he wanted to take care of her and little Linda. Far more fond of him than she'd ever been of Tyler Parnell, Amy accepted his proposal.

Word came that her brother Lucas was dead. There were no particulars other than the fact that he had been killed in a knife fight in a Paso del Norte saloon by a crazed Indian. She knew she should let Baron know their brother was dead, but she had no idea how to contact him. She'd heard nothing from Baron in over a year; for all she knew he was dead too.

The war finally ended and a beaten, bedraggled Doug Crawford came home on foot. He walked straight out to Orilla, and his thin face lighted up happily when Amy ran out to meet him. Sweeping her up into his arms, he made her promise to become his wife just as soon as he could make enough money to take care of her. Desperately lonely, sincerely fond of Doug Crawford, she agreed. And looked forward to a degree of peace after so many years of turmoil.

But Doug had been dead serious when he spoke of making some money before they were wed. Not three months after he'd come home, he left again, heading south for old Mexico. A highly paid mercenary officer in Maximilian's army, each month he sent back money and promised he would soon be home for good.

He'd be back to take care of her and little Linda. She'd never again be alone.

Never be alone again. . . .

A sound, very faint but intrusive in the desert silence, brought Amy abruptly back to the present. Startled, she turned her head and listened.

She heard nothing. But a sudden feeling of unease washed over her. The downy hair at the nape of her neck rose. Her throat grew inexplicably tight.

Amy slowly lifted her eyes.

15

The Indian stood naked in the sunlight.

Too stunned to move, too frightened to scream, Amy completely froze, transfixed by him.

A long white scar slashed down his chiseled face, from high prominent cheekbone to firm jawline. His bare feet were apart, muscular arms crossed over his smooth, hairless chest. A wide cuff bracelet of gold and turquoise gleamed on his dark right wrist. Naked save for a brief loincloth covering his groin, his thick raven hair falling to his wide, bronzed shoulders, the tall, lean Indian stood like a magnificent statue on the rocks above.

Calmly watching her.

A cloud passed over the sun, casting the Indian into deep shadow, leaving Amy in a pool of bright light. A sudden breeze stirred from out of the west and brought with it the familiar sound of the rustling leaves of cottonwoods and ripples on the river's calm surface.

Only there were no cottonwood leaves.

There was no water.

A lone white dove sailed down from out of the darkened sky and wet its beak in a fine mysterious mist that had begun to bubble and spray from the barren rock on which the mute Indian stood.

When the graceful dove took flight, the powerful muscles began to dance in the Indian's long, lean legs. He leapt down from the rock.

The sudden movement shocked Amy into action. Terrified, she shot to her feet and ran for Rojo, her heart hammering in her chest. As she grabbed up the reins and lunged up onto the gelding's bare back, the Indian reached her.

As swiftly as a striking serpent, his hand shot out and his long fingers encircled her bare ankle, the gold and turquoise bracelet on his wrist catching the sunlight, momentarily blinding her.

Too frightened to look into his scarred face, Amy shouted hysterically to Rojo. The big sorrel immediately bolted into motion, tearing her ankle from the Indian's firm grip.

Not daring to look back, but certain the savage was in hot pursuit, Amy wildly slapped the long reins from side to side on the sorrel's neck and dug her bare heels into his sleek flanks.

Eyes wild, great lungs pumping like a bellows, the sorrel thundered straight across the hostile plain, jumping over jutting rock and dead mesquite and tall spiky cactus. Amy leaned low over his neck, expecting a deadly arrow to rip into her back at any second.

Silently cursing herself for riding alone so far from the ranch, she wondered frantically if the aging horse had the stamina to maintain his rapid pace. Could he outrun the Indian's mount? Even if she made it to the hacienda, what then! There was no one there to help her. Juana and Linda—thank God—were safely on their way to New Orleans. Magdelena and Fernando had gone into Sundown. There were only a handful of vaqueros left on Orilla, and they were stationed far out at the line shacks, miles from headquarters.

No one was home.

The blood beating loudly in Amy's ears could not shut out the distinct sound of drumming hoof-beats close behind, echoing Rojo's. Clasping a handful of the gelding's coarse mane, Amy ventured a look back over her shoulder.

And almost choked on her fear.

Not twenty yards behind, the Indian, astride a huge black stallion, galloped steadily after her, easily keeping pace. His back ramrod straight, his thick raven hair tossing about his scarred bronzed face, he pursued her with calm, chilling menace.

Amy turned back and pleaded with Rojo to go faster. But the aging animal was stretched to his limit and was laboring valiantly to hold his present gait. His foam-flecked mouth open, his tongue lolling out, Rojo labored for breath and already his withers were lathered.

And they were still miles from Orilla.

A terrible picture flashed through Amy's churning mind: the bare, mutilated bodies of Shirley and Nell Crawford, victims of wild renegade Apaches. The savage after her was surely a Mescalero Apache. If he caught her, she'd meet with the same fate as the Crawfords.

Her hands cold with fear, she clung to the reins and Rojo's mane and prayed that the end would be merciful and swift. She didn't mind dying, but everyone in the Southwest knew the dreaded Apache delighted in making their captives suffer first.

Mindless of the dust blowing into her eyes and mouth and her unbound hair whipping about her face and her skirts billowing up around her thighs, Amy kicked wildly at Rojo's sweaty belly. After what seemed an eternity, she saw the big pink hacienda rising from the desert floor ahead.

Feeling a small measure of relief, she wondered if she could dismount and make it into the house to the loaded Winchester before he caught her. Seconds after spotting the hacienda, Amy blinked back the wind-caused tears and saw, approaching the hacienda from the south, a contingent of mounted men.

Drawing closer, she saw they were a detail of Juarez's Mexican army and her heart leapt with joy. Frantically trying to swallow so that she could call to them, she lifted an arm and waved madly in an effort to attract their attention.

She was sure she'd been successful when a soldier at the head of the column shouted out an order and the detail halted. At closer range Amy immediately recognized a silver-haired soldier at the head of the command as an old Orilla hand. It was the one-eyed Pedrico Valdez.

"Pedrico!" she shouted jubilantly. "Pedrico Valdez! Oh, thank God, thank God."

Pedrico and the Mexican soldiers would save her. Her worries were over. A smile lighting her dusty, tear-streaked face, Amy brought the lathered Rojo to an abrupt halt, hurriedly slid from his back, and ran anxiously toward the mounted Pedrico Valdez.

But as Amy ran toward Pedrico, the Indian astride the shimmering black stallion rode quietly up and raised his right hand. Every eye in the detail snapped around and came to rest on him.

Wordlessly he issued an order. The soldiers rapidly dispersed, including Pedrico Valdez.

"No!" screamed Amy, totally baffled. "Don't leave me, Pedrico. Come back here!" She ran after the departing troops, stumbling, shouting frantically for them to help her. They continued to ride away, deaf to her tearful pleas. Disbelieving, she stopped running and her worried eyes flicked to the mounted Indian.

The half-naked warrior calmly sat his horse, staring fixedly at her. For one brief moment their gazes locked. Then Amy gasped in fear when he threw a long, bronzed leg over his mount and dropped agilely to the ground.

She whirled about and ran for the house, knowing he was right behind her. She raced up the front walk and onto the porch. She had reached the door when he caught up to her. His long fingers clutched at her billowing skirts, and roughly he slammed her back against his hard, powerful body.

Amy's slender form struck the Indian's with such fierce suddenness, the wind was temporarily knocked from her. Gasping for air, she felt him yank her arms up high over her head then press his warm palm to the center of her diaphragm, rhythmically applying pressure until her breath returned.

He lowered her arms and Amy instinctively looked up over her shoulder into a hard-planed face with mean black eyes, a vicious white scar slashing down a smooth bronzed cheek all the way to his cruel mouth.

She screamed loudly and pulled away. She dashed into the house while the sound of his strange, haunting laughter followed her. Sobbing, she stumbled up the stairs and into her room, quickly bolting the door behind her.

Turning about, she leaned her trembling back against the heavy door and waited, her breath short, her heart racing. Any second he would climb the stairs. Would be in the hall, outside her door. She strained to listen. Heard nothing. Nothing but the sound of her own labored breath.

Amy waited. And waited.

The sun went down and still she waited, sagging against the door, her body tensed, her legs weak and stiff.

Twilight crept over the desert and over the big empty hacienda. The spacious bedroom grew steadily darker. And still she waited, on edge, expectant, rigid. Knowing that any minute the deadly savage would tire of his game and break down the heavy carved door.

It never happened.

When the first streaks of pink light spilled into the room the next morning, Amy awakened, aching and disoriented from dozing on the floor beside the door. Looking about her at the undisturbed room, she wondered briefly if she had imagined the whole thing. A tall, lean Indian? A spraying waterfall? The rustling of cottonwood leaves?

Amy shook her head and for a long moment remained as she was.

It made no sense that a renegade Apache had followed her all the way from Puesta del Sol and then had not harmed her. Even more puzzling was a detachment of well-armed Mexican soldiers scattering with just one look from a lone unarmed Apache.

Amy stiffly rose, cautiously unbolted the door, and cracked it open. She peered out and, seeing nothing, opened the door wider. She looked one way and then the other. She finally ventured out into the silent hallway and saw no one.

But at the upstairs landing of the wide hall, she looked out the tall window and saw a uniformed Mexican militia surrounding the hacienda. Her brows knitted, she scanned each face but did not see the Indian's.

After returning to her room, she hurriedly freshened up, then went downstairs, hoping to find Pedrico Valdez. A polite young soldier stationed on the west patio looked up and smiled when she came outdoors.

"We beg your humble pardon, *señora,* for our intrusion on your property, but—"

"Never mind that," Amy said. "Pedrico Valdez? I need to speak with him immediately."

The young man lifted his shoulders in a shrug. "I am sorry. Lieutenant Valdez ride into village with our superior officer. They will return late today, I think."

"Tell Lieutenant Valdez I wish to see him the moment he returns."

"Ah *sí.* I tell him. *Sí.*"

"*Gracias.*" Amy turned to leave, stopped, and said, "Tell me, when you and the troop arrived here yesterday, did you see a renegade Apache on my land?"

The young man made a face. "No, oh, no, *señora.*" He smiled broadly then, and added, "You are not to worry. We not going to let Apache near you!"

Nodding, Amy again said, *"Gracias,"* and went back into the hacienda.

Inside, she met Magdelena, coming out of her room. The older woman stopped, surprised.

"Why are you up?" she said, giving Amy the once-over. "And why you look so tired? Like not sleep at all."

Amy said, "I didn't sleep too well."

"And it is no wonder. All these soldiers on Orilla. How long they going to stay and how are we supposed to feed them?" She paused, shook her head, then gestured at Amy. "You get back upstairs and change your clothes. I will not have these troops say Magdelena not take good care of this family!"

"Mag, you and Fernando didn't see any Indians when you got home last night, did you?"

Magdelena frowned, stepped forward, and laid a hand on Amy's forehead. "You feeling feverish? I know it, soon as I see you, I know you are sick. Should never have left you alone here."

Amy brushed Magdelena's hand away. "I feel fine. I'll go up and change." Deciding against telling the overly protective servant and friend about the strange encounter at the river, Amy turned to leave.

By noon Amy was a little less edgy.

The warm sunny day passed uneventfully. Magdelena went about her chores in the kitchen, singing loudly as usual. Old Fernando, reliving his own glorious youth, spent the spring afternoon outdoors talking with the young troopers.

As the shadows lengthened and the sun began

its slow descent, Amy relaxed completely. Real or imagined, the Indian had departed. She felt foolish for having been so frightened. Still, it was comforting to have dozens of well-armed Mexican soldiers guarding Orilla. She had no idea how long they intended to stay. But it was obvious they had no intention of leaving immediately.

Tired from her sleepless night, Amy decided a hot bath and a book in bed was precisely what she needed. Choosing a handsomely bound leather edition of Victor Hugo's *Les Misérables*, she had started up the stairs when all at once she heard a loud pounding on the front door.

Frowning, she went back down. A pair of burly soldiers stood on the porch. When she asked what they wanted, they grabbed her arms. Her book crashed to the floor. Forcefully they took her from the house, across the porch, down the front walk, and to a pair of waiting horses.

Amy hotly demanded the two bullies free her at once. She would report them to their commanding officer! They would be severely reprimanded, perhaps punished. They paid no attention to her threats and demands.

Rudely she was thrust up into a saddle, and one of the soldiers swung up behind her. Enclosed in his arms, she was taken atop the galloping horse straight down to the tall ranch gates on the property's borderline.

Stunned and disbelieving, Amy found herself, moments later, standing on the dusty ground directly beneath the ranch gate's high white arch. Her wrists were bound tightly with a lariat, her arms jerked up over her head, the rope tossed over the high supporting beam and tied securely.

Then, without a word, the troopers remounted and rode away. Frantically Amy called after them, begging them to return and to set her free.

But the soldiers were gone.

Bewildered, Amy pulled and twisted to free herself, succeeding only in burning her tender wrists raw on the restraining rope. Angered and afraid, she wondered what this was all about. Did they know—and hold it against her—that her fiancé was fighting under Maximilian against their army of liberation? What did they plan to do with her? What was going on? This was insane!

Straining against her bonds, Amy stood facing the dying sun, dreading nightfall. Hating the thought of darkness. Praying someone—anyone—would come for her.

And, just as the blood-red sun became a fiery ball on the western horizon before her, a lone rider approached from the east behind her. Amy could not see the rider. She could only hear the clatter of the horse's hooves striking the hard ground as the rider steadily cantered closer.

And closer.

16

Straining to listen, Amy heard the rider leisurely cantering closer, as if in no particular hurry. All at once the great sense of relief she had felt on first hearing the approaching hoofbeats now changed to disturbing doubt.

Confused and suddenly terrified, her whole body stiffened when the rider at last reached the arch and pulled up on his mount. The horse snorted and pawed the earth, but the rider made not one sound. Waiting for him to speak, Amy found that she was speechless, unable to ask who had come.

Finally saddle leather creaked as the rider dismounted, and Amy felt her throat constrict with fear. The sound of his approaching footfalls seemed magnified as the rider slowly walked toward her, gravel crunching beneath his heels. When he reached her, he stopped abruptly. Still he did not speak.

Amy could not see him, but the heat of his body was so fierce, she was keenly aware that he was standing directly behind her.

Very, very close.

Hearing his calm, even breathing just above her right ear, Amy instantly knew that it was the Indian. She envisioned the tall, lean warrior as he had been at the river. Half naked and highly dangerous.

Despite the tightness of her throat and the pounding of her heart, Amy summoned up all her reserves of spirit and strength.

"Who in God's name are you?" she said with as much authority as she could muster. "What do you want? I demand an answer!"

Her answer, when finally it came, was a low, masculine laugh followed immediately by a hand placed on the collar of her yellow-and-white calico dress.

Amy swallowed hard and her entire body lurched reflexively when long fingers brazenly curled down inside her white collar, warm fingers that brushed her flesh almost caressingly. The palms of her trussed hands began to perspire with nervous anticipation and dread. Again she was rendered speechless as she stood staring into the blinding rays of the hot, dying sun while the savage's fingers curled around her collar.

But she screamed at the top of her lungs when those strong fingers gave her collar a brutal yank, ripping the fabric. She tried to pull away, arching her back, her toes barely touching the dust and gravel as she fought desperately to avoid his frightening touch.

It did no good.

Effortlessly he tore the back of her calico dress apart clear to her waist, then pushed aside the ruined garment, unmoved by her screams or the violent trembling of her slender body. Amy's horror escalated when she heard the silk of her chemise being ripped away, leaving her back completely bare and exposed.

She spasmed in uncontrollable terror when her mysterious tormentor trailed his forefinger slowly down her naked back, from the nape of her neck to her waistline. Her skin turned cold from his hot touch.

Then, miraculously, he left her.

For a minute.

He strolled away. Back to his waiting horse. When he returned, he slowly circled around in front of Amy, allowing her to at last get a good, long look at him. Shaking like a leaf in the wind, Amy stared, transfixed. Just as she'd done at the river.

Tall. Lean. Thick raven hair. Mean black eyes. High, slanting cheekbones. White scar slashing down his left cheek. The gold and turquoise bracelet on his right wrist.

It *was* the Indian!

But his thick blue-black hair did not hang loose around his dark, chiseled face. It was secured with a narrow white leather band at the back of his neck. And he was not naked; the skimpy breechcloth had been replaced with a captain's dress uniform!

Pale blue, perfectly tailored tunic stretching across wide shoulders, the brass buttons glittering in the fading desert sunlight. Crisp white trousers hugged his lean flanks and hard, muscular thighs. Tall, gleaming black boots reached to his knees.

Booted feet apart, he stood directly before Amy, the attitude of his tall body suggesting supreme arrogance. In his dark right hand he loosely held a coiled whip. His narrowed black gaze silently commanded Amy to raise her eyes to meet his.

At last she did, though she trembled with fear.

And when their gazes collided, his hard mouth stretched into an evil smile and the long vicious scar on his cheek pulled and flashed starkly white against the darkness of his face. As he smiled he idly tapped the coiled black lash against his hard-muscled thigh, a gesture that further unnerved Amy.

Clenching her teeth to keep them from chattering, Amy stared up at the tall, strange man with frightened, questioning eyes. Purposely tormenting her, he stood for a long, silent time, back-lit by the fading sun, rhythmically slapping the whip against his leg.

When at last he spoke, it was in a voice low and rich.

"My soldiers address me as El Capitán. You knew me by another name." Puzzled, Amy shook her head in denial as she stared at him. Again he smiled. "Ah, Amy, Amy, so you've forgotten? Then allow me to refresh your memory."

Deftly he flipped open the brass buttons going down the center of his tunic. When the blue jacket fell open, Amy caught a glimpse of a heavy gold medallion resting on his dark, hairless chest and felt all the air leave her body.

In one fluid masculine movement, he shrugged out of the uniform blouse and released it to the dusty ground. Swiftly he pivoted around to show her his scarred back, compliments of her brothers. And her.

"Tonatiuh!" Amy gasped in stunned disbelief.

He spun about to face her, his dark face as ungiving as stone.

"No!" he said, his voice as deadly cold as his face. "Never call me that again. Only those I love and trust may use my Aztec name. To you I am El Capitán Luiz Quintano."

"No, no," Amy murmured, tears filling her eyes, clogging her throat. "You are Tonatiuh! Dear God, you're alive. Oh, Tonatiuh, I thought you were—"

"Dead?" he interrupted. "I'm sure you did, Mrs. Parnell. You and your loving brothers did your best, but—"

"No, no," Amy repeated, shaking her head. "Tonatiuh, you must let me explain."

"There is nothing to explain, Mrs. Parnell," said Luiz, and again he tapped the coiled whip against his leg.

Crying openly now, Amy said, "Y-yes, there is . . . there is. I-I had to do it, I had to. . . ."

"Had to?" he interrupted. His jaw hardened and his eyes were like black shards of glass. "You had to what? Make love to me and then humiliate me? Have me whipped and left for dead in the desert? Marry the man you'd been seeing behind my back?"

"No, no. There was no one but you, Tonatiuh," she cried, her face blood red with emotion. "I swear it. Only you, but my brothers . . . they would have killed you—"

"Killed me?" he said fiercely, silencing her. "You are the guilty one, Mrs. Parnell. You killed the young, foolish boy who worshipped you. He is dead!" He looked at her and in his black eyes was such naked hatred Amy knew that nothing she

could do would change what he believed or the
way he felt about her.

She tried all the same, but it was no use. At last,
shaking her head, she sadly murmured, "Oh, my
dearest, I saved your life but lost your love."

"You lost a foolish boy's love. I am not that boy. I
am El Capitán Luiz Quintano and a stranger to
you."

Her tear-filled eyes sweeping over the planes of
his hard, hawklike face, searching in vain for the
dear, boyish countenance of the young Tonatiuh,
Amy said softly, "I have known you all of my life."

"You don't know me at all," he said coldly.

With that he uncoiled the long black bullwhip
and quickly moved around in back of her. Expecting to feel the flesh-ripping blow from the whip
any second, Amy gritted her teeth and resolutely
stared at the flaming horizon, the fiery skyline
undulating before her tear-blurred vision.

For a long, silent time they stood unmoving,
bathed in the sun's blood-red glow. She with
raised, bound wrists and naked back and aching
heart. He behind her, whip in hand, black eyes
locked on the delicate ivory back, vulnerably bare
and appealingly pinkened by the desert's dying
light.

Luiz lifted the whip high. And bought it singing
down. Amy instinctively flinched when it
cracked, kissing the air not an inch from her naked back. Her breath erupted in choking sobs and
she wept uncontrollably when suddenly Luiz
sailed the evil-looking lash away, took a sharp
knife from the waistband of his white trousers,
and cut the rope holding her.

Her bound wrists fell before her and, jerking

with fear and emotion, Amy swayed and almost fell. Luiz caught her and pulled her to him. Holding her back against him while his arms encircled her, he cut the punishing rope bindings from her reddened wrists. Her hands fell to her sides and once again the two stood unmoving. He behind her, feeling the trembling and softness of her slender body against him. She leaning wearily on him for support, the heat and hardness of his tall, lean frame totally foreign to her.

Luiz lifted her up into his arms and carried her to his waiting horse. He sat her across the saddle and swung up behind her, immediately touching his bootheels to the black stallion's flanks. The big mount shot away and Amy, her cheek cradled against Luiz's hard, bare chest, continued to sob, her tears wetting his dark flesh.

He took her straight to the hacienda.

When they arrived at the house, Mexican soldiers loitering on the grounds wisely averted their eyes as their bare-chested commanding officer, El Capitán, dismounted before the big adobe mansion and carried the beautiful blond woman up the long front walk and disappeared inside.

The big house was quiet.

In the dimly lighted downstairs corridor, the pair encountered no one. All was silent in the hacienda. Luiz paused only a moment in the brick-floored hallway. He gazed hurriedly about, then climbed the stairs with Amy in his arms. At the second-story landing, he decisively turned to the west wing and headed straight for the master suite. The suite Amy had years ago taken as her own.

With sure purpose, Luiz walked into the suite and kicked the heavy door closed behind him. He crossed the spacious room to the tall double doors thrown open to the gentle April breeze and stopped. He stood there holding Amy in his arms, as if in a deep trance, staring fixedly into the dying sun while its paling glow tinted them both a vivid lavender.

Amy's sobs had stopped. The tears had dried on her hot checks. Drained, she wanted nothing more than to have this tall, cruel man leave her immediately. She wanted him out of her sight, now and forever. He had been right when he said she didn't know him. She didn't know this man at all and she didn't want to know him. He was a heartless stranger and she was deathly afraid of him. And yet . . .

Her swollen eyes on the magnificent Sun Stone resting on the stranger's dark chest, Amy braced a hand against his shoulder and squirmed to be free.

Luiz came out of his trancelike state.

A muscle jumping in his rigid jaw, he lowered his gaze to Amy and felt his belly tighten.

He said, looking pointedly at her throat and delicate white shoulders, "Not even I; a murderous savage, could bear scarring such perfection. But perhaps another form of punishment is suggested."

17

———
————
———

Luiz heard her catch her breath and knew that she was genuinely afraid of him. In his arms her slender body stiffened and the soft hand pushing on his shoulder increased its pressure as she struggled to be free. Her aversion to him was no surprise, nor was it a deterrent. In truth, the fact that this cold, deceitful woman despised and feared him heightened his desire to possess her beautiful body.

He looked into those familiar blue eyes and for an instant there was a chilling flash of memory—tied up, helpless, lashed, and laughed at by the young girl he had loved more than his own life. The vivid recollection turned Luiz's black gaze icy-hot. He bent his dark head and kissed Amy forcefully, his mouth hard and brutal upon her soft, trembling lips.

Fully realizing his intention, Amy tried vainly to free her lips from his. She turned her head from side to side and with her fists she beat on his back and shoulders. But his hot commanding mouth remained fused with hers as he slowly lowered her feet to the floor. As soon as her toes touched the deep beige carpet, Luiz pulled Amy roughly against his tall, hard body, holding her effortlessly to him with one muscular arm around her waist.

His blazing kiss continued, a deep, invasive kiss of such blatant intimacy Amy felt as if her entire body was being violated. His wet, silky tongue was plunging deep inside her mouth. Amy was overwhelmed and terrified by such fierce animal power and passion.

When at last his cruel mouth freed her bruised lips, it took Amy an instant to regain her lost breath and collect her scattered wits. Reason returning, she swiftly lifted a trembling hand and gave his scarred cheek such a stinging slap the sound was like a pistol shot in the quiet, shadowy room.

"You can't do this to me! I will not allow it!" she shouted loudly, pulling away and reaching frantically for the low-riding bodice of her torn dress.

Luiz lifted a hand and rubbed his tingling jaw, the expression in his eyes still that unsettling combination of coldness and heat. Those strange, hypnotic eyes watched detachedly as Amy edged cautiously around him, moving behind him. Luiz did not turn. He remained as he was, standing before the balcony doors, rubbing his face.

Her heart drumming with excitement and hope, Amy hurriedly crossed the room to the door. When her fingers wrapped themselves around the gleaming brass knob, she could hardly keep a triumphant shout of relief from escaping her lips. Anxiously she turned the knob and yanked open the heavy door.

She was as good as free!

At that instant a pair of strong, dark hands slipped quickly around her waist, beneath the ruined dress, and Amy was too surprised even to scream as those capturing hands met in front and the fingers laced tightly together over her bare midriff.

Unceremoniously she was pulled back inside the room and the door was again kicked closed by Luiz's booted foot. Holding her to him, he said calmly, "I can do anything I please to you, Mrs. Parnell. And anything is exactly my intention."

His long fingers came unlaced. His hands moved up to cup and lift her bare, quivering breasts. When his palms settled warmly over the soft, satiny crests, Amy's fear fled and her fiery spirit fully surfaced.

No man could ride back into her life after ten years and mete out this base brand of punishment. She was no spineless young innocent to be bullied nor jaded harlot to be casually used.

Furious, Amy half turned in his embrace, whipped her head around, and sank her sharp teeth into Luiz's bare shoulder, biting him viciously. He made no sound, but his hands released her breasts and Amy immediately spun all the way around to face him. She was livid and at just that moment wouldn't have been afraid of the devil himself. She most certainly was not afraid of El Capitán Luiz Quintano.

Her face red with rage, her teeth bared like an animal's, she shouted at him, "I will kill you before I allow you to rape me!"

"You won't kill me," he said with easy confidence, reaching out and drawing her to him. His hands clasped the sides of her head, holding it in a vise from which she could not escape. He tilted her face up to his. His lips lowering to hers, he murmured, "And I won't rape you."

His hot, hard mouth again covered hers, but this time Amy had her guard up. Her lips were tightly shut against any invasion, and she was determined to put an end to his loathsome physical aggression. While his warm lips and wet tongue and white teeth toyed provocatively with her firmly closed mouth, she held her dress up with one hand and with the other she feverishly clawed at his bare back and his chest, raking the smooth bronzed flesh with sharp punishing fingernails.

It did no good.

He was totally indifferent to her scraping nails and to her furious attempts to get away. With single-minded purpose, he continued to kiss her, nipping at her soft lower lip, sucking it into his mouth, drumming his tongue against the barrier of her teeth.

When finally he tired of her unresponsiveness and raised his dark head, Amy threatened, "It's no use, El Capitán! I will scream and Magdelena and Fernando will come running."

"No, my dear, they will not," he said with cool authority.

"Yes, they will! You'll see, all I have to do is—"

"I have taken care of any interruptions, Mrs. Parnell. The night is all ours and I assure you we will not be disturbed."

Amy's uneasiness returned. "You're lying. They're just downstairs and I—"

"No." He gently shook his dark head. "Both your servants are in the east wing of the hacienda." He smiled then, a satanic smile that caused the white scar on his cheek to pucker and pull. "I have you all to myself."

She had no doubt he spoke the truth. He had planned the whole thing and now here she was trapped, alone in the silent west wing with a man bent on revenge. Sexual revenge.

She said as much to him. "You can lock me up here for the rest of my life, but it will do you no good! I will never submit to you, never! Your touch is repulsive to me. I hate you! Do you hear me, I hate you!" she exclaimed with a snarl, panic rising. "I will hate you for all eternity!"

"So be it," he said, shrugging wide, bare shoulders.

"You're not a man! You're nothing but an uncivilized animal with no sense of decency and I-I—" The fierce new light that sprang into his dark eyes stilled her sharp tongue and Amy knew she had said too much.

His strong chin jutted menacingly. His long arm shot out. He grabbed the bodice of her torn dress and chemise and yanked both down to her waist. Amy screamed and crossed her arms protectively over her bare breasts.

Passion and hatred flashing in his dark eyes, he wrapped his fingers around her wrists and pulled her covering hands away. Looking only at the firm ivory breasts rising and falling rapidly, he said, "You think me an uncivilized animal?" A hint of pain flickered in his eyes for a second before he added, "Then I shall love as a savage."

And forcing her arms down to her sides, he wedged a knee between her legs and held her immobile as his lips dropped to her throat. His teeth grazing the soft flesh below her ear, he spread kisses of fire down the side of her throat.

"No!" she pleaded, as his dark face moved steadily down toward her bare left breast. "Noooo," she cried, when his hot, open mouth enclosed the soft, sleeping crest and he sank down on one knee before her. "No . . . dear God . . . no," she breathed as he sucked and her nipple became an erect point of sensation. Tears of shame and self-disgust slid down Amy's flushed cheeks as she stood pinned against the door while the final glow from the setting sun tinted the room and both of them in a soft pastel gloaming.

"I hate you," she whispered, her knees watery, her heart pounding with passion and despair. "I do, I—I . . . hate . . . you . . ." she repeated the words, feeling they were true. But then how could she stand there in her own home and allow a man she detested to kiss her breasts?

Luiz raised his head, looked into her flushed face. Their gazes locked and held.

"I want you to stop," she said, trying to reason with him. "You have humiliated me enough. Please, let me go."

Accusingly he touched his forefinger to a stiff nipple. "Your body doesn't want me to let you go."

With that he gently eased her trapped hands from the restraining sleeves of her ruined dress. Amy winced when he impulsively kissed her warm, moist underarm.

His mouth returned to her breasts. Amy hated herself as much as she hated him because his teeth raking across her taut nipples, his tongue licking their stiff, sensitive peaks, his lips sucking vigorously, brought a tingling, forbidden pleasure that made the rest of her body feel warm and pliant and eager for his touch.

Plagued with guilt, led by passion, Amy continued to stand with her back against the door while El Capitán Luiz Quintano, kneeling before her, kissed her swelling, aching breasts as if he could not get enough, would never let her go.

Vainly telling herself that she was going to stop him before he went any further, Amy lifted her trembling hands to his dark head. The slender fingers that had earlier clawed at his scarred back settled almost lovingly into the thick raven locks, forgetting her intent was to tear his burning lips from her breasts.

Luiz raised his head and again their eyes locked in the dim light. Amy saw absolutely no tenderness in the depths of his fathomless black eyes, only an unbridled lust that both frightened and excited her. That fear escalated when his deft fingers found the hooks of her dress, the tapes of her petticoat and underwear.

He swept all her garments down to her hips and his mouth returned to her flesh. Amy felt the involuntary jumping of her thighs as his lips and tongue pressed burning kisses to her quivering stomach. Her face flaming hot, her breasts pinkened from his kisses, Amy was thoroughly confused. How could it possibly be that she was more sexually aroused than she had ever been in her life?

It couldn't.

She wasn't.

Reasonable fear was freezing her in place, not unreasonable attraction.

Her head, her heart, and her body all waging

battle with each other, Amy stood there, grateful that the summer sun had finally set and that the room would soon grow totally dark and hide her shame and embarrassment.

Amy was unconsciously surrendering to Luiz, although she did not yet realize it. Luiz was slowly, expertly draining away her will and taking over her body.

If Amy did not know it, Luiz did.

While he brushed kisses to her ribs, her navel, her prominent hip bones, he slowly, skillfully eased the tattered clothes down over her flared hips.

As the fabric slipped dangerously low, Amy stirred. Logic intervened and she lamely protested. Luiz changed his tactics. He knew women. No more precious moments spent at gentle seduction, it was time to frighten and excite her again.

Luiz roughly shoved Amy's torn, twisted garments right down to her knees and paid no mind to her gasps of shock and indignation. Instead he looked up at her and coldly commanded, "Step out of these things."

Brought rudely back to reality, Amy's high brow knitted with alarm. She stared at him, shaking her head, attempting to push him away.

"Now!" he ordered fiercely.

Amy, eyes wide, obeyed.

She stepped out of her shoes, then clung to Luiz's bare shoulders and stepped out of her clothes. He swept the discarded things aside and turned back to peel the white cotton stockings down her shapely legs. Amy could be grateful for only one thing—that the dusky twilight had finally deepened into darkness.

It had grown so dark in the room, she could hardly see him, which meant he couldn't see her clearly either. She could make out only the dark head, the wide shoulders, as he rose before her, turned, and walked away. Amy took a step forward and heard his deep, cold voice cut through the darkness.

"You hold still. *I'll* tell you when you can move."

Amy sank back against the door. She began to tremble. What was he up to now? Where was he going? A match flared across the room and a candle flickered to life, casting soft honeyed light on the harsh planes of Luiz's bronzed face. He returned to her, carrying the silver candleholder with its brightly burning white candle.

He stood looking down at her, lifting the candle high, allowing his dark, penetrating eyes to slide over her bare, slender body. Amy felt the heated touch of those ebony eyes as if his hands were on her. She shivered and tried to cover herself.

Luiz smiled and set the candleholder on the floor beside her. Waiting tensely to see what he would do next, Amy watched him again walk away. He went straight to the canopied bed, yanked down the spread and covers, and tossed them onto the carpeted floor. He swept all the pillows off the high bed, leaving the mattress free of everything save the ivory silk sheet stretching across it.

Luiz stood beside the bed, his eyes on Amy. He took the wide gold and turquoise bracelet off his wrist and laid it on the marble-topped night table. He lifted the heavy gold medallion up over his head and laid it beside the bracelet. He removed the sharp knife from the waistband of his white trousers. He stood there for a long moment, as if deciding, then came back to her.

Bracing a hand on either side of the door, trapping her, he leaned down and kissed her mouth. He kept kissing her until Amy swayed helplessly to him. Her arms went around him, her hands clinging to his back and her soft, bare breasts pressing insistently against his hard chest.

Only then did Luiz release his grip on the doorframe. His hands touched her waist briefly, then his right one moved down to cup her firm, rounded buttock before slipping into the crevice between. Amy flinched when he touched her. She tore her mouth from his and pushed on his chest.

His hand cupped the back of her neck, beneath her long blond hair, and he drew her back to him. He crooked a long arm around her and urged her toward the bed. Amy balked.

She looked at the big, empty bed and realized that if she willingly allowed him to take her there, she would be as vile as he.

Luiz read her thoughts.

"Yes," he said, his voice a mixture of coaxing and contempt, "if you share your bed with a primitive savage, then what does that make you, my lovely Mrs. Parnell?"

She opened her mouth to answer but the words were swallowed up in his capturing lips. Fiercely, provocatively, he kissed her and his hands lightly, gently caressed her slender, naked body, pressing her to him, molding her soft curves to his tall, hard frame.

A master of passion, Luiz drew Amy toward the bed, not stopping until the backs of his legs touched the mattress's high edge. Before Amy

had time to catch her breath from his kiss, Luiz sat
down on the bed, pulled her between his spread
knees, but made her remain standing. He turned
her so that she stood at a right angle to him and
the bed.

With one hand resting on the small of her back,
the other on her flat stomach, Luiz said, "You're
not yet gotten into bed, Mrs. Parnell. Leave now if
you must." He paused, then added more softly, "If
you wish."

Amy stirred and made a move to leave him, but
she never got away. Both his hands slipped
swiftly, seductively between her legs, one from
the back, the other from the front, and met.
Within seconds his long, skilled fingers were doing
forbidden, marvelous things to Amy that literally
set her afire.

"What . . . what are you doing to me?" she
murmured, then drew a long, slow breath
through her mouth, her eyes closing with ecstasy.

"Making you mine," he replied, his fingers
gently touching concealed, sensitive female flesh
in an intimate exploration that shocked and excited Amy.

"No . . . Luiz . . . no . . ." She breathed
raggedly as his fingers daringly stroked and
probed, easily finding the pleasure points, making
her squirm and sigh in erotic bliss.

When Amy began to writhe uncontrollably and
twist and press her pulsing flesh eagerly into
Luiz's gloriously tormenting hands, he stopped,
lifted his glistening fingers up before her flushed
face, and said, "You are hot and wet and ready for
me. Tell me you are. Say it."

Amy shook her head.

"Say it, Mrs. Parnell. Say the words, 'El Capitán, I am hot and wet and ready for you. Make love to me.'" His hands gripped her narrow waist and he turned her to face him.

Her breath coming fast, her need for him out of control, Amy said anxiously, "El Capitán, I am hot and wet and ready for you. Make love to me." She looked into the blazing black eyes and saw a passion that matched her own. "Please. Now."

His smile of triumph was satanic, pulling the scar on his cheek. Amy didn't care. This handsome, hawk-faced man had succeeded in making her so hot she had to have him, no matter what he thought about her. Nothing mattered but the fierce hunger he had awakened in her.

Pressing a kiss to the undercurve of her breast, Luiz said, "Take off my boots."

Immediately Amy fell to one knee before him, tugged on the highly polished tall black boots, and set them aside. Eagerly she rose, wanting—needing—his hands back on her. Luiz drew her to him, sat her down on his left knee, took her hand and placed it directly atop the rock-hard erection straining against his tight white trousers.

Through the fabric, Amy could feel the intense heat and hardness of him. Awed, she awkwardly caressed him and heard him murmur close to her ear, "You want it, it's yours." He pressed a kiss to her shoulder. "But you must take it."

"You . . . you don't mean . . ."

"I do. I undressed you. Now you undress me."

Amy didn't have to be told twice. A white-hot desire consuming her, she anxiously undid the buttons of Luiz's trousers, then rose from his knee and ordered him to stand up.

He obeyed.

Amy's loose blond hair swung into her face. Irritably she pushed it behind her ears and gripped the waistband of his pants. Her large, smoldering eyes following their descent, Amy peeled the crisp white military trousers and linen underwear down over Luiz's slim hips, automatically pausing when his thrusting masculinity sprang free.

Her hands clinging to the half-lowered trousers, she stared at the surging male flesh rising from a dense growth of raven curls and was afraid.

She trembled with a new kind of fear. It wasn't that she was afraid of being physically hurt by his huge, rigid erection. She was deathly afraid of the power his potent maleness would hold over her. Still, fear could not compete with raging desire. She wanted him. Had to have him.

Frenzied, Amy shoved the trousers to Luiz's knees and said, "Step out of your pants."

Luiz obligingly did so, kicking them aside with his foot.

And then they stood there facing each other, the tall white candle from across the room casting its flickering light and shadows over their naked bodies.

18

He did not pull her hurriedly into his arms.

Breathless with desire, Amy stood naked and trembling before the tall, commanding El Capitán Luiz Quintano.

There was none of the easy closeness she had once shared with the considerate young Tonatiuh. Gone was the beautiful, sensitive boy with whom she had shared sweet moments of gentle lovemaking. In his place now stood a coldly handsome man whose strong sexual magnetism made her sense, fearfully, that sharing his bed would be a different experience from any she had ever known.

But Amy had no idea just how different.

An accomplished lover, capable of controlling his desire and his body, Luiz was in no mad rush to obtain fulfillment. At least not his own. If Amy remembered their youthful moments of fumbling, frenzied passion, so did he. He was determined to show this devious blond beauty that the lovesick youth who had been so much in awe of her he was incapable of holding back was gone. Gone the way of lost innocence and unrequited love, and blind, unquestioning trust.

He would show her this very night that he could arouse her, possess her, and bring her to deep, satisfying release, again and again, while calmly maintaining his present state of rigid sexual readiness.

So Luiz did not pull Amy hurriedly into his arms. He stood unmoving, his bare, bronzed feet apart, allowing his hot black eyes to slide caressingly over her beautiful, unclothed body. And allowing her to get a good, slow look at him.

At just the right moment he put out his hand to her, palm up. Anxiously swallowing, Amy laid her shaking hand atop his and caught her breath when his strong fingers closed firmly around the fragile bones.

His black eyes holding hers, Luiz very slowly drew her to him. When their naked bodies were very close, but not quite touching, he dropped her hand and allowed his own to fall to his side. And again they stood perfectly still, a scant two inches apart. So close their heated flesh responded involuntarily to the intoxicating nearness.

Luiz's straining masculinity stirred outward and pressed Amy's quivering belly, evoking a soft sound of wonder from her parted lips. Instinctively she moved closer to the awesome jerking power, so close that the taut nipples of her swelling breasts touched and teased at Luiz's smooth, hard chest.

But his long arms remained at his sides as Amy's nervous fingers moved up to grip his bulging biceps and she eagerly pressed her pelvis to his. Beside herself with desire, Amy's hands moved up his shoulders and around his neck as she closed her eyes, rose to her toes, and pressed burning kisses to his coppery throat.

He stayed as he was for a few minutes more

while the incredibly desirable woman clung to him, undulated against him, and teasingly bit and licked his slick throat.

Working hard to keep just the right note of indifference in his low, sure voice, Luiz said, "Would you like to lie down now?"

Her unbound blond hair pleasantly tickling his chin, Amy nodded against him, her lips reluctant to release his flesh.

"What was that? I didn't hear you."

Her voice almost a sob, she murmured, "Yes. Please. Let's lie down."

Luiz's hands at last left his sides, moved up to her slender waist. He did not urge Amy down to the mattress. He turned around, so that his back was to the ivory-sheeted bed. He lifted a hand up to her golden tresses and wrapped a long thick strand of the shimmering hair around the back of his hand and urged her head up and back.

Amy's eyes opened and she looked up at him. Mesmerized by his dark, handsome face, which bore a strange kind of intensity, she watched as his lips languidly descended to hers. It was a slow burning kiss of such compelling potency, Amy felt as if she were already a part of him as Luiz leaned back and together they sank down across the bed. He stretched out on his back and she lay atop him. And still the kiss continued.

The next half hour was spent in arousing play as Luiz allowed Amy to acquaint herself fully with his long, lean body. She did just that. She squirmed erotically atop him while he kissed her and touched her and murmured forbidden sexual promises that brought her to a dangerous boiling point.

He switched their positions so that he was atop her. His dark, chiseled face and wide sculpted shoulders looming just above, he moved his slim hips between her parted thighs. He slid down and carefully positioned himself so that only the smooth tip of his blood-engorged shaft was touching her slick swollen sweetness.

"Open your eyes and look at me," he softly but firmly commanded. Amy's eyes restlessly fluttered open and she looked up at him. While their gazes locked, Luiz took her hand in his, drew it down, and wrapped her trembling fingers around his erection. His hand fell away. Amy gripped him and anxiously guided him into her.

And sighed with the incredible bliss of it.

Perfectly judging her readiness and need, Luiz waited only seconds before beginning the deep, rhythmic thrusting her overheated body demanded. Immediately Amy felt herself being swept into a vortex of carnal pleasure. She clung to Luiz, experiencing a spiraling sensation of ecstasy so frightening she screamed. The buffeting pain-pleasure was unlike anything she'd ever known.

And then a sweet explosion of heat washed over her, leaving her weak and happy and glowing. Her arms wrapped around Luiz's neck, her breath coming in pants, Amy licked her dry lips and smiled foolishly and felt every muscle in her sated body slacken totally.

Watching, Luiz kissed her parted lips. Amy felt her heavy arms slipping from his neck to the softness of the mattress. Relaxed, she let her gripping knees fall from Luiz's body and waited for him to roll away from her.

But Luiz did not roll away.

He stayed as he was and as Amy's rapid heart-beat began to slow and her limp body began to come back to life, she realized that he had not yet attained release, he was still hard within her.

Lost in the impenetrable blackness of his eyes, Amy lay very still, looking at him, not sure how to handle the situation. Nothing like this had ever occurred before. Not in her bedroom. It had always been the other way round. Tyler had always quickly, selfishly attained his release, then fallen asleep leaving her unsatisfied.

Surprisingly, she felt herself rapidly growing excited again, lured by the heat of his eyes on her face, the hardness of him expanding inside her. Amy, enjoying anew the building of sexual excitement, impulsively lifted a hand up behind his head, gave the narrow white leather band securing his hair a quick tug, and shivered with pleasure when the thick raven locks swung forward and tickled her face and bare shoulders.

Luiz began softly kissing Amy's lips, her delicate shoulders, her breasts, and soon she was bucking up against him, fevered once more. Again he easily guided her to total satisfaction, and this time the depth of her climax was even greater.

Luiz slid from her, pushed his black hair back off his face, gathered her to him, and gently soothed her. But when she had calmed and lay relaxed against him, she realized—this time with an increasing sense of unease—that he still had not attained release.

Her head resting on his shoulder, face pressed to his chest, Amy pondered the puzzling cause.

Did he not find her attractive? Did she not excite
him? Was she incapable of giving him total ecstasy? It never for a minute entered Amy's head
that he had held back on purpose.

Amy did exactly what Luiz Quintano knew she
would do. She stirred, lifted her head a little, and
began pressing soft, sweet kisses to his shoulder.
He folded his hands beneath his head, yawned,
and closed his eyes. Frowning, Amy raised herself
up a little more, put her hand to his ribs, leaned
over him, and trailed kisses across his chest.

His black eyes slitted open. Luiz calmly
watched Amy as she attempted to excite him.
Sweetly assaulted by her increasingly aggressive
hands and mouth, Luiz wondered at her seeming
sexual ignorance.

Didn't she know that he was still so aroused he
was in physical pain? That he was only waiting for
her to grow excited again? Apparently she did
not, so Luiz writhed, his dark, lean body sliding
sensuously about on the slick ivory sheets. Teasingly he tumbled about on the bed and was
overjoyed that the beautiful determined woman
followed, bent on her task of exciting him.

Amy grew highly aroused as she chased Luiz
around the bed, kissing his smooth, hard chest and
flat belly and boldly toying with his pulsing erection. She was again so aroused that when Luiz
reached out and effortlessly lifted her astride him,
she was in the full flush of desire and lustfully slid
fully down onto him.

Her soft buttocks moved stirringly against his
hard cock, and Luiz had to use every ounce of his
dwindling control to keep from exploding within
her. Her hands clinging to his rib cage, Amy

tossed her head back and her breathing deepened. She pressed her pelvis down on his and moved on his so hotly, so sweetly, he knew he couldn't possibly hold out much longer.

At that moment Amy looked into his eyes, spoke his name, and Luiz started to spasm. His started hers and together they came in a rush of wild delirium that left their hearts pounding, their bodies slick with perspiration.

Amy crumpled helplessly to Luiz and they lay unable to move for several long minutes, the candlelight playing over their limp, moist bodies.

Amy felt a sweet exhaustion claim her. It was impossible to move. She told herself she should get up. Should take a bath. Should put on a nightgown. Should straighten the bed, retrieve the pillows and the covers from the floor.

She stayed where she was and was grateful when Luiz finally eased her over onto her back, kissed her mouth, and stretched out beside her. Amy's heavy eyelids fluttered as she sleepily studied the pleated ivory-silk canopy above.

She gave a gentle little sigh of satisfaction and fell asleep.

In the wee hours of the morning, when the candle had burned down and guttered and the moon had risen, Amy awakened. With difficulty she opened her eyes. Staring up at the pleated white silk canopy above her, she wondered why she felt so tired. She was exhausted. She lay flat on her back, one knee bent, the sole of her foot on the mattress.

Amy stretched out her bent leg. She lifted a hand to rub her stomach and found that it was

bare. She lifted her head an inch off the mattress
and looked down at herself. She was sleeping naked. She never did that. Why was she naked? And
why was she lying across the bed instead of with
her head where it belonged? Where were her pillows and bedcovers?

It all came back in a rush of remembering and
Amy cautiously turned her head and saw him.
Captured and framed in a wedge of pale moonlight, Luiz lay stretched out on the silk ivory
sheet, the silvery beams washing over his lean,
dark frame.

Her heart thumping, Amy cautiously examined
every shadowed plane of the hard, handsome face
with its strong, chiseled features, long, sweeping
eyelashes, white slashing scar, and cruelly sensual
lips. Studied every bare inch of the once-familiar
body.

He was a stranger.

A stranger who looked dangerous even as he
slept. Even asleep, he did not appear to be totally
relaxed and vulnerable. There was a coiled tension about his long, hard-muscled body, as if he
was ready to spring and strike.

Amy involuntarily shuddered.

Her eyes touched the muscled shoulders, the
smooth chest, and slid lower, over his corded ribs
and flat belly to that part of him she most feared.

Her face flushed hot and her bare stomach fluttered nervously as she stared at the flaccid flesh at
rest amid the blue-black curling hair of his groin.
Vividly she recalled what that harmless-looking
organ was capable of when fully erect.

Shivering, Amy made a move to rise.

In the blinking of an eye Luiz bolted up, imprisoned her wrist in a tight, painful grip, and forced her back down to the mattress. Then he was above her, his wide, bronzed shoulders looming close, his black, luminous eyes flashing in the darkness.

He said not one word, but commandingly drew her into his close embrace and lay down once more on his back. In seconds he was again asleep with Amy helplessly trapped inside his arms. She lay there in the moonlight, listening to his deep, even breathing, feeling the steady beating of his heart beneath her cheek.

Exhausted from their bouts of lovemaking, she dropped back off to sleep. When next she awakened, bright sunlight streamed into the room. Remembering immediately, she turned her head. She was alone in the bed.

Grateful for that, Amy raised herself up on one elbow, pushed her heavy hair from her face, and looked around. The big room with its cream-color walls and deep beige carpet looked just as it always did. The french doors were open to the cool April morning, the heavy ivory drapes tied back. Across from the bed, she saw the fireplace of gold-streaked ivory marble and above the mantel a gold-framed mirror that reached the ceiling. Arranged before the fireplace was the long, comfortable sofa covered in ivory brocade flanked by the twin wing chairs of lush beige velvet.

All was in place. Except for a silken heap of discarded bedcovers and fluffy feather pillows just beyond the foot of the massive four poster. Through the open door leading into the large dressing-bathroom, she saw a movement. Hurriedly jerking the sheet loose from the mattress to cover herself, Amy sat up as El Capitán Luiz Quintano entered from her bathroom. Dressed in a pair of snug buff-hued trousers, a crisp white shirt, wide red sash around his trim waist, and polished knee-high boots of soft brown leather, he strode forward.

Freshly shaven, his long, raven hair secured at the back of his neck with a narrow leather string, he nodded to her as if he saw her every morning of his life. His casual indifference after such a night of shameful intimacy was too much for Amy.

He came and stood beside the bed, smiled coldly, and said, "Don't look so troubled, Mrs. Parnell. Last night meant nothing to me. I was only amusing myself."

Hurt and heartsick, Amy recognized the stinging words she had once used to dismiss him. He had come to pay her back. That's all last night had meant to him.

Her innate spirit rose and she scrambled up from the bed to face him. Standing before him, clutching tightly at the covering sheet, she shouted angrily, "Fine! You got what you came back here for, El Capitán, now get out! Leave Orilla. Get off my land!"

Luiz gave her an amused smile. "Your land? *Our* land, *chica*. Orilla is owned jointly by me." The smile left; his handsome face hardened and his black eyes turned wintry cold. "I am tired. My troops are tired. Orilla will serve as my headquarters until our return to battle." He turned to leave. At the door he paused, pivoted to face her, and added, "As long as I occupy this hacienda, you will share my bed."

19

Amy watched the door close after his departing back and felt her anger blaze as white-hot as her passions had burned in the darkness of the night. Trembling with rage, she looked about for something to throw at the door.

Her eyes fell on the Sun Stone lying on the nighttable. Her face set, she released her hold on the covering sheet and allowed it to fall to the beige carpet. Naked, she snatched up the shiny gold medallion. Tears of frustration filling her angry blue eyes, she hurled the Sun Stone across the room with all her strength.

"You forgot your precious amulet, you savage bastard!" she shouted hotly, then immediately choked in startled surprise.

At the exact instant she released the medallion, her bedroom door opened and an unsmiling El Capitán stood framed in the portal. His right hand shot out with swift dexterity and plucked the flying Sun Stone from midair.

His narrowed black eyes locked on her, he calmly closed the door and unhurriedly crossed to her. Tensed, her pulses pounding, Amy blinked back the tears and watched as he slowly bore down on her. Suddenly all too aware of her own nakedness, she sank to her knees to retrieve her discarded sheet. And winced loudly when his foot came down squarely atop it. Jerking vainly at the pinned sheet, Amy glared at the polished brown boot carelessly resting atop the ivory silk.

Her intolerant gaze slid up the long, lean leg. Sinewy muscles bunched and stretched the fine beige fabric of his tight trousers and Amy, swallowing, felt another emotion mix with her anger. Resolved that she'd not be affected by this cold man's raw masculinity, she quickly lifted her eyes to his face. She felt a stirring of fear push aside her anger and her attraction to him.

El Capitán appeared irate and dangerous.

The high, slanting line of his cheekbones seemed more pronounced than ever, the chiseled cleft in his chin somehow menacing. His mouth, chilly and closed, was lifted at one end into something not quite a smile, not quite a sneer. His chin was held level in a pose of remarkably frank arrogance.

Amy gasped when he reached down, wrapped his fingers around her upper arm, and drew her to her feet. She tried to pull free. He refused to let her go. He forced her close against him, raised his hand up in front of her, and opened it.

The gold Sun Stone rested atop his palm. The heavy chain was laced through his long, dark fingers. He dropped the medallion and let it swing back and forth before Amy's taut face.

There was about him a frightening quality of cold-bloodedness when he said, his voice barely above a whisper, "Perhaps to you I am a barbarian. A crude savage. You find the beliefs and customs of my people worthy only of your ridicule."

His restraining hand moved from her upper arm, slid almost caressingly up beneath her hair, and clasped the back of her neck. "The Sun Stone is sacred. You will touch it only when I give you permission. Understood?"

Amy said nothing.

Luiz's strong fingers tightened on her neck. "I said do you understand me?"

"Y-yes. Yes, I understand you," she replied grudgingly, unsure of what might come next.

"See that you don't forget," he cautioned levelly.

With that El Capitán lifted the chain, draped it over his dark head, and allowed the gleaming medallion to fall around his neck. He then ordered Amy to unbutton his white shirt, place the Sun Stone inside, and rebutton the shirt.

In silence, she obeyed, hating him, fearing him. Her fingers shaking, she worked at the buttons of the freshly laundered shirt. It parted down his dark chest to reveal the long red claw marks her sharp nails had left on him. Staring at the vicious-looking red welts, Amy caught her breath.

She heard him say, "I've teeth marks on my shoulder. Would you care to examine those as well?"

Amy shook her head, started to place the medallion inside his shirt, and hesitated. Her eyes lifted to meet his. He nodded. "Yes, Mrs. Parnell. You may touch the Sun Stone. You have my permission."

Amy's fingers closed around the medallion. She slid it inside the open shirt, onto the warm, bare flesh directly over his heart. She quickly rebuttoned his shirt, anxious to have him gone and to put on her clothes.

El Capitán thanked her. He reached out, picked up the razor-sharp obsidian knife from the night table, and held it out to her. "If you must throw something at me, may I suggest this." Amy stubbornly refused to take the knife. He took her hand, placed the knife's shiny handle in her palm, and wrapped her icy fingers around it.

He stood insolently before her, his arms at his sides, silently inviting her to stab him if she dared. Amy was tempted to do just that. Her chin lifted, her delicate jaw hardened. Her eyes flashed with rage and excitement. Her stiff fingers tightened on the knife's slick hilt as she contemplated how rewarding it would feel to swiftly plunge the deadly blade into him.

Recklessly she said, "Were I as uncivilized as you, I would do it." She lifted the knife, touched its point to the left side of his chest, and added, "Correct me if I'm mistaken. Didn't your people —the barbaric Aztec—use just such a knife to carve out the beating hearts of their helpless victims?"

Luiz showed no emotion. "That's true. But then you, my naked Jezebel, need no knife. You cut out the beating hearts of your victims with far deadlier weapons." His black eyes held a dangerous light as they slid accusingly down Amy's bare, seductive curves. Suddenly he smiled and added, "A heart can be cut out but once. So I am in no danger."

Ignoring the knife point still pressed directly to his heart, El Capitán leaned close and brushed a kiss to the side of Amy's throat, inhaled deeply, and said casually, "I've had water drawn. You need a bath, Mrs. Parnell. You smell of me."

He turned and confidently walked away while Amy stood fuming, the knife in her hand, her gaze on his cocksure back. Eyes ablaze, she lifted the knife high, but didn't throw it. Sighing, she allowed him to leave unharmed, then carefully placed the knife back atop the table beside his gold and turquoise bracelet.

Her nerves raw, her body spent, Amy felt the hot tears sliding down her cheeks as she rushed across the room, threw the bolt lock, and turned to sag wearily against the heavy door. Almost frantically she pushed away and hurried toward her big bathroom, anxious to cleanse his scent and his touch from her flesh.

Once in the hot, soapy water, Amy vigorously scrubbed herself. A bar of jasmine soap in one hand, an abrasive washcloth in the other, she rubbed and washed and scoured until her skin was pink and tender. Just when she felt certain she was as clean as she'd ever been in her life, another lewd picture of last night's indulgence flashed through her mind and she began scrubbing once more.

When she felt as if she were in danger of scraping away all her skin, Amy rose and stepped from the ivory marble tub. She reached for a towel and, catching sight of herself in the mirrored bathroom walls, flushed, recalling El Capitán's arrogant promise that he intended to make love to her in this mirrored room so that he might watch. She too, could watch. She frantically snatched the huge white towel from the rack and swirled it around her body to cover her nakedness.

She could think of nothing more disgusting than to watch herself make love in a mirror! Especially with a cold-hearted, hot-blooded lover who was more animal than man. The prospect of participating in such an indecent act was revolting. Not in a million years would she do something so sordid and depraved!

Amy hurriedly dressed then found she didn't want to go downstairs. Reluctant to risk running into El Capitán, she remained in her room, pacing.

She was miserable. And confused. All she had ever dreamed of, longed for, hoped would happen, had finally come to pass. Her beloved Tonatiuh was alive! He had come home to Orilla after all these years. Yet sadly, ironically, his unexpected return had made her even more unhappy than this sudden disappearance.

Sighing, Amy stood before the open french doors. Her sad blue eyes scanned the sea of soldiers beyond the yard, searching for that one coldly handsome bronzed face amid all the others. She found it.

El Capitán stood lounging against his big black stallion, a long arm thrown over the creature's saddled back. His blue-black hair glistened in the morning sunlight. Leaning down to listen to an amusing story told by one of his men, his dark face broke into an appealingly boyish grin. Amy felt a painful squeezing of her heart.

She felt so terribly guilty. There was not one, but two reasons for her overwhelming guilt. First, she was the one responsible for Tonatiuh—the sweet, gentle Indian boy she had known and loved—becoming the cruel, uncaring creature he now was. Second, by giving in to the sexually compelling officer last night, she had betrayed her fiancé, Douglas Crawford.

Amy was overcome with remorse. No kinder, gentler human being lived than Doug Crawford. No man had ever been as protective, as understanding as he. His big heart would be broken if he knew that while he was soldiering with Maximilian deep in the interior of Mexico—fighting so he could make enough money to take care of *her*— she was making profane love to a man who had no more regard for her than if she were one of the whores so favored by her late husband, Tyler Parnell.

Her gaze fixed on the tall, lean officer, Amy watched as Luiz swung up into the saddle and rode away alone. She stared until he and the big black were no more than a speck on the horizon. Only then did she draw a long, relaxing breath, turn, and go back inside.

Despite the fact her tormentor had ridden away, Amy, after unbolting the door, peered cautiously up and down the long corridor before stepping outside. Taking a few more calming breaths, she lifted the skirts of her pink-and-white striped cotton dress and moved toward the stairs.

Descending the wide staircase, Amy wondered just how much she should tell Magdelena. She was tempted to fling herself into the older woman's comforting arms and cry out her despair. To tell of the long, terrible night she had spent at the mercy of the vindictive El Capitán Quintano.

She knew she couldn't do that.

She had been raised by a proud father to keep her personal troubles from the servants. As close

as she was to Magdelena, she had never—not once
—told the trustworthy Mexican woman exactly
what had happened all those years ago.

Only that there had been trouble and the Sullivan brothers had sent Luiz away. She herself had
sworn she was happy to become the bride of Tyler
Parnell. She'd gone on with the pretense of being
the contented young wife, never revealing to anyone that she was unhappy. That her young heart
was broken. That never a day, an hour, a minute
passed that she did not wonder if her beloved
Tonatiuh was dead or alive. Nor did she ever di-
vulge that her husband spent more of his nights
with other women than he ever spent with her,
and that she was relieved he did.

At the base of the stairs, Amy squared her slender shoulders.

No, she wouldn't tell Magdelena about last
night, but surely the older woman would know. El
Capitán had bragged about moving Magdelena
and Fernando to the east wing saying that the two
of them had the west wing all to themselves for
the night.

Magdelena was a smart, intuitive woman. She
would put two and two together and her motherly
instincts would make her want to intervene on
Amy's behalf.

Amy felt a little better.

Magdelena would protect her from the evil El
Capitán. There would be no more nights like the
one past. Her Magdelena wouldn't allow it.

Amy found Magdelena in the kitchen. She was
carefully slicing fresh fruit and artfully arranging
it on a china platter. As she worked, she sang a
beautiful Spanish love song. She looked up and

smiled broadly when Amy entered. Amy couldn't believe her ears when the older woman dropped what she was doing, put her hands on her spreading hips, and said, "You mean to wear that dress today?"

Amy frowned. "I have it on. Of course I plan to wear it."

"No, no, Amy. Is not the right one for this special day." Magdelena wiped her hands on her apron and came forward. "Come. We go back up and find something more suitable."

"More suitable for what?"

Magdelena's dark eyes sparkled.

"For sharing lunch with the handsome El Capitán Quintano!"

20

"For sharing lunch with . . . I have no intention of having lunch with this arrogant Mexican officer," Amy said firmly.

"Such foolish talk, Amy Sullivan Parnell. We do not speak of some stranger. *Dios,* Luiz is the sweet, pretty little boy who once live here. This is his home!"

"That sweet, pretty little boy is a cold, disrespectful man who last night—" Amy caught herself and her words trailed off. Frowning, she gave a dismissive wave of her hand.

Puzzled, Magdelena stared at her. "He do what to you? Spend some time with old childhood friend. This is a crime? I do not understand you. You are the one who has changed, not Luiz." She shook her head back and forth. "Times like this, I do not know you."

Amy forced herself to soften her expression. She smiled and said, "Magdelena, its been ten long years since Tona—since Luiz Quintano left the Orilla. No one need remind you of all that has happened since then."

"No. Much has changed but"—Magdelena's brown face broke into a wide smile—"I remember sweet young boy and girl who were together constantly that last summer. I not forget the times I packed lunches so you two could ride to river and spend the afternoon playing in the water. You remember, Amy?"

Amy drew a slow, deep breath. "Yes," she said. "I remember."

"Were you not the best of friends?"

The best of friends? My, God, Mag, didn't you realize that we were lovers? That we spent every hot afternoon making love at the river? Didn't you have any idea what was happening between us? Don't you know what happened here last night?

"We were the best of friends," Amy said softly.

"Then what is wrong? Why you not wish to have lunch with Luiz? He will be disappointed."

"He'll get over it."

"I think not. Bless his heart, he come to me late yesterday afternoon. He say he wish to spend entire evening with his old friend, Amy. Say he missed you. Say the two of you wanted to visit and laugh and catch up. Asked if Fernando and I mind sleeping in east wing so as not to be disturbed. I tell him we glad to do it."

"How courteous of you," Amy said sarcastically.

"Hmmmp! Time you show a little courtesy." Magdelena reached out and touched Amy's arm. A questioning look came into her large, dark eyes. "My children not enjoy themselves last night?"

Amy could feel herself flushing. "Well, yes, we . . . it was . . ." She cleared her throat. "We had a nice visit. But, let's face it, one can only hash over old times just so long. I believe Luiz Quintano and I have said all we have to say to each other."

Unconvinced, Magdelena said, "Ah, now that is very hard for me to believe."

Flustered and on edge, Amy suddenly snapped, "Have you forgotten I am an engaged woman?"

Magdelena suddenly grinned impishly. "No. Have you?"

"I most certainly have not!" Amy answered too quickly, her voice an octave too high. "I—I have a headache, I'm going to lie down for a while."

"What about your lunch?"

"I'm not hungry."

"Amy have a terrible headache, Luiz," Magdelena apologized when the tall, dark man took his place at the table shortly after noon. "She say I am to tell you she is very sorry. She had looked forward to having lunch with you." Color suffused Magdelena's dark face, and she hoped this imposing young man could not sense that she was fibbing.

Luiz was fully aware that the Mexican house woman was not telling the truth. But he said nothing. He was fond of Magdelena, had spent more than one happy hour in her kitchen when he was a boy, "licking the pan," she had called it. And sampling huge wedges of freshly baked pies. Or tearing off chunks of tender, succulent roast beef straight from the oven. And learning dozens of Spanish love songs from the romantic woman whose voice was as warm and pleasant as her aromatic kitchen.

Hers was a good, pure heart. By lying to him now, Magdelena was trying to spare his tender feelings, thinking him to be the same shy, sensitive young boy who had left Orilla ten years ago.

Luiz said easily, "I'm sorry to hear Amy isn't well. Convey my concern."

"I will do that." Magdelena said.

Looking at the strikingly handsome young officer seated at the table, she did not see a chilly, dangerous man, as Amy did. She still saw the innocent young boy who was dear to her heart.

Gazing fondly at him, Magdelena set a plate of sliced fruit and cold chicken before him, placed a basket of freshly baked bread nearby, and once again apologized. Her face wearing a worried expression, she said, "I wish I could feed you tender Orilla beef for lunch like in the old days." Sadly she shook her head. "We have beef seldom now. The ranch . . . the cattle . . ." Her shoulders lifted in a shrug. "Our river, the Puesta del Sol, dried up. Then the long drought come. Everything die. Times are hard, Luiz." She started to move away.

Luiz caught her arm and drew her back. He flashed Magdelena a brilliant, boyish smile that reminded her of happier days gone by.

"Don't worry, Mag. Things change. You will see."

Warmed by that dazzling smile and longing to believe things would change, she nodded happily. "Ah, *sí, sí,* my boy is back. Things will be better. Much better." She turned to leave.

Luiz pushed back his chair and rose. "Don't make me eat alone, Mag. Have lunch with me."

She whirled around and stared at him. "Me? Why, I couldn't . . . That would not be proper."

Luiz, continuing to smile, put an arm around her thickening waist and gave her an affectionate squeeze. He led her around the table and pulling out the chair, urged her down into it, then pushed it back up to the table while Magdelena continued to weakly protest. "I really shouldn't. . . ."

"Stay right where you are," Luiz softly commanded as he backed away and moved to the swinging door connecting the kitchen with the dining room. After nudging it open with his shoulder, he disappeared inside. In minutes he was back, bearing a filled plate and a glass of wine, which he placed before Magdelena.

He reclaimed his chair, shook out his napkin, draped it across his trousered right knee, and said, "I appreciate this, Mag. I hate to eat alone."

Charmed and flattered, Magdelena smiled broadly and whispered, "Luiz, Luiz! This is not done! What would people say?"

"I won't tell if you won't," he answered, and winked at her. Magdelena laughed and nodded her agreement. "Besides, I'm counting on you to tell me all that happened while I was away."

Magdelena was not accustomed to drinking wine at any hour, much less at noontime. Nor was she used to having her favorite boy back home. The combination made her unusually light-hearted. And light-headed. And Luiz was able to draw her out, to get her to talk about things she'd not talked of for years.

The casual attitude of his relaxed lean body, his seeming placidity, belied the keen alertness with which he noted every word she spoke. Long after the meal was finished and coffee had cooled in their cups and Luiz had lighted his second cigar, the pair remained as they were, seated at the table, speaking of the past.

Or, rather, Magdelena spoke and Luiz listened.

Most of what she told, he already knew. He knew that the ranch was almost worthless since the river had dried up. He knew that Lucas Sullivan had been killed in a Paso del Norte knife fight. He knew about Amy's marriage to Tyler Parnell and Parnell's subsequent death. He was even aware that Amy was to wed the widower Doug Crawford, a big, likable man he remembered as being happily married with a child.

But some things came as a surprise. Until now he hadn't known that Amy had a daughter. He had not heard that the Apaches had killed Crawford's wife and child. Nor did he know that Magdelena's daughter, Rosa, had run away with Baron Sullivan and was now dead.

"And Baron?" he gently questioned, after expressing his sympathy.

Her dark eyes flashing with hatred, Magdelena said, "I am sure he is still alive. Evil lives forever!"

Luiz gave no reply. He guided Magdelena back to more pleasant topics, and soon she was laughing again and couldn't believe it when he said, "Mag, my men will think I've deserted. It's nearing three o'clock."

Magdelena clasped her hands to her cheeks. "No! Where did the time go?"

Luiz smiled, pushed back his chair, and rose. "I too enjoyed it. Very much. Now, if you will excuse me."

She sighed and watched the tall, dark man walk away. Then, talking to herself in rapid Spanish, Magdelena began clearing away the dishes and planning what she would serve for dinner.

* * *

Amy had no idea that El Capitán was inside the hacienda. It was the middle of the afternoon and she assumed he was in the field with his men. When the tall cased clock struck three, she was in the dim *sala,* the shutters closed against the afternoon sun.

Her back to the room's wide entrance, she stood at the cold marble fireplace, carefully dusting a porcelain figurine that rested on the mantel. Holding the valuable object in one hand, she meticulously flickered a feather duster back and forth over its shiny surface when suddenly she sensed a presence just behind her.

She tensed and waited. And told herself she was being foolish. No one was there. She was alone. Her imagination was playing tricks on her.

She trembled when she felt his breath upon her ear.

"Mrs. Parnell," he said, the timbre of his voice a strange mixture of warmth and coldness. "I missed you at lunch."

Her fingers tightened on the porcelain figurine. She coldly replied, "And you will miss me at dinner, El Capitán."

"No, my dear, I will not. I have invited my lieutenant, Pedrico Valdez, to join us for the evening meal. You will be there."

Amy carefully replaced the figurine atop the mantel. She laid the feather duster alongside it. She turned to face him and immediately felt her bravado slipping away. He stood so close their bodies were almost touching and he refused to step back. Tall and menacing, he had Amy trapped.

Unnerved by his nearness, Amy found herself helplessly nodding when he said, "Think anything you please of me. It does not matter. But tonight, before Pedrico, you will behave like a lady."

The irony struck her. This ruthless man was telling her how to act. It was too much.

Summoning up all her courage, Amy said, "I am neither the mistress of *your* house nor the hostess to *your* guests. You cannot make me obey you."

A smile on his lips, a dim flame in his black eyes, Luiz lifted a hand to Amy's face. He ran his finger along her pale cheek. She trembled. She attempted to stand still but could not. Luiz's hand moved up to stroke her gleaming hair, then his fingers burrowed into the flowing tresses and he raised her face more fully to his. He let his black eyes drink from hers.

He said, "You are the hostess at my table. The mistress of my home." His imprisoning fingers tightened their hold on her hair. "You *will* obey me. You will make yourself beautiful. You will wear your most luxurious gown, your finest jewels. Magdelena will help you dress. You will meet me downstairs at precisely eight-thirty. And you will be charming to our guest."

Lowering her eyes to the level of his brown throat, she said, "I will have dinner with you and Pedrico this evening."

Her mind already racing, she was thinking past the evening, past the dinner. With a dinner guest in the hacienda, she might well be able to escape to the safety of her room—bolt herself inside— while El Capitán graciously shared cigars and brandy with Pedrico after the meal. The prospect filled her with hope.

Lifting her eyes back to meet his, she said, almost warmly, "Yes. I'll be more than happy to join you for dinner this evening."

El Capitán kicked his chair back six inches from the Brazilian walnut table to make room for his long legs. He glanced at Amy, and the look was unbearably cold and detached.

It was dusk outside and dark in the hacienda. Flickering candles in the silver candelabra cast eerie light over the large, quiet dining room. Shadows danced on the high ceiling and on the harshly planed face of the dark, unsmiling man with whom Amy was reluctantly sharing the evening meal.

Her back stiff, she sat very still, very erect on the padded, tall-backed chair of elaborately carved walnut and worn wine velvet. Her freshly shampooed blond hair was parted in the middle with long curls falling over one bare shoulder in the latest fashion. A wide lavender band was arranged coronet style across the back of her head.

Her gown was a flattering vivid lavender hue, woefully out of style. Cut to a deep, low V at the bosom, the skirt was very full, measuring eight yards about the bottom edge. It was so long it swept the carpet when she walked. The lavender gown was intended to be worn over several crinolines and starched skirts, as had been the fashion of the late fifties. Rosettes and ruffles and velvet ribbon trim further dated the aging costume.

Amy felt both foolish and angry.

By dressing up and dining with the sinister El Capitán and her old servant, Pedrico Valdez, she was willingly participating in a ridiculous masquerade. She should never have agreed to this unpleasant travesty. Should have flatly refused, just as she had refused having lunch with him.

Stealing cautious glances at the intimidating officer whose honed muscles curved and pulled beneath the perfectly tailored uniform, Amy told herself the farce would be over in an hour and she could flee to the safety of her room. She didn't care if an infuriated El Capitán pounded on her bedroom door all night, she would refuse to allow him inside.

Ignoring the chiseled-faced man across from her, Amy lifted her stemmed crystal wineglass, took another cooling swallow, and favored the one-eyed Pedrico with genuine smiles and pleasant conversation.

Amazingly, the meal passed quickly and Amy, seizing her opportunity, said, "I'm sure you gentleman would like to go into the *sala* for brandy and coffee."

"That sounds delightful, Miss Amy," responded the smiling Pedrico. He looked at Luiz. "El Capitán?"

"Yes," Luiz said, rising to circle the table and pull out Amy's chair. "Mrs. Parnell can play the piano for us."

Amy's head snapped around and she was about to tell him she had no intention of playing any out-of-tune piano. But a warm, firm hand laid on her bare shoulder silenced her. Damn him to hell! He was taking full advantage of the fact that she, as well as he, had been reared to never raise a voice before either servants or guests. His infuriating smile told her she was correct.

In the living room she sat stiffly on the stool and

let her fingers move unfamiliarly over the ivory keys she had not touched in years. She stopped in midchord when she realized the piece she had automatically begun to play had once been El Capitán's favorite song when they were young.

If Luiz noticed, he did not show it. Amy chose a newer tune. Half an hour later she got up, walked to the two men, and when both rose, she smiled and said, "Pedrico, I hope you'll excuse me. I enjoyed the evening. It is wonderful to see you again."

The one-eyed soldier grinned and bowed his silver head. "Señora Amy, thank you for having me. We will meet again, *sí?*"

"Indeed." She turned to Luiz. "Good night," she said, her heart pounding, fearing he would stop her. He didn't.

She floated out of the room, almost lighthearted. It was all she could do to keep from running across the brick-floored corridor and up the wide staircase. Exercising a bit of the same control El Capitán practiced, she made herself slowly ascend the stairs.

She reached the heavy carved door of her bedroom and a smile of triumph lifted her lips and made her blue eyes sparkle.

But once inside, when she turned to throw the heavy bolt in place, her smile vanished and her eyes widened in disbelief. Foolishly she stared at the door, reaching out and running her hand over its surface.

The bolt had been taken off the door!

Horrified, she stood frozen in place, shaking her head, then quickly came to her senses. Any minute the man responsible for this high-handed deed would walk through the door. She had to leave. Now, before he came upstairs.

Amy whirled about. She raced across the carpet and into her dressing room. Hurriedly she snatched up a fresh nightgown and tossed it over her arm. She had to flee immediately to another room, one she could lock.

Racing against time, she dashed out of the dressing room, raced across the bedroom, and anxiously yanked open the door. And bumped squarely into the hard, ungiving chest of El Capitán.

Pressing her back inside with his lean frame, he closed the lockless door. His chill black eyes on her face, he plucked the filmy nightgown from her, opened his hand, and allowed it to flutter to the carpet.

He said, "There will be no locks between us save the one of your faithless little heart, Mrs. Parnell."

"You son of a bitch! You took off the bolt! You cannot do this to me."

"Ah, but I have."

Luiz's hands came up to the sides of her throat. With gentle pressure he tilted her head back, bent down so that his lips were nearly touching hers.

A hint of savage sexuality in his black eyes, El Capitán's cruel, hot mouth brushed Amy's, the scent of brandy on his warm breath.

He murmured, "Tonight you will make love to me in front of the mirrors."

"I will not!"

"You will."

She did.

21

―――――
―――――

It was later that same night that Amy decided she had to escape. Leave Orilla. And him.

As she lay in the moonlight beside the sleeping El Capitán, her face still hot with shame, Amy began to make plans. She would have to wait until tomorrow. She longed to leap up out of his bed and flee this minute. But she knew it was out of the question.

If she so much as made a move to rise, those hard glittering black eyes would be on her, open and brimming with violence. She didn't dare try it.

So she lay there naked in the night with El Capitán. Trapped by a bronzed hand lying possessively spread atop her stomach and a long leg hooked over hers, Amy tried to focus solely on her upcoming escape. It was near impossible.

The heat of his bare body burned her skin and made her constantly aware of his nearness and his power. And, try as she might, she couldn't blot out the erotic pictures that kept rising in the darkness.

Amy shut her eyes tightly. It did no good. She saw the two of them reflected in the mirrored bath. Just as he had so arrogantly predicted, she

had given in. After countless heated kisses and
persuasive caresses, she had willingly allowed him
to carry her into the mirrored bath and undress
her fully. Then he had stripped off his tall gleaming boots and uniform.

He had made slow, exquisite love to her while
he sat on a velvet stool with his knees spread wide,
his bare brown feet on the deep carpet. Holding
her astride his lap, her legs draped over his hard
thighs, he had gently commanded her to open her
eyes, to watch, just as he watched.

So aroused she would have obeyed any command, Amy had done just that. Watched. Every-
where she had looked—over his shoulder, behind
her, to either side—she had seen a pale-skinned,
wild-looking woman panting and tossing her head
and eagerly grinding her hips and pelvis against a
dark-skinned man of such physical beauty and superb animal strength the mere recollection was
enough to set her pulses pounding, her bare belly
to involuntarily contracting.

Amy winced in shock when the dark hand lying
on her stomach began to move, to stroke gently.
Her head snapped around. El Capitán was looking
at her, those hot black eyes aglow.

"I—I thought you were asleep," she murmured.

"Your desire," he said in a low, soft voice,
"awakened me." He rolled a muscular shoulder
up from the mattress as his long fingers gently
raked down through the triangle of blond curls to
intimately touch her.

"You are mad! I never—"

"Don't lie to me, sweet," he gently interrupted.
"You want me. I felt the quivering of your belly

beneath my hand." His dark face lowered to hers. "It's all right."

Mesmerized by those gleaming eyes, Amy vainly tried to deny what they both knew was the truth. "I don't want you. I don't. I hate your hands on me." She squirmed, her body already afire from his skilled touch.

El Capitán paid no attention to her denials. With one well-placed forefinger he continued tenderly caressing her while he looked into her eyes and murmured seductive endearments in perfectly accented Castillian Spanish.

Finally he said, "Kiss me, sweetheart, and tell me you want me."

Amy shook her head. "No. No, I won't. Never."

His hard, handsome face came closer, so close his breath was hot upon her cheek. "One kiss. That's all. Just one kiss, *querido.*"

Amy moaned, lifted a hand to his thick raven hair, anxiously drew his mouth down to hers, kissed him hungrily, and murmured against his burning lips, "I do want you. I do, I can't help myself."

"I know," he said.

And made love to her again.

Amy didn't get very far when she tried her escape the next day. El Capitán's troops had been alerted that Mrs. Parnell would likely attempt to leave the ranch alone. It was not to be allowed. She must be constantly protected. If the lovely widow chose to go into the village, his trusted Lieutenant Pedrico Valdez would accompany her. If she tried to leave by herself, she was to be detained and brought immediately to their commanding officer.

It was just after two in the afternoon when Amy, furious and struggling, was brought against her will into the downstairs library by a couple of determined young Mexican troopers. Once inside, the soldiers released her, turned, and left, closing the heavy door after them.

The shutters were pulled and fastened against the sun, making the paneled, book-lined library quite dark. Amy felt a presence in that dim room and knew that it was El Capitán. The hair lifted on the nape of her neck and she blinked and squinted, trying to locate him.

From out of the shadows came that deep, sure voice.

"Over here, Mrs. Parnell. Behind the desk."

"You won't get away with this!" Amy said, her hands clenched, her heart hammering. "I am not your prisoner. I will come and go as I please, damn you!"

His voice came from the shadows. "Ah, but you are my prisoner. You will come and go only as I allow. And"—she heard the scraping of the chair legs on the brick-tiled floor—"you will be punished when you disobey me."

Amy shuddered but bravely said, "Stay away from me. I will scream at the top of my lungs!"

"Go right ahead," he said, circling the desk and moving slowly closer.

"I have some rights here!" she declared, wishing her voice would not quaver so.

"Of course you do."

"I will tell Magdelena and Pedrico!"

"What are you waiting for?" He reached her

and stood looking down at her. His white shirt was
half open. His bronzed chest gleamed with a fine
sheen of perspiration. When he carefully lifted
the Sun Stone up over his dark head and put it
into his trouser pocket, Amy swallowed hard. He
had never looked more dangerous.

Fearfully she looked up into his black eyes. Heat
radiated from them. Amy trembled involuntarily
and whimpered helplessly when his long, powerful arms came around her and pulled her into his
close embrace, crushing her against the hard
length of him.

"What do you want of me?" she whispered bro-
kenly against his shoulder.

"Everything," he said.

Amy's punishment for trying to run away was
an hour in the hot afternoon darkness of the silent
library with her cool captor. And just as always—
against her will—his carnal punishment became
her guilty pleasure.

Their perspiring bodies slipping and sliding
sensuously together, the dueling pair made wildly
abandoned love as if they could never get enough
of each other. Finally sated, they lay entwined,
their damp, limp bodies sticking to the soft black
leather of the library's old worn couch.

His hand stroking Amy's long, flowing hair, El
Capitán said in the dim silence, "It is impossible
for you to elude me."

Her cheek resting on his chest, the sound of his
slow, heavy heartbeat beneath her ear, Amy replied softly, "I *will* escape you. And just when you
least expect it."

* * *

A week had passed since El Capitán and his troops had arrived to occupy Orilla. During that week Amy had not been off the ranch, save for the afternoon of her failed escape. She knew that if she did not soon go into Sundown, people would begin to wonder and worry about her.

She was certain the news had spread that Quintano and his soldiers were headquartered at the ranch. If she failed to put in her weekly appearance in town, ugly gossip might spread as well.

Much as she hated to do it, Amy went in search of the arrogant El Capitán. It was midmorning. She found him alone on the west patio and hesitantly approached.

He sat, his long legs stretched out before him, staring broodingly into space.

Amy cleared her throat.

His dark head swung around and for a second he stared right through her. Then he nodded, came to his feet, and said, "To what do I owe this honor, Mrs. Parnell?"

"I've come to ask if I might go into town this morning." She hated herself for sounding like a frightened child begging a stern parent for permission.

"Why, certainly you may. I'll have Pedrico drive you. How long do you plan to stay?"

At his prying, Amy's temper quickly flared. "How should I know how long I'll stay! Am I to account for every minute of my days?"

El Capitán smiled, causing the white scar on his cheek to contract. "No. I suppose every minute of your nights will do, Mrs. Parnell."

Amy glared at him. "You are disgusting and despicable and depraved."

"And what does that make you?"

"Damn you to eternal hell!"

Of the silver-haired Pedrico, Amy asked the questions she would never have dared put to El Capitán. Minutes after Pedrico helped her up onto the high seat of the umbrella-shaded buckboard and they headed down the palm-lined drive toward the tall ranch gates, Amy sighed and relaxed for the first time in a week.

Touching the aging man's forearm, she said simply, "Please, Pedrico. Tell me all you know."

The gentle, one-eyed man nodded.

He told Amy of how he had searched in vain for the young, injured Luiz after her brothers had left the boy for dead, deep in the Mexican desert. He told of finding the clothes and the boots with the silver initials.

"But no Luiz," Pedrico said, shaking his silver head as if he still could not believe it.

He continued his search for over two years, riding in and out of small Mexican settlements, asking questions, studying faces, looking endlessly for Luiz, knowing somehow that he was still alive. But, alas, the boy had vanished into the air.

Finally he had given up all hope of ever finding him. He supported himself working in gold mines and on cattle ranches and in cantinas across Mexico.

Nodding, Amy listened intently as Pedrico said, "And when Mexico was invaded by the French, I joined Juarez's army of liberation."

He fell silent. Amy prodded, "But El Capitán?

Why do you follow him? Pedrico, he is not the same Luiz we knew long ago. He is a cold, callous man who—"

"Señora Amy," Pedrico interrupted, fixing her with his one good eye, "I would give up my life for El Capitán Quintano! You do not know what it was like. We owe everything—our very lives—to him."

"I don't understand. What do you mean?"

Pedrico turned his eye back to the horses. "Our brave but untrained detail was cut off from the main forces. Lost and scattered. Afraid and unsure where to turn." He shook his head and began to smile. "Then, just when we were surrounded by the French and all seemed lost, a mighty warrior rode down from out of the hills. An Indian with a white scar down his face and long scars across his back. It was El Capitán!

"He commanded us to form a line behind him, and his presence was so compelling, we did not hesitate. We fought through enemy lines back to rendezvous with the main army. It was not until he had led us to safety that I realized El Capitán was Luiz Quintano."

"And did he tell you where he had been all those years?"

"No, *señora*, and I did not ask him. El Capitán is a very private man."

"Yes. He is."

Amy listened politely while Pedrico continued singing the praises of a man he knew to be honorable and fearless. It was more than evident that Pedrico's loyalty to El Capitán Quintano was unshakable.

Amy inwardly sighed.

She was doomed to live in her private hell while those around her were blind to her torture. Pedrico and Magdelena and even old Fernando looked at El Capitán with admiring eyes. They welcomed his presence on Orilla and were eager to please him.

And she was far too proud to admit what had happened—what was continuing to happen—between her and the cold-hearted commander. She couldn't tell anyone that she was being held sexual captive in her own home.

Amy lifted troubled blue eyes to the scattering of small, square adobe buildings on the near horizon. She took a long, deep breath, pinched her cheeks to bring out their color, and prepared herself to meet and visit with merchants and old friends who must never guess the truth.

22

Sundown, Texas, was built around a main plaza, in the Spanish style of cities south of the border. The plaza was actually nothing more than a dusty square with a few backless benches and a smattering of sparse shade from spindly cottonwoods planted a quarter of a century ago.

On the south side of the plaza, the tall white spires of St. Mary's Cathedral rose to meet a generally cloudless blue Texas sky. Next door to the mission, the Sundown jail was—for the moment— empty of occupants, a situation that would likely change come nightfall.

On the square's west side, adjacent to St. Mary's, a low, flat, sand-color adobe building took up the entire block. Large square pilasters supported the building's slanting porch roof and from one of the porch's high beams hung a large white sign that said Mac's.

Mac's cavernous hall housed a combination dry goods store, apothecary, grocer's, saddlery and tack, furniture emporium, and post office. Mac, a big-fisted, big-bellied Irishman, always wore a large white cloth apron tied around his middle and a brace of loaded Colt .44's in a low-riding holster atop it. He smiled more than he frowned and his blue eyes twinkled often with merriment. He feared no man, but his tiny Mexican wife, Lena, and their four small dark-haired, dark-eyed boys easily bullied the stocky, good-natured Irishman.

A string of noisy cantinas, louvered-doored saloons, and round-the-clock gambling dens kept the genteel ladies of Sundown away from the plaza's north side. There were, however, women who did not avoid that lively part of Sundown. They made their living there.

Above the most boisterous saloons were the brothels where it was whispered a gentleman could "conduct himself in a most wicked and licentious manner so long as he had the money." The women who supplied the pleasure were voluptuous, scantily clad, and eager to show the boys a good time.

On the plaza's east side were a dentist, the undertaking parlor, the telegraph office, a barber shop, a ladies' millinery, and Sundown's only hostelry, La Posada.

Several modest adobe dwellings, a couple of big-frame boardinghouses, and a handful of imposing haciendas lined the narrow, dusty streets leading into town.

One such hacienda, a big, impressive home surrounded by a high, elaborate wall of pink adobe blocks and intricate ironworks, sat alone and apart on the road leading into town from the south.

Passing it now, Amy glanced up at the red-tiled roof of the big mansion and frowned. She couldn't leave town without seeing Diana.

Diana Clayton, a strikingly pretty twenty-two-year old brunette, had been educated in the East and had returned to Sundown only when her father, the wealthy owner of several productive Mexican gold mines, had passed away in the winter of '64.

Diana was cheerful, intelligent, and always good fun, if somewhat spoiled and self-centered. Amy and Diana had been drawn to each other from the first time they'd met. Which had been in Mac's.

Amy, on her weekly trip into Sundown, had been filling a list of essentials when Diana Clayton had called to her from across the room. The outgoing brunette had come rushing over, holding up a green-and-yellow flowered calico dress she had taken off a rack from Mac's ladies' finery section.

"What do you think?" she demanded of Amy.

"Do you want the truth?" Amy smiled and lifted her perfectly arched eyebrows. Diana nodded. Amy shook her head. "Absolutely dreadful," Amy said decisively.

"I fully agree," Diana replied, pressing the garment to her curvaceous body and laughing gaily. "I can see I won't be able to find anything decent to wear in Sundown." She tossed the dress aside, stuck out her hand, and said, "Diana Clayton. And you're Amy Parnell. Have you time to stop by for a cup of tea or coffee before you leave town? I'm dying of boredom and feel I shall go quite mad if I don't spend an hour with someone my own age. Here, let me take that basket. My carriage is just outside. We can drink wine if you prefer, or even iced tequila. Will you come?"

"Lead the way," Amy said, eager to hear about Diana's exciting life in distant, glamorous New York City.

From that morning, the two women had been friends. They had seen each other at least once a week, usually at Diana's mansion. They had sipped Madeira and gossiped and laughed together like two young girls. Diana had spoken openly of the torrid four-year love affair she had conducted while living in New York. The gentleman was, she assured Amy, quite handsome and quite wealthy. And quite married. Amy had neither judged or censured.

Now, as Amy passed by the walled Clayton hacienda, she realized she was in no frame of mind to see Diana. In fact, she was in no frame of mind to see anyone. But she had no choice. Unless she wanted the gentry guessing her guilty secret, she would be obliged to conduct her life routinely.

"Pedrico, first I'll be going to Mac's to pick up a few items."

"*Sí, señora.* I will stop in and say hello to Mac."

Amy smiled at Pedrico. "Fine. Then if you'd like to have a drink or play a game of poker in one of the saloons, it will be okay with me."

The one-eyed man shook his head vigorously. "No. I must wait for you, *señora.* Right in front of Mac's."

Amy tried to keep the irritation from her voice. "I don't think you quite understand, Pedrico. For years I have been coming alone into Sundown to shop and to visit my friends. I may stay in town for several hours. There is simply no need for you to—"

"*Por favor,* Señora Amy. Is no trouble. I do not mind the wait."

"It's his idea, isn't it?"

"His? Pardon?"

"El Capitán," Amy said flatly. "He told you to watch me. Didn't he?" Pedrico lifted his shoulders in an apologetic shrug. Amy ground her teeth and sighed. But then she quickly smiled, patted his shoulder, and said, "I'll make no trouble, Pedrico. I've grown up since the old days."

The Mexican laughed and nodded his silver head, fondly recalling the young willful girl from the past. "Si," he said. "It is hard for me to believe that little Amy is now a grown woman with a child of her own."

"Yes, well . . . After I've done my shopping at Mac's, I will walk over to La Posada and visit with any of the ladies who happen to be in Sundown."

"Ah, sí. Sí."

"Then, on our way home, I will want to stop at the Clayton hacienda on the—"

"I remember the old Clayton home. The pretty Señorita Diana has returned home from the East."

"Oh? And who told you that? El Capitán?" Amy snapped, feeling inexplicably annoyed. An unpleasant thought flitted through her brain. Had the pretty and sophisticated Diana Clayton already caught the eye of the darkly sensuous El Capitán?

"No." Pedrico shook his head forcefully. "It was not El Capitán. I do not think he would remember the Clayton girl. She was only a child of twelve when he was . . . when he left Orilla."

Her head beginning to ache slightly, Amy nodded. "Well, it really doesn't matter. Unless I run into Diana at Mac's or La Posada, I'll want to go by and see her."

The sidewalks and shops and saloons of Sundown were filled with the blue-uniformed soldiers of El Capitán's command. In Mac's, the big Irishman's grin was wider than ever and his wife, Lena, speaking rapid-fire Spanish, cheerfully bustled about, waiting on the restless young men who had plenty of time and money.

"Ain't this something, Miz Amy?" said Mac, adjusting his worn gunbelt beneath his girth. "I've taken in more money in a week than I usually make in a month." He lifted his round, balding head joyfully. "Yes sirree, we're mighty happy to have Quintano and his men in Sundown."

Amy had no choice but to smile with the happy Irishman. "And we're quite pleased to have the captain and his men at Orilla."

"I reckon you are. How long's it been since Luiz left here? Eight, ten years? He was just a kid then. Why, I bet you was sure surprised to see him again after all this time."

Amy's smile remained firmly in place. "You have no idea."

And so it went.

The town was abuzz. While people living farther north might have wondered at the warm reception extended the Mexican soldiers, here, close to the border, it was commonplace. The young, spirited soldiers of Benito Juarez's army of liberation couldn't have been more welcome had they worn the uniform of the United States Cavalry.

The merchants of Sundown, their businesses suffering from years of drought in southwest Texas, looked on the influx of the free-spending Mexican soldiers as a godsend. The highly visible presence of the troopers in and around Sundown was equally embraced by the families living in that remote, dangerous region where the threat from renegade Apaches was as constant as the dust storms that rolled across the barren plain. Then, too, more than one fanciful young girl and lonely war widow was all aflutter over the invasion of the handsome young soldiers.

Several females came into Mac's as Amy shopped. All were full of questions, from Miss Minnie McDaniel, a seventy-six-year-old hard-of-hearing spinster, to Katie Sue Longley, a freckle-faced, red-haired fourteen-year-old barber's daughter.

With good grace and an easy smile, Amy answered all their questions. When Judy Bradford and Glenda Thurston and Sally Byers came hurrying in, out of breath, saying they had just heard Amy was in town, she knew the serious questioning was about to begin.

But it didn't begin in earnest until Judy, Glenda, Sally, and Amy met Diana Clayton in the sunny cedar-beamed lobby of the big white stucco hotel, La Posada. While Judy, Glenda, and Sally listened intently, the brash Diana asked the very questions they—young wives and mothers all—had been dying to ask.

"Tell us everything, Amy Sullivan Parnell!" Diana wasted no time in urging Amy and the others to the hotel's spacious dining hall where she pointed to a large linen-draped pine table against the far wall. Shoving Amy down into a chair and eagerly taking the one beside her, Diana said, "We've all seen him and we want to know the truth. So far, from what I've been able to learn, he sounds fascinating."

"He's dangerous," Amy said thoughtlessly, "if that's what you mean."

Diana's eyes shone with excitement. "Really? Is he as savage and as sexy as he looks? Has he tried to make love to you? Doug will be terribly jealous when he hears! Is El Capitán staying right there in the hacienda with you? Do you think he would come to dinner at my home?"

Determined to maintain her fragile self-control, Amy smiled, tilting her blond head, and said, "Let me see. I believe the answers, in order, would be, 'I've no idea. No. No. Not really. And why don't you ask him?' "

They all laughed. Amy laughed with them. And prided herself on giving nothing away, even when Diana and the others refused to speak of anything but the soldiers and their darkly handsome commander throughout a long, leisurely lunch.

She was more than a little relieved when the meal finally ended and the time came to leave. Outside on the stone porch the ladies said their good-byes, promising to meet again in a week, and Amy and Diana watched the others hurry away.

Blinking in the strong afternoon sunlight, Diana took Amy's arm and said, "Come home with me so we can really talk."

"I'd love to, Diana, but I must get back to the ranch."

"No! Why, it's just past three o'clock. You never leave this early."

"I know, but . . ." Amy looked across the street, across the plaza. The buckboard was still parked in front of Mac's. "One of the soldiers drove me into town and I—"

"Who? El Capitán?" Diana's eyes were round. "Is he waiting over there in the buckboard? Oh, my lord, I'll walk over with you and—"

"Diana," Amy interrupted. "No. It isn't he. For heavens sake, you're behaving rather irrationally."

Taking no offense at her friend's remark, Diana laughed. "I'd like the opportunity to really behave irrationally." She took Amy's arm. "As I said earlier, I was in the millinery shop when El Capitán and his troops rode into Sundown that first day. Attracted by the noise, I hurried to the door and saw, at the head of the command, the most handsome, the most dangerous-looking man I've ever laid eyes on."

"Yes, yes, so you told us."

"That long white scar down his cheek. Mmmmm, mercy. I wonder where he got it? And who gave it to him."

"I've no idea."

"He was astride a magnificent black stallion and he held himself ramrod straight." Diana shivered, remembering. She quickly continued. "There was alkali dust on his brown face and in his black hair. And the back of his blue tunic was soaked with sweat."

"That's all very interesting, Diana, but I—"

"His white trousers were so tight I could see the muscles of his thighs pulling and bunching and I—"

"Diana, I have to go!" Amy's head was pounding now.

"Darn, I do wish you could . . . well, all right, but do me a favor. Tell El Capitán that the dark-haired woman who waved to him from the door of

the millinery shop would be honored if he would
join her at her home for dinner some evening
soon. Any evening. Will you do that?"

"Yes. Yes, I'll tell him."

"Good! Oh, there's William now with my carriage. Can we drive you around to the other side
of the plaza?"

"No, I'll walk."

"Suit yourself." Diana hugged Amy. "I enjoyed
lunch, see you next week." She laughed and
added, "And give my regards to El Capitán. Until
I can personally give him my *best.*" She was still
laughing when her driver helped her up into the
gleaming black victoria.

When at last the carriage rolled away, Amy released a deep sigh of relief. She was completely
wrung out. Her head throbbed. Her lunch had not
agreed with her. She wanted nothing more than
to get back to Orilla for a bath and a nap before
dinner.

Amy lifted the skirts of her simple cotton dress
and stepped forward to cross the dusty street. She
hurried across the plaza where soldiers were buying hot tamales and roasting ears and sugary
pralines from a stooped old Mexican vendor. Feeling the heat of the sun beat down on her aching
head, Amy finally reached the far side of the
square.

Waiting for a trio of mounted men to ride past,
she looked toward her waiting carriage and saw
Pedrico's black-booted foot resting atop the
brake.

Thank goodness he was there waiting. They
could leave immediately for the ranch.

Amy eagerly crossed the street and circled

around behind the buckboard. She was just about to call his name when the seat dipped under his moving weight and he swung down to the sidewalk directly in front of her.

To her stunned surprise, Amy found she was not looking at the kindly, one-eyed Pedrico Valdez. The dark, chiseled face before her had two eyes, both of gleaming obsidian. And a long white scar slashing down the left cheek, a scar that was puckering from the lifting of wide, sensuous lips into a devilish smile.

El Capitán.

23

His head cocked to one side, he stood there, handsome as the devil, his habitual air of egotism as offensive as ever. He was quite obviously enjoying her look of startled surprise and discomfort. Was insolently waiting for her angry protest at his presence. Eagerly anticipated watching her make a spectacle of herself.

Well, the cocksure bastard could wait until hell froze over! She *was* a fool, of that she was certain. But she'd be damned if the entire population of Sundown would perceive her as such.

After a split second of astonishment, Amy regained her self-control. Like a great stage actress performing before her most critical audience, she stood before him looking cool, unruffled, even pleased.

Tilting her face up to his, she favored him with one of her most winning smiles and said, "Ah, Capitán. How kind of you to wait all this time. I hope you haven't been too uncomfortable out here in this warm April sunshine."

Not waiting for a reply, she calmly brushed past him toward the buckboard's front seat.

"Not at all," came his deep, resonant voice. And before she could climb up into the buckboard, his strong fingers encircled her waist. He easily lifted her up onto the high padded seat, his hands remaining on her waist for one heartbeat too long.

Amy was keenly conscious of people watching them, so she smiled serenely, settled her long skirts about her feet, and waited as her tall tormentor unhurriedly circled the buckboard, then swung up into the seat beside her, purposely moving too close to her. So close his shoulder and hip were touching hers. When he allowed his right knee to fall against hers, she released a quick breath but did not flinch.

All eyes remained on them as El Capitán unwrapped the long reins from around the brake handle and coaxed the team forward. Her head throbbing, her stomach afire, Amy continued to smile and to nod to old friends and acquaintances. And wondered miserably whether the entire community of Sundown was blind to the true dark nature of El Capitán Quintano. Clearly he was an idolized hero in his own hometown. No one suspected he was a cold, cruel conqueror who held her—even this very minute—against her will.

He drew open looks of approval and admiration from old and young alike, and Amy, casting stolen glances at him, found it remarkable that the dark chiseled face that loomed so menacingly above her own each lust-filled night appeared decidedly less hard, less evil now as he smiled disarmingly and nodded to the people lining the streets.

For a brief instant there was that engaging boyish quality that had been so devastatingly appealing years ago.

Amy was not fooled.

If she wore a mask of agreeableness and repose, so did he. These people thought they knew Luiz Quintano. They didn't. Only she knew the real El Capitán, a man so cold and heartless she felt a chill skip up her spine from the dreaded knowledge that she was to be alone with him—all the way back to Orilla.

Amy was never sure whose smile vanished first, hers or his. All she knew was when finally they reached the edge of town and she scooted as far from him as possible, turning angrily to confront him, his face had lost any illusion of affability.

Amy nervously licked her lips and ran her tongue under her teeth. "What have you done with Pedrico?"

His piercing black eyes settling on her mouth he said, "Sent him home. He's no longer a young man. You stayed a long time in town; the desert already grows hot." His hooded gaze returned to the road.

"Everything you say is true. And I'll supply you with some further truths." Amy's chin lifted, but her voice remained level. "Pedrico will get no younger. The desert will get no cooler. And I will continue to tarry in Sundown—or anywhere else I choose—for as long as I please."

Amy quickly curled her fingers around the edge of the seat to brace herself against what she knew would come. His dark head would snap around and he'd fix her with those mean black eyes and tell her she would do just as she was ordered.

But he didn't.

El Capitán never behaved as Amy anticipated. For a long moment he was silent, his attention seemingly on the road ahead. Finally Amy saw the almost imperceptible lifting of his wide shoulders, and he said, "Since you know most everything, then I'm confident you're aware the Apaches are again riding down out of the hills and causing mischief."

Slowly he turned to her. His eyelashes swept low over surprisingly gentle eyes, and he asked, his tone as tender as his eyes, "Have you any idea what the Apaches would do to a woman like you should they catch you alone?"

It was the first time Amy had seen even the slightest trace of sensitivity in the impervious commander. It caused her heart to race with excitement.

She wasted no time in stinging him with a hateful barb. "The same thing you do to me every night?"

A curtain of coldness immediately dropped over his handsome face and any residue of gentleness was swept away by it. At once all was deathly still and quiet in the afternoon heat, the steady *clip-clop* of the horses' hooves the only sound in the strained silence.

Amy automatically inched farther away from him, far enough that her right arm was no longer beneath the big umbrella shading the seat.

His silence unnerved her. She would have much preferred that he shout and threaten like a normal man provoked. His cold, mute rage was far more menacing, and Amy cowered under the silent power of it.

When finally he spoke it so startled Amy, she jumped.

Without turning to look at her, he said quietly, "The danger from Apaches is the reason I object to you riding out alone. I need not remind you of the atrocities for which they're famous."

Off balance as always when she was with him, Amy nodded and said, "No. I understand."

She waited for him to say more, but he did not. They rode on in silence, a summer-warm breeze suddenly stirring, blowing from out of the west. Dust devils danced across the desert floor and Amy, frowning, bowed her head against the gusts of wind and sand that stung her face.

El Capitán paid no attention to the blowing dust. Effortlessly controlling the skittish horses, he was presented with the opportunity to study the unhappy woman seated beside him. From beneath dark lashes he did just that.

He searched for defects—for anything that would prove that this woman was not the girl he had dreamed of for years—but there were none. Her golden hair, though restrained now in a white crocheted snood, was as long and silky as ever. Her pale skin was still smooth, young, and glorious to touch. Her high, intelligent brow gave her a look of haughty aloofness. Most appealing. Her eyes—those magnificent sky-blue eyes—still flashed and signaled her eruptible passions. The mouth was a perfect Cupid's bow of such sweetly curving sensuality she looked, constantly, as if she needed to be soundly kissed.

His narrowed, scrutinizing gaze drifted down to her delicate, white throat and lower, to her firm, full breasts pressing insistently against the snug bodice of her clean, starched, but slightly faded cotton dress. Her waist was trim. Beneath the full skirts, her flaring hips and pale thighs were nothing short of perfection.

He forced his eyes back on the road.

She was breathtakingly beautiful.

He told himself he was glad. More than delighted to find her still so temptingly lovely. He could now enjoy her beauty as never before, since he no longer cared. Since she meant nothing to him.

Until he was summoned back into battle, he could possess her whenever he chose. Could undress her at will and leisurely admire her naked golden charms. Could relish their hours of heated lovemaking for exactly what they were: gratifying physical release. Sweet, meaningless diversion.

And always, regardless of how intense the joy, the ecstasy would involve only his body; it would never touch his heart. Never. And when it came time to ride away, she'd be cast aside and quickly forgotten, just as she'd forgotten him that last summer of his youth.

After what seemed a lifetime to Amy, she realized they were finally back on Orilla land. But they were not headed for the hacienda. They were moving steadily upward over the sloping land toward the northeast. She turned and gave El Capitán a questioning look and opened her mouth to speak. Those icy black eyes kept her from saying anything.

The buckboard topped a gentle rise and Amy saw dozens of El Capitán's men working out in the hot sunshine. Their tunics and shirts cast aside, their bare, brown backs gleaming with sweat, they were vigorously shoveling, digging in the long-unused dirt- and debris-filled canal.

The buckboard rolled past the working men who shouted and called to them. El Capitán pulled up on the reins, stepped down, and walked over to speak briefly with his men. When he returned, Amy, refusing to ask what the troopers were doing, said, "Will you take me home now?"

"Not quite yet," he replied. "First we will go to the river."

"The river?" Amy started shaking her head. He was taking her to the river! To the dead, dried-up Puesta del Sol! "No!" she said forcefully, her high brow knit. "I do *not* want to go to the river. There's nothing there. The river's been dry for years. Take me home."

"You'll be home by sunset." And on he drove.

The jostling buckboard bumped on over the rough, arid ground, steadily climbing toward the river. Angry and tired, Amy held on to the seat and gritted her teeth. Every time his hard shoulder bumped hers or she was jiggled and bounced against him, she grew more exasperated.

She wanted to go home. She wanted to get away from El Capitán. She was hot and thirsty and miserable.

But she forgot her misery as the buckboard rolled to a dusty stop on the flat rocky bank of the river. A sound—familiar, yet one she'd not heard for years—drew her attention. The frown of annoyance leaving her face, Amy's mouth fell open and she turned her head to listen.

Water!

The sound of rushing water. Falling from above and splashing into a pool below.

El Capitán lifted Amy down from the buckboard. She clung to his hard biceps and gave him a wide, questioning look. He remained silent. He set her on her feet and released her. Amy stood, staring at him.

Suddenly she whirled about, lifted her skirts, and ran toward the streambed, the blood starting to beat in her ears, her heart thumping against her ribs.

In seconds she stood on the smooth flat river-bank, her lips parted in awe, her unbelieving eyes lifted high above to where roaring, rushing water spilled over the jutting boulders and cascaded into the river below. A river that was again flowing with cold, clear water.

Amy's hands went to her hot cheeks. She shook her head, closed her eyes, opened them, and still she saw the majestic waterfall, the limpid running river.

"But how . . . ?" Wildly she spun around and bumped squarely into the tall, hard frame of El Capitán. The first thing her eyes fell on was the glittering gold Sun Stone resting on his bronzed chest. A shiver raced through her. Her knees turned to jelly and she felt she might fall. His strong hands came up to steady her. Slowly her wondering eyes lifted to meet his.

His answer was to take one of her cold, soft hands and bring it up inside his shirt. He placed the splayed fingers directly atop the Sun Stone. Then his own hand fell away.

Amy swallowed hard.

Beneath her palm was the hard, precious metal of the Sun Stone. And under her sensitive finger-tips was the hot, smooth flesh and thundering heartbeat of its enigmatic owner.

The Sun God.

24

It was early morning.

Dawn was creeping over the Chihuahuan desert.

Luiz Quintano, alone out on the far northern reaches of the ranch, sat unmoving, astride his saddleless black stallion, Noche. His unblinking gaze sweeping over the vast expanse of land, Luiz felt his bare chest swell with pride, his heart thump against his ribs.

Orilla.

His Orilla.

The Orilla he had missed so desperately all those empty years away from its arid, desolate, glorious beauty. Orilla with its sagebrush rangelands and stark furnace deserts and cool distant mountains and blue sky that wrapped itself around him.

And its pervasive silence broken only by the moan of the desert winds. Sweet solitude; a soothing balm for the troubled soul.

Luiz took a deep, long breath of the dry, clear air.

How many times had he dreamed of being back here in this, his native land. How many restless nights had he paced the floor in crowded, noisy cities, unable to breathe, unable to sleep, longing for the quiet of his desert home. How many days had he spent in thankless labor or tedious idleness, yearning to be atop a swift mount, herding a sea of bawling longhorns toward the branding fires of Orilla's holding pens. How many stifling afternoons had he envisioned plunging into the cold, clear waters of Puesta del Sol.

While the eerie gray light of a soon-to-rise sun bathed the endless acreage of his beloved Orilla, Luiz, for the moment, was again the young, happy boy he had been. The last decade had never happened. He was again seventeen and the best horseman on Orilla.

A broad smile appearing on his dark, chiseled face, Luiz suddenly slapped his stallion's withers and said loudly, "How about it, Noche? Think I can still do it?"

The big black neighed loudly and danced in place, and Luiz began to laugh. "The hell you say," he shouted.

And then, with easy agility and complete self-confidence, Luiz leapt to his feet to stand atop the mount's bare, glistening back. Making certain his moccasins were placed in exactly the right position to ensure good balance, the breechcloth-clad Luiz bent his knees a couple of times, then carefully sprang up and down until he was comfortable with his stance.

His toes—within the soft moccasins—curling to the slope of Noche's back, Luiz purposely relaxed all his muscles. He concentrated on his body becoming but an extension of the mighty stallion's. They would no longer be two separate units. They would become one perfectly coordinated vessel of grace, power, and speed.

And when the transformation had taken place, it was unnecessary for Luiz to give Noche the command to move. Just as the man had become the stallion, the stallion had become the man. Noche nickered and immediately set off. He went into an easy lope, the symmetrical movement of his sleek powerful body totally harmonious with the sleek, powerful body of Luiz.

His raven hair blowing wildly about his head, the muscles in his bronzed legs and wide shoulders flexing like well-oiled springs, Luiz effortlessly kept his equilibrium, loving the sting of the wind on his face, the sense of the ground rushing by.

His deep laughter echoed across the dusty flats and rugged arroyos as the sheer joy of performing this old boyhood feat of derring-do brought back long-forgotten pleasure.

If horses could laugh, then the responsive beast beneath Luiz's feet was surely laughing too, as together they went into a rapid, dusty gallop, speeding across the barren rangeland, racing headlong toward the gun-metal gray of the horizon.

And even as happy horse and laughing rider sped across the wild, untamed tablelands, Luiz was charting the course of Orilla's future. Already the desert was beginning to bloom. Soon, in a few short weeks, tobasa grass would again cover the bare, crusty floor with a carpet of green. Newly bought cattle would graze contentedly and fatten. Trusted vaqueros would ride the far ranges. Orilla would again be as it was in its glory days and his

promise would be fulfilled. A promise made to his
father, Don Ramon—a promise to the dead.

It was all possible.

Now that the river again flowed.

Those were the thoughts filling the head of the
laughing man standing atop the thundering stallion in the dawn light.

The thundering horse, not the laughing man,
decided when it was time to end the sport. But the
man instinctively knew—grinding flesh and bone
beneath his moccasined feet telegraphed the message—that the frisky, playful stallion, hoping to
catch his rider off guard, was contemplating an
abrupt halt aimed at tossing Luiz head over heels.

Luiz was not to be deceived.

Continuing to laugh, he tried hard not to relay
his own strategy to leap from the fun-loving stallion's back just in the nick of time.

No longer thinking and moving as one being,
man and beast had again become separate entities, and a competitive test of wills now existed
between them. Each attempted to anticipate the
other's every intent.

Luiz was never quite certain who won. But seconds later he went careening over the stallion's
head, did a limber somersault on the hard ground,
rolled immediately to his feet, and spun around.

Directly before him Noche was rearing triumphantly and whinnying loudly enough to be heard
all the way to the hacienda. Luiz, standing with
his legs braced apart, put his hands on his slim hips
and cocked his head to one side.

Smiling, he looked up at the big horse and said,
"What are you carrying on about? I knew it was
coming." He lifted his hands to brush at the dust

and dried mesquite beans clinging to his bare chest.

Noche moved forward, nudged at Luiz's chest, and made blowing, snorting gestures, as if to clean his master.

"No." Luiz shoved his velvety muzzle away. "You don't get off that easily, my friend. I want a bath and you are taking me to the river."

Noche's great head swung right back to Luiz's bare belly and the steed acted as if he was going to bite the only man who had ever been atop him. Luiz knew he wouldn't do it. He reached up and grabbed the mount's coarse forelock. He gave it a hard yank and ordered, "The Puesta del Sol and be quick about it, or you'll be sold to the U.S. cavalry at Fort Bliss before sunset."

Minutes later Luiz was slicing naked through the cold, clear waters of Sunset River. An hour later, as the sun was beginning to peep over the earth's curve, he was back at ranch headquarters.

After throwing a long leg over the horse's back, he dropped to the ground and headed for the white stucco barn where he stabled Noche. Long abandoned, the stall and fenced lot around it was set apart from Orilla's many other outbuildings. Luiz had selected it for that very reason. A man of privacy, he sought the same privacy for his prized stallion.

The big beast docilely followed the man into the stable and made soft sounds of gratitude when Luiz took a bucket down from a peg on the far wall and filled it with oats. There was not time to rub Noche down. They had played too long on the plain. Luiz had to hurry if he was to be dressed and back outdoors before the household awakened and his troops began to rouse.

Leaving the contented stallion to feast on his breakfast of oats, Luiz moved quickly toward the ranchhouse. Inside, he silently ascended the stairs of the sleeping hacienda. At the wide landing he turned west.

He stole into the master suite, automatically glancing at the bed. A skein of silky blond hair, a bare ivory shoulder, and a well-turned hip was all he saw of the woman slumbering there on her stomach. Curbing the desire to slide back into the bed and make love to her while she was still warm and drowsy with sleep, Luiz quickly dressed.

Amy didn't rouse until he was leaving. She caught only a flash of the immaculate man with black hair, dark face, white shirt, military-beige trousers, and gleaming boots. Luiz opened the door and left, never knowing she had awakened.

Amy did not get up at once.

She reached for the worn cotton robe lying across the night table beside her, turned onto her back and draped the robe modestly over herself, still uncomfortable with her own nakedness. Her eyes on the ruffled silk canopy above, she stretched and yawned and silently acknowledged that sleeping bare *was* more comfortable.

Or would be, if not for the fact that she was obliged to share her bed with a naked stranger. A fierce, hot-blooded man whose strange habit of removing all covers and all pillows from the bed left her, each night, without even a top sheet to hide herself from his black, penetrating eyes.

"The river," Amy murmured aloud, suddenly recalling yesterday's trip to Puesta del Sol and the

expression she'd seen in those hypnotic black eyes
when El Capitán had placed her hand on the Sun
Stone. "My God, the river *is* flowing again and it's
because . . . because . . ." Amy sat up straight,
threw her legs over the bed's edge, and forcefully
shook her head. "No! It can't—it can't be. He had
nothing to do with it. Nothing. I am being ridiculous!"

But Amy's breath was short and a chill skipped
up her spine. Her modesty temporarily forgotten,
she dropped the robe, pushed her long tumbled
hair behind her ears, and stared into space, seeing
again the rushing waterfall, the rapidly flowing
river.

And the tall commanding man with the gold
medallion resting on his chest.

Amy shivered, then told herself it was because
she was stark naked. Good Lord, Luiz Quintano
was a mere man. Flesh and blood. Human. Incapable of performing miracles. Possessed of no su-
pernatural powers, for heaven sake!

Or was he?

While the words Sun God kept repeating themselves over and over in her brain in an unsettling
litany, Amy impatiently dressed, made up her
bed, and hurried downstairs to find Magdelena.

So excited that she eagerly disregarded her own
strict rule of never discussing anything personal
with a servant, Amy breathlessly revealed to Magdelena everything that had happened the day before, leaving out nothing. She told of El Capitán
driving her home from Sundown. Of seeing his
troopers dredging out the old canals. Of the rushing waterfall, the swirling river. Of the captain

placing her hand on the Sun Stone; of the unforgettable expression in his eyes.

And when, breathless, Amy had finished, she
asked, "What do you make of it all, Mag? Have I
imagined the whole thing? Is it possible the dried-
up river is actually flowing again after all this
time?"

The sturdy Mexican woman smiled and said,
"How long, Amy, since the river dry up?"

Amy squinted her eyes and caught her bottom
lip behind her top teeth, pondering for a moment.
"I'm not sure, but it was years ago. Eight, maybe
ten."

Magdelena looked Amy straight in the eye.
"The river dry up at exactly the time young Luiz
leave Orilla."

A crease appeared in the middle of Amy's brow.
Her lips fell open. For a moment she was speechless. Finally she laughed nervously and said, "You
can't actually believe . . ."

"Sí, I do believe," Magdelena interrupted.
"Luiz's mother, the Aztec goddess Xochiquetzal,
perform miracle and bless this ranch with water
twenty-seven years ago. Then, when her son was
cast off Orilla, she take the water away. Now he is
back . . ." Her words trailed off and she lifted her
shoulders in a shrug.

Amy gave no reply. Lost in thought, she turned
and left Magdelena's kitchen. She was still pensive
later that morning while she went about scrubbing the floors in the hacienda's wide downstairs
corridor.

Long blond hair pinned atop her head and covered with a bandanna, and wearing an ancient,
faded work dress, Amy was down on her hands

and knees. A basin of water was beside her, a large, stiff-bristled brush in her right hand.

Vigorously she scoured away the tracked-in dirt from the smooth red bricks. Perspiration dotted her upper lip and wisps of wilted hair curled around her cheeks. She paused for a minute, wiped her damp face with the back of her hand, then sat back on her heels and undid the top buttons of her bodice.

Hot and tired from her labor, she sighed and went back to work, her thoughts still on the flowing river. Totally preoccupied, she had no idea anyone was within a mile of her.

El Capitán stood in the wide hall, not ten feet away. Temporarily blinded from coming in out of the brilliant sunlight, he hadn't immediately seen her. He had stopped short when Amy sat back on her heels and unbuttoned her dress. When she went back down on all fours and began scrubbing the bricks, his face went rigid. It so rankled him to see her working like a servant, he bore determinedly down on her, a muscle jumping in his hard jaw.

Amy looked up just as he reached her. His hand shot out, wrapped tightly around her upper arm, and hauled her to her feet with such swift force, her head rocked on her shoulders.

Mouth agape, she found herself looking up into the dark, disapproving face of the clearly angry captain.

"Never," he said through thinned lips, "are you to scrub floors." He took the brush from her and dropped it. "Do not let me catch you at it again."

Her own anger immediately flared. Amy snatched her arm from his firm grasp and said spitefully, "If you don't want to catch me at it, then I'd suggest you stay out of the house!"

"You are *not* to do this—or any other menial work—again. Where are all the help?"

"The help?" Amy laughed at the absurdity of his question. "You're looking at the help, Captain."

"You have no servants?"

"Oh, sure. I've servants all over the place. So many they're constantly underfoot, but I do so enjoy scrubbing floors." She shook her head disgustedly and said, "Magdelena and old Fernando. That's it. So, if you'll excuse me now."

"Why didn't you tell me this?"

"Would it have changed anything?" She gave him a wilting look and sank back down to her knees to pick up where she had left off.

"Get up," he commanded.

"I have work to do."

"I won't allow it."

"You have no choice," she replied, going for the brush.

He coolly kicked it out of her reach. "I said get up."

Fire flashed from Amy's narrowed blue eyes. She looked up at him and hissed, "And I said no!" Then quickly went down on all fours and crawled toward the brush.

She didn't get far.

An arm of steel went around her waist and she was scooped from the floor so swiftly she hardly realized what had happened. She found herself pressed back against his tall frame, trapped. Instinctively she struggled, kicking at him and clawing wildly at the muscular arm holding her so tightly she could barely breathe.

"Be still now," he said with that icy calm she had come to recognize as being far more dangerous than any sudden explosion of anger. "Be still."

At once Amy gave up the battle, feeling the latent force of his masterful nature, the strength beneath the calm surface. She stood still and stiff in his embrace, fearing him, hating him. Hating herself for fearing him. It seemed to Amy they would stand there forever, he with his back against the wall, she forced to stand flush against him, so close that the gold Sun Stone on his chest was cutting into the flesh of her left shoulder.

Abruptly he released her.

Amy quickly stepped away, refusing to speak or to look at him. She held her breath until he pushed away from the wall, turned, and started down the long corridor. Only when she was certain he was actually leaving, that he was nearing the heavy front door, did she slowly turn around.

Glaring after him, she ground her teeth in angry frustration, then silently mouthed the words "I hate you."

And then almost swallowed her tongue when El Capitán, as if he had read her mind, said over his shoulder, "And I've the scars on my back to prove it."

25

My Darling Linda and Dearest Aunt Meg,

Your letters arrived this morning and I've read both over at least a dozen times.

It sounds as though the two of you are having a wonderful time; how I wish I was there with you. The ballet and the opera in the same week! My goodness, Linda, I'm afraid you'll never want to come home to Orilla.

Things are just as usual here. The weather is hot and dry, the big hacienda quiet and empty. The days are long and the nights are longer. I am so lonely I . . .

Amy abruptly threw down the quill pen and wadded the half-written letter up in her fist. sighing loudly, she dropped it atop the desk and rose. She would try again later. She couldn't bring herself to finish. Couldn't make herself write one more lie.

Everything the same. Indeed!

Nothing was the same. Nothing. Not even the restful solitude of the old hacienda.

Two weeks ago, on the very day El Capitán had found her scrubbing the floors, he had made a complete inspection of the hacienda, his critical eye missing nothing. With Magdelena and old Fernando in his wake, he strode purposefully through the many rooms, including those long shut off and unused.

Seeing firsthand just how much the splendor of the old mansion had faded, he threw open dry-rotted shutters, yanked down dusty, tattered drapes, studied threadbare carpets. Carefully, his face inscrutable, he examined the floors and the walls and the ceilings.

And made the decision then and there to restore the large Spanish-style adobe dwelling to its former grandeur without further delay.

So now there was a great flurry of activity every day in the hacienda as El Capitán's barechested troops hammered and sawed and painted. Laid new carpets and hung heavy drapery and moved in new furniture.

Half a dozen smiling, chattering female Mexican servants—hired by the captain—worked industriously, polishing and dusting and singing.

And scrubbing floors.

Magdelena and old Fernando couldn't have been happier; both were in all their glory. El Capitán had put Magdelena in charge of the six Mexican servants, declaring unequivocally that she was solely responsible for making sure they kept the place spotless and sparkling.

Then, noticing that the stooped Fernando's sun-wrinkled old face had taken on a hurt expression, the captain had turned directly to the aging servant and, addressing him in flawless Spanish, said, *"Compadre,* can I count on you to oversee the workers in their monumental task of renovating the hacienda?"

"Sí, Mi Capitán, sí," Fernando said eagerly, his watery eyes lighting with pleasure.

Skeptically watching the exchange, Amy experienced an unfamiliar surge of gratitude toward the tall commander. The cold, callous man *did* remember how to show kindness—at least with the servants and his elders. Catching herself reluctantly admiring him for his thoughtfulness, Amy turned away.

The restoration of the hacienda was not the only thing changing on the big sunland spread. With the flowing of the river and the dredging out of the irrigation canals, grass was sprouting up on the barren pastures. Rail cars filled with bawling cattle arrived daily at Orilla's private spur. Vaqueros who had worked the ranch in days gone by heard the news and wandered back, eager to work for the man they had known as a boy. A man they now considered the *Patrón* of Orilla.

Amy watched all the activity with a mixture of pride and despair. She was grateful, of course, that the river now flowed, that cattle would again graze the far meadows, that the ranch would once more prosper. But she was alarmed as well. Surely El Capitán would not be spending such great sums of money—money she wondered how he had come by—if he did not intend to return to Orilla permanently when the French had been finally routed and Mexico was free once more.

The prospect chilled her.

A shout from below her open balcony doors drew Amy's attention. She did not recognize the voice. It was a sentinel calling excitedly to alert El Capitán.

Amy stepped out onto the balcony in time to see a youthful trooper reining his lathered horse to a halt. Taking care to remain concealed, she watched the tall, long-legged captain walk leisurely out to meet the dismounting courier.

She heard the messenger anxiously announce, "A dispatch from Presidente Juarez, Capitán."

Luiz took the missive and read it, his dark face displaying no emotion. Holding her breath, Amy waited. Surely he would reveal its contents and make some comment to the messenger.

He did not. He thanked the young soldier, dismissed him with a crisp military salute, and Amy was left to wonder.

Was he being called immediately back into battle? Would he, and all his troops, be leaving within the hour? Was the nightmare about to end, her life about to return to normal?

Amy left her room and hurried downstairs, hoping to learn what was in Juarez's orders.

El Capitán walked in the front door just as Amy reached the base of the stairs. She automatically stopped and stood there waiting expectantly, a couple of steps up the staircase.

He looked up, saw her, and unhurriedly crossed to her. His handsome face giving nothing away, he put a booted foot on the first step of the stairs and draped his forearm over the polished banister. His hand was mere inches from Amy's face, and in those long bronzed fingers was the folded manila missive.

The orders from Benito Juarez, President of Mexico.

He never mentioned the dispatch. Instead, he casually inquired if she intended to make her weekly visit into Sundown.

Stiffening immediately, afraid he intended to

drive her, Amy shook her head. "No. No, I wasn't planning on—"

"Pedrico is waiting with the buckboard." He took his arm from the banister, his foot from the stairs. He placed the yellow missive in his shirt pocket and stepped around her to start up the stairs.

Frowning, Amy grabbed his arm. "Are you sure Pedrico will have the time?" She held her breath.

"All the time in the world," El Capitán said, and proceeded up the stairs.

Longing to strangle him, Amy stormed across the foyer and out the front door.

In less than an hour Amy had finished with her shopping in Sundown. Leaving Mac's cavernous store, she was glad it was still early. She would go to the Clayton hacienda for a nice long visit with her good friend, Diana.

If anyone could cheer her up, it was Diana.

Contemplating a lazy, pleasant afternoon with her troubles forgotten for a while, Amy was smiling as she crossed the stone porch outside Mac's. The sound of familiar feminine laughter from across the plaza attracted Amy's attention. She would recognize Diana's throaty laugh anywhere.

Continuing to smile, Amy lifted a hand to shade her eyes from the sun and squinted toward the source of that warm laughter. The smile froze on her face.

Standing directly before the double-doored entrance of La Posada Hotel was the laughing Diana. The person responsible for her laughter was Capitán Luiz Quintano!

Amy felt her face go hot then cold, her stomach do a crazy cartwheel. Wishing she could look away, incapable of doing so, she watched as El Capitán smiled disarmingly down at Diana, his teeth flashing starkly white against his dark face. As he smiled he was gesturing, making a slow, graceful downward sweep with his right hand, inches from Diana's voluptuous body, as if he were telling her that she was lovely from head to toe.

Knowing how the gorgeously gowned Diana responded to compliments, Amy was not surprised when the dark-haired beauty, smiling flirtatiously up at the tall officer, reached a small gloved hand out to Luiz's chest, and playfully toyed with a gleaming brass button on his uniform tunic.

Rooted to the spot, wishing she could turn away, Amy continued to watch as Luiz nodded his dark head affirmatively, gallantly took Diana's arm, and escorted her into the white stucco hotel.

A dozen vivid pictures flew through Amy's brain.

The two of them—Luiz and Diana—sharing a long, intimate lunch. Sipping champagne and gazing into each other's eyes. Staying long past the hour when the dining room closed, then tipsily making their way out to Diana's fancy carriage for the short ride to her hacienda where they . . . they . . .

Amy rushed anxiously toward the buckboard, grateful that Pedrico was there waiting. She wanted only to get out of town as quickly as possible. Surprised she had stayed such a short time in Sundown, Pedrico, guiding the team around the plaza, asked innocently, "Shall we go to Señorita Clayton's hacienda, *señora?*"

"No," Amy snapped, violently shaking her head.

Taken aback, Pedrico's brow wrinkled. *"Problema,* Miz Amy?"

"No. Everything is fine."

Back at Orilla Amy paced all afternoon. And as she paced she told herself she was being foolish. What did she care if El Capitán and Diana had discovered each other? She didn't. She was glad. Relieved. Maybe with the distraction of the willing Diana, the captain would no longer find it necessary to torture her each night.

Yes, an affair between the man-hungry Diana and the lustful Capitán would make Amy happy. *Very* happy!

The long, warm afternoon dragged on and the very happy Amy had a throbbing headache. She didn't feel like going down for dinner that evening, a meal she was sure she would be eating alone since the cold man with whom she usually dined would be having his dinner at the Clayton mansion.

Amy stopped pacing as the idea struck her.

At last an opportunity to look for Juarez's dispatch! Hurrying into the large dressing room to begin her search, Amy felt little guilt. The white shirt Luiz had worn that morning was lying draped across a chest. She eagerly snatched it up, then sighed when she found the pocket empty.

Annoyed, she dropped the shirt to the floor and riffled through all his neatly pressed military uniforms, sticking her hands into every pocket. Nothing. She pulled out the many drawers of the tall chest, lifted crisp folded shirts, looked beneath stacks of linen underwear and mens' stockings.

She flipped open the square leather box where he kept his jewelry. His wide gold and turquoise cuff bracelet was there. Some silver shirt studs. A gold pocket watch and chain. A lone ladies' ear screw of rubies and diamonds.

Amy slammed the lid shut.

Frustrated, she lifted his tall boots, turned them upside down and shook them. She felt in the toes of his soft doeskin moccasins. She ran her fingers around the sweat band of his rarely worn hat.

She looked in every conceivable place where a man might hide an important piece of paper. Either he had destroyed the message or he had it on him. Most likely the latter. He knew very well she was dying to find out if he had been ordered back into battle. So, naturally, he would spitefully keep it from her until the last possible minute. The bastard!

There was a gentle knock on the door, and one of the fresh-faced Mexican servants brought in a cloth-covered tray. Amy, lifting the corner of the pink linen cloth, casually inquired if El Capitán had returned. And knew the answer was no even before the servant girl firmly shook her head as she backed away.

Not the least bit hungry, Amy left the tray untouched.

Again she paced restlessly. She continued to pace until long after the sun had set and she was totally exhausted.

Bedtime came and still she was far too jumpy to sleep. It made no sense. For the first night since he and his soldiers had come riding onto the ranch, she did not have to fear his coming to her bed. She should feel nothing but blessed relief!

Amy took a long, hot bath, tensing every time the old house creaked or a sudden sound broke the night silence. She still half expected Luiz to come striding into the dressing room ignoring her demands for privacy.

It didn't happen.

Amy drew on a long white nightgown, turned down the silken covers on her bed, and prepared for the best night's sleep she had had in ages. It was wonderful to wear a nightgown like a decent woman, to sleep in a bed with nice, fat pillows and a covering sheet.

Sighing, she blew out the lamp beside the bed and lay back on the comfortable pillows. The moon—almost full—had risen. Its silvery light streamed in the open balcony doors, bathing half the spacious room with an incandescent glow, completely framing the heavy carved door.

Amy moaned aloud as vivid memories rushed in to overwhelm her.

On that very first night with Luiz, she had stood frightened and submissive against that door in the bright moonlight while he undressed her. Amy turned away, pressed her face into the downy pillows, and vowed she would forget that night and every other profane night spent in his arms.

But sleep refused to come. After tossing and turning for the better part of an hour, Amy rose from the bed. Tired and on edge, she strolled out onto the balcony and looked out over the flat, moon-silvered landscape.

In the distance she saw little puffs of dust hanging in the air. Then she heard the echoing hoofbeats. Finally she saw horse and rider steadily approaching the hacienda.

Moonlight touched the pair and revealed a sleek black stallion with a sleek dark man on its back.

Noche and El Capitán.

Amy clung to the balcony railing, her heart beating wildly with fear and with dread.

Or was it anticipation?

26

May 5, 1866.

The day dawned sunny and warm and perfect in the deserts of far southwest Texas. The sky was a bright breathtaking blue with only a handful of high-sailing cumulus clouds casting shadows on the cool mountain peaks far to the south. The air was dry and still, but comfortable, not yet oppressive with the scorching heat of summer.

Newly delivered foals galloped on spindly legs, chasing after their mothers across Orilla's grassy highland horse pastures. On the flats, longhorn cattle munched contentedly on newly sprouted tobaso. At the hacienda, a red-tailed hawk abandoned his holding pattern to swoop down and drink from the new birdbath Pedrico had built out back on the wide flagstone porch.

Excitement was in the air at Orilla on that sunny morning in May, both inside the big house and out in the whitewashed stucco bunkhouses where El Capitán's troops were billeted.

Cinco de Mayo.

Since the fifth of May four years ago when determined Mexican soldiers led by General Ignacio Zaragpza and the young brigadier Porfirio Diaz had humiliated the French military force attacking their fortified city of Puebla, all Mexicans—wherever they might be—celebrated the anniversary of this important victory.

Knowing just how much this date meant to his troops, El Capitán Quintano was hosting a big *Cinco de Mayo* celebration blow-out at Orilla. The gay festivities were to begin at twilight.

By midmorning Magdelena and her chattering young help were at work preparing the evening's outdoor spread, a feast certain to win the unanimous approval of hungry young soldiers.

The menu included mountains of soft flour tortillas wrapped around strips of hotly spiced beef. Savory enchiladas *verde* covered with thick melted goat cheese. Bubbling pots of *frijoles rojos* seasoned with red chili peppers. Tostadas, crispy tortillas spread with shredded chicken, cheese, and salsa. Green corn hot tamales loaded with tangy beef. Fiery chili con carne packing enough punch to bring tears to the eyes of the unwary. Quesadillas, a pair of fried tortillas with a thick layer of Menoniha cheese in between. And, of course, gallons of burning-hot salsa for dipping crunchy tostadas.

For dessert, Magdelena's special light-as-a-cloud hot sopaipillas with warm, sweet honey, exquisite *flautas,* those small dainty pastries filled with dark sweet chocolate and rich whipped cream. Warm, golden flan, the delicious custard so loved by all Mexicans. And plates of sweet, sugary pralines loaded with large pecan halves.

Along with the abundance of good foods, there were gallons of tequila, barrels of *cerveza,* and cases of Madeira and bourbon to quench the revelers' thirst. Entertainment was planned as well.

Not one but two mariachi bands would play, and a trio of talented flamenco dancers were coming all the way from San Antonio to perform. Pretty *señoritas* from the village had been invited to the fiesta as welcome guests of the troopers.

The site El Capitán had chosen for the festivities was the flat open plain on the Spanish-style hacienda's west side, just beyond the stone-floored patio and vast side yard. A small wooden platform had been constructed as a stand for the musicians and entertainers. Long buffet tables were already in place to hold the food. Stacks of dry mesquite kindling had been gathered to build a giant celebration bonfire come nightfall.

By sundown all was ready.

And everyone was ready.

Everyone but Amy.

Amy had no intentions of attending the *Cinco de Mayo* fiesta. She had not been consulted on planning the party, nor would she have participated had she been asked. The night, the feast, the celebration—it all belonged to El Capitán. It held no appeal for her.

Now, as dusk crept over the old many-roomed hacienda, the entire household staff—including Magdelena, the servant girls, Pedrico, and even old Fernanado—had gone out to join in the festival. Amy was alone in the *sala*, reading a book by lamplight as if the evening was in no way special.

She paid no attention to the steady stream of carriages arriving at Orilla to discharge excited female guests. She ignored the occasional shouts of the troopers or the laughter of women that carried faintly on the still May air.

Her blue eyes remained on the pages of her

book, pretending concentration, her demeanor one of total absorption. Her pretense became real as the engrossing tale she read drew Amy slowly, steadily into its captivating fantasy.

The sounds from outside receded and Amy was fully swept back to another time and place where brave knights and their fair ladies presided over mighty kingdoms.

Lost in Scott's world of derring-do and sweet magical romance, Amy could almost hear her own handsome White Knight softly speaking her name. She sighed gently and her lips turned up into a smile. Then she realized with a start that it was not her imagination. Someone *was* speaking her name. Fingers tightening on the book, the smile leaving her face, Amy slowly raised her eyes.

He stood framed in the arched doorway, his hands gripping the polished woodwork on either side. He was looking straight at her, a satanic gleam in his black eyes. His shoulder-length raven hair was secured with a white leather band behind his neck. A snowy white shirt of lace-trimmed batiste stretched across his wide shoulders, pulled tautly over hard biceps, revealing the darkness of his chest, bare beneath the delicate fabric.

The golden Sun Stone had been left upstairs.

A pair of tight black twill charro pants were molded to his slim hips and long legs, their cuffs breaking perfectly atop the instep of his polished back boots. Around his slim waist, a belt of silver conchos flashed in the twilight.

He was no apparition. No mythical knight come to spirit her away atop a shimmering white charger. He was the devil's own, come here to torment her, raw flesh-and-blood masculinity with penetrating black eyes, cruelly sensual mouth, and utterly splendid physique.

And he never wanted to whisk her away to any place other than his bed.

El Capitán spoke, breaking the silence. Coolly he invited Amy to attend the *Cinco de Mayo* celebration. With him if she wished.

Coldly Amy informed the tall, lean man that she had no desire to go with him and promptly turned her attention back to her book. Unruffled by her refusal, Luiz nodded, turned, and unhurriedly walked away.

Amy continued to read after he had gone. But the utopian tale of honorable knights and chaste ladies had lost its appeal. When finally she'd read the same paragraph half a dozen times, she gave up and laid the book aside.

Sighing, she rose and roamed restlessly about the big silent *sala,* searching for something to do, some way to occupy herself. She rearranged a bouquet of wild marsh pinks resting in a huge alabaster porcelain vase atop the cherrywood piano. She straightened a silver-framed picture on the wall. She brushed a piece of lint from the back of a rust-hued velvet upholstered chair.

She sighed again and left the lonely living room to wander aimlessly, stopping briefly in the deserted kitchen, taking a nibble of this, a bite of that, before conceding she had no appetite.

At nine o'clock Amy climbed the stairs to the master suite and made a face of annoyance as soon as she stepped inside the darkened room. Through the open balcony doors the sounds of music and shouting and laughter was far more intrusive than downstairs.

Amy was drawn across the room. She stepped onto the balcony and looked out at the crowd, her eyes searching. Swarms of men and women were laughing, talking, eating, and drinking. All were obviously enjoying themselves. After several minutes of scanning the sea of faces, Amy gave up. Turning away, she went back inside, sarcastically muttering aloud, "I hope you're having a grand time, Quintano!"

Quintano *was* having a grand time.

While from the balcony, Amy searched in vain for his dark, handsome face, Luiz stood with his back to her, carefully sprinkling salt atop his left hand.

"*Salud!*" he said to the cluster of admirers surrounding him.

"*Salud!*" they echoed loudly as he put out his tongue and licked the salt away, took a large bite out of a lemon, then turned up a glass of fiery tequila and emptied its contents.

His admirers applauded. A bearded young trooper hurried forth to refill his superior's glass as Luiz sprinkled more salt atop his hand. One of the pretty San Antonio dancers, moving suggestively close, placed her hand possessively to the small of Luiz's back.

The mariachis played. Guitars and violins and trumpets provided loud, spirited music for the all-Mexican crowd's favorite dances. *El galope. El Bule. El vals de la escoba.*

Everyone participated. Including El Capitán.

Between the rousing dances he drank tequila and ate tortillas and effortessly charmed the women.

The San Antonio entertainers took the stage to perform a flawless flamenco, the two attractive women dressed in glittering red sequined gowns, the man in dark bolero jacket, red cummerbund, and tight trousers. The handsome trio pleased the shouting, whistling crowd, and no one applauded their performance more vigorously than El Capitán Luiz Quintano.

Darkness cloaked the desert.

Torches were tossed onto the big pyramid of mesquite branches. Fire roared to life, shooting bright orange flames high into the black night sky. The party grew wilder as the liquor flowed and the celebrating Mexicans yelled and yipped and whistled and laughed. Amorous couples openly kissed and embraced as they danced. Jealousies flared. Fistfights broke out. Knives flashed. Shots were fired into the air.

Everyone was having a wonderful time.

Everyone but Amy.

Attempting to sleep, she lay wide awake, the bedroom tinted an eerie shade of orange from the brightly burning bonfire below. Exasperated, she got out of bed and again went onto the balcony to watch the boisterous merrymaking.

A lone couple, framed in the intense glow of the giant bonfire, was dancing while a ring of approving spectators clapped and shouted and hooted.

A tall, lean man and a voluptuous Mexican woman. Their bodies touching provocatively, their hands raised above their heads, fingers snapping castanets, feet stamping the hard-packed earth, they were looking into each other's eyes.

Amy needed no one to tell her that the tall, graceful dancer was El Capitán Luiz Quintano. Her intense gaze fastened on the handsome pair; she experienced an immediate flare-up of jealousy, just as she had when she'd seen Luiz escort her friend Diana Clayton into the La Posada.

Amy quickly turned away, telling herself she didn't care what he did, whom he danced with. Or to whom he made love.

She went back inside. But the sight of the beautiful red-gowned dancer pressing her full breasts boldly to Luiz's chest remained.

The air inside the bedroom seemed close, stuffy, stifling. There was no night breeze and Amy was uncomfortably warm. Her long white nightgown stuck to her prickly skin and she felt miserable. Telling herself she badly needed a breath of fresh air and that there would certainly be no harm done if she wandered down to the fiesta just for a few brief minutes, Amy hurried toward her dressing room.

After stripping off the hot nightgown, she dropped it where she stood and quickly slipped on a fresh white cotton chemise and some underwear. She yanked down a heavy, ruffled petticoat, shook her head decisively, and tossed it aside. It was far too warm for petticoats and cotton stockings. Besides, she would only be outside for five or ten minutes, then she'd come right back up and go to bed.

Amy chose a white Mexican-style blouse with blue embroidery on the yoke and a drawstring around the sleeves and gathered bodice. She drew on a full skirt of blue-and-white flowered cotton, made a face at herself in the mirror, then grabbed a wide, long sash of vivid scarlet silk and tied it around her small waist. She slid her bare feet into soft kid slippers, ran a brush impatiently through her long blond hair, and rushed from the room.

Attempting to appear casual and at ease, Amy ventured down to the party. El Capitán spotted her at once. But he did not go to her. Amy felt foolish and out of place. She wished she had never come. She was in agony.

After only a few miserable moments, Amy, her face hot with embarrassment, turned and started to leave. Anxiously pushing her way through the crowd, she gasped when someone caught her arm.

She whirled about and found herself face to face with El Capitán, his long dark fingers sliding down to encircle her wrist and draw her closer.

"Let me go," she said with calm authority.

"Dance with me, Mrs. Parnell" was his easy reply.

"No. I can't. It . . . it's getting late. . . ." Her words trailed weakly away as her senses were assailed with his powerful presence.

His white shirt was damp with perspiration; it clung to his dark chest and shoulders. The effect was disturbingly appealing. His hard, handsome face glistened in the firelight.

The not-unpleasant scent of liquor on his warm breath, Luiz leaned down and said, "One dance. Then you're free to go."

He masterfully drew her into his arms as the band began to play a haunting Spanish love song. But Amy refused to put her arm around his neck. She refused to look at him. She stood stiffly in his embrace, unwilling to make a scene but wanting him to know that dancing with him was the last thing on earth she wanted.

Luiz simply smiled, amused by her futile attempts at coldness. He drew her slowly closer, wrapping a long arm securely around her waist, knowing she could no more resist him than he her.

His pulse quickening as he felt her soft curves settle against him, he closed his eyes and inhaled deeply of her perfumed hair, totally comfortable with their relationship. If she was not, well, that was her misfortune.

The beautiful woman in his arms looked almost angelic with her long golden hair and her limpid blue eyes and slender, lovely body. He knew better. She was a conniving little imposter. The well-respected young widow was anything but strait-laced and honest.

In his arms she was a fiery, responsive lover. That she was a liar and a cheat meant nothing to him. Nothing at all. She was another man's heartache, not his. What he wanted from her, she gave him. And she would give it to him tonight, freely and eagerly.

Luiz began the slow, sensual steps of the dance. Amy had no choice, she followed his lead, but her left arm remained hanging limply at her side. She was determined to remain indifferent, wanted him to know she had no intention of staying.

But her temple was pressed to his cheek. Her eyes fell on his gleaming bronzed throat just as his hand moved up to caress the bare flesh of her shoulder and she felt her resolve start to melt. And knew, miserably, that he had somehow sensed it.

El Capitán abruptly stopped dancing. He leaned back to look down at her with sultry black eyes. He smiled sexily and urged her arms up around his neck.

"Mi palomacita," he murmured huskily, his Latin blood beginning to heat from her nearness. "My little dove, I want you to stay here with me. And you want to stay. You want me. When will you admit it?"

Amy wondered if he was a little bit drunk. If not he would surely never have asked such a question. He would have known the answer.

"El dia que me muera. The day on which I die!"

27

"Ah, so sad, so sad," he murmured softly, and then smiled easily. Stung by her cutting remark, Luiz was determined not to let her know. And determined that before the evening ended, he'd have her shamelessly admitting that she did want him.

"You make fun of me," she accused.

"No, Mrs. Parnell," he replied, his dark gaze holding hers, "It *is* sad. I want you. I want to hear you say you want me. But there's so little time . . ." He shrugged his wide shoulders and left the rest unsaid.

Amy's heart immediately leapt in her chest. He was leaving! The dispatch from President Juarez he'd received four days ago and about which he'd never revealed the contents—it was his orders to lead his troops back into battle. He was telling her this was to be his last night.

An involuntary tremor raced through Amy's slender body. Her slippered foot came down atop Luiz's instep. Her tensed body slammed into his.

"I—I'm sorry," she apologized. "I'm so clumsy tonight. Forgive me."

"It is all right." His voice was low, soft. "I have

you. I won't let you fall." And his cold jet eyes grew unfamiliarly warm.

His hands spanned her rib cage, the thumbs lightly grazing the sides of her breasts. He drew her closer and pressed her face gently to his hard shoulder. Amy didn't see the devil lurking in the depths of those changing black eyes.

Nervously she wet her lips. "Ah . . . when you said there's so little time left, did you mean . . ."

"Shhhh," he gently interrupted, and pressed his smooth cheek to hers. Amy felt his long silky lashes stir restlessly against her face and knew his eyes had closed. "If I'm to have you for only one dance," he whispered, "let me enjoy it while I may."

Amy automatically nodded, stirred by an unusual tenderness in his voice and by the unsettling emotions his tone evoked, emotions she did not fully understand.

Held closely in his arms, Amy felt her taut body relaxing, molding itself to his. He was an expert dancer, smooth and easy to follow. She moved perfectly with him to the slow, provocative beat of an achingly pretty Spanish love song.

Her arms locked behind his dark head, her eyes sliding closed, Amy was affected by the moving sentiment of the ballad and by the knowledge that the leanly muscled arms holding her so tightly would soon hold her no more.

He was leaving!

El Capitán Luiz Quintano would rise at daybreak and ride right out of her life. After a few days—or weeks—it would be just as if he had never been here. In time her terrible guilt would fade.

Everything would be as it had been before. Her existence would be as it had been before the fear, before the shame, before the ecstasy.

Before El Capitán.

Routine. Respectable. Safe.

Lonely.

The beautiful love song ended. Luiz's hands dropped away from Amy. He took a step back.

"I enjoyed the dance," he said gallantly, now the polite Spanish grandee. He smiled winningly and added, "But it made me very thirsty. Are you thirsty?"

"A little," Amy admitted, knowing she should return to the hacienda at once. But wanting to stay here with him far more.

With a gentle hand on her arm, Luiz guided Amy through the rowdy crowd toward one of the liquor stations. When they stood before a table loaded with bottles, some overturned, some empty, he asked if she had ever tasted tequila. Amy shook her head. She had never tasted anything stronger than wine. She told him as much.

Luiz reached for a full bottle of tequila. He had no trouble persuading her to say yes to one small jigger of the fiery, potent liquor distilled from the desert's hearty century plant. He poured, handed her the full shot glass, and Amy started to turn it up immediately.

He laughed.

"Wait," he said, and reached out to stay her hand. "You have to do this right."

"I do?"

"Give me your left hand." Amy frowned but held out her hand. Luiz sprinkled salt into her palm, picked up a slice of lemon, and instructed,

"Lick the salt from your hand, take a bite of this lemon, *then* drink your tequila."

Amy looked skeptical, but put out her tongue and gingerly touched it to the salt in her palm. Luiz held out the lemon and she dutifully took a bite, immediately making a sour face. He smiled and motioned for her to drink. She turned up the glass and drank down the tequila as if it were orangeade. As soon as she swallowed, her eyes grew wide with horror and began to water. She fanned herself frantically, drew in anxious gulps of air, and looked up at Luiz as if he had played a dirty trick on her.

He caught her to him, brushed his lips to her temple, handed her a glass of cool water, and said, "I am sorry, *querida*. Are you all right?"

Feeling the liquor's fierce heat spread through her chest and out into her arms, Amy was shocked by its powerful and immediate effect. Already her head was beginning to feel fuzzy and she wondered if she had heard him correctly. Had El Capitán really called her sweetheart?

She clutched her throat and said, "I'm not sure. I feel strange. My fingers and toes are tingling."

Luiz was charmed.

With her flushed face, her unbound golden hair spilling around her bare shoulders, a splayed hand gripping her burning throat, she looked adorably young and appealing. For a second he was overwhelmed with the fierce desire to pull her to him and kiss away the hurt.

A muscle twitching in his jaw, he said, "Perhaps we'd better dance."

He grinned and, lifting a dark hand, he slipped only the tip of his little finger beneath a wayward lock of shimmering blond hair and gently pushed it back off Amy's face.

And again they danced.

Couples near them smiled and greeted them and loudly thanked El Capitán for giving such a wonderful celebration. Soon a trio of laughing, shouting troopers excitedly approached the pair and everyone stopped dancing to watch the fun.

One of the trio drew out a clean white handkerchief and tied it securely around Luiz's right wrist. Amy was puzzled, but he didn't seem to be. He was laughing, the white scar on his cheek coloring slightly, his dark eyes glowing.

When the trooper looked at Amy and said, *"Con permiso, señora?"* Amy turned questioning eyes to Luiz.

"Give him your left wrist, *querida*."

Amy was dubious, but she presented the smiling trooper with her wrist. Thanking her, he swiftly tied it to Luiz's bound wrist and the whole crowd applauded enthusiastically.

While the thunderous applause continued, Luiz turned his head, spotted Lieutenant Pedrico Valdez and motioned him over. He quietly spoke to Pedrico, who nodded. Luiz put his lips close to Amy's ear and explained that everyone was having a good time. To be assured of having another dance soon, the hosting couple was *amarrado*—tied together with a handkerchief. They would not be untied until a guest promised to redeem them by giving a *baile del desempeño*. A dance of redemption.

Nodding with understanding, Amy said, "What if no one agrees to give a dance of redemption?"

"Then we must stay tied together forever."

A shiver swept through Amy's body as she looked up into those hypnotic back eyes and considered the scintillating prospect of being tied to him forever. The almost mystic attraction of this coldly handsome man caused her legs suddenly to tremble uncontrollably.

"I think the tequila has made me a little dizzy," she quickly told him.

"Ah, *querida,*" he whispered softly, drawing her into his arms, "I was hoping it was me."

And again they danced.

This time with their wrists tied securely together. By song's end, they found themselves dancing near the blazing bonfire. The flames hot on their faces, they looked steadily into each other's eyes, barely conscious of those around them.

In minutes they were covered with a sheen of perspiration, their faces shiny wet, their clothes damp and clinging to their perspiring bodies.

But they were not bothered by the fire's glowing heat. Heat of a far more potent kind was slowly, enticingly enveloping the swaying, silent pair.

The one tequila she'd consumed had taken the edge off Amy's initial nervousness. She no longer glanced warily about, concerned with what people might think. She wrapped her free arm around Luiz's neck and allowed her body to melt against his, marveling, as always, at the hardness and strength of his long, lean frame.

After a few stirring dances, Luiz offered Amy more tequila. She eagerly accepted. When he gave her a shaker of salt, she coyly sprinkled the salt into his hand instead of her own. Then, looking straight into his eyes, she put out her tongue, touched it to his palm, and heard his sharp intake of breath. She lifted her head and smiled at him. While he stared intensely at her, Amy drank her tequila and set the glass aside.

She then picked up the shaker and carefully sprinkled salt into her own hand. She sweetly offered it to him. Luiz made no move to take her hand. Her glistening lips parted and she lifted her hand closer to his dark face.

"Lick," she said, her gaze holding his. "Lick it,"

And she thrilled to the pull and play of hard muscle beneath his white shirt as his fingers enclosed her wrist and he lifted her hand as his face lowered.

She squirmed with pleasure from the first electric touch of his silky tongue to her sensitive flesh. Luiz took his time. Leisurely he licked and kissed and sucked at her tingling palm until Amy felt warm and weak, her heart fluttering with excitement. Her eyes on the dark head bent to her, she held her breath, praying for him to stop so she could collect her scattered wits.

El Capitán didn't stop until his lips and tongue had licked away every last tiny grain of salt. When it was all gone, he teasingly bit her palm with sharp white teeth. Bit her hard enough to make her wince.

He lifted his head and stared at her. Amy trembled when he drew her tongue-wet palm to his chest and pressed it flat over his heart.

A heart that was beating almost as rapidly as her own.

He kept her hand there while he picked up his glass of tequila and tossed it off in one fiery swallow.

"Dance with me, *querida*," he said, and licked a missed grain of salt from his full lower lip.

And so once again they danced.

Or if they did not actually dance, they stood with their arms around each other, seductively rocking together, moving steadily closer to the brightly burning bonfire. Unspoken was the shared strangely compelling desire to gravitate nearer and nearer to the fierce heat of those beautiful, deadly flames. Some driving force drew them toward the raging inferno. Swaying together, they moved slowly but steadily around the huge fire, seeking privacy. They found it on the far side, a place to be alone together, to allow smoldering passions to surface fully.

Dancing perilously close to the blaze, flirting with its fury, the hot pair relished the pain-pleasure that belonged to them alone.

Privacy was theirs in the middle of the crowd. The intensity of the fire's heat kept the other guests well away from their sweltering arena of growing desire. They were free to touch and be touched; to engage in a dance so brazenly erotic, they were as pagans who knew no shame.

It was sweet torture.

They were burning up. On fire for each other. Hotter than they'd ever been before. Their bodies were feverish, temperatures steadily rising.

There was not a dry thread on either of them. They were soaking wet with perspiration, a condition they found curiously stimulating. An added aphrodisiac. The heaviness of soaked fabric pressing against burning flesh that already tingled with sensation was highly arousing.

Through the wet, heavy gathers of Amy's clinging blue-and-white skirt, she could feel the hot power of Luiz's fully formed erection pressing insistently against her stomach. Her breasts swelled against the tight yoke of her white Mexican blouse, her taut nipples rubbing against the solidness of Luiz's broad chest.

Amy licked her lips and slid her free hand between their scorching bodies. Brazenly she unbuttoned Luiz's white shirt, pushed the soggy fabric apart, and exhaled as she pressed her aching breasts to his sweat-slick skin. She wished that she could push her blouse apart and feel his hot naked flesh against her own. She shuddered with emotion.

She shuddered more deeply when Luiz put a hand into her hair, urged her head back, and bent to drink away the beads of perspiration pooling in the hollow of her glistening throat. When his flaming lips slid up to her ear, he said raggedly, *"Querida,* I cannot stand much more of this. I will have to take you right here where we stand."

Her breath coming fast, Amy's forehead sagged against his gleaming chest. "Why do we wait? Let's leave."

"We can't."

Her head came up off his chest. She looked into his eyes. "We have to. We can't. . . . Dear God, not here."

Luiz groaned and his black eyes were tortured. He jerked their tied wrists up before her face. "Until someone unties us, custom requires that we stay at the dance."

"No . . . no. What if no one unties us?" She closed her eyes and pressed her hot face into the curve of his neck and shoulder. "I want you so badly. I don't think—"

"What, *querida?* What did you say?"

Amy lifted her head and looked pleadingly into his eyes. Her spread hand anxiously caressing his bared chest, she murmured breathlessly, "I said I want you. I want you to make love to me." Her eyes closed in frustration. "I hurt from wanting you so badly."

"*Mi querida,*" Luiz said, his voice low and soft.

Her confession was what he'd been waiting all evening to hear. He didn't remind Amy of what she'd said earlier, that the day she told him she wanted him would be the day on which she died.

Instead he drew her hurriedly back to the other side of the fire and kissed her closed eyes so she wouldn't see him lift his free hand high into the air. It was the signal for his sentinel to come at once.

Pedrico saw Luiz's raised arm. He smiled, dropped his cigar, crushed it out under his bootheel, and stepped down off the platform. In seconds he was standing beside the couple who danced alone and apart before the roaring fire.

Smiling, he informed them that a charming señorita Maria Guerrero had graciously offered to redeem them. She would give the *baile del desempeño* at her home in exactly three weeks.

Swiftly he untied their wrists, bowed, and backed away while Luiz said, "*Gracías. Gracías, amigo.*"

While Pedrico clapped for silence, Luiz hastily rebuttoned his damp shirt. Then a hush fell over the crowd as Luiz turned and stepped forward. Addressing the throng, he said in perfect Castilian Spanish, "Four days ago I received a dispatch from our *presidente*, Benito Juarez. My orders and yours are to remain in ready reserve here at this command post. So, *mis amigos,* enjoy yourselves. There will be no reveille sounded on this post come daybreak."

Cheers went up. Luiz immediately turned to Amy.

His back to the crowd, he ignored the whistles and shouts, his undivided attention on her.

"Now say it again," he ordered firmly, the shooting flames of the bonfire reflected in his black, penetrating eyes. "Say you want me."

"I want you," Amy whispered, and it was almost a sob. "I want you. Take me, *Mi Capitán.*"

28

Amy watched the muscles in his gleaming throat work as he swallowed with obvious difficulty. The expression in his glittering eyes became a strange mixture of passion and tenderness. The hard lines of his mouth softened into sensuous fullness.

For once his impenetrable cloak of coldness fell completely away. The inflection of his voice registered a surprising vulnerability when he said, without a trace of sarcasm, "And I want you. More than I've ever wanted anyone or anything in this world."

"Luiz," Amy murmured, her trembling hand slowly lifting to his chest.

He reached for her hand, laced his long bronzed fingers through her slender white ones, and said, "Come with me."

Amy didn't ask where but nodded eagerly, willing to go anywhere with him. Willing to do anything with him. Because she felt exactly as he did. Never had she wanted anyone or anything the way she wanted him tonight.

Hurrying to keep up with his long, supple strides, Amy gave no thought to the guests and what they might conclude. Her usual fanatic need to keep her private life her own was swept away on a tide of rising passion.

She was not, on this warm May evening, the wise, unshakable, level-headed young widow about whom there had never been a breath of scandal.

She was half tipsy from the fiery tequila and totally intoxicated by the dark, compelling man decisively leading her away from the party. The likelihood that their departure would cause whispers and speculations concerning her behavior had no effect on Amy.

It didn't matter. Nothing mattered but the fierce need to be in this man's arms, to feel his sleek naked body against her own, to look unwaveringly into those magnificent dark eyes while he masterfully brought her to ecstasy.

Luiz didn't take Amy back to the hacienda. Drawing her along with him, he quickly circled the roaring bonfire and headed in a northwesterly direction, away from the *Cinco de Mayo* celebration. Away from the ranchhouse.

Hard-packed dirt crunched beneath their feet as they skirted the perimeter of Orilla's many bunkhouses and outbuildings. They continued on across the flat desert floor until, moving down a gently sloping incline, Amy saw, rising in the moonlight, the red-tiled roof of a barn set apart from the others. It was the stable where Luiz kept his prized stallion, Noche.

The big black caught their scent and began whickering long before they reached the corral's tall fence. He was there waiting when Luiz threw open the gate and handed Amy inside. Noche was glad to see them. He wanted to play, but his master ignored the spoiled stallion.

As soon as the gate closed behind the pair, Luiz took Amy in his arms and kissed her. Noche whinnied his outrage and nudged forcefully at Luiz's back. When the passionate kiss ended, the stallion followed the pair across the sandy lot, biting at Luiz's shoulder.

"What's wrong with him tonight?" Amy asked as Luiz guided her toward the stucco stable.

They stepped in out of the bright moonlight and Luiz backed Amy up against the wall, ran his hands down her slender arms and said, "He's jealous."

"Of me? Noche's never been jealous of me."

"Not of you. Of me." His eyes flashed in the shadowy dimness.

"I don't understand," Amy said, her fingers eagerly working at the buttons of Luiz's white shirt.

"He knows why we're here." Luiz's hands moved up, clasped the sides of Amy's neck. His thumbs made slow, caressing circles in the hollow of her throat.

"You're teasing me," she said, not quite sure he was. Her head fell back against the wall and she looked into Luiz's flashing eyes. "Noche couldn't know . . ."

Luiz's warm lips covered hers, silencing her. It was a hot, open-mouthed kiss, but it lasted only a few seconds. His lips moved to Amy's closed eyelids. He told her, "The stallion knows. He mounts Orilla's mares in this barn."

Amy felt her face flush hotly. The blood began to pound in her ears. But over its roar she could hear the nervous stallion. His low, plaintive neighing had become frenzied whinnying as he pranced restlessly back and forth just outside the open stable door.

Luiz paid no attention to the stallion's loud protests. He pulled Amy's white Mexican blouse free of her skirt's tight waistband and drew it up over her head.

His heated gaze touched her breasts, covered only by the clinging damp satin of her lace-trimmed chemise. Luiz dropped the blouse. He shrugged out of his wet white shirt and Amy saw the muscles bunch and stretch under his glistening bronzed skin.

Finding it suddenly hard to breathe, she said, "Maybe we should leave Noche in peace. Go to the hacienda."

Eyes almost savage, Luiz stepped closer. He wrapped his fingers firmly around Amy's wrist and brought her hand up to his flat, naked belly. Slowly, while he looked into her eyes, he slid her hand down his body. Past the silver concho belt, over the rough black fabric of his trousers, until it rested directly atop the rock-hard erection threatening to burst from his pants.

"I can't make it to the house," he said, almost as surprised by his statement as Amy was.

His sexual control was usually unfailing. He could and had maintained a rigid erection for great lengths of time, bringing the woman in his arms to climax after climax before seeking his own. Not this night. Not with this golden-haired woman whose lightest touch sent jolts of electricity through him. Not with this angel-faced Delilah who had been his first and only love.

He was far too excited, wanted her far too much.

"It has to be here," he said honestly. "Right here and right now."

"Yes, oh, yes," Amy murmured breathlessly, moving her knee against the inside of his thigh and sliding curious fingers up and down the hard, hot length of him. Thrilling to his trembling response to her touch.

Abruptly Luiz gripped her wrist and pulled her hand away. He cupped the back of her neck beneath her long blond hair, drew her forcefully to him, and kissed her with all the hunger and passion he felt for her. When their burning lips separated, he immediately turned her about so that he was standing behind her, her slender body pressed back against his tall frame.

While the black stallion pawed at the earth and neighed loudly less than six feet from where they stood, Luiz asked in a deep, emotion-shaded voice, "You know how horses make love?" His hands cupped her bare shoulders. Amy's lips fell open. She drew a quick breath as his fingers plucked at the lacy straps of her chemise, peeling them down her arms. She didn't answer. Visions of big, excited stallions mounting restrained, frightened mares flashed through her mind, and she was at once repelled and aroused. The blood beat in her ears.

But above its roar, she could hear the frenzied Noche whickering and racing wildly around the big corral, his sharp hooves striking the hard earth with a thudding vengeance.

Luiz went on in that deep, sensual voice. "First the stud bites the mare."

He lowered his dark face to the curve of her neck and shoulder. His open lips settled on her pale, dewy skin. He kissed her, moving his tongue enticingly in a warm, wet circle. He opened his mouth wider and sank his sharp teeth into her soft flesh. Amy trembled, threw her head back, and felt all the air leave her lungs when the slippery satin fabric of her chemise whispered down over the curve of her erect breasts and settled at her waist. She squirmed and made a soft little whimpering sound in the back of her throat.

Luiz sucked at the delicate flesh of her throat, then slid his lips to her ear and murmured seductively, "After he bites her, the stud nuzzles and gentles his mare."

His warm, dark hands filled themselves with Amy's bare, swelling breasts. His fingertips gently plucking at the passion-hardened nipples, he kissed and nuzzled the side of Amy's throat while she stirred and thrashed, excited, aroused, unable to hold still.

Continuing to kiss and caress her, Luiz skillfully maneuvered her farther into the dim stable, toward the room's center where scattered hay made a soft carpet on the plank wood floor. Pressing her steadily forward with his ungiving body, he kept her locked to him while Amy softly panted and wriggled and half fought against what she knew was going to happen.

They reached the middle of the barn. Luiz stopped and stood there unmoving, pressing soothing kisses to the struggling woman until she settled back against him in surrender and laid her head on his shoulder.

"When the mare no longer tries to flee or to

kick him"—Luiz spoke again—"the stud knows
that she is his and he covers her." His hands gently
squeezed her bare breasts and moved down to
her rib cage. "Are you mine?"

"I . . . yes. Yes, I'm yours."

"You'll let me take you like a stud covers a
mare? Let me make love to you in that position?"

Luiz fell silent then, holding his breath, waiting.
Her hands clutching frantically at the black twill
fabric stretching across his hard thighs, her head
lolling to one side, nervous breaths coming fast,
Amy finally whispered, "Yes. Yes. Take me like a
stallion takes a mare. Be my stud."

A deep, new surge of sexual excitement raced
though Luiz's lean body. Her words alone very
nearly brought on his shuddering release. He
stood there almost afraid to move. Then Amy
turned in his arms. Her hard-nippled breasts
brushed against his chest as her bare slender arms
came up around his neck.

She whispered in the darkness, "Will you show
me how? I'm not sure I know exactly. I never—"

"Ah, baby," he murmured, the blood scalding
through his veins. "I'll show you, sweetheart. I'll
show you."

For a long, frozen moment they stood looking at
each other. And then, as if by unspoken agreement, both took a step back and began hurriedly
undressing. While the black stallion continued his
manic sprinting and neighing outside in the
bright moonlight, the eager, excited couple in the
dim stable frantically stripped.

Unwanted clothing was peeled off and sailed
carelessly away. Luiz was totally naked within seconds and Amy was bare except for the long red

sash tied around her waist, a stubborn knot that refused to loosen. Making little sighing sounds of frustration, Amy looked to him for help. Luiz immediately swept her hands away and took over.

But the knotted sash was damp and refused to budge.

Luiz wasted no more time. He wound the long sash around his hand and drew her against him. He kissed her upturned face and said into her mouth, "It's all right. I'll take care of it."

He again turned her to face away from him. He slid the red sash around her narrow waist until the unyielding knot was at the small of her back. He drew the sash's long streamers behind his own back, crossed them, brought the ends around, and tied them at his waist.

He urged Amy close back against him. His face pressed into her golden hair, he said, "I like this. I like you tied to me."

"Me too," she whispered breathlessly, turning her face toward his. "Yes, me too."

Her eyes closed when Luiz's hand, warm and sure, moved down over her bare belly to the triangle of moist curls between her legs. For a sweet, brief time he simply cupped her, pressing her firmly back to the throbbing erection stirring against her bare bottom.

Then his long skilled fingers gently raked through the golden curls and Amy exhaled a long shuddering breath as he began caressing her in just the way he knew she most liked.

He had, on their first night in bed, easily found the key that unlocked her surprisingly fierce passions. Now, as his fingers touched that sensitive spot, he found it already swollen and silky wet.

"Sweet baby," he murmured. Placing a bare brown foot between her ankles, he nudged her feet farther apart. When there was ample room for both his feet between hers, he slowly urged her to her knees, going down with her.

Naked save for the crimson sash binding them together, they knelt there in the pale moonlight that spilled through the open stable door. Amy sighed with pleasure as Luiz's hot lips pressed kisses to her sensitive back and he murmured endearments in three languages—English, Spanish, and the Aztec tongue, Nahuatl.

The fire in her blood burned brightly. So brightly that when Luiz urged her over onto all fours, it seemed the most natural thing in the world, the ideal way to love and be loved. The red sash pulling tautly between them, Luiz knelt behind her, his heart hammering in his naked chest.

One hand settling on the curve of her hip, he gripped himself, slid the smooth, swollen tip of his throbbing masculinity into her waiting warmth.

Cautiously he sank into her. Both gasped with pleasure. He withdrew, almost completely, before thrusting once more. Deliberately taking it slow and easy, Luiz did not give her all of himself. Wary of hurting her, he slid only a little of his rigid length into her.

It was enough to make Amy want more. Rolling her hips in an unconscious effort to draw more of him inside her, Amy sighed and moaned and bowed her bare back, her breasts swaying back and forth with her excited movements. Frustrated, she suddenly became aware of Noche's savage whinnying just outside the door and heard the laughter and shouts of party guests who were no more than a hundred yards away up the incline.

Like a flash of heat lighting, reality washed over her. And with it, shock. Was this actually happening? Was she, Amy Sullivan Parnell, naked and on all fours, making love in a barn like an untamed animal while an excited stallion whickered a few feet from her and a hundred people were but a stone's throw away?

Luiz, sensitive to her every nuance, felt the change in her body and knew what had happened. And knew exactly what to do about it.

"There's no one in this world but the two of us, sweetheart. Nobody else." He kept his voice low and calm. But his temples throbbed and he was consumed by his feverish lust for her. "Just us, *querida.*"

Inch by inch he let himself sink more fully into her, increasing the length of his strokes, allowing his hardness to fill her completely. And driving away any worrisome traces of logical thought.

Amy's body and mind immediately responded. The stallion, the crowd, her misgivings faded away. There was nobody but the two of them, their slick bodies fitting together so perfectly, so deliciously.

Amy sighed and her hips began that rolling, rhythmic gyration that made the man linked to her groan with heightened pleasure and whisper his encouragement and praise. His was the only voice she heard.

The palms of her hands, her knees, and her toes crushing the hay on the floor, her unbound hair spilling into her eyes, Amy was like some wild, untamed being, totally lost in physical pleasure.

Her lover knew it, was inflamed by her absolute abandon, and longed to give her even more pleasure.

Luiz leaned forward, gripped Amy's shoulders and pulled her up. They knelt there together for an instant, with him still inside her while he told her how beautiful she was, how sweet. Then he sat back on his heels, bringing her with him, and spread his knees wide. He settled Amy's bare, soft bottom on his muscular thighs, placed a gentle hand around her throat, and urged her head back to his shoulder.

He said softly, "Never have you pleased me more." He brushed a kiss to her temple. "Never have I wanted to please you more."

"You please me." She sighed. "Too much."

"Never too much." His voice was low, husky. "Never enough."

"I—I couldn't stand any more pleasure," she told him, and meant it.

Then found out that she could.

While Luiz's gentle fingers stroked the graceful curve of her throat, he laid his free hand on her stomach. And he began to stroke the tiny line of barely visible golden fuzz that led from her navel downward. While he stroked, he continued to buck his pelvis rhythmically against her buttocks, plunging his painfully swollen maleness high up into her.

It was glorious.

Amy squirmed and panted and thrilled to the magic fingers stroking her throat, her belly, and to the awesomely hard male flesh so thoroughly impaling her. With the elevated pleasure came lowered inhibitions.

And with lowered inhibitions, the quest for even more pleasure. Turning her face into his, Amy whispered, "Do you really want to give me more pleasure?"

"I'll do anything to make it so, *querida.*"

"You know what I want you to do," she said brazenly.

He did know, but he told her, "I want to hear you say it. Ask me for it. You will get it."

Without shame or hesitation, Amy did just that. She said the words she'd never spoken. She asked him aloud and never knew how much it excited him. She gave a soft little wince of ecstasy when, promptly complying with her graphically spoken wish, Luiz put his hand between parted thighs, found that slick, distended little nub of ultra-sensitive female flesh, and began expertly caressing it.

"Ohhhhh . . . Luiz," Amy murmured. "Luiz, Luiz, Luiz."

"I know, baby. I know."

El Capitán Luiz Quintano sat on his bare heels on the hay-covered floor of Noche's stable and made hot, unorthodox love to Amy Parnell in the May moonlight. Sweat glistened on his bronzed body. His pelvis lifted and lowered, thrusting into her. His fingers stroked, coaxed, circled. His deep voice caressed, praised, encouraged.

Between murmured words of passion, he gritted his even white teeth, struggling to hold back his release until she was totally fulfilled.

Her sweet-scented hair whipping about in his face, her luscious, fevered body slipping and sliding so splendidly on his, her sweet childlike voice whispering his name was almost more than he could bear. He could not hold back much longer.

Amy began to breathe rapidly through her mouth and she gasped, "Noooo . . . Luiz . . . I . . ."

"Yes!" he persuaded, feeling her deep contractions starting, gripping him tightly. "Yes, baby, let it come. Let it come."

Seized by a joy so intense it was frightening, Amy couldn't have stopped it had she wanted. Her hot body out of control, she screamed out his name in her mounting ecstasy. It was the sweetest of sounds to Luiz. He could let himself go at last. He pumped madly into her, staying with her, giving her all he had. As her wild, wrenching climax was coming to an end, his own exploding release began and his loud groans of joy joined her dying cries of elation.

29

That same full May moon that shone on the two passionate lovers kneeling in a hay-strewn stable on Orilla spilled into a garishly decorated bedroom on San Francisco's rollicking Barbary Coast. While nymphs and satyrs of ivory plaster cavorted on the high ceiling above their heads, a flesh-and-blood nymph with coppery skin and raven hair frolicked with a debauched, insatiable golden-haired satyr.

His liquor-clouded blue eyes following every lewd movement of the dark-haired woman's supple body, the blond man sat naked on a red satin bed, his knees apart, a long cigar in one hand, a glass of Kentucky bourbon in the other.

The woman, at his command, danced for him. Had been dancing for more than an hour. She was hot and tired and rivers of perspiration washed over the ample curves of her copper-hued body. Her thick black hair, parted in the middle, fell to her hips and was tangled and damp. It slapped at her shiny face and shoulders as she spun and writhed and contorted her agile body into obscene poses for the blond man's benefit.

Her name was Nacori. A half-breed, she had been born twenty-four years ago to a fifteen-year-old Mimbreño Apache mother and a fifty-one-year-old English father who had come to America to head up a British-owned ranching operation.

Ranching proved not to be to Sir Alfred Whittington's taste, nor was the prospect of being father to an Indian child. When his young Apache companion's belly grew round with his child, Sir Alfred cast her out and sailed back to England where his sedate, horse-faced wife and family of five awaited.

The pregnant Apache girl wandered back to her people. Her baby was born in Chief Mangas Colorado's camp in northern Mexico and was cherished by his whole band. The child, Nacori, grew into a lovely girl and was sought after by the bravest of the young warriors.

Nacori's mother taught her the English she'd learned from the rancher, and told her of the fine home where she'd lived with Nacori's father, but warned her half-white daughter that only heartbreak awaited in that other world.

Married and widowed twice by the time she was twenty-two, Nacori longed to see for herself what the white world was like. In the darkness of a hot summer night, she stole away from camp. Unfortunately her path soon crossed that of a trio of Mescalero Apaches. They took her to their cool uplands camp high in the Chisos mountains. There their tall, lanky chief, a hideously ugly man they called Snake Tongue, took one look at the pretty, light-skinned woman and ordered his braves to bring her to his wickiup.

All Nacori's screams and protests fell on deaf ears. Within minutes of riding into camp, she found herself being pushed inside Chief Snake

Tongue's dim wickiup. Terrified, she blinked and spun about, searching for the tall, ugly man who had followed her inside.

The ghastly Mescalero chief with the beady black eyes, huge, bulbous nose, and slashing, grotesque mouth from which an incredibly long tongue habitually darted—hence his tribal name—was so close she could feel his body heat.

Nacori tensed. From out of the silence came the sound of his buckskin trousers being dropped to the floor. In seconds he stood before her, naked from the waist down, his ugly, frightening face now concealed behind an equally ugly, frightening devil's mask.

It was a hideous carved mask with horns made of deer antlers dipped in crimson, a long leather tongue and ferocious fangs, and eerie marble eyes with slits below to see through.

Frozen with horror, Nacori screamed when the chief roughly tore away her doeskin dress and undergarments. She fought for a time, but managed only to annoy him. His long, evil-looking tongue darting out over the limp leather tongue of the devil's mask, he flung Nacori atop a bed of buffalo furs and followed her down.

At the first touch of his long wet tongue on her bare left breast, Nacori spasmed in revulsion. It was only the beginning of a long, hot afternoon in which, inside the dim, tightly closed wickiup, the chief in his devil's mask slowly, methodically licked every inch of her writhing body.

When there was not one spot left—not the soles of her feet nor the palms of her hands nor the deep insides of her ears—that the chief had not thoroughly licked, he flopped over onto his back and ordered her to climb astride him. Willing to do almost anything to have the nightmare end, Nacori settled herself on the chief's straining member, ground her hips, and in seconds heard his shout of satisfaction.

Anxiously she slid off his body and was rising to her knees when he caught her and drew her back.

He said in Apache, "You will stay here with me. You will be my woman." When she wildly shook her head, he picked up a sharp knife, put it to her bare throat, and repeated, "You will be my woman."

From that day forward, Nacori was Chief Snake Tongue's woman. She was watched constantly. Everyone knew that the chief prized his woman for her fine looks and light skin. He was partial to light-skinned women. He had once captured a full-figured white woman and had so worshipped her, it was said he actually loved her to death. No one knew for sure what had really happened, but the white woman, after less than a year with the chief, had grown so thin and sickly it was no surprise when she died.

Nacori was of stronger stuff. She did not grow skinny. She did not get sick. She did not die, although there were times when she wished she was dead. She never let the chief know how she felt. She cleverly pretended, within weeks of her capture, that she was mad about the ugly, depraved chief.

Steeling herself, she became constantly affectionate to the man whose tall, bronzed body was a study in male perfection, but whose face was repulsive. She pretended she couldn't stand having him out of her sight. She followed him about as a worshipping dog might, her adoring gaze always fixed on his monstrous face.

When with him in the privacy of their wickiup, she indulged his every perversion as if she enjoyed it. She lay sighing and moaning for hours at a time, feigning pleasure while he licked her as if he would never get enough.

Nacori remained with Chief Snake Tongue for eighteen months before she finally got a clear opportunity for escape. The entire band was convinced of her devotion to the chief, so well had she played her part. And so, on a cloudy gray day in January, after spending the long afternoon coddling the naked chief, Nacori stole from his arms as he lay napping, hurriedly dressed, and walked, unchallenged, right out of the camp.

Her heart pounding with hope and excitement, she easily cut the fastest pony out of the remuda, climbed on its bare back, and rode down out of the hills.

It took more than two months to reach San Francisco, but that was where Nacori had always dreamed of going. It was one of the few cities she had heard of. She loved the big, noisy place at once and, seeing all the finely dressed gentlemen crowding the wooden sidewalks, Nacori was resolved to so beguile one of the rich dandies that he would beg her to be his wife.

On her first night in the teeming city, she met the man of her dreams. A tall, good-looking dandy with vivid blue eyes and gleaming blond hair came strolling out of a place called El Dorado, practically bumping into Nacori.

He flashed her a dazzling smile and Nacori felt her heartbeat quicken. When he politely took her arm and asked if she'd like to go inside with him, she couldn't believe her good fortune.

"Yes. Yes, I would," Nacori tried to enunciate the words distinctly so that he wouldn't know she'd spent all her days in the wilderness with uncivilized savages. She suddenly hated the soft doeskin dress she wore and decided, as he took her arm to guide her inside, that she would cut off her long black hair and dress it some fancy way atop her head.

Inside Nacori's lips fell open in wonder. She'd never seen anything so grand in all her life. They stood in a large, square room, the walls covered with costly paintings of pale nude women in suggestively abandoned postures. The furniture was dark mahogany, the lights above their heads sparkling crystal chandeliers. At one end was a raised platform draped with bunting and colored streamers. An orchestra played loudly from atop the platform.

At the other end was a bar and behind it were huge mirrors of cut glass. Scattered throughout the room were gaming tables on which huge stacks of gold and silver coins rested. Behind each table sat a dealer, nattily clad in black and white.

Awed by the riches surrounding her, Nacori clung to her tall blond gentleman's arm and followed him to the far side of the crowded room. He reached out, swept back a curtain of scarlet muslin, and handed her inside a small private booth with a long low couch.

Without a word he shrugged out of his tailored gray suit jacket and began unbuttoning his white shirt.

Nacori blinked at him, but asked, "You wish me to be your woman?"

"Yes," he said, and smiled at her, a smile so radiant, Nacori was filled with happiness. He failed to add that he wanted her to be his woman only for the next fifteen minutes.

Half an hour later, when he was buttoning his trousers, Nacori sprang naked from the couch and said, "You will take me with you to your mansion?"

He chuckled and told her, "Darlin', the only mansion I have is a rundown old hacienda in southwest Texas. If I ever go back there, I'll take you with me."

Now, five months later, Nacori knew all about her lover's Texas home, had questioned him at length when he was drunk and in a talkative mood. She dreamed of returning there with him one day to be the mistress of his big mansion, to present him with beautiful blue-eyed children.

That the possibility of such an occurrence was remote did not dampen Nacori's fond daydreams. Not did the fact that her beautiful lover had so little money that she was called on to sell her body to many of the fine gentlemen who gambled at El Dorado or the Parker House or the Empire or the Arcade or any one of a dozen gaming palaces on the Barbary Coast.

She didn't mind so much. For the most part the gentlemen were clean and smelled nice, and they were generally easy to please. Entertaining a different one every night was not half as bad as when she'd spent all her dreadful nights with the horrid Chief Snake Tongue.

And besides, the money she made had afforded

them this fancy hotel room with its red satin bed and red-and-gold flocked walls as well as the custom-cut suits for her blond gentleman lover. Soon all this would be behind them.

Earlier this evening, as Nacori entertained a big, raw-boned Texan, she had learned some thrilling news, news she would share with her lover as soon as he allowed her to stop dancing.

At last her handsome blond sweetheart snapped his fingers loudly. Nacori ceased dancing, her limbs weak, her body drenched with sweat.

She smiled and said, "My love, I have exciting news for you!"

"Later," he said. "Can't you see I'm in no mood for talk."

Nacori nodded happily and came to him. She started to put her arms around his neck, but he stopped her.

"On your knees," he ordered. She obeyed, sinking immediately to the carpeted floor between his spread legs. She heard his loud groan of pleasure when she clasped him with her hands, licked her dry lips, and then enclosed him in her wet, warm mouth.

Afterward, she wiped her mouth across her forearm and said, "Now may I tell you my news?"

He smiled at her, twined his fingers through her wild hair, and said, "Tell me."

Nacori told him what she had heard. That a customer, familiar with the land and the people of southwest Texas, had heard that his huge ranch, the Orilla, was again prospering. A half-breed Spaniard had led a troop of Mexican soldiers onto the ranch and had taken it over. A long dried up underground river was running again, grass was growing, cattle were getting fat.

She talked and talked and he listened with more interest than he'd ever shown before, his blue eyes narrowed in concentration.

Her hands affectionately rubbing his hair-dusted thighs, Nacori asked, "Will we go there now? Will we return to your big hacienda and be rich landowners? Will I have fine dresses and jewels and satin-lined bassinets for our children? Will I?"

"Will you . . . what? I wasn't listening."

"Baron, my only darling, will we go back to Orilla now?"

His fingers left her tangled hair. He brushed her hands from his thighs. He callously pushed her away with a foot to her chest. He stood up and said, "*I* may go back to Orilla. You? You think I'd take a half-breed whore home to Texas?"

Her face framed in a patch of shimmering moonlight, she stared at him. Hot tears sprang to her eyes and washed down her smooth copper cheeks.

"But I thought . . . what . . . what shall I do?"

Baron Sullivan put his hands on his knees, leaned down so that his face was inches from hers.

"You could always go back to Snake Tongue," he said, the square of bright May moonlight capturing his smiling face and making a silvery crown of his shiny blond hair.

Fifteen hundred miles away, high in the Chisos Mountains of Texas, that same bright May moonlight shone down on the high meadow camp of a small band of Mescalero Apaches.

It was well past midnight. The camp was silent and peaceful. The Apache families were inside their wickiups, sleeping soundly.

Chief Snake Tongue was not inside his wickiup nor was he sleeping soundly. He was at camp's edge, beside a gurgling stream. He was stretched out naked in the shimmering moonlight with a pretty, young Apache woman.

The chief was wide awake, and he was unhappy.

The woman was one of the camp's prettiest young maidens, but she did not please him. Any more than the three others who had—one at a time—come and gone from his wickiup earlier in the evening.

When, unsatisfied, he had sent the last woman away, one of his braves had reminded him of the full, white moon, then quickly suggested that the chief take a woman he'd not yet had out in the meadow beside the stream. Beneath the high, full moon, she would appear almost as a white woman.

"Yes!" the chief had said excitedly. "Her skin will be pale white. Who will it be? Who have I not had? Who is pretty enough?"

The brave who had made the clever suggestion spoke up. "My sister, Doe Eyes, is thought to be fair to look on. She would be honored to have this opportunity to please you."

"Wake Doe Eyes and send her to me at once!"

Now, lying on a blanket in a patch of day-bright moonlight, Chief Snake Tongue was annoyed. He had spent more than an hour with Doe Eyes. She had cheerfully offered her body for his pleasure, had willingly done everything he had asked of her.

She *was* a pretty girl and her firm, melon breasts and strong thighs were good to look on and to taste, but he was not satisfied. Although the moonlight made her appear appealingly lighter than she was, it was not enough. She was still very much an Indian woman with dark skin and dark hair and a submissive attitude.

Abruptly Chief Snake Tongue stopped licking Doe Eye's toes. He dropped her foot heavily to the blanket and ordered her to leave. Hurt and disappointed, Doe Eyes gathered her discarded clothing and went running in tears back to her wickiup.

Moments later the entire camp was shocked awake by the sound of a bugle blaring in the night. Alert warriors reached for their guns and raced outside, and frightened women drew their children around them and waited.

Casting a black outline against the moonlit sky, Chief Snake Tongue, wearing his devil's mask, blew on the old bugle taken in a long-ago raid on white soldiers. When he blew on his bugle, it was the signal for every man in camp to drop what he was doing and swiftly assemble before their chief.

Snake Tongue lowered the bugle.

He stood, his feet apart, the marble eyes of his mask glittering, the red horns appearing almost black. He darted his long tongue out atop the mask's leather tongue, making him look like a horned devil with two tongues.

Suddenly he threw his horn down. He snatched off his devil's mask and slammed it to the ground.

Locking his hands behind his back, the chief marched back and forth before his waiting men. As he marched, he told them that he was not a content man. Told them that he was never going to be fully content until he had what he wanted.

The chief stopped pacing. He darted his tongue out of his slashed mouth several times. Then he gave them their orders.

"Bring me a white woman. I don't care where you get her. Snatch a settler's daughter. Attack a stagecoach. Steal a rancher's wife. I want a pretty white woman with silky yellow hair and skin as white as milk."

The braves all muttered and shuffled and looked at each other.

The chief's voice raised to a eye-squinting shout. "Get me a white woman!"

30

Amy was awakened the next morning by the touch of warm May sunshine on her face. Wondering why she was so incredibly thirsty, and why she had such a terrible headache, she slowly opened her eyes. Pushing her tangled hair off her face and rising on one elbow, she groggily looked around.

She was alone in the master suite. Naked on the big white bed swept clean of pillows and covers, exactly as she was each morning. Except that the sun was higher and hotter. She had obviously overslept.

Swinging her long, slender legs to the carpeted floor, Amy reached for a silver pitcher of cool water on the night table, searched in vain for a glass, shrugged bare shoulders, turned up the pitcher, and drank thirstily.

Sighing, she then lifted the silver pitcher higher, carefully rolled it back and forth across her pounding forehead, then lowered it and pressed it to her breasts and bare midriff. The touch of the cold silver against her too-warm flesh made her gasp and quiver.

It also shocked her into remembering.

Everything.

Amy's eyes widened in horror and her lips automatically formed the word no, though no sound came. Hugging the icy-cold pitcher to her, she shivered and shook her head and tried desperately to deny what had happened. She'd had a dream; that was it. She hadn't . . . she would never have . . . oh, my God. . . .

A tiny straw of hay fell from Amy's tumbled hair.

Amy recalled reading alone in the *sala* and looking up to see El Capitán standing in the archway. Dressing hurriedly and going out to the celebration. His taking her in his arms for a dance and telling her there was so little time. Making her assume that he was leaving.

The bastard! He had purposely led her to believe that he had been ordered back into battle. Had made her think that he would be gone with the sun and she'd never see him again. He'd planned the whole thing! He had arrogantly supposed that if she thought he was leaving, she'd let down her guard entirely and . . . and . . .

More memories rushed in.

Licking salt from El Capitán's hand and he from hers. Dancing again and again with him, forgetting anyone else existed. Tied to him . . . with a handkerchief. The heat of the bonfire making them hot. Perspiring profusely. Leaving the party and . . . and . . .

With shaking hands Amy carefully placed the silver pitcher back on the night table. She pressed her trembling knees tightly together and hugged her arms to her sides. She shut her eyes and felt a sob of despair building in her tight throat.

Behind closed eyelids, she saw a shameless pair of human beings, naked and bound together with a red silk sash, mating in the hay on the stable floor, exactly like animals.

The strangled sob tore from Amy's throat.

They *were* animals. *She* was an animal. There in the arms of El Capitán—a man who openly held her in contempt—she was a shameless animal. Why? What was wrong with her? Could her sanity have totally departed?

Dear God, what am I going to do? I am trapped in this unending nightmare!

For the first time, Amy noticed the neatly folded yellow dispatch lying on the night table beside the silver pitcher. She knew immediately what it was. El Capitán's orders. The orders she'd searched for in vain.

Amy's delicate jaw hardened as she reached for the dispatch. Quickly she read it. Sure enough, El Capitán had been ordered to remain at his present post. Rage rose red hot in Amy. He'd left the dispatch there to mock her.

Again he had made a fool of her. Again he had shown her that against him she was powerless. He could make her do anything, say anything, be anything he wanted.

Trembling with self-loathing, Amy laid the yellow Juarez dispatch back on the night table and rose to her feet. Suddenly it came to her that she must get away this minute. He was *not* going to leave, so she had to! She couldn't spend one more night on Orilla.

Amy hurried to the dressing room. She badly needed a bath, but there was no time. By the slant of the sunlight coming in her room, it was surely midmorning. El Capitán would return any minute, walk right in while she bathed, pull her to her feet, and . . .

Amy dressed as quickly as possible. She yanked a carpet bag down from a shelf and hastily stuffed extra clothes and underwear into it. Then realized she couldn't take anything without raising suspicions. Her heart thumping against her ribs, she peered out into the hall and, seeing no one, stepped outside. She fairly flew down the stairs and through the empty dining room.

Amy hadn't counted on Pedrico being in the kitchen with Magdelena. Her face turned crimson when she saw the pair drinking coffee at the table. She felt like a naughty child about to be lectured.

But instead they both smiled warmly, and their eyes twinkled as if they fully approved of her behavior. Perhaps they didn't know. Maybe they, like everyone else, had been having such a good time last night, they never noticed when she and El Capitán slipped away to the stables.

"Good morning," she said with as much composure as she could muster.

"Señora Amy." Pedrico politely rose from his chair.

"You need a big breakfast today," said Magdelena, chuckling as she poured a cup of steaming black coffee. Handing it to Amy, she told her, "I will fix you a special—"

"I'm not hungry," Amy interrupted. She glanced nervously about and added, "I . . . ah . . . thought I'd go into town this morning." She took the cup of coffee.

Magdelena's hands went to her hips. "Why you go into Sundown? We need nothing. There is so much food left from the fiesta we will never eat it all."

"Yes, I know." Amy kept her voice level. "I was thinking . . . You could fill a small hamper with the leftovers and I'll take it to Mac and his family."

"You need rest, you look like . . . like . . ." Magdelena lowered her eyes for a second. Then said: "You sure you feel up to going into town?"

"I feel fine," Amy snapped. She turned her attention to Pedrico. "You'll drive me?"

"El Capitán has gone for a ride," Pedrico said, smiling. "As soon as he returns, I will drive you to Sundown."

"No!" Amy declared irritably. "I do *not* want to wait until El Capitán gets back. I want to go now."

"But, *señora*, why the hurry? If you will just—"

"I am going into Sundown, Pedrico. If you refuse to drive me, then I will drive myself!"

Pedrico and Magdelena exchanged glances. Magdelena said, "He will drive you if you insist. I'll pack the food; it will not take a minute."

Not half an hour after Amy and Pedrico had driven away from the hacienda, El Capitán, astride his big stallion, returned from his morning ride. After dismounting, he led Noche into his special corral, holding the long leather reins in one hand, a brilliant bouquet of orange Mexican poppies in the other.

One-handed, Luiz removed the barebacked stallion's bridle and stepped inside the dim barn to hang it on a peg. Blinking to focus, Luiz stepped farther into the barn. His eyes fell on something lying on the hay.

Carefully he laid his bouquet of poppies aside,

stepped forward, and crouched down on his heels. His dark face broke into a smile of pleasure as he reached for the shimmering red silk sash. A sash that had been cut into.

His fingers toying with the ruined silk, he draped it across one knee and fondly rubbed it as a sweetly erotic vision flashed through his mind.

A naked, beautiful Amy on all fours in the hay, the long red sash tied around her waist and around his own as they made love.

Later, still tied together with the silk sash, they had lain in the hay touching and kissing until they wanted each other again. They began making love, this time facing each other, Amy beneath him. Face to face. Eye to eye. Heart to heart.

The sash had pulled and bound and grown uncomfortable.

"Cut it," she had whispered, her lovely eyes looking into his, her silky legs wrapped around him. "Cut the sash, darling." She thrust her pelvis up to his. "We'll still be bound together."

He had removed a knife from his discarded boot and sliced the lovely sash away from her slender waist. Then she had taken the knife from him, slipped its point under the red silk tightly pulling against his ribs, and severed it.

Now, as Luiz slowly rose to his feet, he carefully folded the butchered sash, opened the middle button of his shirt, and slipped it inside. His eyes shone with amusement as he stepped out of the stable into the bright sunshine. Crossing the sandy lot, he stopped abruptly, snapped his fingers, turned, and hurried back inside.

He stooped and picked up the bouquet of vivid orange poppies. Flowers he had picked for Amy.

When he crossed the west stone patio, Luiz felt like an excited young boy. Looking nervously about inside the wide corridor, he heavily exhaled with relief to find it deserted. He climbed the stairs, taking them two at time, his heart beginning to beat erratically.

Outside the heavy carved bedroom door, he raked long fingers through his thick black hair, looked down to check his appearance, and lifted his hand to knock.

Then lowered it without doing so.

After turning the knob, he silently stepped inside, then closed the door behind him. His eyes went at once to a big white bed. Seeing it empty, he frowned. But his smile quickly returned.

Amy was probably soaking in the tub after the night they'd shared. He could think of no better way to spend the remainder of the morning than watching her bathe leisurely.

Gripping the Mexican poppies in both hands, Luiz crossed the room, softly calling her name. But when he reached the white marble bath, he saw only his own reflection in the mirrored walls. The tub was empty.

The slightest trace of unease took the edge off his feeling of well-being. His hands fell to his sides as the premonition that she was gone gripped him. He turned on his heel and went back into the bedroom. Nervously tapping his thigh with the bouquet he stood beside the rumpled bed, remembering how the two of them had quietly climbed the back stairs at five that morning, half dressed, laughing, eager to get into their bed.

His black eyes narrowed. Luiz bent and plucked a tiny piece of straw from the white silk sheet. He tossed the bouquet of poppies on the bed and went downstairs to find Amy.

And knew that he would not.

Amy wasted no time. As soon as Pedrico had pulled up in front of Mac's big general store, she was out of the buggy and on the wooden sidewalk, saying "You needn't come in. This will take a while."

Not waiting for a reply, she dashed inside, relieved to see none of El Capitán's troops. She caught sight of Mac behind a counter, hurried over, and asked the big Irishman if his oldest son, Raul, could run an errand for her.

Mac laughed good-naturedly. "If you can wake him. He's asleep in the sun out behind the store. Where did his mother and I go wrong?" He laughed and Amy laughed with him as she turned and hurried away.

Amy anxiously shook eleven-year-old Raul awake. The boy rubbed his eyes and blinked, but listened as Amy told him to go at once to the livery stable, hire the best horse they had, see that it was saddled, and bring it right back to the rear of the store. She pressed money into his palm.

The barefoot boy took off running and was back within minutes, leading a powerful-looking saddled roan gelding. Pleased, Amy took a shiny gold coin from her reticule, handed it to Raul, and said, "This is yours if you will do me one last favor."

"*Sí, señora?*"

"Go back to sleep."

"Ah, *sí, sí.*" Raul shoved the gold coin into his pants pocket, curled up like a cat in the sun, and closed his eyes. But he opened one eye into a slit and watched as Amy mounted the roan and rode away toward the west. When the sound of hoofbeats and the dust kicked up by the roan had disappeared, Raul yawned, touched the gold coin in his pocket, and went back to sleep.

Two hours later a worried, remorseful Pedrico Valdez returned to the ranch. Standing in the buggy and applying the whip to the tired team, he flew through Orilla's tall white archway.

El Capitán, immaculate in a snowy white shirt, sky-blue uniform trousers, and gleaming black boots, paced back and forth on the shaded west patio. He had been pacing for the past hour. He saw the cloud of dust on the horizon and felt his heart lurch in his chest.

Arms crossed, feet apart, he was waiting in the drive when Pedrico brought the horses to a plunging halt in the gravel. El Capitán stepped forward to meet his lieutenant.

"*Dios*, Capitán! It is all my fault. I should never have—"

"Lieutenant Valdez," Luiz calmly cut in, "tell me what has happened."

"She's gone!" Pedrico shouted apologetically. "I drove her to Sundown against your wishes and Señora Parnell is gone!"

Conditioned to conceal his innermost emotions, Luiz said evenly, "Come, *amigo*. You need a drink. Then you will tell me all."

Pedrico did just that. He listened intently as El Capitán issued orders in a low, level voice.

"Have one of Orilla's fastest horses saddled."

"You do not wish to ride Noche?"

Luiz shook his head. "No. Apaches' don't shoe

their horses, *amigo*. Noche is shod. Make my mount a paint."

"Dios!" Pedrico hurriedly crossed himself.

"Gather supplies—blankets, extra clothes, candles, water, weapons. Go now!"

Minutes later El Capitán came downstairs. He was out of uniform. A pair of soft buckskin trousers clung to his lean flanks and long legs. A matching buckskin shirt with fringe around the yoke and down the sleeves stretched across his wide shoulders. A low-riding gunbelt was buckled around his slim hips, a Colt .44 in the holster. His knee-high black boots had been replaced with a pair of soft brown cowboy boots. A neckerchief of vivid blue was tied at his throat.

Wringing her hands and crying, Magdelena followed him out of the house and onto the porch. He turned and said, "Stay here, Magdelena. And stop worrying. I'll bring her back."

Unable to speak, the weeping, heavyset woman lifted the tail of her apron, wiped her red eyes, and watched the tall buckskin-clad man move down the front walk to the drive.

"Let me search with you?" Pedrico asked as Luiz mounted the big paint pony.

"No, my friend." Luiz looked down at the older man's pain-etched face. "You must be in command here until I return."

Pedrico objected. "I am not trustworthy, Capitán."

Luiz leaned down from the horse, gripped the older man's shoulder, and said, "No man on earth is more trustworthy, *amigo.*"

Before Pedrico could reply, Luiz righted himself, wheeled the paint about, and kicked him into a trot. Pedrico stood looking after him, tears blurring the vision of his one eye. He blinked and tried to swallow the growing lump in his throat.

A gentle hand touched his shoulder. He turned his head and saw Magdelena standing beside him. Wordlessly his arm went around her shoulders and they stood there clinging to each other.

Watching until they could no longer see El Capitán. Then they turned and went back inside.

31

Her long blue skirts billowing in the wind, Amy beat it out of Sundown atop the big roan gelding. Never looking back, she slapped the long reins from side to side and violently kicked the mount's flanks. Leaning low over his neck, she raced him across the barren desertland, the rapid beating of her heart in tempo with his sharp hooves striking the packed earth.

She didn't slow the pace until the peaceful little village of Sundown had been left far behind. Only then did she pull up, bringing the well-trained horse to halt atop a broad, barren mesa, two miles west of town. While the horse shook his head about and danced restlessly in place, Amy stood in the stirrups and lifted a hand to shade her eyes against the glare of the noonday sun.

Reining the roan around in a slow deliberate circle, she carefully pondered which way she should ride. She had her final destination firmly in mind: New Orleans, Louisiana. She would take the train to Galveston, then hop a riverboat to New Orleans. She'd go to her Aunt Meg and daughter Linda and stay there until the cruel El Capitán and his troop left *Orilla*. Poor Magdelena would be frantic . . . she'd worry about that later.

Amy looked about.

Far to the west, on the Mexican border, was Paso del Norte. To the north was the Guadalupe mountain range with the highest peak in all Texas, ironically called El Capitán. Amy shuddered and quickly turned away from its stark, cold summit. To the east lay the town of Pecos, Texas. South was the Davis mountains and the Big Bend of the Rio Grande. And the Mescalero Apaches.

Amy sighed with indecision.

East or west? If she chose Paso del Norte she'd lose precious time traveling in the wrong direction. But if she headed east to the small town of Pecos, she might be noticed and reported to El Capitán when his search for her began. Nobody would pay her any attention in the wild border town of Paso del Norte. She could likely board an eastbound train as soon as she got there.

Amy turned the horse in full circle, again kicked him into a gallop, and headed west. She was a long way from Paso del Norte—at least sixty miles. Still, she figured if she rode hard and stopped for only short periods of time to water and rest the roan, she would reach The Pass within twenty-four hours.

She rode through the thick silence of the afternoon, her head throbbing, her back aching. The sun's harsh rays burned her fair skin and the dust made her eyes sting and water. She was hungry; she'd not eaten since yesterday at lunch. Worse, she was terribly thirsty, and she had no water. By the sound of the blowing, lathered roan, he too was thirsty.

Silently Amy promised herself and the winded gelding that if they kept going, she would soon spot a ranchhouse located on some remote rise of land. Or a shallow water hole. No need for worry.

On she rode.

The sun had lost some of its sting and was starting its slow descent toward the western horizon when Amy caught a glimpse of something moving in her side vision. She turned and looked to the south, never slowing the roan's steady pace.

At first she thought it was only a fast-moving dust devil swirling up out of the burning sands. But the cloud of dust grew larger, moved closer, and finally horses emerged from out of the whirlwind. Amy immediately began slowing the roan, her parched throat already tasting the nice cool water from canteens the riders surely carried.

The contingent thundered closer and Amy's lips fell open in astonishment. For a split second she was totally paralyzed with fear and disbelief. The riders racing toward her were not dressed in chaps and boots and big sombreros. They wore breechcloths and moccasins and feathers in their long black hair.

Apaches!

Her heart seemed as if it would pound its way out of her chest, and Amy's brain screamed for her useless feet and hands to work, but they did not obey. It seemed an eternity that she sat immobile as the warriors closed in on her, the one in the lead opening his mouth to give a long, wailing cry for attack.

Amy screamed and kicked her mount into movement. Across the barren tablelands she raced, her cumbersome skirts flying up into her face, her heels digging into the gelding's belly. She didn't dare look back but knew by the sounds of their horse's pounding hooves and their blood-curdling shrieks that the band of savages was rapidly gaining on her.

The lathered roan gave his best, leaping narrow washes and whipping around scrubby mesquites that scratched Amy's arms and legs. When they reached a wide, shallow ravine, the roan plunged down into it, his hooves flinging up clods of soft, sandy soil. The valiant gelding was struggling up the far side when one of the riders spurred his swift paint into a flying run that lifted it in a wide-reaching jump across the ravine.

The Apache's arm shot out. He grabbed the roan's bit and pulled his head forcefully down. The roan continued his efforts, his forelegs pawing at the sandy incline as he struggled to lunge to its top. Amy had not given up either. She shouted to the laboring roan, kicked his heaving sides, and jerked frantically on the reins, trying to loosen them from the red man's tight grip.

When an arm of steel came around her waist, Amy screamed at the top of her lungs. Tenaciously clinging to the reins, she was pulled from the roan, onto a prancing pony, and crushed to the sweaty, naked chest of a stocky warrior. The Indian backed his pony away with Amy still gripping her mount's reins. Big-eyed and frightened, the roan stumbled and neighed wildly until a knife flashed in the bright sunlight, the straining reins were cut, and Amy was left holding nothing but two useless strips of leather.

Her head banged against her captor's jaw as he wheeled his mount around. Squirming impo-

tently within the brave's clasping arm, Amy
clawed at his chest and shoulders and kicked her
feet and screamed at him to release her.

He did not.

He held her easily in one strong arm as his horse
lunged into a hard, fast run. Soon the other half-
dozen shouting, laughing braves caught up with
them. Racing alongside, they stared at Amy, glee-
fully examining the fighting, screaming white
woman.

They were excited and very surprised to have
found her riding alone in the desert. All were well
pleased with the pale good looks of their terrified,
yellow-haired captive. They nodded to each other
and grinned. Happy with their good fortune, they
jubilantly raced across the dusty flats toward the
cool blue mountains rising majestically against the
violet evening sky.

Their home was on the far side of those rugged
mountains. It was there they were taking the
pretty white woman. They would ride until they
reached the remote alpine camp where their impatient warrior chief waited for delivery of the
pale-skinned, yellow-haired woman he could
make his own.

Chief Snake Tongue.

Luiz rode directly into Sundown and Mac's
store.

Assuring the worried Irishman that everything
was fine, Luiz patiently questioned Mac's young
son. He smiled and ruffled the boy's dark hair
when Raul had told all he knew. All except about
the shiny gold coin buried deep in his pocket.

Thanking father and son, Luiz crouched down

on his heels and studied the shoe marks the hired roan's hooves had left in the sand behind the store. Young Raul squatted down beside him.

"*Señor,*" Raul said, pointing his forefinger, "you see that tiny Y at the right base of each shoe. Yancy the blacksmith give it to all the horses he shoes. That will help, no?"

"That will help, *sí,*" Luiz said, and came to his feet.

Without another word he swung up into the saddle and rode away. It was easy to follow the roan's tracks in that parched, desolate land. Luiz spurred the big paint into a rapid gallop, glancing down occasionally to make sure Amy hadn't suddenly changed directions.

The distinctive hoofprints made a clear trail due west. Relieved she had ridden in that direction, Luiz knew she was heading for Paso del Norte. He figured she had a good two-hour head start on him, but knew he could overtake her. The Pass was sixty miles away. She couldn't stay in the saddle forever.

He could.

And he would. He wouldn't dismount until he had found her. The range-bred paint he rode had the stamina to maintain a punishing pace for hour upon hour. With any luck, he'd find the foolish, fleeing woman before sunset.

Luiz's jaw hardened and his unblinking eyes narrowed. He was more angry than he was worried. And he was more angry with himself than he was with Amy Parnell. The woman he pursued across the parched prairie had again made a fool of him, just as she had all those years ago.

Would he never learn?

Would he never get it through his head that she was a beautiful, conniving temptress who cared nothing for him? That even as she'd lain in his arms last night and called him darling and cried out in her ecstasy, she had done so to throw him off guard so she could run away?

If she wanted to be away from him that badly, perhaps he should let her go. Maybe he should turn back. What difference did it make? What difference did she make?

None. Amy Parnell was a woman like any other; he'd had dozens as beautiful. There'd be dozens more. He need not spend one night alone if he never got her back. The exotic San Antonio flamenco dancer was still in Sundown. A couple of the young, pretty house servants looked at him with unveiled interest. And then there was the bold, rich Diana Clayton. The day at the La Posada when he'd commented on her stylish gown, Miss Clayton had made it clear she would be more than willing to slip right out of it.

Why ride one more mile? Let Mrs. Parnell go where she pleased. Let her stay forever or return when she wanted. Who cared? He had what he wanted. What he had come back for. What was rightfully his. Orilla.

On he rode.

Black eyes squinting against the savage glare of the Texas sun, Luiz held the long reins looped slackly around his hand. His palm rested on his hard belly, thumb stuck down inside the low riding gunbelt. Lulled by the desert quiet and the monotony, and tired from a night of strenuous lovemaking, Luiz closed his burning eyes and slouched comfortably in the saddle. Confident

Amy's trail led straight on to the pass, he relaxed his body and soon dozed.

The sun went down.

A pale pink gloaming lingered in the west behind the distant Franklin mountain range of the towering southern Rockies. Luiz was suddenly jolted awake when the big paint leapt a wide, shallow ravine, his hind legs coming down inches shy of the rim. Hugging the paint with his knees, Luiz remained in the saddle, but he was again wide awake and keenly alert.

The paint bolted forward, cleared the ravine, and galloped on as if he had never broken stride. The man mounted on his back flicked a hurried glance down at the ground and abruptly pulled the paint up as his eyes widened in alarm.

There were no tracks on the desert sand.

Amy screamed until she was so hoarse she could no longer make a sound. She clawed and kicked until she was too exhausted to lift her tired arms or move her weak legs. When her stocky Apache captor shifted her in his arms and cradled her to his massive chest, the effort to lift her head was too great. Amy couldn't do it.

As the sun died and darkness enveloped the desert, Amy's mouth and nose were pressed against the Apache renegade's bare chest, the offensive odor of his unwashed flesh causing her stomach to churn and roll violently. Gagging reflexively, Amy tried to speak, to say that she was ill. But her voice would not work and she was forced to swallow back the hot bile that poured into her raw, burning throat.

New tears sprang to her red-rimmed eyes as

suddenly she was overwhelmed by the contrast of this huge Apache's horrid smell with that of the clean, unique scent of El Capitán. The agonizing thought occurred to her that in last night's darkness she had eagerly pressed kisses to El Capitán's smooth, naked chest, relishing the smell and the taste of his bronzed skin. If she had not so enjoyed being in his arms, she would not now be in the arms of a dirty, uncivilized renegade in tonight's darkness.

Amy squeezed her tear-filled eyes tightly shut. She continued to swallow and to retch helplessly. She attempted to take only shallow breaths so that she would not smell so strongly the stale sweat and woodsmoke and grease of the bare chest beneath her cheek.

Finally the worst of her nausea passed, and with it a little of her strength returned. Enough that she could turn her head away and draw long, refreshing breaths of the cooling desert air.

The sun had gone completely down. Stars filled the night sky and a big, white moon sailed high in the heavens. They were riding fast toward the southeast and already the terrain was changing. The flatness of the desert was giving way to the broken butte country leading into the Big Bend.

Fort Davis was the farthest south Amy had ever been in that wild, immense triangle of Texas bordered by the Rio Grande. There were rangelands surrounding the fort and a few scattered, remote ranches. But beyond the cool, blue Davis range, the rugged Santiago Mountains sliced across the region from northwest to southeast. And on the other side, the true badlands began.

Few white men had dared venture south of the

Santiagos into that uncharted wilderness of rock and desert and mountains. It was said there were canyons so deep and so wide, a man lost inside could roam forever and not find his way out. Indians, outlaws, mountain lions, jaguars, wild horses, and rattlesnakes inhabited the Big Bend of Texas.

None of the species was friendly.

Amy's desperation grew when her stocky Apache captor urged the big paint pony up a rocky outcropping. They were heading up into the foothills of the Davis Mountains. Once these savages had taken her into the Big Bend, all hope would be gone.

Amy didn't want to die down there. No one would ever know what had happened to her. Her darling Linda would have no idea what had happened to her mother. Her bleached bones would never be found and brought back to her beloved Orilla.

Fear and despair giving her a fresh surge of energy, Amy whipped her head around and shouted into her captor's face, "No! Don't take me across the mountains. Stop and kill me here!"

The silent Apache never even glanced down at her. He calmly continued to rein his paint up a long rocky trail as if he had not heard her speak. The horse turned a sharp corner into a narrow arroyo and the bright moonlight abruptly disappeared. Suddenly it was pitch black. Amy could see absolutely nothing. She felt as if she would suffocate.

She heard only the sound of falling pebbles, dislodged by the horses' hooves, and the mad fluttering of a frightened canyon wren. Panic seizing her, Amy, for the first time, considered the horrifying possibility that the Apaches might not mean to kill her. If that was their intent, what were they waiting for?

They had left the open desert and the danger of being apprehended. They need not wait longer. It was dark and they were already entering country so rugged they could leisurely kill her. No one would come along. Fort Davis had been abandoned since the early days of the war; blue-coated soldiers no longer patrolled the region.

They were taking her to their home! Dear God, did they mean to keep her alive? To hold her captive for the rest of her life?

The paint emerged from the thick darkness of the canyon and Amy's breath exploded from her tight chest.

"Please," she pleaded, the bright moonlight offering a degree of comfort, "don't take me to your camp. Have the decency to kill me on this side of the mountains."

No reply. Not a flicker of an eyelash.

Anger swiftly mixing with her terror, Amy doubled up her fist and socked the silent Indian in the stomach. He grunted. And finally looked down at her, his eyebrows drawn together.

"Kill me, damn you," Amy cried, her hoarseness making it hard to shout. "You hear me? Kill me right here, right now. Kill me, take my scalp and go. But leave me here!"

He stared at her, frowning slightly, but making not one sound.

Frantic, Amy raged on. "I want to be buried at home. Surely even you can understand that. When one of your people is killed in battle, you don't leave him behind, do you? Don't you take

him home to bury him? Please . . . please don't
take me down into the Big Bend."

She fell silent, but continued to look directly
into his flat, expressionless eyes, hoping he had
understood, praying that he would grant her wish.
After what seemed an eternity of waiting for a
reply, Amy again shouted at the Apache.

Finally she got a response.

He clamped a broad, dirty hand over her mouth
and clasped her cheeks with thumb and fingers.
Holding her face in his viselike grip, he jerked her
head from side to side so forcefully Amy heard the
bones popping. She tasted blood as her bottom lip
was pressed painfully against her teeth. Certain
that any second her neck would snap and she'd be
dead, Amy grew dizzy. The entire starlit sky undulated above her.

Her eyes slid closed and she saw those stars
exploding in a kaleidoscope of brilliant colors.
Faintly, over a rising roaring in ears, she heard the
Indian's gruff voice. She couldn't understand the
Apache tongue, but his tone was threatening.

Her last conscious thought was that he meant to
kill her. She was soothed by the notion.

Luiz wheeled his horse around, retraced their
steps, and silently cursed himself for falling
asleep.

At the wide ravine he slid to the ground, leaving the paint standing with the trailing reins. He
crouched down on his heels and squinted, studying the sand. The distinctive horseshoe marks
were missing. He rose to his feet, leapt down into
the arroyo, and hurried to the other side. He
climbed out and again went down on his heels.

He felt a sudden cold in the pit of his stomach. There were Amy's tracks and tracks of half a dozen other horses as well. Unshod horses. Luiz jumped back down into the gorge. Cursing the lack of light, he struck a sulfur match and held it low to the ground, seeing it all with a frightening clarity.

Quick as a cat he was up and out of the ravine. He grabbed the paint's trailing reins, put his hand on the pommel, his foot in the stirrup, and swung up into the saddle. He turned the stallion to the southeast toward the serrated mountaintops barely visible beyond the dusk-cloaked desert.

Luiz touched his heels to the paint. The big mount plunged down into the sandy ravine and out the opposite side, and broke immediately into a thundering gallop.

Controlling the paint with his knees, Luiz reached up, tugged loose the narrow leather band that held his hair secured at the back of his neck. He opened his fingers and allowed the thong to fall to the ground.

He slipped the blue kerchief from his throat, lifted it, wrapped it around his temples in a tight headband, and tied it. He bowed his head and let his thick black hair swing forward around his face.

When he lifted his head, the aristocratic Spaniard, Capitán Luiz Quintano, was completely gone. A lean, buckskin-clad Indian with harshly chiseled features, cold black eyes, and wildly blowing raven hair rode across the darkening desert toward the distant Davis Mountains.

And the last stronghold of the Mescalero Apaches.

32

It was noon.

The blazing sun was directly overhead. Its scorching heat had sent even the sidewinders and lizards scurrying for shade. The temperature had soared past the century mark over an hour ago. Not a breath of air stirred the leaves on the juniper trees or carried away the thick choking smoke from dozens of roaring campfires.

At the very center of a small, remote valley, high up in the forbidding Chisos Mountains, a pale, terrified woman was bound to a tall cedar pole beneath the blistering noonday sun. Her wrists and ankles tied to the pole with tight bands of leather, she was on display for the entire band of Mescalero Apaches.

Amy felt the sun's harsh rays burning her face and bare arms. Her wrists, pulled behind her and tied to the pole, were scraped and cut, her hands stiff and numb. Her ankles were rubbed raw and her bare left foot had gone to sleep. It felt as if a million tiny needles were pricking the sole, and she could not lift her foot to stomp away the pain.

Her lips were badly chapped and cracked, her face blistered from the savage rays of the unfiltered mountain sun. Pain hammered at her temples. Her throat was so sore she could barely swallow. Her chest ached from bouts of smoke-triggered coughing. Her stomach rolled, protesting the greasy, half-cooked meat she was given for breakfast.

Since arriving at the Mescalero hideout at mid-morning, Amy had been staked out like some trapped, prized animal for the curious to examine. When her captors had brought her into the camp, everyone—men, women, and children—had come running. All eyes had locked on her.

Her stocky captor had beamed proudly and lifted a dirty hand to push Amy's long, tangled hair from her face so his people could get a good look. At first there was a low, speculative hum, then thoughtful nods, shouts of approval, and a sea of coppery faces all smiling up at her.

Minutes later Amy had found herself lashed to the cedar pole as the Mescaleros built up fires and hurried excitedly about as if some kind of big pow-wow was about to take place.

Among the men there was a lot of staring and talking and pointing, first at her, then toward the barely visible top of an animal-skin wickiup set apart from the others on an elevated location amid the trees.

Amy's gritty eyes lifted to follow their pointing fingers. She could not understand their language, but it was clear they were discussing her, so she supposed they had picked that secluded wickiup as the place they would hold her. If that was the case, she hoped they would soon take her there. After three days of travel in which she had not been allowed out of her captor's sight for a minute, the prospect of a small degree of privacy was incredibly appealing.

A tugging on her skirt drew Amy's attention from the men and the distant wickiup. Amy frowned down at a short, obese squaw who was smiling and clutching at the hem of her soiled blue cotton dress. Amy croaked her outrage when the woman reached underneath and tore a strip of lace from her dirty white petticoat.

Pleased with herself, the fat woman's body shook with laughter and her flat, glittery eyes disappeared into folds of coppery flesh. She turned around and held the lace high in the air, waving it proudly back and forth.

The gesture seemed to be a signal to the other women. They all crowded closer. A tall young maiden stepped forward. She looked into Amy's eyes with unveiled hatred. She reached out, plucked at a blue puff sleeve until it tore loose and sagged down Amy's arm.

It was noon—the beginning of a long, sweltering afternoon of torment for the trussed Amy. The women laughed and rushed at her, tore at her dress and yanked painfully at her long hair. Hour after miserable hour they snatched and tore and tortured, until Amy was left nearly unclothed.

Her blue dress and full petticoat were torn to shreds. All the dress's buttons had been yanked off. Her lace-trimmed chemise had been ripped down the middle. It hung limply, exposing the inner curves of her breasts. Her bare legs and thighs were visible beneath the torn dress and petticoat.

Her dignity and modesty were now completely violated and still the women pulled at her ruined clothes. Amy was sure they would not stop until she was left standing totally naked. She rolled her bloodshot eyes in despair, then closed them against the woman and against the harsh rays of the sun.

The day finally drew to a close, but not the torment.

At sunset a chuckling woman with long black braids grabbed the lacy edge of Amy's drawers and yanked. The delicate lace ripped loose from the satin. The wide band of lace slid down Amy's thigh, slipped over her knee and calf, and whispered down around her bound ankle.

The braided squaw stared at the trapped lace, shook her head, and reached out again. Amy moaned with desperation when the woman clutched at the left leg of her satin underwear.

Just as the delicate fabric began to tear, a man's voice rose above the din and the squaw immediately turned loose the satin underwear. Relieved and puzzled, Amy watched the woman back away.

A sudden hush fell over the bustling camp.

The women seemed to quietly melt away, leaving Amy standing alone, the dying rays of a blood-red sun tinting her bare arms and legs with color.

Amy looked past the retreating women and saw a throng of breech-clothed braves steadily advancing on her.

They too were silent. When the men were twenty yards from her, they halted as one and looked straight at her.

The camp had grown eerily quiet. The children had stopped running and squealing. The babies had stopped crying. Even the dogs had ceased their continual barking.

Baffled, Amy looked cautiously about. She had no idea what was happening, why the women had suddenly left her alone and why everyone had fallen silent.

After countless minutes, while the entire tribe seemed frozen permanently in place, the phalanx of braves parted, making a wide, long path down the middle of their number that led toward the tree-hidden wickiup.

All eyes went to that path, including Amy's.

For a time, nothing happened. Then a tall, lean buckskin-clad man came down that path, the top of his dark head visible above the crowd. He emerged into the clearing and the blood in Amy's veins turned to ice water.

The tall chief paused. He stood with his feet apart and hungrily looked her up and down. Amy's flesh crawled.

His was the most repulsively ugly face she had ever seen. His eyes were small, beady, and glittery, and far too close together. His nose was a huge, bulbous blob on a cadaverous thin face. His mouth was nothing more than a wide grotesque slash in his narrow face. He was smiling evilly and looked as if he were about to drool.

He was monstrously ugly and under his arm he held a more monstrously ugly mask. A ghastly carved devil's mask with long, sharp horns of crimson red, chilling marble eyes with slits below, and a long leather tongue and ferocious fangs.

Amy's heart quit beating when the evil-looking man with the evil-looking mask started toward her. Tall and spare, he walked slowly across the clearing. The way he moved his lean, long body made it seem as if he were slithering toward her, like a slippery snake.

When he stopped directly before her, Amy instinctively cringed and tried to draw away, every muscle contracting in an attempt to escape him and his dreadful beady eyes. Those glittery eyes slid from her frightened face, moved over her throat, and paused pointedly at her breasts.

Amy convulsed with horror when he lifted a hand, slipped it inside the torn satin chemise, and gave her bare, trembling left breast a painful squeeze. She screamed loudly and he released her. His eyes returned to her face. He smiled at her, his slash of a mouth stretching from ear to ear. And then a long, reptilian tongue darted out three or four times in quick succession as he pointed his forefinger at her breast. Amy shuddered with revulsion at the thought.

She fought wildly against her restraints when, his tongue darting in and out like a snake's, he swept away the tattered blue skirts of her dress and groped at her right thigh, attempting to slide his fingers underneath the satin of her underdrawers. Her eyes wild, every cell in her body screaming against the invasion, Amy tossed her head from side to side and shouted at him to leave her alone.

His hand dropped away, but he smiled and shook his head. He spoke, clearly addressing her. Amy could not understand the words, but his actions and attitude made his meaning all too horribly clear. Grinning diabolically, the ugly chief grabbed his crotch, humped it vulgarly against his cupped hand several times, then pointed from himself to her groin and back again. He nodded and darted his tongue out as his glittery eyes shone with depraved lust.

Amy lurched frantically when he moved. He laughed uproariously. He lifted the evil-looking devil's mask, put it over his head, and settled it securely. Those lecherous eyes gleamed at her from under the marble eyes of the mask, and his long tongue darted out atop the mask's leather tongue.

Paralyzed with fear and horror, Amy realized his intention. He was going to rape her. And he was going to do it while he wore the hideous mask.

Abruptly the masked chief turned and walked away. He went back to his assembly of warriors and spoke excitedly to them, turning to look over his shoulder at Amy. Amy strained to hear what he was saying. She couldn't speak the Apache tongue, but gestures and an occasional word of Spanish was enough for her to understand exactly what he was saying.

Chief Snake Tongue told his men that he was more than pleased with the white woman they had brought to him. She was the prettiest one he had ever had. So pretty, he intended to take her for his wife, to father a dozen children by her.

He was going now into his wickiup to wash his armpits and groin and lay out his best fur beds for his new white woman. When he was finished, he would come back out, cut the pretty captive down from her pole, carry her to his wickiup, and make her his woman.

Tongue darting obscenely out of his mask, he hurried off toward his wickiup as the last traces of pink disappeared from the sky. The silence that had descended over the camp with his arrival ended. Braves patted each other on the back, congratulated one another, and looked forward to a long night of glorious celebration.

In minutes drums began to throb and children squealed and chased each other. Dogs barked excitedly and chattering women started preparing the celebration feast. It was a time of great joy in Chief Snake Tongue's Chisos encampment. At long last the perfect mate had been found for their leader. Life would be easier for everyone now that the chief had a pale-skinned woman to lie with each night.

As the last traces of pink disappeared behind the Chisos mountains, Amy pleaded pitifully for someone to help her. Knowing that a fate far worse than death awaited her in the evil-looking chief's wickiup, she cried and begged passersby to cut her loose.

No one paid her any mind. They went cheerfully about their chores, uncaring that she was so terrified she was nearly hysterical. Desperate, she called out to a small naked child. The little girl peered at her curiously, moved closer, and Amy felt a tiny surge of hope spring to her breast.

When the big-eyed child stood directly before her, Amy, jerking with sobs, caught her breath and said, "The leather cords, untie them. Behind my back. My hands, untie my hands."

The child stared at her for a long minute, then wandered around behind her. Amy thought she might explode with elation when she felt the tiny girl's fingers tugging at the leather bands securing her wrists.

"Y-Yes—yes," Amy encouraged, tears pouring down her cheeks. "Untie them and—"

Abruptly the child's hands were ripped away and an admonishing woman loudly scolded, picked up the tiny girl, and carried her off.

Amy slumped in defeat and her head sagged to her chest.

But a loud commotion caused her to lift it immediately. Anxiously she blinked the tears from her eyes, looked up to see what was happening, and died a thousand deaths in that split second.

From out of the darkness the masked chief was slowly, surely approaching her while his people cheered and clapped and urged him on. The beat of the drums grew deafening as the shadowy figure in the devil's mask reached her. He stood unmoving before her, a tall, lean symbol of unspeakable evil and perversion.

Amy couldn't breathe. She was swallowing convulsively, choking. All at once the chief drew a sharp knife from the waistband of his buckskins, and Amy's breath whooshed loudly out of her lungs.

The knife blade flashed menacingly in the firelight and Amy began to scream. The masked chief stepped behind her and slashed the leather thongs binding her wrists to the cedar pole. Her stiff, weak arms fell to her sides and the momentum threw her off balance. She was about to pitch forward onto her face when he was back before her, his flattened palm on her waist, steadying her.

His hand stayed there while he crouched down, cut the leather restraints from her ankles, then rose. Pressing her to the pole with the flat of his hand, he slid the knife back inside the waistband of his buckskins.

"Pl . . . no . . . Please!" Amy sobbed.

He didn't listen.

In one fluid movement he swept Amy from the ground and up into his arms. As she screamed and struggled and pleaded with him, the tall masked chief strode purposefully through the gathering darkness toward the distant wickiup hidden in the trees.

While the drums pounded a savage rhythm and the wild Mescalero braves danced jubilantly around the roaring fires, their lean, bronzed warrior chief in his evil-looking devil's mask carried his squirming, terrified, pale-skinned beauty to his wickiup and ducked inside.

The flap was lowered. The drums beat faster. The white woman's screams grew louder. The people looked at each other, laughed, and nodded knowingly.

Their leader, the powerful Chief Snake Tongue, was already beginning to have his fun. And so were they.

33

He stood there, his black hair blowing back, his face wearing that inscrutable mask that was sheer Indian. Above his high-sculpted cheekbones, his unblinking jet eyes studied her with an almost impersonal intensity.

She could have been a total stranger, for all the emotion he showed—had shown through the long, arduous night. But Amy was not fooled. He was very angry with her. So angry he was rigidly exercising that extraordinary self-control she'd come to recognize. And to detest.

While he stood in a rocklike stance as the first pink light of dawn came from behind him, Amy knew that his tall lean body was tightly coiled with pent-up rage. Despite his adopted air of indifference, she was acutely sensitive to his struggle against the overwhelming desire to seize her and physically punish her.

At another time, under different circumstances, she would have cringed in the face of all that unleashed male rage. Not this morning. No matter his black mood, Amy was so relieved to look on that hard, handsome face she could hardly curb her own desire to reach out and touch the slanted cheekbones, the strong chin, the cruel mouth.

Her clothes in tatters, her long hair tangled, her face dirty and tear-streaked, she stood before the unreachable El Capitán, strangely warmed by his cold eyes, curiously reassured by his barely contained wrath. Nothing he had said or done—nothing he might yet say or do—could alter the fact that he had come for her.

Checking the foolish urge to smile at this brave, angry man, Amy recalled, for the hundredth time, the unforgettable moment when first she had looked on his face last night.

It was just at sunset that Chief Snake Tongue, wearing the hideous devil's mask, had come for her. Cutting her down from the cedar pole, he had lifted her up into his arms and carried her, screaming in terror, to his wickiup.

She was so hysterical, she had hardly realized that he immediately crossed the dim wickiup, slashed through the animal-hide lodge, tossed her roughly over his shoulder, and ran from the camp.

She vividly remembered being bounced uncomfortably, his powerfully muscled shoulder cutting into her stomach and the sharp crimson horn of the evil mask scraping her bare back as she struggled. Swiftly he had sprinted across the timbered terrain as dusk slowly descended over the Chisos.

They came upon a big paint stallion tethered to a leafy juniper, and Amy was immediately lowered to the ground. Confused and terrified, she whirled about and started to run for her life, but the tall chief grabbed her. Holding her with one strong hand clamped around her wrist, he reached up and tore the horrid devil's mask from his head and tossed it away.

She blinked in shock.

The bronzed, handsome face of El Capitán had emerged from beneath the horrid mask and Amy, continuing to scream, stared at him, afraid to believe her tear-filled eyes. She was not given time to wonder at how such a marvel had occurred.

Before she could choke back the sobs and regain her voice, the buckskin-clad El Capitán swiftly untied the big paint, looped the reins back over its neck, turned and lifted Amy up across the saddle.

He swung up behind her and the paint immediately went into motion. The stallion galloped through the towering trees and dense underbrush, quickly putting distance between them and Chief Snake Tongue's wildly celebrating Mescaleros.

Feeling calmer, Amy caught her breath and wrapped her weak, trembling arms tightly around his trim waist. She pressed her cheek to his broad chest, closed her eyes for a minute, and inhaled deeply of his clean, unique scent.

He had come for her! Thank God! The grotesque chief would *not* be raping or killing her tonight! This fearless warrior whose heart beat a slow, sure cadence beneath her ear had saved her! Had walked unarmed right into the hostile camp and carried her away!

Her senses assailed with the scent and feel and power of him, Amy slid a hand around to Luiz's chest. Her dirty fingers crawled up to the laced opening of his buckskin shirt. She nudged the soft fabric apart and smiled when a gold chain winked brilliantly at her. Her fingers curled tenaciously around the heavy chain and she drew out the glittering gold Sun Stone.

With a soft little sobbing gasp of gratitude, she brushed her chapped, parched lips to the cool solid metal. For a time she was content to stay just like that, one hand clinging to El Capitán's back, the other clinging to the Sun Stone.

Oblivious to everything save the all-encompassing power of man and medallion, Amy felt her tired, tense body slowly relaxing as a wonderful sense of well-being replaced the numbing fear she'd known for the past four harrowing days and nights.

The sound of the drums grew steadily fainter, the glow of the campfires against the night sky had all but disappeared. There were no sounds of thundering horses crashing through the forrest. No blood-curdling cries of vengeful, pursuing Apaches.

Amy was certain the danger had passed. Miraculously they had escaped. Now they would ride down out of the mountains and go home to Orilla. She yawned, took a long, slow breath, and raised her weary head from Luiz's chest.

Raising her voice to be heard over the wind, she said, "When are we going to stop for the night? I'm exhausted."

His black eyes flicked to her face for an instant, and Amy caught their almost imperceptible narrowing. He gave no verbal reply. She waited for him to speak. He said nothing. She finally tried again.

"Please, we have to stop. I can't go on." Still he said nothing. His eyes remained on the treacherous trail ahead. Exasperated, Amy explained, "I am too tired to ride farther. We're safe now and—"

"We are not safe." He spoke at last, interrupting. "You will ride as far as I tell you to ride."

It was her first taste of what the long journey home would be like. But she was too tired and too relieved to argue. She merely nodded and snuggled back down on his chest. Maybe he was right. Maybe they should put more miles between them and the Mescalero camp before they stopped.

So she didn't complain when they continued to ride as evening turned into night and night changed to morning, the mountain air growing bitingly chilly. She didn't attempt to make conversation. Luiz's starkly chiseled features, sporadically illuminated by appearing and disappearing wedges of mountain moonlight, wore a cold, impenetrable expression that held her silent.

Intuitively Amy knew it was wise to let him be. It was a long way home; he couldn't remain distant and uncommunicative forever.

Sunrise.

In a high, carefully chosen valley with a narrow, concealed mouth and high protective walls of stone, Amy stood on unsteady legs and faced the tall, unsmiling man who had not spoken all night.

The unsaddled stallion cropped contentedly at the grass inside the hidden canyon, oblivious to any tension between the two humans. Totally exhausted and wanting nothing more than to lie down and sleep, Amy supposed El Capitán was waiting for her tearful apology for causing everyone such anguish.

Shifting from one bare, dirty foot to the other,

she rubbed her badly sunburned face, licked her cracked lips, took a deep breath, and said, "I'm sorry for the trouble I've caused. I thank you for coming after me—for saving my life."

His reply was a quick, dismissive shake of his dark head.

Amy felt compelled to say more. "The chief was a vile, depraved man and I—I . . ." She shuddered and hugged her arms to her sides. "Thank God you got there before the beast could do anything. Did you kill him?"

"No." He spoke at last. "I do not kill brothers."

"You don't—" Amy looked at him as if he had lost his mind. "But he was going to—"

"You must understand the Apaches, my tribal brothers." His voice was conversationally calm. "They are still a primitive people, like children." He shrugged wide shoulders. "Mischievous children."

Amy's tired chin lifted minutely. "Mischievous children? How can you stand there and defend them? They are dirty, uncivilized, bloodthirsty Ind—"

"Indians? Is that what you were going to say?"

"I—I . . . didn't mean that every—"

"The way you and your family feel about my race has never been a secret."

"That's not true. I never . . . My daddy had great respect for . . . Besides, you're not a . . . You are—"

"A breed? A mixed blood? Isn't that even worse?"

"No, it isn't. You are—"

He cut her off. "Your opinion of me is of no importance." For a moment he stared at her in hard-eyed silence then said, "You will do as I say until I get you safely back to Orilla." A muscle worked in his jaw and he added, "After that, I don't give a damn what you do."

"Listen, I realize that you're angry with me, but—"

"Angry?" His voice cut like a knife blade. "I ought to take over where the Apaches left off. I should rape and torture you myself." Suddenly he swung forward, the breadth of his shoulders shadowing her from the rapidly rising sun.

Amy trembled but stood her ground. Still weak and upset from her ordeal, she had had just about enough of this man's high-handed behavior and habitual coldness. Too much, in fact.

"Well, what the devil are you waiting for?" She narrowed her scratchy blue eyes and whipped her tangled hair back off her dirty face. "I'm totally defenseless. So weak and tired I can barely stand. I can't fight you, so have at it! Get it over with! Torture me. Rape me. Kill me. Name your pleasure, El Capitán!"

Her outburst surprised him. "Calm down, I'm not going to—"

"No? Why ever not? To the victor goes the spoils! You snatched me from the chief. Wasn't that because you want the same thing he wanted?"

"That's enough of that," he said, ending the conversation. Shaking his dark head, he moved away from her.

He turned to the gear he'd stacked on the grass. Crouching on his heels, he unrolled his pack, drew from it a pair of soft doeskin trousers and a pale-blue cotton pullover shirt. Tossing them over his arm, he rose.

"There's a shallow spring around that corner." He inclined his head. "Down about fifty feet, in the bottom of the canyon. I'll stand guard while you bathe. Put these on when you've finished." He held the shirt and trousers out to Amy.

Indecisive for only a second, Amy snatched the clothes from his hand and said tiredly, "I don't suppose you have any soap?"

Wordlessly he produced a small new bar of castile, and it was all Amy could do to keep from sighing with pleasure. Suddenly she felt so sticky and miserable she couldn't wait to hurry down to the stream, strip off her torn, soiled clothes, and wash away four days and nights of grime.

While Amy bathed, Luiz, his back resting against the smooth, high wall of rock, sat at the mouth of the narrow canyon with a loaded Winchester rifle across his knees. His alert black eyes constantly moving, he scanned the rugged region surrounding the concealed canyon for any sign of approaching Apaches.

When half an hour had passed, he began to worry.

It was then that Amy came up the draw from the spring. As she rounded the corner of soaring rock and stepped into full view, Luiz, despite himself, stared like an entranced youth.

She had washed her hair. The long golden glory of it, still in damp strands, fell down her back and captured the sunlight. Her face glistened with cleanliness and her sky-blue eyes held a warm, drowsy expression.

The shirt she wore—his shirt—was the exact

same hue as her sleepy eyes, and it clung damply to her clean skin, contouring the roundness of her breasts and the taut, chilled nipples.

The doeskin trousers were appealingly snug over her flaring hips and shapely bottom, but they were far too long. She had rolled them up over her bare, bruised feet. She stood with one knee bent and cocked outward. The leather strings that laced up the pants from crotch to waist were loose, the ends falling over her flat stomach and swinging gently between her long, slender legs.

She stood looking at him, the newly risen sun striking her full in the face. She yawned sleepily. And she asked, "Can we go to bed now?"

Though his heart kicked against his ribs, he said tonelessly, "Sure."

And remained as he was, seated with the rifle across his knees, his eyes locked on her. Never had she looked more blatantly desirable and at the same time so sweetly innocent. His tired, lean body responded automatically. The blood rushed into his groin, expanding it painfully. The heat moved upward attacking every part of his body.

His heart pounded and he could scarcely breathe. His face was so hot it felt as if it were on fire. While he found the physical reaction downright annoying, he understood it and was not particularly concerned. It was lust, pure and simple. She was undeniably beautiful and he desired her body as any healthy man would.

But he experienced another emotion that disturbed him a great deal more than the simple passion she stirred in him. An emotion far more dangerous. An emotion so alien to him, he did not fully recognize it for what it was but was frightened by it.

Sexual hunger he could understand and control. But the strong unbidden yearning to enfold this slender, sunburned, golden-haired woman tenderly in his arms and keep her safe forever—even from himself—was terrifying.

He behaved as every frightened male since Adam had behaved. With unreasoning anger. Anger that he directed at her as if it were her fault, not his.

"What are you standing there for?" he said through thinned lips. "I thought you were tired."

"I am a little tired," she said, then lazily raised her hands, raked slender fingers through her long, damp hair, and shook her head about. Impulsively she bent over from the waist and whipped the clean, shiny tresses forward over her head until the golden hair almost swept the ground.

Unknowing and uncaring that his fierce black gaze was locked on her, Amy stayed in that position for a time, her hands flattened on the grassy ground, her shapely rear pointed skyward.

Her unselfconscious limbering exercise made the angry El Capitán even more angry. Made him mad as hell. Certain that she was doing it just to devil him, he was determined she would not know how well she had succeeded.

As casually as possible, he said, "Better go on inside the canyon, spread the blanket, and go to sleep."

Amy's head came up. Her face was red from the blood rushing to it. Her hair was a wild golden mane spilling around her shoulders, blazing in the sunlight. She cocked her head and looked at him and moved closer. She crouched down directly in front of him and absently slapped at his arm with the long leather lacings of her borrowed trousers.

"What about you?" she asked after yawning.

"Don't worry about me."

"But I do. Surely you—"

"Get on over there." He cut her off. "Mind me now."

She didn't mind him. She continued to crouch on her bare heels, curiously examining his dark, rigid face.

There was a stern, angry look in the black eyes of El Capitán as he sat gripping the Winchester rifle too tightly in his bronzed hands. But it was different somehow from the undiluted anger she'd seen there so often. Now, mixed with the anger was the slightest hint of . . . what? Agony? Fear? Regret?

"Is—is something wrong?" she asked gently.

His face and body suffused with a burning heat, his groin aching, his heart behaving strangely, he managed coldly, "Not a thing, Mrs. Parnell. Not one thing."

34

Amy stirred, opened her eyes, and wondered what time it was. The narrow, steep-sided canyon was completely in shadow, but high above, a slender ribbon of blue sky was bright and clear. She turned her head. El Capitán was not there beside her.

Amy knew a moment of panic. She quickly sat up and looked all around. She opened her mouth to call out and closed it before making a sound. Her voice would carry and echo through the canyon. She had no desire to alert any patrolling Apache.

She got up, stepped off the spread blanket, and anxiously went in search of her mysteriously withdrawn companion. Rounding a bend, she winced silently when her bare right foot struck a sharp, jagged rock. Making a face, Amy hobbled on, carefully picking her away over rock and sand and gravel and tangled underbrush.

She stopped abruptly when she saw El Capitán seated in the exact same spot, in the exact same position, as when she had left him hours earlier. She wondered if he had sat like that, rifle across his knees, vigilantly keeping watch the whole time she had slept.

Amy hadn't made a sound, but his dark head swung round and he looked straight at her. At once he leaned the rifle against the wall of rock and came to his feet. It was then that Amy noticed the sleeves had been cut from his fringed buckskin shirt. His long arms were bare all the way to the shoulder, his hard biceps surging, muscles rippling under the smooth skin.

"You got too hot," she said, gesturing to his sleeveless shirt. And wondered why the meaningless statement so annoyed him.

He advanced on her as if she had insulted him. His bronzed, sinewy presence was so intimidating Amy automatically took a step backward. Again she stepped on a rock, her tender heel coming down directly atop its rough surface.

"Owwww," she murmured, but kept her watchful eyes trained on his set face and continued to retreat.

"Be still," he ordered, and reaching her, went down on one knee before her. From inside the waistband of his trousers, he drew out a pair of soft knee-high moccasins. Draping one over his shoulder, he reached for Amy's right foot. While she held on to him to keep from falling, he set her foot atop his thigh and closely examined it, running inquiring fingers over the soft sole.

Amy's feet were ticklish. She burst out laughing and attempted to pull her foot away. He wrapped his fingers around her ankle and his eyes lifted to hers.

"Laugh a bit louder," he said sharply. "Laugh long enough and you'll draw the Apaches to laugh along with you."

The laughter died in her throat. "Sorry."

"Pull up your pants leg so I can get these moccasins on your feet."

She nodded. "You made me a pair of moccasins from your shirtsleeves."

"It's a long way back to Orilla. You'd never make it barefooted."

"No, I. . . . Thank you. That was very thoughtful."

He said nothing. He slipped the soft doeskin moccasin onto her foot and laced it to just below her knee. He repeated the action with the other foot, then pulled her pants legs down over the newly made footwear and rose.

"Start gathering up the gear," he instructed. "I've seen no sign of an Apache all day. It's midafternoon. With any luck we could be down out of the Chisos by nightfall."

"Have you slept?"

He turned and walked away. Over his shoulder he said "I'll sleep tonight."

She followed after him and laid a hand on his bare forearm. "You can't make it without sleep."

His gaze coldly touched the pale hand lying on his arm and Amy guiltily snatched it away. He told her, "I can make it without sleep. I can make it without food. I can make it without water if necessary." He paused. His eyes became black ice. "And, Mrs. Parnell, I can also make it without you."

Her hands went to her hips. "Well, who ever said you couldn't? Go on without me! Just leave me here and—"

"Get the gear together!"

* * *

It was nearing six in the afternoon.

The pair, riding tandem, were just about down and out of the Chisos. Amy, seated astride and behind Luiz, had her hands locked around his hard waist. They had said almost nothing since quitting the canyon.

Growing increasingly weary, Amy was glad it would soon be nightfall. She was relieved that they had wound their way down out of the Chisos to the wide valley without encountering a single Apache.

She didn't realize just how tense and wary she had been until now when she began to fully relax. She felt that the danger had passed. Sighing, Amy laid her cheek against El Capitán's erect back and closed her burning eyes.

She was almost dozing when a faint flapping sound caused her eyes to open, and she stirred. Her head came up off Luiz's back. She saw two huge black vultures, their wings spread wide, perched on a dead tree ahead. A chill raced up her spine.

It was an omen. She knew it. They still weren't safe.

"Amy, you awake?" Luiz's soft, low voice startled her.

"Yes," she managed, her eyes locked on the pair of hovering buzzards. This cold, unreachable man had called her Amy. He never called her Amy. Something was wrong.

"Can you fall off this horse without breaking anything?"

"What is it?" Amy asked anxiously, feeling the blood turn cold in her veins.

"We have company," he told her calmly.

Her head snapped around. Squinting anxiously, at first she saw nothing.

Then, about a hundred yards behind her, the Apaches came into sight.

"I counted nine of them," said Luiz.

"Then why are we going so slowly?" Her voice grew shrill with fear. "Put the paint into a dead run and get us out of here!"

"Not quite yet," he said, no urgency in his tone. "Now listen carefully and do exactly as I tell you. We are going to maintain our present pace—let them close in. Meanwhile, unstrap our gear from behind the cantle. Reach under my shirt, take the revolver from my waistband, wrap it up inside the gear. Hang the canteen over your shoulder. But first, take the Winchester from the saddle scabbard and hand it up to me."

Amy didn't hesitate. She set to work immediately, knowing whatever his plan was, she must follow it without question.

"You see that beginning string of Santiago foothills rising from the valley floor directly ahead of us?" Amy nodded anxiously but didn't make a sound. "Amy?"

"Yes. Yes, I see them."

"When we have rounded the very first one and are out of the Apaches' sight, let your body go completely limp, fall off this horse, get up and dash up the timbered slopes the minute you hit the ground. Can you do that?"

"Yes. But where will you be?"

"Hopefully drawing the Apaches away from you."

"No, Luiz! I won't let you do that. I'm staying with you. We'll take our chances together."

"Don't argue with me!" His voice had taken on a cutting edge. "Get busy. Do everything I told you, but as you work, hang on tight with one hand. I am fixing to tell this big paint to stretch it out."

A touch of his heels to the stallion's flanks sent the creature into a rapid gallop with an amazing burst of speed. Half a mile behind, nine shouting, shrieking Apache braves madly pursued. Luiz was not worried about them firing their weapons. At least not yet.

They had been ordered to bring the pale-skinned woman back to their chief unharmed. They didn't dare risk a misplaced bullet striking Amy. That had been Luiz's reason for having her ride behind him.

It was a fancy balancing act Amy performed atop the sprinting paint. She managed to get the Colt revolver wrapped up in the blanket, the whole pack rolled back up, and the canteen draped around her neck. She passed the Winchester up to Luiz.

She was ready.

The trees were flashing past. The wind was stinging her eyes. Her heart was pounding with anticipation. She knew that any second El Capitán would give the command for her to fall off the speeding horse and . . .

"Now, Amy, girl," said Luiz, turning his head, and Amy tumbled from the galloping stallion and crashed to the grassy ground. Her elbow struck first, hitting squarely on her funnybone. Fingers of numbing pain shot up the useless arm and Amy dropped the pack.

She jerked it up with her other hand and sprang to her feet. In her protective moccasins, she scrambled quickly up into the dense undergrowth. Low, leafy limbs hit her in the face; a jungle of vicious thorns and barbs slapped at her arms and legs, but she plunged on.

She didn't stop until she had climbed high up the mountain slope. When finally she was so out of breath, her lungs burning so painfully she could go no farther, she sank to the ground, her legs so weak she could no longer stand,

She heard the drumming hooves of the Indians' ponies passing directly below. Luiz's plan had worked! The Apaches had no idea she was no longer riding with him.

Amy wearily dropped the heavy pack to the ground and searched hurriedly through it until she found the heavy revolver. With shaking hand she lifted it. It wavered and dipped and she brought around her other hand to help support the weapon's weight.

Sucking anxiously for air, Amy sat in the dappled shade, the gun raised defensively before her. She jumped reflexively when she heard the first burst of gunfire. The whine of ricocheting bullets striking rock made her fall down onto her belly and flatten herself to the ground. Her weight supported on her elbows, the gun pointed down the mountain, she stared wide-cyed through the trees.

The gunfire blasts continued—rapid and frightening—but growing steadily softer as the Apaches rode farther away. She was momentarily safe, but what about Luiz? Had he avoided that fierce barrage of bullets. Was he hit and badly hurt? Dying? Dead?

No, she told herself forcefully. Had he been hit, the firing would have stopped. He had eluded them. He was an expert horseman and an expert marksman. He would either outrun them or kill them all!

Long minutes passed.

The firing finally stopped and Amy's fear escalated. Had the Apaches killed him, and were they now combing the woods for her? She rolled over onto her back and sat up.

An hour went by. All was silent save the occasional call of a mountain thrush and the yelping of a coyote as dusk settled over the Santiagos.

Amy waited, long after the sun had gone down and the night air had chilled and her densely timbered redoubt grew oppressively dark.

She told herself she had to remain calm. El Capitán knew what he was doing. He was cunning and ingenious. He was not dead! He had eluded the Apaches and he would come back for her. All she had to do was remain concealed and wait. Soon he would come riding up out of the darkness astride the big paint and everything would be all right.

The moon rose high above the trees, but its silvery light could not penetrate the lush canopy of heavily foliaged junipers and tall piñon pines. Her hand numb from holding the revolver so tightly, Amy sat blinking in the thick, pervasive darkness, every muscle in her body stretched as taut as a violin's strings.

They've killed him, her frenzied brain screamed out. He couldn't lose them, couldn't outrun them. They've caught up with him, pulled him down off the paint, butchered and scalped him. Now he was lying out there in the moonlight, dead, his lifeless body growing cold, his unseeing eyes open and staring sightlessly up at the heavens.

Her imagination running away with her, Amy's body began to jerk with fear and anguish. El Capitán was dead. And, once again, it was her fault. She was alone and the mountain was crawling with Apaches and any second they would close in on her and rape her and scalp her and slit her throat from ear to ear and . . . and . . .

The faint sound of a twig snapping nearby brought Amy scrambling to her feet in terror. She blinked frantically in the thick darkness and couldn't see a thing.

The gun wavered. She couldn't hold it level in her cold, shaking hands. She stiffened her arms out straight, but had no idea in which direction she should point the weapon. Her heart beat so fast she could scarcely get a breath.

Frantic, she strained to listen and spasmed with panic when dead chaparral crunched lightly beneath the intruder's foot. She whipped about to face the direction from which the sound had come. Her finger curled around the .44's trigger, she pointed at the wall of impenetrable blackness and waited, trembling, for her attacker to emerge.

From behind her, a hand shot out of the darkness, clamped tightly over her mouth, and she was slammed back against a tall, solid frame. A steel-like arm wrapped around her, pinning hers to her sides. The gun hung useless in her right hand.

Against her ear a deep, reassuring voice whis-

pered very softly, "Amy, it's Luiz. Sorry I had to
frighten you, but I couldn't permit a scream." He
felt her slender, jerking body go slack against his.
He went on, his lips so close to her ear Amy could
feel their warmth, "When I take my hand away,
don't' speak, don't make a sound." Her eyes closing with relief, Amy nodded against his covering
fingers.

Luiz took his hand from her lips, took the heavy
Colt from her hand, and when she turned and
threw her arms around his neck, he held her, his
bare arm around her, comforting her.

When she had calmed, Luiz warned her to remain totally mute. She did but she refused to let
go of him. So, holding her, Luiz looked watchfully
about, his eyes narrowed keenly. He listened and
then whispered against Amy's ear.

"Directly in front of you, exactly eight feet from
where we're standing, there's a big-trunked
ponderosa. Go quietly to that tree. When you
reach it, turn your back to it and step away two
feet." He gently removed her arms from around
his waist.

Amy tiptoed forward to the tree, her hands out
before her like a blind person. When she reached
it, her searching fingers swept over its rough bark,
and she turned around, stepped two feet back
toward Luiz, and waited.

After what seemed forever, he came to her,
placed a gentle hand atop her shoulder, and urged
her to sit down. When she was settled on a
smooth, soft patch of grass, he stepped around
behind her and slowly sank to the ground, spreading his bent knees to enclose her. He leaned his
back against the large tree trunk.

Again his lips touched her ear and he whispered. "I'm here. You're safe. Think you can rest in this position?" She nodded. "Then lean back on me and relax."

Amy didn't have to be told twice. The nights were still nippy at this altitude and the winds seemed to go right through her blue cotton shirt. She needed the heat of his body, so gladly she scooted close against him. She leaned her back against his broad chest. She laid her head on his shoulder and pulled her knees up.

Immediately enveloped by his warmth, she released a sigh of gratitude. It struck her that she was not only warmed by his physical presence. He was showing a surprising degree of warmth and understanding. Was he beginning to thaw? Maybe this shared experience—the two of them alone against the Apaches and the elements—had permanently stripped away his veneer of coldness, had taken the edge off his old anger.

She reached up and laid a hand on his jaw, signaling him to bend down so she could whisper something to him. When Luiz lowered his dark head, Amy put her lips against his ear and said, "Your plan worked perfectly. You're so smart, so resourceful."

She took her hand from his face and Luiz lifted his head without replying. When, half an hour later, she fell asleep on him, he sat there wide awake in the darkness, wishing her hair did not smell so sweet. Wishing she had not turned her face in so that her soft, moist breath was on his throat. Wishing he had not felt so pleased to hear her say he was smart and resourceful.

Gun raised, narrow-eyed gaze constantly

sweeping the pitch-black forest, Luiz mentally steeled himself against the danger. Not the danger lurking out there in the darkness but the danger snuggled sweetly against his chest. He didn't, he told himself, need nor want her approval.

A hint of a sardonic smile touched his lips. Would she still think him smart and resourceful come morning when he told her they no longer had a horse to ride?

They would have to walk home to Orilla.

35

_____

"You did what?"

"I turned the paint loose."

Amy's voice rose sharply. "Do you want to die?"

"On the contrary," Luiz went on in the same unruffled voice, "I want to live. That's why I did it."

It was early morning. The pair stood facing each other across a scrub juniper near the base of the mountain. At first light Luiz had gently shaken Amy awake. In minutes they had gathered up their gear.

"Let's go," he had said softly, and headed down through the dense thicket.

"Ready," Amy replied, following. "Where did you leave the paint tethered?"

"I didn't."

Abruptly Amy had stopped. "Did you hobble him?"

"No." He continued walking.

Frowning, Amy ran after him. She caught up and grabbed his bare arm, stopping his progress. "What have you done with the horse?"

Matter-of-factly, Luiz told her he had to let the horse go.

So now, as the June sun rose to take the chill off

the morning, Amy said doubtfully, "You don't want to die so you turn the horse loose? Forgive me if I'm a bit confused, but you're not making a great deal of sense."

Shifting the packroll on his back, Luiz calmly explained that there had been no other choice. The Apaches had closed in; he couldn't outdistance them. They were firing at him. He managed to get the speeding paint around the bend of a projected foothill.

Temporarily out of their sight, he had wrapped the reins around the horn, dug his heels into the racing paint's flanks, and tumbled from its back. While he slipped up through the trees to safety, the valiant paint continued around the mountain's curve. The Apaches followed, thinking him still in the saddle. By the time they realized their mistake, it was too late.

"Sorry for this inconvenience," Luiz concluded, "but I had to do it." He shrugged wide shoulders.

Nodding, Amy said, "Yes, I can see why you . . . but how will we get home?"

"Walk?" he casually suggested, his slashing black brows lifting quizzically.

"Walk?" she repeated, staring at him blankly. "Walk? Do you know how far it is to Orilla?"

"As the crow flies, seventy miles. Over the mountains, at least a hundred."

"And I'm supposed to walk one hundred miles?" Her hands went to her hips.

"Had you rather stay here?"

"I can't walk that far! Nobody can."

"You're wrong, Mrs. Parnell. I can. I have done it before. Many times." He turned to leave. "Coming?"

Glaring at him, Amy didn't answer. Nor did she follow. Rooted to the spot, she watched him stride away as if he were off on a Sunday stroll. She wanted to brain him. He moved with loose-limbed quickness that swiftly put distance between them. In a matter of seconds Amy lost sight of him entirely as he reached the valley floor below and disappeared around a towering, sun-tinged pillar of rock.

Amy stood immobile for a few more seconds. All at once she was in wild flight, her heart thumping in her chest. Ducking low tree limbs, she crashed through the undergrowth, momentum propelling her rapidly down the steep incline. When her moccasined feet touched level ground, she started calling his name.

"Luiz, wait!" she called. "I'm coming. Wait for me. Please!"

There was no response. She was immediately apprehensive. Dear Lord, he had gone off and left her! What would happen to her now? She could never find her way out of these mountains.

Out of breath, Amy reached the tall column where he had vanished from sight. Anxiously she raced around the sandstone monolith, shouting his name.

"Luiz, don't leave me! Wait, I can walk. I can, and I—" The words died away in her throat and she came to a quick stop.

Six feet from her, El Capitán stood leaning against the smooth granite scarp, his long, bare arms crossed over his chest, a moccasined foot raised and resting flat against the smooth stone upthrust. His dark head was turned her way, the long white scar on his cheek tinted pink in the early-morning sunlight.

Amy released a breath of relief, smiled tentatively, and hurried to him. "I can walk home if you can," she offered hopefully.

His black eyes regarded her with apathy. He pushed away from the sandstone spire, lifted his bare arms, and straightened the vivid blue headband around his temples.

"Let's go."

It was a long, hard morning for Amy.

Determined not to gripe, she gamely followed her mute companion over a nonexistent trail through the most rugged country in all Texas. While the sun climbed high in the cloudless sky and the heat became brutal, she labored up treacherous rocky ridges, peering nervously over sheer drop-offs but keeping her fear to herself.

Without complaint, she crossed deep, sand-bottomed gulches that left her moccasins filled with the fine, gritty sand that got ground under her soles and in between her toes. She picked her way through slashing arroyos filled with tons of loose, heel-bruising gravel. She disregarded the sharp cactus thorns that snagged at her doeskin pants and pricked the flesh beneath. She ignored her long, worrisome hair when it blew into her eyes and caught on tree limbs, pulling painfully at her tender scalp. She uncomplainingly swatted away the deerflies that bit her face, neck, and arms.

She did not ask for a drink of water, even when her throat was so dry it ached and she felt as if her body were growing dangerously dehydrated.

Stumbling up over a ledge of craggy ocher stone at mid-morning, Amy was struck by the knowledge that the tall, lean man she hurried to keep up with did not appear to be hot or tired or thirsty.

Furiously mashing at a blood-sucking insect feasting on her left forearm, Amy squinted at El Capitán, twenty feet ahead of her up the trail. The heavy packroll on his back seemed to be no burden. His wide shoulders were erect; his bare, bronzed arms hung loosely at his sides. The firm muscles of his buttocks stretched and pulled with neat precision beneath his tight buckskin trousers as he moved steadily upward with the sure-footed grace of a great cat.

As if he could feel her eyes on him, El Capitán abruptly stopped and turned about. Standing there above her on a great jagged wall of the mountain, he quietly observed the slender, struggling woman approaching him.

Her face was shiny with perspiration and flushed red by the harsh sun and the strenuous exertion. Her long blond hair was an impossible mass of tangles that fell into her eyes and clung damply to her hot cheeks and neck. She was slapping madly at a vicious black deerfly that had attacked her gleaming throat. Grass burrs clung to the legs of her borrowed buckskins and she was favoring her left foot.

"You all right?" he inquired as she neared him.

Amy had to swallow two or three times to make enough saliva in her dry throat so she could speak.

"Splendid," she said, tossing her hair haughtily from her eyes. "And you?"

For all his seemingly casual attitude, Luiz was a man who missed nothing. He knew she had gone well beyond her endurance but was too proud to

admit it. It was a quality in her he grudgingly
admired while at the same time it annoyed him.

The slightest hint of a sardonic smile touched
his lips and was gone almost at once. He said, "I'm
a little tired."

He stepped forward, reached for her, and easily
swung her up into his arms. Amy was far too
weary to put up any protest. It felt so good to get
off her tired, bruised feet, she sighed and her head
sagged to his shoulder.

Luiz carried her up the steeply slanting mountain of rock to a shadowy cupped-out crater on its
northern face a hundred feet below the summit.
He ducked in out of the bright sunlight, lowered
Amy to her feet, and unceremoniously announced, "We will stay here through the hottest
part of the day."

"Don't do it on my account," she said, swaying
tiredly on weak legs. "I'd just as soon continue."

"Well, I wouldn't," he told her, and shrugged
out of the heavy packroll. After uncorking the
canteen, he held it out to her. Eagerly she
grabbed it, turned it up, and drank thirstily. And
glared at him when he took it from her. Then
shook her head wonderingly when he recorked it
without taking so much as a sip.

"Aren't you thirsty?" she asked, frowning.

"Not really," he replied, although he was. He
was unwilling to admit that their water supply
was running dangerously low and that as May was
the driest season in the Big Bend, they might have
to travel for miles before they found a running
creek.

Amy shook her head and sank wearily to the
smooth stone floor. Scratching at a red, swollen

welt on her neck, she watched idly as Luiz meticulously spread the blanket just inside the cavern's opening. She continued to observe him as he then took several articles from the pack and laid them in a neat row beside the spread blanket.

But she blinked in nervous inquiry when, crouching on his heels directly before the cave's entrance, he said softly, "Now come here, Mrs. Parnell."

Amy swallowed and stared at him, but could not see his face, backlit as he was by the sun coming in the cave's wide mouth. She tensed. What punishment was about to be executed? Now that they had escaped the devilish Apaches and he had her alone in this high, shadowy redoubt, was he determined to be a devil himself? Was he preparing to dole out that unique form of discipline he favored above all others?

"I said come here." His voice filled the entire chamber, it's deep timbre reverberating off the close rocky walls.

"No. I will not come there." Amy spoke in level tones although her pulse beat erratically and her chest felt uncomfortably tight.

He continued to crouch there on his heels, forearms draped across his thighs, not moving a muscle, blocking the only possible route of escape. Filling the entire scope of her vision. Looming large and threateningly before her, like a dangerous predator with his trapped prey. His black eyes flashed like an animal's in the dim light.

"You will. You'll come to me," he said, and his voice was an opiate as he softly summoned her. "Come. I am waiting."

Drawn helplessly by that rich, persuasive voice

and the strong sexual danger he exuded, Amy hesitated for a long breathless moment, fighting the magnetic pull radiating from him. The small cave grew quiet and close. So close she could hardly get a breath. Her hand went to her tight throat.

"I told you to come here." His velvet voice shattered the silence. Amy exhaled loudly, then started toward him, fully expecting him to strip her clothes away and force her down onto the blanket.

Knee-walking across the shadowy space that separated them, she stopped when she was two feet away. Her eyes searching the unreadable mask of his hard, handsome face, she nervously sat back on her heels.

Luiz moved at last. He held out his hand to her. Licking her lips, Amy laid her hand atop his upturned palm. His strong fingers closed around hers and Amy felt an icy heat immediately envelop her. While a chill tickled her spine, jolts of searing electricity shot through her body.

She looked into the awesome eyes, feeling their power and their heat. And she waited.

36

Amy waited. Resigned. Eager.

Waited for El Capitán to pull her commandingly into his arms and crush her to his hard chest. Waited for that cruel sensual mouth to hotly cover her cold trembling lips. Waited for those strong bronzed hands to sweep the clothes from her tense body.

Waited for the punishment.

Waited for the pleasure.

His black eyes glittering in the half light, El Capitán said softly, "I am going to make you feel better."

Amy trembled. Knowing exactly what he meant, she simply nodded in helpless, halfhearted surrender.

And learned, once again, that the dark man who wielded such potent animal magnetism was ever a puzzling paradox.

He did not draw her roughly into his embrace and fiercely kiss her and strip her clothes away. Instead, he tended her as a loving parent might minister to a wayward but adored child.

He carefully sat her onto the spread blanket and Amy, legs stretched out before her, leaned back on stiff arms and watched from beneath veiling lashes, baffled by the mystery that was El Capitán Luiz Quintano.

She puzzled over it while he painstakingly plucked all the grass burrs and cactus stickers from the legs of her buckskins. In seconds, however, she was biting her bottom lip and trying hard not to laugh as he removed her moccasins and began dusting the gritty sand from her feet, getting them as clean as he could without water.

Her feet were incredibly ticklish and despite his stern, reproving glances, Amy laughed out loud when his long fingers dislodged sand from between her toes and he leaned over her lifted foot to blow the loosened particles away.

When both her feet were sand-free, Luiz reached for the canteen. From the row of neatly stacked articles he had taken from the pack, he withdrew a clean white handkerchief. After wetting the handkerchief with a couple of douses of the scarce water, he corked the canteen and turned to her.

Amy's laughter ceased as the wet handkerchief touched her open lips. Luiz carefully washed her flushed, dusty face, drawing the cloth gently over her cheeks, her chin, her nose. He pressed it to the limp, hot hair above her high forehead; he blotted the wispy hair at her temples; he washed the insides of her small ears.

He lowered the handkerchief to her throat and bathed away the grime and grit. His hand went inside the opening of her soiled blue shirt and Amy felt the cooling cloth move soothingly out over her shoulders, her collarbones, the beginning swell of her bare breasts.

Luiz withdrew the dampened handkerchief.

"Give me your hands," he commanded.

Amy sat up and presented the right one to him. He gently washed it, and her arm, going up under her shirtsleeve, all the way past her elbow. Then she gave him the left arm.

When he had finished, he tossed the handkerchief aside and reached for a small tin of salve, snapped it open, and dabbed his little finger into it.

He went in search of insect bites on Amy's pale flesh. His black eyes intense, he examined all her exposed flesh—and some that was covered—and promptly applied the warm, thick salve to even the tiniest of telltale red dots.

Amy was amazed at how swiftly the worrisome itching and stinging vanished. One quick, light touch of his salved fingertip to the tiny bites brought instant relief.

"Ummmm, that feels so good," she murmured gratefully. "That salve is miracluous. What exactly is it?"

His black eyes never lifting from the ivory arm he was doctoring, Luiz said, *"Iztac-patli."*

"No wonder I've never heard of it." She smiled.

"It's an old Aztec medicine made from exotic plants." He gave her the names of five.

"I see," she said, and studied his face thoughtfully. Puzzled, she asked, "But where did you get it?"

His face gave nothing away. "I am Aztec." His black eyes flicked up to hers. "Or had you forgotten?"

"No. No, I hadn't. But I don't—"

"Never question the *ticitl.*" His full lips suddenly stretched into a faint smile. "The doctor."

"No, of course not. But I'm curious where you got the—"

"All done," he interrupted, and, wiping his hands, recapped the tin of salve.

Amy knew it was useless to continue the questioning. Still, her curiosity remained. Where could he have gotten an ancient Aztec potion made of plants whose names were totally foreign to her?

Her thoughts were pulled from the riddle when Luiz picked up a strong-bristled brush, rose, stepped around her, and sank to the blanket behind her, trapping her between his long legs. For the next half hour he gently brushed away all the snarls and tangles from her long blond hair. When it lay smooth and orderly around her shoulders, he tossed the brush aside.

"Tip your head back a little," he said.

She did and he pulled all the gleaming gold hair atop her head and then expertly plaited it into one long, plump shiny braid that fell down her back. He took the white leather thong he had laid out and wrapped it around the braid's tip.

"Isn't that better?" he asked, leaning his dark face up alongside hers.

She turned her head to the side and looked at him. Smiling, she said, "Much better, thank you. Where did you learn to braid a woman's hair?"

His reply was a harmless tug on the golden braid and a shrug of wide shoulders. But Amy continued to wonder as he rose to his feet and moved toward the mouth of the cave.

He was too adept at the intimate tasks he had just performed. Far too capable of brandishing a hairbrush and plaiting long hair.

From out of the blue came a worrisome image

that had troubled her dozens of times. The unsettling sight of El Capitán and Diana Clayton entering the La Posada Hotel, all smiles. What had happened between them that day? What was continuing to happen between them?

Mentally Amy shook herself. What difference did it make now?

"Better get some rest while you can." Luiz's voice broke into her thoughts.

"Yes," she replied. She drew the long braid over her right shoulder and stretched out on the blanket. "You should rest as well."

"I will," he told her, and continued to stand at the cave's mouth, his gaze sweeping out over the surrounding hills and wide valley below. "Soon as I'm comfortable the Mescaleros haven't picked up our backtrail."

"Mmmmm," Amy murmured, folding her arms beneath her head. She closed her eyes, her breathing soon deepened; she fell asleep. Sometime later in the afternoon, she half awakened. Her arms came down from beneath her head. She laced her hands together atop her stomach. Her eyes partially opening, she saw that Luiz still stood, unmoving, at the cave's mouth.

Framed alone against the sky, he appeared to be carved from polished stone. The classic male profile, the thick raven hair, the superb physique. He was a magnificent work of art that took her breath away.

For long, enjoyable minutes Amy watched as if in a dream, entranced by his wild masculine beauty, waiting for the slightest movement to prove to her he was actually flesh and blood and not a cold, lifeless sculpture.

After what seemed forever, she caught the minute blinking of his thick black eyelashes. She smiled, closed her eyes, and went back to sleep.

Luiz's dark head swung around.

He knew that she had been watching him. Now he watched her. Watched until he was certain she was sleeping soundly. Satisfied that she slumbered deeply, he reached up behind his head, grabbed the collar of his buckskin shirt, and in one swift movement drew the shirt up over his head and off.

Silently he walked to the blanket. After sinking to his knees, he withdrew the Colt from his waistband, laid it beside the pallet, then leaned over Amy, gently lifted her head, and slipped his folded shirt beneath. Sighing softly in her sleep, she turned onto her side and her lips fell open over perfect white teeth.

Luiz automatically smiled, caught himself, and frowned. He stretched out beside her, folded an arm beneath his head, and draped the other across his bare belly. His aching muscles began to relax. Bone-tired, he felt as if he could sleep forever but knew he could not, that he had to get them down to Terlingua Creek by nightfall or they would be completely without water.

Setting his mental alarm clock for four that afternoon, he closed his scratchy eyes and exhaled heavily.

The exhausted pair slept as morning changed to afternoon and the blazing sun moved across the cloudless sky, steadily changing angles, spilling light more fully into the high mountain cave.

El Capitán had anticipated that occurrence and had placed the blanket accordingly. The sleeping couple remained in cool, dim shadow. All the same, at some point in the hot, still afternoon, Luiz came awake. It was not the sun or the dry heat or the threat of Apaches that disturbed his slumber.

It was Amy.

He had dreamed about her. Had dreamed that her golden hair was so long it reached the floor. Dreamed that they were on a cloud drifting through the heavens. Dreamed that she was naked, but her long, thick hair was spread about her so that he could see nothing of her beauty. Dreamed that he plaited her hair into a long rope of spun gold so he could leisurely admire her bare charms.

She had gladly allowed him to look upon her unclothed beauty and had teasingly tickled him with the long, braided hair, drawing it over his mouth, his chest, his belly until he was weak with wanting her.

But when he reached for her, she smiled strangely, swiftly wrapped the golden braid around his neck, and choked him with it, laughing in his face. The sound of heartless laughter was the last thing he heard as darkness engulfed him.

The dream had been so real Luiz felt his heart pumping violently against the bare skin of his chest. He swiftly turned his head and saw Amy lying there beside him, her face angelic, the golden braid falling over her breasts.

She looked sweet and completely harmless, but she was not. She was the most dangerous woman he had ever known, and he was afraid of her. Foolishly he had let his guard down since the moment he had carried her from the Mescalero camp.

She was getting under his skin.

Again.

He must not let that happen. If he did, he'd have nobody to blame but himself. It was all right for her to wrap her pale arms and legs around his body, so long as she never got her hands on his heart.

Luiz's eyes narrowed as he stared at her. Suddenly the impulse to hurt her was so strong in him he was appalled by it. His fists doubling, his entire body tensed with the pressure. At that moment, Amy awakened to see a pair of mean jet eyes looking at her. Alarmed, she rose to an elbow. "Is something wrong?"

A muscle contracted in El Capitán's dark face. He tore his gaze from her, rolled to a sitting position, and said, "It's time we leave. We have to get to Terlingua Creek by nightfall."

Amy had no idea what had caused the complete change in him. She knew only that the kind, caring companion who had doctored her insect bites and braided her hair had been left behind in that high cupped-out mountain crater.

The sullen man walking ahead of her atop a high, flat plateau had not spoken since they had quit the cave. Now, as the sun went down behind the mountains and the thin, dry air began to cool, Amy was dying to know how much farther it was to the creek. But she didn't dare ask. And he, of course, volunteered nothing.

It was dusk when finally they did reach Terlingua. The sight of all that clean, clear water brought a smile to Amy's face. Not so the captain. He continued to scowl and avoid her, and when she said, "I know it will be cold, but I've a good mind to take a bath," he shrugged as if he didn't care what she did.

Well, fine. She didn't care that he didn't care. The hell with him. He certainly was not someone whose opinion she valued. Making faces at his rigid back, Amy unrolled the blanket from their pack, tossed it over her arm, and headed around a curve in the creek.

The chill of the water took her breath away, and after only seconds in its icy depths, Amy was sure her body was turning blue. She swam to the bank and climbed out, shivering violently when the night air hit her wet flesh.

She snatched up the blanket and swirled it around her shoulders. Then she stood there, huddled under the blanket, her teeth chattering, her body trembling. She knew she had to get dressed, but she was so cold she couldn't bear the thought of it.

Amy saw a small reflection of light coming from around the bend where Luiz was setting up camp. Her chilled face lit with a smile. He had built a fire. She could warm herself before she dressed. Eagerly Amy gathered up her clothes and started toward the light.

She came around the creek's curve, saw him, and stopped before he caught sight of her. Shirtless, he was crouched on his heels feeding kindling to the blaze. Firelight danced on his naked torso. His hair swung forward, black as the night sky.

Luiz felt her presence and came to his feet.

Smiling tentatively and hoping his mood had softened somewhat, Amy started toward him. "The water was icy," she said conversationally. "I almost froze before I could get out."

She reached him and realized immediately that nothing had changed. Or it if had, it was for the worse. He looked at her with cold contempt, and there was about him that aura of suppressed violence.

As Luiz looked at Amy, he felt his anger and frustration grow. It seemed she delighted in torturing him. It was evident she was bare beneath the blanket. Apparently she was all too aware of his weakness, knew full well he was incapable of seeing her naked without wanting, needing, having to make love to her.

Damn her to hell!

She would *not* get the better of him. He could govern his emotions—and his hungers—as well as any man alive. Let her strip and dance around the fire for all he cared. He wasn't about to touch her.

Not tonight.

Not ever again.

37

His low-lidded stare was colder by far than the water that had left her shivering. A vein throbbed violently on his firelit forehead and an entire network of pulsing veins stood out in bold relief on his long, bronzed arms.

His hands were doubled up into tight fists at his sides and Amy was struck by the notion that he actually wanted to hit her. Instinctively she moved back a few steps.

Out of his reach, she said, "I'll go back down to the stream and get dressed."

"Stay where you are," he ordered evenly. "I'll turn my back."

He pivoted about and Amy hurriedly dressed, keeping a wary eye on him. His back to her, Luiz's black eyes were tightly closed. He ground his teeth viciously. His short fingernails cut into the palms of his hands. He sternly ordered his body not to misbehave.

It didn't listen.

After what seemed a lifetime to him, Amy said she was dressed. Luiz released a pent-up breath and half turning—but not looking at her—said in clipped tones, "I'm going downstream for a bath."

The icy water felt good to his tense, fevered

body. He swam back and forth across the wide frigid stream until his breath was short, his limbs exhausted, and the raging heat had left him.

In charge once more, he dressed and returned to camp. Across the fire, they shared a silent supper of beans, jerked beef and bread, keeping their eyes on their tin plates. Then slept back to back, each pretending the other did not exist.

Late the next morning, after crossing grassy meadows and endless flats of cactus and creosote, they were at the barrier ridges of the Santiagos. They had not spoken all morning. The tension between them was growing hourly.

Luiz's pointed coldness had fostered a like chill in Amy. It was obvious that the only thing he wanted was to have her out of his sight. Well, she wanted him to know that the feeling was mutual.

The sun was high and hot when they began the ascent into the rocky, broken country of the Santiago foothills. That's when the trouble really began. Luiz nimbly climbed over the uneven ground and fallen boulders, showing no mercy, not stopping to offer a hand.

Struggling to keep up, Amy did not ask for his help. She knew he was waiting for her to do just that. Well, he would wait until hell froze over. She would make it through this hostile country under her own steam if it killed her.

She ignored him when, pausing on ridges above, he turned smugly to look back down at her. She paid him no mind when once he stretched out on a rim high above, pretending to be napping. She disregarded his implied warning that if she did not hurry, he would leave her behind.

But when her lungs were burning so she felt they would explode, and her legs were too weak to climb up one more ledge, Amy shouted up to him, "I am stopping. Feel free to go on without me."

And she didn't take one more step. She slumped down to the ground, leaned back against a smooth rock, and closed her eyes. She did not open them even when she heard him swiftly coming down toward her, dislodging pebbles as he descended.

Steeling herself, she laid her head back on the boulder, stretched her legs out straight, and yawned lazily.

Eyes closed, she knew the second he reached her. Felt the overpowering presence that caused the downy hair to lift on her forearms. She was determined to keep her eyes shut, even when she knew without doubt that he was standing directly before her, scowling at her.

But she couldn't quite do it.

Tentatively she opened her eyes then gasped. He *was* standing over her. Almost on top of her. His moccasined feet were planted firmly on either side of her hips, arms at his sides. With her head back, she was looking directly at his groin.

While she helplessly stared, he slowly dropped into a crouch before her. Straddling her with his knees bent and widespread, he further directed her attention to the straining crotch of his buckskins.

Guiltily she tore her eyes away, annoyed by such blatant flaunting of his masculinity. When he lifted his hands and gripped the rock on either side of her, she was further irritated by a quick glimpse of the dark hair under his arms.

Angry and upset, she said, "You are suffocating me! Move back, damn you!"

"As soon as you agree to get on up the trail."

"I'll agree to nothing," she told him, meeting his gaze.

"We'll stay just as we are until you do."

"No," she said, "we will not."

"Yes," he assured her, "we will."

"I don't think so," she replied confidently, knowing it was virtually impossible for anyone to remain in his uncomfortable position for long.

"I guarantee it," he coolly assured her.

"We'll see," she said smugly.

"You'll see," he corrected her and remained crouched astride her.

And so began a foolish test of wills that would last for the next hour. Amy was miserable. A gust of hot wind blew a grain of sand into her left eye. She badly wanted to rub it but her hands were resting on her thighs with El Capitán's hard buttucks poised not an inch above them. She didn't dare risk brushing against him, so she was forced to sit there and suffer.

No sooner had her eye quit tearing than her nose began to itch. Then a drop of perspiration started at her hairline and slowly, maddeningly worked it ticklish way down the side of her face. When finally it dripped off her chin and she sighed with relief, she had a sneezing fit.

Through it all, Capitán Luiz Quintano remained as he was, not moving a muscle, seemingly in total comfort crouched there on his heels, spread knees and long arms enclosing her.

Amy finally conceded defeat.

"If you will kindly move off me, I'll try to go on."

By early afternoon they reached Persimmon Gap, one of the two small breaks through the rugged Santiagos. Leading the way, Luiz guided them into its wide mouth. A hundred yards inside, he stopped so abruptly that Amy, her head down, bumped into him.

Startled, she stopped short and said, "You trying to scare me half to death?"

"Quiet." He laid his forefinger to his lips.

"What is it?"

"Be still," he said. He dropped to his knees, leaned over, and laid an ear to the rocky ground. Frowning down at him, Amy didn't dare make a sound. When he came to his feet, took hold of her elbow, and guided her swiftly toward the ribbed wall of the canyon, she felt her heart rise to her throat.

"Apaches?" she whispered anxiously, hurrying over the uneven floor of fallen boulders and loose gravel.

"Apache, singular," he told her, "I heard only one horse. Likely they've sent out scouts all through the mountains and one has picked up our backtrail."

They hid behind a tall sandstone outcropping, Luiz urging Amy into a narrow passageway between the high promontory and the gap's rocky wall. After taking the packroll from his back, he tossed it behind her, drew out the Winchester, then left her there with the caution not to make a peep.

He scrambled up the sandstone spire and chose

a spot where he was concealed but could see anyone entering the canyon. Soon Amy could hear
the sound of horse's hooves striking the rocky
earth, drawing steadily closer. She sank farther
back into her close-walled hideout, hunched her
shoulders, pressed her hands between her knees,
and squeezed her eyes tightly shut.

She almost jumped out of her skin when Luiz
came skidding down the hillock. Wordlessly he
took her hand and pulled her from her hiding
place, then reached for the pack.

Whispering, Amy said, "Have they seen us? Are
they coming?"

"No Apaches," he told her, handing her the
Winchester and searching through the pack for a
length of rope. "A horse. A wild horse." He almost
smiled then and added, "We'll ride back to Orilla
after all. Come on."

Hurrying after him, Amy said skeptically,
"Don't be ridiculous. You can't catch a wild
horse."

"I can if you'll just keep quiet."

Lowering her voice, she said, "And even if you
could, what good would it do? If it's wild, we can't
ride it."

He didn't answer. They rounded the tall spire
where they had hidden, coming back out into the
main corridor of the gap. Luiz looked about, spotted a flat, overturned boulder large enough for
them both. He took Amy's arm and propelled her
to it, lifted her atop its five-foot height, then
climbed up and ordered her to lie flat on her stomach.

Immediately he stretched out on his belly beside her and within seconds the horse came fully into view. A red sorrel mare, she was as large as a stallion and looked every bit as powerful. Her mane hung in wild profusion over her sleek neck and her long tail swept the rocky ground.

The mare caught their scent and stopped immediately, fifty yards away. Amy, squinting at the shimmering horse in the distance, couldn't believe it when Luiz puckered his full lips and produced a low whistle.

The mare's ears went back flat against her head. Luiz whistled again and shot Amy a look when the curious mare trotted toward him. As the sorrel approached, she whickered nervously and Luiz began to talk to her in a low, crooning voice.

Inquisitive yet frightened, the mare stopped short when she was still twenty yards away. High nostrils flaring, eyes wild, she whinnied and tossed her head about, her body trembling with excitement.

While Amy lay completely still, Luiz continued to speak to the skittish mare, his voice low, encouraging, persuasive. The nervous sorrel stood her ground, would not come one step nearer. Urgently he chanted to her, gentling her, reassuring her.

Still she refused to move forward. Planting her feet firmly, she blew and snorted loudly while he continued with his litany of encouragement. Finally it worked. Slowly the mare came toward him, her big eyes watchful, her ears laid back.

"That's right, sweetheart," Luiz praised, "come to me. I won't hurt you. Come on, now. Let me pet you. I'm harmless, pretty girl."

Amy watched, awestruck, as the jittery mare, as if she understood every word, pranced toward the man so commandingly beckoning to her. Though a little hesitant, the mare was plainly intrigued. Slowly she came prancing to him, but stopped thirty feet away, unsure, sensing danger.

With a swiftness that left the mare and Amy stunned, Luiz bounded to his knees, threw the rope, sailing the loop high into the air. Startled, the sorrel jumped sideways and stuck her head straight into it. When she realized she was caught, she went crazy with fear.

Luiz leapt down from the boulder and went to her, holding tightly to the rope, drawing the slack around his elbow. The sorrel reared and whinnied, her eyes walling, her entire body shuddering.

Rising to her knees, Amy watched while the competent horseman gentled the terrified mare. Within minutes Luiz had reined in all the rope's slack and had his arm around the sorrel's neck, patting her. His lips near her laid-back ear, he murmured softly, telling her that she was a proud and beautiful specimen and the last thing he wanted to do was harm her in any way.

As badly as they needed a horse to ride home, Amy found herself meanly hoping the big sorrel would not be swayed by his murmured words and gentle hands. Watching the pair, she told herself the wild, magnificent beast was one female who would put El Capitán in his place! Just let him try mounting her! He would quickly find himself bucked off to the rocky ground before he could put his full weight down. And the beautiful, untamed mare would race right out of the canyon, leaving him behind without a backward look!

Amy held her breath when Luiz, clinging to the mare's thick mane, threw a long leg over and mounted her. The sorrel didn't like it. She bucked frantically, neighed shrilly, snorted violently, and carried on something awful.

But the man on her bare back stayed with her, clamping his long legs around her expanded belly, holding tightly to rope and mane, refusing to let the lady unseat him.

"No," Amy tonelessly murmured, "no . . . Don't let him do this to you. Don't you see he's determined to make you his, to bend you to his will."

It took a surprisingly short amount of time for Luiz to do just that. Not fifteen minutes after climbing on the sorrel's bare back, the mare had stopped trying to buck him off. Praising her, Luiz rode her around in a wide circle, teaching her how to respond to the pull of the rope, the touch of his knee, showing her that he truly did not mean to hurt her.

When the mare was completely calm—completely his—he rode her over to the flat rock where Amy waited. With a touch of his right knee to the sorrel's withers, he turned her and drew alongside the boulder.

One hand holding the rope, the other riding his thigh, he sat and looked at Amy, waiting for her to speak. Longing to smack that smug, dark face, she said nothing.

"Would you like to ride with me, or do you prefer to walk to Orilla?" he said, the tone of his voice leaving little doubt he would allow her to walk if she gave him any trouble.

Hating him for his eternal confidence, hating the foolish mare for falling so easily under his spell, hating herself for needing either one of them, Amy grudgingly nodded.

"I would like to ride," she said.

"With me?"

"With you."

The words had hardly passed her lips before he reached for her. While the docile mare swished her long tail, Luiz plucked Amy from the rock, sat her astride in front of him, and drew the packroll up and onto his back. He wheeled the sorrel about and the trio set out northward through Persimmon Gap.

If Luiz had expected any commendation for his almost miraculous act of capturing and quickly breaking the wild mare, he didn't get it. Amy was totally silent, withholding any acknowledgment of his feat.

The vulnerable, boyish side of the dark, enigmatic *capitán* had halfway expected her to be impressed. He thought she would at least comment on his prowess, his expertise with horses.

Stung that she withheld even one word of praise, he told himself she was just being an obstinate bitch. *Como siempre.* As usual. No matter. If he so chose, she would be his, totally. If he wanted her to be. And, when he left her, she would beg him to stay.

A hint of a smile touched his lips and he thought confidently, *I can break you just like I broke this beautiful mare, Mrs. Parnell.*

For a change Amy was the one who read *his*

mind. She knew exactly what he was thinking as if he had spoken it aloud.

"Never!" she coldly informed him, startling him so he jumped. "It will be a cold day in hell when you can break me, El Capitán!"

38

Things went from bad to worse.

No one could anger El Capitán as quickly and as completely as Amy Sullivan Parnell. And the fact that she could so anger him made him deathly afraid of her. And because he was deathly afraid of her, his anger grew fierce.

In turn, El Capitán's fierce anger made Amy fear him. And the fact that she feared him made her furious.

So it was two angry, frightened people who rode the sorrel mare northward. As the mare carried them through the high-walled Persimmon Gap, neither spoke a word, though the thoughts running through their heads were identical.

Luiz, his jaw set, his narrowed black eyes on the trail ahead, told himself that he would *never* touch the golden-haired witch again.

Amy, chin jutting, teeth clenched, swore to herself that she would *never* allow the raven-haired bastard to touch her again!

Silent, they rode through the quiet afternoon. At sundown they camped on the flat rim of a *barranca*. Thirty feet below, at the ravine's bottom, cold, clean water welled up from a spring. But neither Amy nor Luiz trusted each other—or themselves—enough to undress for a bath.

They spent a restless night, each finding it impossible to sleep. Clouds drifted over the moon, casting their hard bed into darkness. The wind rose to whine mournfully around rock outcroppings and through canyon crevices, rustling the thick chaparral, the sound eerie in the black silence.

Their progress was good the next day. When dawn broke over the mountains they rose and moved out, anxious to be on their way. By noon they left the Santiagos behind, stopped and ate alongside a small offshoot of Alamito Creek, dozed for an hour in the shade of a cottonwood, then set out again.

It was sunset when they reached the tall pink palisades bordering Fort Davis. Fifty yards out, Luiz pulled up on the mare, but they remained mounted. Amy, staring at the ruins of the once-bustling fort, spoke for the first time in twenty-four hours.

"My lord, what on earth . . . ?"

"Your playmates," came El Capitán's voice from over her shoulder. "Mescaleros burned the fort when the soldiers were pulled out during the war."

Amy shook her head and sighed wearily. "I thought we would find comfort and safety when we got here."

Luiz rope-reined the sorrel forward. "Maybe we will. Looks like they missed one of the officers' quarters." He pointed to the northwest.

Amy looked in that direction. At the base of the towering rock walls rising abruptly from the canyon floor, a lone building stood amid the fort's ruins, its porch roof fallen, doors and windows missing. It looked like a mansion to her.

Inside, debris was strewn throughout the one room, a table was smashed into splinters, broken glass was scattered over the plank floor. But on opposite walls were narrow bunks, complete with worn mattresses. Luiz tossed their packroll on one of the cots and swiftly cleared away the clutter. He told Amy that, if she'd like a bath, a stream noted for its clear, pure water ran through the canyon alongside the fort.

Amy haughtily informed him that she was well aware of the *Limpia* and its crystal-clear water, but had no intention of taking a bath. His reply was a lifting of his wide shoulders as he turned to leave.

"Where are you going?" she asked.

"Down to the Limpia to wash up."

"But it's getting dark."

"I'm not afraid of the dark," he told her, stepping out the door and walking away.

"I'm not either," Amy assured him, flopping down on one of the cots and folding her arms over her chest as dusk settled over the silent, ghostlike fort. From outside she heard the neighing of the sorrel mare and the soft words of El Capitán. Then nothing.

She sat alone in the darkening officers' quarters, feeling tense and on edge. Certainly she was not afraid of the dark. Never had been, even when she was a child. But here in this remote, destroyed fort, she was not actually safe. Apaches had been here before. Suppose they returned?

Amy remained seated on the cot for as long as

she could, attempting to calm herself. They had, she reminded herself, ridden miles from Snake Tongue's Chisos camp.

The recollection of the horrid chief made her spring from the bed, dash across the room, and fly out the door. Enough light remained of the dying day to find her way to the Limpia and Luiz. She considered calling out to him, thought better of it. If Indians were around, she didn't want to alert them.

She reached the gurgling stream and followed its banks toward the sound of splashing water. She stopped momentarily when she heard a horse nickering from around the next bend. Puzzled, she advanced cautiously and heard a man's deep laughter.

Bottom lip caught between her teeth, Amy tip-toed curiously around the curving streambed. Circling a cottonwood, she stopped short and her lips fell open.

She couldn't believe her eyes. The last traces of light revealed a laughing man and a nickering horse out in the deep center of the stream, swimming about like carefree children. Shaking her head, Amy watched as Luiz grabbed the mare's long tail and the mare joyfully swam forward, towing him after her.

Luiz abruptly released the sorrel's tail and disappeared beneath the surface of the water. Watching closely in the swiftly dying light, Amy grew nervous when long seconds passed and he did not emerge. So did the sorrel. The mare kept tossing her head, looking back over her shoulder, wondering what had happened to her new playmate.

All at once, up lunged Luiz out of the water, dark head and bare shoulders slicing the waters a foot ahead of the startled mare. He had dived down and swum between the mare's churning legs, underneath her belly, and surfaced directly in front of her. Confused, the mare nickered nervously until Luiz wrapped his long arms around her wet, slippery neck and laughed.

The strange pair continued to play for a few more minutes, and Amy realized she was smiling foolishly as she spied on them. Her smile disappeared when, without a warning, Luiz swam to the bank, rose, and walked out of the water.

Stark naked.

The obedient mare followed her master out of the stream, and for the next five minutes man and mare stood in the last of the twilight, shaking the residue of water from their glistening bodies.

It was the man's bare body that held Amy's rapt attention. Wishing she could turn and run, afraid if she made a quick move she might attract his attention, she was forced to stand there while he lifted his long arms and swept the wet raven hair back off his face.

When he ordered the mare to pick up his discarded buckskins, Amy didn't wait to see if the sorrel obeyed. As quietly as possible she turned and fled, waiting until she was around the bend before breaking into a run. Sprinting through the enveloping darkness, she reached the ruined fort, shot across the abandoned parade ground, and dashed anxiously into the officers' quarters.

Choosing the first cot her eyes fell on, she dove into it, hurriedly spread the blanket over herself, and closed her eyes tightly.

Her heart was still pounding from the run when El Capitán came through the door. He paused just inside. Amy supposed he was looking her way, determining if she was asleep. When he moved, Amy inwardly sighed with relief. He was going to his cot across the room. She had not been caught.

Luiz did go to his cot, but he did not lie down. He removed the Colt from the waistband of his pants and laid it on the bunk. He mopped at his damp chest with his sleeveless buckskin shirt and stared at Amy.

Then, Indian-silent, he crossed the small room, leaned down, and tapped Amy on the shoulder. She bolted up, eyes wide, and found herself face to face with El Capitán. He stood there like an animal crouched to spring, his black eyes flashing in the darkness.

"I don't like it when people spy on me," he said in low, level tones.

Horrified, she replied nervously, "I have no idea what you're talking about!"

"Yes, you do," he accused gently. Then: "If you want to see me naked that badly, I guess I'll just have to oblige you." His hands went to the laces of his buckskins.

"No!" she shouted. "Don't you dare take off your pants!"

"Ah, is it *your* pants you'd like me to take off, Mrs. Parnell?"

"Stay away from me," she hissed loudly.

"With pleasure," he softly replied.

The next day was another long one, passed in strained silence. They descended out of the cool Davis Mountains, down the grassy sloping mead-

ows. At sundown they stopped on a high, flat plateau and looked out over the barren deserts below.

Neither said a word. Both were aware that they
would be home before another sunset. Just one
more day of this forced togetherness and then it
would end forever.

Anxious to reach Orilla, and knowing that their
progress would be slow over the scorching desertland, they rode on long after the sun disappeared
and the moon had risen. Keeping the mare to a
slow, steady walk, they tediously edged their way
home.

The next day was every bit as uncomfortable as
they had supposed. By midmorning the desert
was like a furnace, the dry, still air so hot they felt
as if they were breathing fire. Luiz knew how to
survive in the desert. By ten o'clock he had found
them a sanctuary to den up in through the hottest
part of the day.

Back on the trail by two that afternoon, the sun
was still brutal, but they were determined to
make it to Orilla by night. They had ridden but a
mile when a great cloud of dust loomed on the
northern horizon. Luiz pulled the mare up and
squinted.

From the billowing cloud emerged a uniformed
patrol. Shimmering in the heat thermals like a
giant mirage, the uniformed troopers, out searching for the captain and Orilla's mistress, thundered forward. At their head, leading the rescue
operation, was the one-eyed Pedrico Valdez.

There was much shouting and joy and the first
thing Amy knew, she was no longer atop the sorrel mare with Luiz. She was riding behind a young

trooper on an iron-gray stallion. Clinging tightly
to the soldier's waist, she looked about and saw El
Capitán astride a blood bay gelding. The faithful
sorrel mare followed.

Amy quickly turned away. She was free of him
at last. No more long hours enclosed in his arms
atop a moving horse. No more sleepless nights
lying beside him in the darkness. Her running
away had proved successful after all.

In the past few days, the captain had made it
clear that he no longer desired her. Good! Tonight
she could sleep alone in her bed with half a dozen
pillows and a silky top sheet and soft downy covers. And she wouldn't be concerned that the door
could not be locked.

It was sunset when Amy spotted the tall arched
gates of Orilla looming against the pale lavender
sky, and up the hill, the twinkling lights of the old
Spanish-style hacienda.

Amy was almost as glad to see Magdelena as the
stocky Mexican woman was to see her. Tears
streaming down her brown cheeks, Magdelena
drew Amy into a smothering, motherly embrace
and thanked the Almighty in sobbing Spanish for
sparing a life so precious, for returning this child
of Orilla safely home.

After a sumptuous meal of which Amy ate little,
she put up no argument when Magdelena ordered her upstairs for a hot bath, then straight to
bed. Yawning, Amy took one last sip of coffee,
rose, stretched, hugged Magdelena one more
time, and left the big dining room.

Shortly after Amy's departure, El Capitán, fresh
from his bath in the bunkhouse, entered the haci-

enda's wide corridor. He saw the lights in the dining room, heard voices, and assumed that Amy was having dinner.

Here was his opportunity to collect some of his clothes without having to ask her permission. The borrowed white trousers he wore fit his slim hips and long legs, but the shirt was too small. On his feet were the shredded moccasins he'd worn for the past week.

He stole quickly up the carpeted stairs and into the mastersuite. Inside, the room was empty. A lone lamp burned beside the turned-down bed. Luiz kicked off the dusty moccasins and walked, barefoot, into the spacious dressing room.

He removed the too-small shirt, tossed it aside, and was reaching for a fresh one when movement caught his eye. He swung around.

Amy stood in the doorway between the bath and the dressing room, her golden hair pinned atop her head, a large white towel wrapped around her body. Her blue eyes flashed fire.

Luiz was about to apologize for the intrusion. To tell her that if he had known she was in her room, he wouldn't have come upstairs. To say that he was sorry and assure her it would never happen again.

But Amy didn't give him the chance. So his remorse turned swiftly to anger when, jumping to conclusions, she said hotly, "If you had one ounce of decency, you wouldn't have come here!"

Provoked, he replied, "If you had one ounce of honesty, you'd admit you want me here."

39

—
—

"To hell with you!" she said heatedly. "I do *not* want you here. I never wanted you! Never!"

His ice-cold black eyes flashed with a predator's intent and he advanced on her. "You are lying, Mrs. Parnell."

Amy backed away, a hand clinging protectively to her covering white towel. "I am not lying!" She moved from the dressing room and into the mirrored bath. "Get out of here, damn you!"

"Not yet," he said, looming tall and dangerous before her, "not quite yet."

Realizing too late that she had foolishly goaded him, Amy quickly tried another tack. "Look, I'm sorry. It's just that you startled me. Please, go. You don't really want me so—"

"You're right," he said, stalking her until she was trapped against a mirrored wall, "but you want me, Mrs. Parnell."

She couldn't believe her ears. Was he totally insane? "Such appalling conceit," she said, her anger flaring white-hot. "You actually believe that every woman—"

"Not every woman," he cut in. He reached out and curled his long bronzed fingers around the top edge of her covering towel. "But you are one who does."

"You wish!" she snapped, and clawed viciously at his intrusive hand.

Unbothered by her assault, Luiz gave the towel a forceful snap and watched as it fell open. Amy grabbed frantically at it, but he was quicker. He gripped both sides and framed her nakedness with the white towel, his black eyes glinting threateningly. He pulled her to him.

As Amy struck at him as best she could with her arms pinned inside, he said in a low, seductive voice, "Ah, Mrs. Parnell, you believe you're fighting me, but you're actually fighting yourself." He felt the slash of her long nails draw blood on his right cheek, but continued speaking in the same calm tones. "You needn't fret, sweetheart. I'll give you what you want. What you need."

Amy shouted, "I don't want you. I do not need you!"

"You honestly feel that way?"

"Yes, damn you to hell, I do."

He shook his dark head and told her, "I will have you crying out in ecstasy within the half hour, Mrs. Parnell."

There was no time for thought or warning. Swiftly he gathered her closer with the towel, bent his dark head, and captured her open lips. The long, intrusive kiss began, and the smoldering sexual heat that always existed between them blazed to life. The kiss was penetrating, furious, overwhelming. Still, Amy valiantly struggled against the naked desire he so suddenly evoked in her. But his hot lips and probing tongue drew all

the strength from her until finally she was motionless in his arms.

As the hot, harsh kiss continued, her bare
breasts swelled, the hard-rising nipples pressing
against his naked torso. The gold Sun Stone was
caught between them, and it cut into her pale
flesh.

Continuing to kiss her, Luiz lowered the white
towel until it caressed only her hips. Arms freed at
last, Amy neither fought him nor wrapped her
arms around his neck. Her hands fell limply to her
sides. Finally his lips lifted from hers but hovered
there an inch above.

Amy said defiantly, "I don't want—"

His mouth dipped back to hers, silencing her.
Gripping the towel, he drew her pelvis flush
against his own. Exerting pressure, then relaxing
it, he drew her forcefully against him as he rocked
his slim hips forward, then pushed her back as he
withdrew, repeating the action again and again.

Kissing her hungrily, Luiz stood in the mirrored
bath and led Amy in an erotically rhythmic dance.
Knowing she was enjoying this foolish bit of
foreplay, he continued with the teasing game.

But without the towel.

He released the towel and it fell to the carpet at
Amy's bare feet. He filled his hands with the soft,
rounded cheeks of her bottom and, not missing a
beat, drew her pelvis to him as he thrust his own
forward. Through his tight white pants he could
feel her honeyed heat. He pressed closer, permit-
ting the abrasive fabric of his white trousers to rub
against her sensitive flesh.

Still, when he lifted his mouth from hers, Amy
murmured, "I don't . . . I don't need you."

His released her buttocks. He swept his strong hands over her damp, slender back and slid them underneath her arms. Then, taking her breath away, he stretched his powerful arms straight upward holding her suspended in the air before him.

"No!" Amy arched her back. Her fingertips danced restlessly atop his muscular shoulders, and her bare toes curled into his trousered knees. She said softly, "Please . . . put me down."

"I will," he said as he drew her to him and brushed a kiss to her bare belly. "I'll put you down."

Continuing to hold her high in the air, he left the mirrored bathroom, walked into the spacious bedroom, and carried her straight to the bed. He put a knee on the mattress, laid her across the silky ivory sheet and, following her down, half lay atop her.

His mouth descended to hers again. He kissed her aggressively, his tongue thrusting deeply. While he kissed her, he swept the top sheet, the fluffy ivory comforter, and all the lace-trimmed pillows from the bed.

When he lifted his dark head and gazed into her eyes, Amy said weakly, "Don't do this, Captain. Go now."

"Soon," he replied. Then: "Take the Sun Stone from around my neck. I don't want to hurt you." Amy made no move to comply. Luiz lowered his mouth to hers once more, gently nipped at her bottom lip with sharp white teeth, and said, "Then both the Sun Stone and I will make love to you, Mrs. Parnell."

He kissed her lips, her throat, her shoulders, his

thick dark hair ruffling against her chin, the heavy medallion sliding down over her ribs.

"I don't want this," she murmured, and tried to rise, but his knee was pinning her to the mattress. He trailed kisses down her torso, around each full, firm breast, then enclosed a diamond-hard nipple in his mouth and sucked on it as if it were a delicious sugary treat.

Amy's breath caught in her throat. Her eyes opened and closed and she slowly raised a hand. But before she could place her fingers on his dark head, Luiz allowed the wet nipple to pop from his mouth and he moved on.

Downward.

His hand on her waist, he kissed her flat belly. Amy gasped, partially from the pleasure of his mouth, partially because the heavy Sun Stone had slipped between her parted thighs and was lying against the most intimate part of her anatomy.

The Sun Stone's shocking location was no mistake. While Luiz probed her navel with his tongue and licked the faint line of pale wispy hair that led down to the blond triangle, he held the gold medallion in his palm and pressed its warm shiny metal gently to her.

She realized it finally when he lifted his dark head, gazed into her eyes, then drew the gleaming medallion up before him and kissed it. Sliding it along its heavy chain, he shoved it over his shoulder to rest on his scarred back.

His black eyes holding hers, he told her, "My mouth will feel even better."

Knowing his intent, Amy said, "I won't let you."

Brushing a kiss to her left hip bone, he said, "I didn't ask your permission."

As deftly as any sleight-of-hand magician, he
took her hand, drew her up into a sitting position,
slipped off the bed, and knelt between her parted
legs. His long bronzed fingers tightly gripping her
knees, he said, "Watch me this time, Mrs. Parnell.
Watch while I love you this way."

"No . . . I won't . . . I—"

Amy did watch as his dark head lowered and he
began purposely tormenting her. His mouth went
to the inside of her left knee, he kissed it, then
languidly kissed his way up to the warm inside of
her thigh. A hair's breath away from the golden
curls he stopped short, raised his head, and ordered, "Kiss me."

And he knew all the power again belonged to
him when Amy anxiously cupped his dark face in
her hands and kissed him hungrily, hotly, thrusting her silky tongue deep into his mouth. He tore
his mouth from hers, sat back on his heels, and
kissed her right knee. And as before he slowly
teasingly kissed and licked and nipped his way up
to the borderline of golden pubic hair.

By now Amy's back was arched, and her breath
was coming in short, little pants. Her breasts were
full and aching, her belly contracting involuntarily. Between her parted thighs, guarded by
that abundance of thick blond curls, the tiny nub
of sensitive female flesh was slick from the wetness of her passion, swollen with the escalation of
her appetite, throbbing with the evidence of her
need.

She was hurting in a way only he could make
her hurt. Aching in a fashion she'd never experienced until he had taught her the meaning of
unbridled lust. Craving to have that heated

mouth pressed to her until she no longer hurt or ached or craved.

Luiz continued to torture her. He nuzzled his nose and mouth into the downy curls between her thighs, dabbed at the tight, moist coils with his tongue, teased at the burning flesh beneath, blowing cooling breaths over it. When he knew that Amy could not stand much more, he lifted his dark head and looked into her glazed blue eyes.

"Please . . ." she breathed, "kiss me. Kiss me."

"Where, sweetheart?"

"You know where."

"Show me."

"Here," she said, and eagerly put her fingers on the wet, throbbing flesh between her legs, knowing no shame or embarrassment. A loud breath exploded from her when his hot mouth immediately covered her fingertips. For a few seconds Amy didn't move her hand.

It was the strangest of sensations—the sweetest of sensations. His tongue licking her fingertips while her fingertips touched her burning flesh. When she started to move her hand away, Luiz stopped her.

His fingers encircled her wrist and he murmured, never lifting his head, "Let it stay."

So she did and the peculiar, but pleasing, ritual continued; a highly erotic game whose only object was to prolong her pleasure. With his tongue, Luiz pressed strongly against her fingertips, in turn pressing her fingertips against that tiny nub of pleasure. Then he probed between her slender fingers, the tip of his tongue forcing them apart, hungrily questing for the swollen sweetness beneath.

As adventurous as he, Amy eagerly played the game with him. If his goal was to get his tongue beneath her covering fingers, then hers must surely be to keep that delving tongue from gaining entrance. It was a glorious, erotic delight played with total abandon.

The game lasted but a short time more because one of the participants grew so incredibly hot, she could no longer battle her opponent, not when the only thing she wanted was the same thing he wanted.

To have his hot mouth and stroking tongue directly on her responsive flesh.

Always attuned to her slightest wish where sexual pleasure was concerned, Luiz released her wrist and Amy immediately withdrew her wet fingertips. She sighed with wondrous bliss when his open mouth settled hotly in their place.

At once he began to slowly, lovingly stroke her with his tongue. Amy, watching just as he had suggested, felt the heat of her body raging out of control. His tongue was spreading fire and she felt as if she would burst into flame where he touched her.

"Yes, yes . . ." She moaned and her fingers entwined in his dark hair. Frantically she pulled him to her, spreading her legs wider, thrusting her pelvis up and forward, feeling the unmistakable beginnings of her coming climax.

Luiz's hands went under her, gripped the cheeks of her bottom, and he lifted her as his dark face sank more fully into her. Hungrily he feasted on her, his tongue licking, lashing, circling, driving her half out of her mind. Amy writhed and panted and bucked against him, feeling as if the

center of the entire universe and all that mattered
in it was located between her legs. Enclosed in his
hot, sensual lips.

It began then, a release so deep, so frightening
in intensity, Amy pulled at the hair of Luiz's moving head and tears of sexual hysteria sprang to her
eyes. The climax went on and on, the delirium
spiraled up and up and Amy cried out, not caring
who might hear, not remembering there was anyone to hear but this raven-haired master of loving
whose bronzed face was buried between her
thighs, drawing the ecstasy from her with his marvelous, magical mouth.

At last the final explosion of heat came and Amy
shuddered and screamed from its potency. Luiz
kept his mouth fused tightly to her until the tiny
aftershocks had stopped and her tenacious fingers
had released their desperate hold on his hair.
Only then did he lift his head, brush one last kiss to
her belly, and rising, gently lay her back across the
bed.

Slipping the heavy gold medallion back over his
shoulder and onto his chest, he stood looking at
her.

She was limp and dazed. Her eyes were half
closed, her long golden hair swirled out around
her head like a silky fan. One slender arm was
bent, a hand lying open beside her serene face.
Her long shapely legs remained as he had left
them, parted wide, exposing the feminine charms
to which his mouth had paid homage.

A hint of a smile touched his glistening lips. She
was completely sated. Completely mastered.
Completely submissive. He could go now and

leave her. Leave her to leisurely consider, and ultimately admit, that he had been right.

She wanted him. Just as always. He could make her want him anytime.

Yes, he would leave her and he had better go immediately, so she wouldn't know just how badly he wanted her, needed her.

"I'm going now," he announced casually as he backed away, retreating languidly so that she would know he was completely cool and calm.

"Not yet," Amy said, her lethargy falling away. She sprang up from the bed. "Not just yet."

She went to him so swiftly, he was startled. She smiled up at him while her fingers curled into the waistband of his white trousers. "You can't leave now. Not when you still want me so badly, Captain."

"Want you?" Luiz shook his head and shrugged indifferently. Smiling confidently, he said, "You're mistaken, sweetheart. I don't want you." He attempted to brush her hand away from his waistband.

"You're lying, Captain." Amy's smile was as confident as his. Continuing to grip his waistband tightly, she leaned to him, put out the tip of her tongue, and gave a flat brown nipple a teasing lick. "You want me. You need me."

"No. I don't," he said, swallowing hard, "I—" The words choked off in this throat as Amy, paying no attention to his denials, sprinkled kisses over his smooth bronzed chest and boldly placed her free hand atop the erection revealed by his tight-fitting white trousers.

Running her fingers along the restrained fullness, she looked up into his eyes and said, "What's this then, Captain?

He shuddered involuntarily. "Don't. For heaven sake—"

"No, for your sake, *Mi Capitán.*" Pressing him back with her bare, slender body, she urged him toward the bed, her hands never leaving him, her lips and tongue at his broad, bare chest. When the backs of his legs touched the bed's edge, Amy gave him a shove. He fell onto his back and she swiftly climbed atop him.

Straddling him, she said, "I can have you calling out in ecstasy within the half hour, Captain."

She leaned down and kissed his mouth, his chin, his throat, and try as he might, Luiz could not bring himself to forcefully push her away.

Her teeth nipped playfully at his throat and she ordered, "Take the medallion off, Captain, I don't want to hurt you." Luiz shook his dark head. "No?" she said. "Then both the Sun Stone and I will make love to you."

"You've had your fun, Mrs. Parnell. Let it go now."

"But, Captain, you've not had yours."

Amy clasped the gold disk in one hand, the heavy chain in the other. She pulled it over his face, jerked it free of his dark head, and promptly draped it around her own. The glittering medallion swung appealingly between her full, naked breasts.

It fell onto his chest when Amy lowered her face and pressed open-mouthed kisses to his ribs and belly, licking a path along the line of thick black hair going down his middle. He exhaled heavily when her small, deft hands went to the buttons of his trousers.

His heart began to pound as she slid the buttons from the buttonholes, put her hands to the sides of the waistband, and, slipping off him to stand by the bed, ordered him to lift his hips. He did and she swiftly peeled away his trousers and linen underwear, not stopping until she had taken them completely off and tossed them across the room.

At once she was back astride him, settling herself on his hard thighs. Hands spread on either side of his body, she bent back to him, strategically lowering the swinging golden disk so that it fell and slid down over his straining masculinity.

"No . . ." he murmured, but she wasn't listening. While her lips and tongue played on his flat belly, Amy took the Sun Stone in her palm and gently, knowingly rubbed it up and down the length of his throbbing erection.

His breath was coming in short, loud spurts and he was groaning softly. Amy eased the Sun Stone's chain up and off him, lifted her head, gave the golden medallion a kiss, and swung it over her shoulder to rest on her back.

"My mouth will feel even better," she told him.

"No. You've never before . . . I won't let you."

Amy slid off the bed. Luiz quickly sat up, shaking his head. She pushed his legs apart and fell to her knees between them.

"I didn't ask your permission," she said. Her hands gripped his hard thighs and she added, "Watch, Captain. Watch me while I love you this way."

"No, damn it . . . I . . ."

But Luiz did watch as her golden head lowered

and she began to torment him sweetly. She started at his right knee and kissed her way up his hair-dusted thigh to its warm inside. She stopped an nth of a degree from where the thick raven curls swirled around his pulsing erection.

She raised her head and ordered, "Kiss me."

Luiz groaned helplessly, cupped her cheeks in his hands, and kissed her hotly, hungrily, the taste of her still on his lips and tongue. Amy tore her mouth from his and sat back on her heels. She kissed her way up the inside of his left thigh, then she nuzzled her nose and her mouth in the dense black curls of his groin. She put out her tongue and dabbed at the tight, crisp coils. She teased at his rigid burning flesh by blowing cooling breaths up and down the hard, hot length of him.

She kept it up until his breath was labored, the muscles jumping involuntarily in his hard thighs. Hoarsely he said, "Please . . . kiss me . . . kiss me."

"Where, Captain?"

"Jesus God, you know where."

"I don't. Show me."

Eyes clouded with passion, Luiz gripped himself. "Here."

Her mouth was on him immediately, atop the long bronzed fingers wrapped around himself.

"Let it stay," she commanded when he started to move his hand. She clutched his wrist, and just as he had done with her, she licked his squeezing fingers and forced the tip of her tongue in between to touch the rigid male flesh.

The game lasted for an even shorter time than when he had played it on her. His bare chest heaved, his heart thudded, his clutching hand trembled, and the long fingers loosened and fell away. Amy released his wrist and Luiz gripped the edge of the mattress when her soft lips pressed the gentlest of kisses to the base of his pulsating erection.

She put out the tip of her tongue and slowly, sweetly licked her way up the length of him to the smooth head. Her hands came up to gently cup him and she pressed a wet, warm open-lipped kiss to the smooth velvet tip.

Her soft hands clasping him loosely, Amy lifted her head and shook her long blond hair back off her face as her eyes met his. Holding his tortured gaze, she ran her forefinger back and forth over the glistening tip of all that awesome male power.

And felt her own power overshadow his when she said, "Tell me the truth, Captain, do you want me?"

"Jesus, yes!" He groaned in desperation and groaned again as Amy bent to him. "Ahhhh, Amy, Amy. . . ." He moaned as her warm, wet lips enclosed him.

At once she began to slowly, lovingly draw him into her mouth. Luiz, watching, felt the heat of his body blaze out of control.

"Yes, yes . . ." He moaned and his fingers entwined in her silky golden hair. Frantically he pulled her to him, spreading his legs wider, thrusting his pelvis up and forward, feeling the unmistakable beginning of his release.

Amy felt it as well. She drew him more deeply into her throat, determined she'd give him a climax unequaled by any he'd ever known.

Knowing he was only seconds away from exploding fulfillment, Luiz tried to pull her up. But

Amy refused to be dissuaded. She stayed with him and when his release came, there was no doubt in her mind that he had never before experienced anything to compare.

"Noooo . . . Ohhhh. . . . Ahhh. . . . Oh God, oh yes, yes . . . Baby, yes . . . Baby . . . babeeeeeee!"

The Sun God shuddered.

40

And so their heated sexual affair continued, just as before. But the handsome hard-faced captain never missed an opportunity to remind his naked blond beauty that no matter how hot their passions flared or how glorious their shared fulfillment, the splendor was entirely physical. It never touched his heart. *She* never touched his heart.

Amy was just as adamant.

Even as she lay naked in his arms, night after hot night, thrilling to the erotic pleasure he provided and bringing him to equal ecstasy, she looked dauntlessly into those hypnotic black eyes and firmly informed him that while he had conquered her body, he had never penetrated her heart.

Still, Amy suffered as never before. Far more disgusted with herself than with the uncaring, hardened man, she guiltily relished the hours spent in the arms of the highly sexed Captain. Their heated lovemaking was nothing like it had been when they were young.

Then they had both been innocents and they had learned together. They'd been awkward, unskilled, and unknowledgeable in the arts of offering and obtaining total fulfillment.

Not so this hard-faced man. An extremely skilled lover, El Capitán was capable of bringing her to total release in any number of ways. In their frequent sessions of lovemaking he had coaxed her into doing things she had never done with her husband. And she had learned, to her guilty delight, that she was not repulsed. She derived incredible pleasure from every intimate act they performed, from each shocking physical expression of carnal hunger in which they so enthusiastically indulged.

Nonetheless she constantly told herself she hated the cruel Captain. Hated sharing his bed because it was unforgivably sinful to do the things they did when neither cared one whit for the other. Hated him for making her the wanton she had become. Hated the steamy nights she behaved so shamefully.

But, if there was one thing Amy hated more than the nights Luiz made love to her, it was the nights when he did not. A master at meting out torment as well as pleasure, El Capitán kept her constantly off balance. As if he could look right into her tormented soul, he sensed the times when she most desired his touch.

And he withheld it.

On long, hot, sleepless nights when she most wanted him—needed him—Luiz did not come to her bedroom. Knowing she was watching, waiting, he strolled leisurely about the hacienda grounds, his lighted cigar like a beacon in the darkness.

Other nights he did come to their room. To strip and sleep naked beside her. To stretch and sigh and make her want him.

And never touch her. Knowing she was in agony, burning for his body. Then, when she least expected it, when the fever in her blood had cooled a little, he would commandingly seize her and take her to sexual paradise again.

It was on such a night that El Capitán, brushing a kiss to the sole of Amy's bare foot, rose from the bed, stepped into his trousers, and said, "Stay right where you are. I'll be back."

He left the room. When he returned he was carrying a tall stack of large boxes, which he placed on the bed before her. Amy, sitting up against the headboard, gave him a quizzical look.

"For you," he said, and placed one of the boxes across her naked knees.

As curious as a child, Amy lifted the lid, handed it to him, pushed back the folds of tissue paper, and withdrew the most stunningly beautiful evening gown she had ever seen in her life.

A shimmering creation of champagne taffeta, the tight bodice was cut low off the shoulder with a row of bias folds. The waistline was raised—in the very latest fashion—and the skirts were the new, narrower kind, flared out in the back.

Amy could not hide her delight. Her blue eyes shone with wonder as she held the lovely gown up before her, admiring it.

To herself, more than to him, she murmured, "I've never seen anything so beautiful. It's been . . . I don't recall the last new gown I—"

Luiz reached out and took the gown from her. "Get up and try it on."

Amy immediately bounded off the bed. "I suppose I'll need a corset and a chemise and petticoats and—"

"Tonight you need wear nothing under it." He took her arm and turned her about, then raised the dress up over her head and lowered it. He smoothed it down over her curves and deftly hooked up the low, tight bodice, then ordered, "Turn around."

Her hands reverently skimming down over the taffeta skirts, Amy turned to face him. Eyes aglow, she said, "It fits perfectly. As if it had been made especially for me."

Luiz said, "It was made especially for you."

"It was? But how did you . . . ?"

"I met your friend, Diana Clayton, in Sundown late one afternoon. She was dressed handsomely. The way I wanted to see you dressed. She gave me the name of her couturier in San Antonio. I sent one of my men with your measurements to San Antonio with orders for a dozen frocks."

Temporarily forgetting the true nature of their relationship, Amy said, "You mean you went to the hotel with Diana and all you did was . . ."

"What else?" he said, and she caught a definite hint of smugness as he surmised she had been jealous. He added, "How did *you* know I was in the hotel with Miss Clayton?"

"Ah . . . never mind that . . . May I look at the rest?" she asked, stepping away from him and lifting the lid on another large box.

A gorgeous apricot silk with a daring horizontal neckline. Next an ice-blue faille with pagoda sleeves and delicate lace around the deep V neck. A high-throated yellow satin with long tight sleeves, tight bodice, and a back that was open almost to the waistline.

Luiz stood with a muscular shoulder against the

bedpost, his black eyes hooded, watching as Amy excitedly examined the new gowns. She was, he thought indulgently, totally, endlessly female. She made no fraudulent, halfhearted attempt to conceal her joy at having these pretty new clothes to wear.

Standing barefoot in her champagne satin gown with her tousled blond hair falling into her face, she looked very much like a child. Like a thrilled little girl who had just come down to see what Santa had left under the tree.

All at once his heart squeezed painfully in his chest and he remembered too well when she was a little girl. A curious, pigtailed little girl who had followed him around, asking a million questions, tagging after him constantly, always wanting to know what he thought about this, what he thought about that.

Amy grabbed up the yellow satin and said, "I believe I'll try this one next. What do you think?"

She turned questioning eyes on him and for a second he was Tonatiuh, twelve years old and worshipped by this eleven-year-old blond girl. A muscle danced in his jaw and he shook his head.

His eyes fell on the ivory swell of her full breasts above the satin gown's low bodice. She was no child, nor was he. He took the yellow gown from her and tossed it aside.

"Try them on tomorrow," he said, moving closer. His hand settled on her bare shoulder, then slowly moved down to cup her right breast. He released her and swiftly stepped from his trousers. Naked, he leaned down, kissed her open lips, and said, "Let's make love."

"You'll have to unhook me" was her reply.

"No," he told her, "leave the dress on."

"No! We'll crush it!"

He sat down on the bed, pulled her to him, pushed the front of her full taffeta skirts up around her waist, and drew her down astride his lap. The taffeta rustled as he guided himself into her. Knowing they were wrinkling her beautiful new gown, Amy frowned.

But not for long.

In minutes the sound of the rustling taffeta competed with her soft sighs of pleasure and she found that making love in an expensive evening gown was great, decadent fun.

Theirs remained the strangest of relationships as the hot Texas summer wore on. Each long, blistering day they went about in front of the servants and the soldiers as polite strangers. Each evening they dressed for dinner, Amy in her fine new gowns, El Capitán in his dress military uniforms. Seated stiffly at opposite ends of the long dining table, their nerves grew ever more taut and raw.

And when the sweltering nights came, they exploded in a blaze of passion, both resolved that their hearts and souls would not be offered along with their willing flesh.

Luiz continued to behave as if Amy meant nothing to him. But that was not entirely true. The more he held her in his arms, the more he cared. And the more he cared, the more distant he became. His aloof manner was met with determined coldness from Amy.

Except in his bed.

There she could not keep the protective cloak of ice around her. On the hot summer nights, she continued to give in to greedy pleasure, just as he did. But despite those unforgettable nights, Amy was certain she actually despised him.

Until one blistering August day when a lone, pale rider came cantering up the long graveled drive of Orilla.

41

It was the hottest part of the day.

The old hacienda was silent. The servants were asleep in their quarters. Siesta time at Orilla. No one was awake in the big adobe mansion. Except Amy.

The heat had kept her from sleeping. Even with the shutters and drapes closed against the harsh August sun, it was stifling hot in her darkened bedroom. It hadn't bothered her while she and the Captain spent the first part of siesta time making love.

She'd hardly noticed the discomfort, despite the fact that they were both covered with perspiration after the first few kisses. In truth, that had added to their pleasure. It was somehow very sensual for their bare entwined bodies to be slippery wet.

With sweat glistening on his powerful bronzed arms, Luiz had held her. When his release came, beads of sweat flew and his raven curls shook.

But, afterward, when he had fallen asleep, Amy had lain there beside him, bothered by the stuffiness of the room, the stickiness of her body. Silently she had stolen from the bed, sponged her heated flesh, dressed, slipped from the room and down the stairs.

Now she stood on the stone porch, watering her thirsty, withered oleander bushes.

She saw the cloud of dust on the horizon and set the spouted pail aside. Curious, she crossed the big porch, lifted a hand to shade her eyes, and watched as a lone rider cantered toward the hacienda.

He rode right in out of the glare of the sun, pulled up on his steed at the edge of the yard, dismounted, and stood for a long moment, looking thoughtfully at the hacienda. Then he swept the hat from his head and Amy's hand flew up to her heart.

Tall and slim, the man strolled up the front walk toward her, his pale golden hair gleaming in the sunlight, his smile as bright and as counterfeit as ever.

"Baron." Amy's lips formed the name, though no sound came. The selfish, villainous brother she had not seen for years was coming up the walk, and her first and only thought was of Luiz Quintano, asleep upstairs in her bedroom. What would happen when he awakened? When Baron learned he was there?

"Baron," she said, finding her voice. "I can't believe it." She stepped forward to greet him, her mind racing. "You should have let us know."

Baron, looking much older than his forty-one years, stepped onto the stone porch. His once-handsome face was pale and puffy, the riveting blue eyes dulled permanently from liquor and debauchery. Once a meticulous man, his worn clothes were frayed and dirty, and they hung loosely on his too-thin frame.

But that smile, aimed at winning the coldest of hearts, was still brilliant and firmly in place.

"Glad to see me, are you, little sister?" He reached for her, but Amy sidestepped him.

"You must be hot and tired, Baron," she said, gesturing nervously. "Sit down here in the shade and I'll bring you something cold to drink. How does that sound?"

Baron raised a blond eyebrow and remained on his feet. "Why would I want to stay out here when I can go inside where its cool?" He advanced on her. "Yep, I think I'll go upstairs and take a bath, get some of the trail dirt off me."

"Wait!" Amy said, blocking his way. "I . . . ah . . . can't we visit awhile first and then—"

"What's this, now?" His smile broadened and he shook his head accusingly. "You never had two words to say to me before. Why all this sisterly interest now?" He reached out and touched a long golden curl lying on Amy's left shoulder. "Why, Amy, have you got yourself another hot-blooded Mexican stud to warm your bed while old Doug's down in Mexico with Maximilian, playing soldier?"

"No, of course not. Don't be—"

"I bet that's it," he interrupted. "I bet you've got some José or Carlos or Jesus putting it to you every night. What about it, little sister? Still humping the vaqueros?"

"Stop it, Baron! Don't speak to me like that."

"I'm going inside," he told her casually. Amy, frantic, whirled about and rushed indoors ahead of him, trying to think what to do.

Hurriedly she crossed the brick-floored corridor, hoping to draw her brother into the *sala.* But when Baron paused just inside the front door and moved no farther, Amy looked first at him, then at what he was staring at.

At the top of the stairs stood a bare-chested Luiz Quintano, Colt .44 in his raised hand. Seeing the hatred flashing in his black eyes, Amy automatically shouted, "Dear God, no! Luiz, don't, he's my brother!"

Holding her breath, she watched as his bronzed arm slowly lowered. Immediately a shot rang out and a bright blossom of blood appeared on Luiz's dark chest. Amy screamed in horror, but before she could move, a second shot was fired.

As if in a dream, Amy turned to see Baron Sullivan, a smoking revolver in his hand, crumple to the brick floor.

Magdelena, her face a mask of hatred, came calmly forward, still clutching the smoking gun. Unable to move, to think, Amy stood rooted to the spot, her heart pounding with fear and horror, while the Mexican servant who had never harmed anyone or anything moved purposely toward the dying blond man.

His blue eyes clouded with pain and shock, Baron, clutching his stomach, murmured, "Mag . . . Magdelena, honey. Why . . . ?"

"Once I love you with all my heart," she said, standing above, looking down at him. "Then you kill my baby, my Rosa. Now I kill you." She slowly raised the gun.

"No!" Pedrico's voice cut through the tension and penetrated. He threw open the front door, hurried inside, and tore the gun away from Magdelena. Sobbing, she collapsed against him.

Amy's horrified gaze was on her brother. She watched, unmoving, as Baron Sullivan gasped his last breath. Amy did not go to him. She did not burst into tears. She did not experience so much as one fleeting second of sorrow.

"Luiz!" she screamed, and flew up the stairs.

Her high brow drawn in lines of worry, her body weak with exhaustion, Amy Sullivan Parnell sat at the bedside of the wounded Captain Luiz Quintano, refusing to allow anyone else to tend him.

It had been three days since the tragedy.

Amy had lived a lifetime in those three terrible days. An hour after the shooting, Doc Gonzales had arrived from Sundown to remove the bullet from Luiz's chest. It had been touch and go for the next forty-eight hours. Finally, this morning, as the sun rose on another long, scorching Texas day, Luiz's black eyes had opened and he had asked for water.

Now, as the sun was going down, Amy sat in the gloom and studied the dark, still face on the ivory pillow. His prominent cheekbones seemed more pronounced, as if already he had lost weight.

Brows knitting, Amy leaned closer. She peeled the ivory sheet down from his bandaged chest to his waist. She placed a gentle hand on his bare stomach. His belly was concave below his ribs. If he didn't soon start taking nourishment, any remaining reserves of strength would ebb swiftly away.

Amy patted his sunken stomach as if he were a

sickly child, and she shook her head in despair. She drew the sheet back up over his chest and shoulders and tiptoed from the room. Outside, she raced down the stairs, forgetting that she was tired.

In the kitchen she found Magdelena.

The Mexican servant, seated at the table, hands laced atop it, raised her graying head and looked up when Amy came hurrying in. It was the first time the two women had been alone since the catastrophe. Great tears sprang to Magdelena's eyes and rolled down her fleshy cheeks.

Rising she said, "I kill your brother. I will leave Orilla. I will go tomorrow."

"This is your home, I want you to stay," Amy said, meaning it. Her tired arms opening wide, she stepped forward to comfort her lifelong friend.

Crying openly, Magdelena sobbed. "Can you ever forgive me for what I've done?"

"There's nothing to forgive," Amy soothed, patting her shaking back. "Put it from your mind and we will never speak of it again."

"*Dios*, you are a good, kind woman," Magdelena said gratefully. She pulled back to dab at her eyes with her apron.

"I am neither." Amy blinked back her own tears. "Now I need your help. El Capitán must eat something soon or . . ."

"I fix strong beef broth for him already. I warming on the stove. He is awake?"

"No, but I mean to wake him. I am going to feed him whether he's hungry or not."

Nodding, Magdelena said, "Dr. Gonzales said

Luiz is lucky the bullet missed his heart. He will
be okay, no?"

"I don't know; I am worried, Mag. Doc Gonzales said this afternoon that Luiz is not coming
around as he should. He said it's as if Luiz isn't
fighting. As if he doesn't care whether he lives or
dies."

"You must make him care," Magdelena said,
and hurried to dish up the steaming broth.

Amy did make him care.

She woke him that evening and insisted he allow her to feed him a few spoonfuls of the nourish-
ing broth. That simple act of human kindness was
the beginning of a profound change between the
pair.

It was during Luiz's convalescence that cruelty
was replaced with kindness. Lust with love. Revenge with regret.

For two long weeks Amy was never out of his
sight for more than a few moments at a time. She
did everything for him, refusing offered help from
Magdelena and Pedrico. She fed him, she bathed
him, she shaved him, she changed his bandages.
She tended his every need and did so with kindness, patience, and good cheer.

In turn Luiz was the model patient. He worried
about *her* health. He tried to persuade her to rest
more, to leave him, to let him take care of himself.
He thanked her genuinely for everything she did
for him, no matter how small the favor.

Early one afternoon Amy saw the pain in his
black eyes, though he said nothing. He never
complained. It was more than she could bear to
see him hurting. The doctor had left plenty of

laudanum, but she could never persuade Luiz to take any. So she did what she had done more than once since he was wounded. She added a few drops to a cup of hot tea and made him drink it.

Within minutes he had gone to sleep, and he slept the long, hot afternoon through. Sleeping deeply, resting peacefully in a drug-induced slumber. Amy, in her usual chair beside his bed, watched him as a protective mother would watch her only child.

As she watched him, a tightness closed around her chest. He was so beautiful, so very beautiful. His face, turned toward her, was unlined and smooth and perfect, save for the white scar down his cheek. He looked like a young, innocent boy. Like the young, innocent boy she had adored a lifetime ago.

All at once the need to touch him was so great Amy slid from her chair. On her knees beside the bed, she slowly, carefully peeled the ivory sheet down to his waist. Being very careful not disturb the bandaged wound, Amy placed an arm across him and laid her cheek directly atop the bare right side of his chest.

Sighing softly, she allowed her hands to lightly, lovingly clasp his naked ribs. Inhaling deeply of his cherished scent, she closed her eyes and murmured softly, "My darling, I'm sorry, so sorry. Everything bad that ever happened to you is my fault."

Her eyes fluttered open, but her cheek remained pressed to his warm chest. Her lips formed his name against his smooth, bronzed flesh and she simply spoke his name over and over again. His name, not El Capitán's. Not Luiz's. But his real name. His only name as far as she was concerned.

Tonatiuh.

"Tonatiuh, my Tonatiuh," she softly whispered. "Tonatiuh. Tonatiuh. Tonatiuh." She sighed. "My love, my only love, my Tonatiuh. Tonatiuh, Tona—" Amy abruptly stopped speaking as a hand touched her, settling gently on the crown of her head. All the breath left her body as long, firm fingers entwined in her hair. She was afraid to move, afraid to speak, afraid to hope.

Amy slowly lifted her head and saw those magnificent black eyes swimming in tears. It touched her more deeply than anything that had gone before. She began to cry.

And she sobbed aloud when the tears spilled down his dark cheeks and he said, "Don't cry, darling. Kiss me. Kiss me, Amy. Kiss your Tonatiuh hello."

42

"My love." Amy sobbed as he gently pulled her to him with his good arm.

His mouth covered hers in the first tender kiss they had shared since the days of their youth. Luiz tasted the salt of Amy's tears and his heart kicked painfully against his wounded chest. Slowly, lovingly, he kissed all her tears away.

But new tears streamed down her flushed cheeks as their lips separated and Amy said, "I've hurt you so much. I'm sorry."

"Shhh, sweetheart." His hand cradled her head. "I'm the one who is sorry. I've been cruel. I've made you suffer, and for that I will never forgive myself."

Both began to talk at once, anxious to assure the other that all was forgiven. Punctuating each rushed, broken sentence with eager, healing kisses, all that had been locked in their hearts poured out. Explanations were offered and accepted. Forgiveness was sought and extended. Love was confessed and embraced. Both cried unashamedly and their tears washed away the last bitter traces of misunderstanding and distrust.

Finally Amy laid her head on Luiz's chest and sighed peacefully. And she said, "Please, my love, you must tell me of the night my brothers took you from Orilla. How did you survive? Who saved your life?"

Luiz smiled and brushed a kiss to her forehead. And he said, "The Sun Stone."

Amy didn't doubt him for a second. If her beloved Tonatiuh said the Sun Stone had saved him, then it had. "Go on," she coaxed, eager to hear everything.

His voice low and even, Luiz said, "It was midnight when Baron and Lucas left me for dead in the deserts of northern Mexico. Baron hatefully threw the Sun Stone at me. It landed several feet from where I lay. Its brilliance drew me like a magnet. I crawled to it, knowing only that I had to reach it, to hold it in my hands.

"Finally I made it. I recall vividly my fingers closing around the golden disk. The next thing I remember was waking in a vast underground cave filled with stalactites and stalagmites and strange, unnatural limestone formations. The first sound I heard was the soft tinkling of bells. My vision was blurred, but when it cleared, I saw, seated on the stone floor beside me, my beautiful mother, the last princess of the Aztec.

"She wore a magnificent robe of scarlet silk and there were tiny gold bells sewn all around the skirt's hem and around the edges of the long, loose sleeves. The golden bells tinkled with every move she made. She lifted her right hand and laid it to my cheek.

"And then the goddess Xochiquetzal spoke and her voice was rich, melodic. She said, 'Tonatiuh, my only son, you are in the chamber called *El Pavika*. It is here that important rituals have been held for centuries. One is testing the bravery of our young boys who are left alone in the darkness.'

"She smiled then and lifted her elegant hand to brush her long black hair back from her face. 'You, my son, my Tonatiuh, withstood a much worse test than darkness.' The smile left her face and her eyes turned icy when she said, 'The white man's whip.' At once her smile returned and she praised me. 'And the gods tell me you never made a sound.'"

Luiz fell silent then, remembering that day. Amy hugged him tightly and, looking into his eyes, told him she was just as proud of him as the goddess Xochiquetzal. She vowed she would kiss those scars left by the whip until she wore them completely away with her adoring lips.

At that Luiz laughed, and Amy thought she had never heard anything quite so wonderful. Or seen anything quite so enchanting. His white teeth flashed and his black eyes twinkled and his hard facial features softened dramatically. He looked incredibly young and carefree. It caused her heart to sing.

"Woman," he said, looking at Amy's soft, lush mouth, "I can think of better places for your lips."

"You are shameless," she teased, and snuggled happily back down to his chest, lacing her hands and leaning her chin atop them so she could look at him. "Tell me more. Tell me about every minute of every day and night you were away from me."

Luiz told of spending two years with his mother and her court. Then sailing abroad to learn of his Spanish heritage. Determined to keep nothing from her, he told of killing her brother, Lucas, in

Paso del Norte. Self-defense, the judge had ruled.
The long scar on his cheek was from Lucas's slashing knife.

He looked into her eyes and saw no shock, no
censure. She simply nodded and let her gaze caress the long white scar.

They talked and talked, clearing up once and
for all anything that might still be puzzling. Or
troubling. There was only one secret Amy withheld. Had he asked, she would have told him the
truth.

They kissed and sighed and fell into easy, relaxed silence. It was Amy who first spoke again.

"Tonatiuh?"

"Yes, sweetheart?"

"Doug Crawford thinks I'm here waiting for
him."

"I know," Luiz said softly. There was a note of
deep sadness in his voice when he added, "We are
ill-starred, dear Amy." He pressed her closer. "I
found you only to lose you again."

"I love you," she said. "I've always loved you.
What are we going to do?" She hugged him
tightly and buried her head in his chest.

He said, "I'd like to say that we will go away
together and forget anyone else exists. We'll find a
place where no one knows us and we'll start over
from the beginning. You'll get to know me and
I'll—"

"I have always known you, Tonatiuh," she said
with a sudden softness, her mind reaching back to
a time tender to them both.

"Yes, you have. So you know what we must do. I
have obligations; I am an officer in Juarez's army
of liberation. And I must now lead my men back

into battle." He paused, waited for her to speak, and when she did not, he continued, "You, sweet love, have obligations too. A young daughter who wouldn't understand if her mother ran off with a half-breed. Doug Crawford has known enough tragedy. He will be a good husband and father."

Crying softly again, Amy sadly looked into his eyes. "But what about us? You and me?"

Luiz swallowed hard. "We've wasted so much time. Let's waste no more. For as long as I am here, let's live as if we'll be together always." He smiled at her, then added, "And we will be, sweetheart. I told you a long time ago that you are my *tonali*. My fate. My destiny. You will be a part of me for as long as there's breath in my body."

"That's just talk. It's not enough, Tonatiuh. I love you. I want you. I don't care about the others. Just you . . . just you . . ."

But even as she said the words, Amy knew it was hopeless. Love, no matter how deep, could not change everything. Could not completely alter the past and all that had happened since.

Neither mentioned parting again.

They pretended the bliss they shared would last forever. They spent every moment of every day and night together, and the hours were golden, precious, unforgettable.

Magdelena knew and jealously guarded their much-needed privacy. She cautioned her well-run household to let the pair be. To stay out of their way.

When one evening Magdelena went outdoors to take the breeze on the east patio, she looked up and smiled as Pedrico approached and asked if he might join her.

They spoke of the couple upstairs and it was Pedrico who said, "They deserve a few hours of happiness."

"Yes," Magdelena said. Then: "Did you know that . . . ?"

"That they were lovers all those years ago? Yes, I know. And Linda, is she his?"

"She is," Magdelena said. "Amy has never said as much, but I am a woman and women know. And Linda looks hauntingly like Luiz."

Nodding, Pedrico drummed his fingers on the wooden chair arms. He cleared his throat needlessly.

"Magdelena?"

"Yes?"

"Perhaps Luiz and Amy are not the only ones who have earned a little happiness." Magdelena stared at him, wide-eyed. Pedrico nervously stroked his thin mustache and said, "My life has been a lonely one. I believe yours has been also. Do you think . . . that is, would you consider waiting for me, Magdelena? When this conflict ends, I want to come back here. Orilla is the only home I have ever known."

Surprised, flattered, Magdelena self-consciously smoothed her untidy graying black hair and smiled almost girlishly.

"I will be here, Pedrico. Waiting."

With Amy for his beautiful, caring nurse, Luiz quickly mended. Soon he was almost back to full strength and could have taken care of himself. But he chose not to let on. It was far too pleasant having Amy fuss over him.

On a hot afternoon in early September, a rare

cloudburst broke over the desert. Thunder boomed loudly, lightning flashed, and torrents of rain splashed against the tall bedroom windows.

Inside, Luiz was propped up against the bed's headboard, smiling boyishly while Amy, soapy sponge in hand, bathed him. Along with the bath there had been plenty of teasing and laughter and fun. Luiz laid his head back and inhaled deeply, a contented man.

"I love the smell of the rain on the desert," he said. "It makes me want to . . . to . . . Amy . . . honey, what is it?"

Suddenly Amy looked up at him with great tears in her eyes. After dropping the soapy sponge back into the china basin of water, she picked up a large white towel and pressed it to Luiz's gleaming chest.

She had to tell him. She could keep the secret no longer; it wasn't fair to him.

"Linda is your child, Tonatiuh. She's yours. Your black eyes, your dramatic coloring, your wild beauty."

"Sweetheart? You mean that when—"

Forcefully Amy shook her head. "I was carrying your child when Baron and Lucas drove you from Orilla. That's the reason I married Tyler Parnell. I didn't know what else to do."

"Well, of course you didn't, honey. You were just a child yourself. Oh, God, Amy, Amy."

He reached for her, but she said, "Wait. There's something I want you to have." She rose and crossed to the tall mahogany bureau. She took out a porcelain music box, flipped it open, and while it played, she withdrew a fragile gold locket and returned to the bed.

She held it out in her spread palm and said, "Open it, Tonatiuh."

Carefully he opened the small gold locket and stared, unblinking, at the tiny photograph of a startlingly beautiful young girl.

"This is . . . ?"

"Yes. Our daughter, Linda. I want you to have this."

Amy draped the delicate gold chain around his neck and fastened it behind his head. The locket fell into the hollow of his bronzed throat. At once, Luiz removed the heavy Sun Stone from around his neck. He draped it over Amy's head and placed the gold medallion between her breasts.

He pulled her into his arms and said, "Our daughter is almost as beautiful as you, my love." A near flash of lightning illuminated his dark face. The following thunder rattled the windows. "I am eternally sorry for all the unhappiness I have caused, for the unnecessary cruelty I have shown you. I love you, Amy. I will love you forever." His arms tightened around her. "Sweetheart, a dispatch arrived today. Marching orders. We leave in the morning."

"Then you must take back the Sun Stone," she said, and raised her head, "so you will be safe in battle."

"No." He stopped her when she started to remove it. "You must keep it. It is a part of me." What he left unsaid was that his safety mattered little since he could never have her. "If the rain stops, will you ride with me to the Puesta del Sol at sunset?" Unable to speak, Amy nodded and kissed his bare chest.

And that night, when the skies had cleared and

a million stars dangled in the darkness like diamond pendants, the pair rode his strong black stallion, Noche, up to their private bend in the river. There in the silvery moonlight they made love one last time; it was almost spiritual.

Their bodies still combined, Luiz pressed his hands onto the grassy banks and eased himself upward to get a better sight of Amy. His black eyes shining with love, he said, "We will not meet again. But you go with me; I go with you."

"Yes, my only love," she answered, "my darling Tonatiuh."

At sunup the next morning, El Capitán Luiz Quintano, in full military dress uniform, stood beside his restless black stallion addressing his mounted troop. His back to the salmon-colored hacienda, he stood with his booted feet apart, wide shoulders erect, hands clasped behind him.

When the short speech ended, he drew the stallion's reins up over its great head and started to mount. But he stopped, turned, and saw her coming toward him, her golden hair a shimmering halo in the early morning sunlight.

Mindless of the soldiers and servants, Amy crossed the yard's dewy grass and then the dusty plain where he waited. Her hand clutching the heavy Sun Stone resting on her bosom, she reached him.

Luiz looked at her, committing to memory every perfect feature. He said nothing. Nor did she. His arm encircled her and drew her to him. Their embrace was brief but full of meaning.

As if they would never see each other again.

43

When El Capitán and his troop had ridden out of sight, Amy sighed, turned, and went back into the hacienda.

Already it seemed empty. Amy felt lost. She didn't know what to do with herself. She moved aimlessly about the silent rooms, half listening for the deep voice she would hear no more, half looking for the dark face that was forever gone.

When the long summer day finally drew to a close and a full, white moon rose over the desert, Amy climbed the stairs to her suite. Inside, she leaned back against the door and let her searching eyes slide around the big, lonely room.

There was nothing there to indicate a virile man had recently occupied it. No shirt stud rested atop the mahogany bureau or on the nighttable. No trousers were tossed carelessly over a chair's back. No gunbelt was buckled around the tall bedpost.

Amy pushed away from the door, went into the dressing room. Here it was the same. No blue military uniforms. No black gleaming boots. No snowy white shirts.

Nothing.

Amy wearily prepared for bed. A clean white

nightgown had been laid out just as always. Smiling suddenly Amy did with the gown what El Capitán had done every night. She picked it up, tossed it aside, and undressed.

Naked save for the Sun Stone around her neck, Amy crawled in between the ivory silk sheets, blew out the lamp, and settled back on the fluffy pillows. She sighed and stretched her slender legs out full length. She pulled the silky sheet up over her breasts. She told herself it was splendid to be allowed the luxury of sleeping with pillows and sheets and downy comforter.

And then cried because she would gladly have given them up forever if she could have slept the rest of her nights in El Capitán's arms.

Late the next afternoon Doug Crawford, leading a small detail of Maximilian's cavalry, rode through the tall white ranch gates of Orilla.

Magdelena was the first to see the mounted soldiers. She called to Amy. Amy hurried outdoors and squinted at the approaching detail. She saw the leader's flaming red hair blaze in the summer sunshine.

"My God . . . Doug," she murmured soundlessly. "It's Doug. He's come home."

She automatically unbuttoned the bodice of her dress and slipped the Sun Stone inside. Then she drew a deep breath, lifted her skirts, and ran forward to greet the big, kind man who loved and trusted her.

Doug Crawford swung down out of the saddle, scooped Amy from the ground, and swung her around. When he lowered her to her feet, he said,

"Honey, I'd just about forgotten how pretty you are."

"It's good to see you, Doug," said Amy.

And it was.

Doug Crawford had a kind, gentle nature. He spoke softly, his Southern drawl barely audible at times. His smile, when he looked at her, was genuine and pleasant, adding to the softness of his facial expression.

It was not until she and Magdelena were serving lemonade to his thirsty men that Doug caught Amy alone in the kitchen and said, "Honey, I can't stay but a couple of hours. We ride from here to form up with a large force near Chihuahua City."

Amy's breath caught in her throat. Chihuahua City! That's where Luiz had headed. "Can't you at least spend the night and—"

Abruptly he pulled her into his close embrace. "God, how I'd like to. Amy, Amy," he said, and his arms tightened around her, pressing her to his massive chest and pressing the concealed Sun Stone against her breasts.

Plagued with guilt, Amy's eyes filled with tears. Against his muscular shoulder, she said, "Doug, there's something I must tell you." She pulled back to look at him.

Doug Crawford smiled and said, "Honey, there's only one thing I want you to tell me. Say you'll be here, waiting for me when I come back to stay."

Amy's tears overflowed and spilled down her cheeks. "I'll be here," she said, then added, "And I will try to be a good and decent wife to you, Doug."

"Honey, you're all I could ever want in a wife."

Smiling, he drew her protectively close and said, "My men razzed me about being such a fool in love I'd ride all the way up here just to see your pretty face one last time."

By sundown Doug Crawford and his men had left Orilla. Long after their departure, Amy stood alone in the twilight, silently asking God to forgive her her sins and to watch over both men.

The following days were long and agonizing for Amy. News was slow coming out of Mexico, but finally word reached Sundown that Juarez's rebel army had been marshalled and was waiting for the attacking French troops. A bloody siege had ensued. Chihuahua City had fallen. But not before there were heavy casualities on both sides.

There was nothing Amy could do but pace the floor and wait. Magdelena understood perfectly. She too paced and worried. One breathtakingly clear September morning, the two women heard the clatter of horses' hooves striking gravel. Both flew outside and stood holding hands while the lone rider cantered up the palm-lined drive.

"Pedrico!" Magdelena cried and, dropping Amy's hand, hurried down the walk to meet him. Amy stayed where she was while the aging couple embraced. It was when they started toward her that Amy commanded her racing heart to slow its beating, her watery knees to continue supporting her.

Unable to speak, she turned anxious, questioning eyes on Pedrico's dark face.

Pedrico took her hand. "I am sorry, Señora Amy. Captain Douglas G. Crawford was killed leading the last mounted charge. He died a hero."

Amy swayed but stayed on her feet. Barely above a whisper, she asked, "And Luiz?"

"Missing," Pedrico said. "El Capitán is missing." Amy paled visibly and Magdelena put an arm around her slender waist. Pedrico hurried on, "So many dead, but many more captured. We can continue to hope, to believe that—"

"Yes, of course," Amy said with little conviction, "we can hope. Now, if you'll excuse me . . ."

"Wait, *Señora,*" Pedrico said. He reached inside his soiled tunic and produced an envelope-shaped chamois bag. "Before El Capitán rode into battle, he told me to give this to you if—if—"

Inside the chamois envelope was a will, written only hours before Luiz had gone into battle. A wealthy man, with priceless treasures from his Aztec mother and wise investments made with his Castillian cousins, Luiz left all he had to Amy. With the exception of one small portion of Orilla. If Amy was agreeable, the handwritten will stated, Pedrico Valdez was to have the far southwest corner of the huge Sunland spread.

Pedrico was so touched he could not speak.

Amy gently touched the aging Mexican's face and said, "I'm only sorry I didn't think of it myself, Pedrico."

"Gracias, señora."

"De nada," Amy said, then turned to Magdelena. "Mag, please have the girls pack my bags. I'm going to New Orleans to bring Linda home."

Two days later Pedrico and Magdelena stood on Orilla's private railroad spur and said good-bye to Amy.

Hugging the frowning Magdelena, Amy said, "You are not to worry. As soon as I reach Galveston, I'll take a river steamer across the Gulf. When I arrive in New Orleans, Aunt Meg and Linda will be there to meet me."

"Promise me you and Linda will come back home soon," said Magdelena.

"We will. Now it's time to leave," Amy said. She turned, took the conductor's hand, and climbed the portable steps.

When the locomotive picked up speed and moved out of sight, Pedrico turned and said, "Magdelena, this may not be the most romantic time or place to ask, but will you do me the honor of becoming my wife?"

The stocky, graying woman looked up at the slender, silver-haired man. She said, "Ah, Pedrico, are you sure this is what you want?" She looked off toward the horizon. "You are a landowner now, a true grandee. You can have a fine lady."

Pedrico's one eye twinkled. He took Magdelena's hand, drew it to his lips, and kissed it. "My dear Magdelena, to me you have always been a fine lady."

44

Amy stood at the railing of the paddlewheeler, *Creole Lady*, and watched as the bustling New Orleans levee came up to meet her. A large crowd waited on the landing. A smiling black boy, seated atop a tall stack of cotton bales, enthusiastically played a banjo. People clapped their hands and tapped their feet. Everyone was in a holiday mood.

Amy eagerly searched the smiling faces below. She began to wave and shout when she spotted her beautiful, dark-eyed daughter jumping up and down on the wooden wharf. Pink cotton-candy dress swirling up around her olive knees, thick, dark hair spilling around her slender shoulders, Linda looked as if she had grown a foot since leaving Orilla.

Blowing kisses and waving, Amy shifted her gaze to the well-dressed woman standing beside Linda. She gasped. She hardly recognized her dear Aunt Meg. Meg had always been pale and slender, but the woman whose gloved hand rested atop Linda's shoulder was deathly pallid and as thin as a rail. Beneath a small, fashionable straw hat, the hair that had remained a pale gold for so long had turned completely to silver.

It meant nothing, Amy told herself. After all, it had been a few years since she'd seen her adored aunt. Meg Sullivan had aged, just as she herself had aged.

The *Creole Lady,* her whistles blasting, paddlewheels churning up a thick, white foam, moved gracefully into her berth on the levee and the next thing Amy knew, she was rushing down the long gangplank and straight into the outstretched arms of her excited young daughter.

They rode through long tree-lined boulevards of the Crescent City, all talking at once, and by the time the carriage pulled up in front of Aunt Meg's St. Charles Street home, it was nearing dinnertime. After old Stella's passing, Meg had never replaced her, so she took off her hat, dropped it on the table in the foyer, and announced she would prepare the meal while mother and daughter visited.

"Wait," Amy said, and touched Meg's thin arm. "Aunt Meg, you look a little tired. Let me cook dinner, I've learned to—"

"Nonsense," said her aunt, smiling warmly. "Linda and I have been planning this meal all week." She winked at Linda.

Reluctantly Amy allowed the frail-looking woman to fix dinner. She sat in Meg's pleasant parlor and listened attentively while her talkative daughter filled her in on the most adventurous summer of her life.

Later, after Linda had gone up to bed, Meg, sharing a cup of strong black tea with Amy, looked at the younger woman and said, "Amy, dear, you are more beautiful than you've ever been in your life."

"Oh, now, Aunt Meg."

"It's true. How long has it been? Three years since you and Linda last came to visit." Meg studied Amy thoughtfully. "You were always a pretty girl, but now . . . it's . . . you . . ." She laughed softly and added, "Dear, you look for all the world like a woman who has learned the sweet mystery of love. I'm so happy for you . . ." She stopped speaking and a hand went to her bosom. "Amy, darling, what is it?"

"Oh, Aunt Meg, I—I—" Amy shook her head.

"What, child?" Meg set her cup aside and moved quickly to the sofa beside Amy. "Tell me what's troubling you."

Amy told her. Told her the truth. Told of the summer she'd spent with Luiz Quintano. Told her she loved him, had always loved him. Told her that Linda was Luiz's child. Told of the terrible guilt she was feeling because of Doug Crawford.

To her relief, Amy found that her prim and proper aunt did not scold or lecture or even appear shocked. Instead Aunt Meg put her slender arms around Amy and soothed her, saying all the kind, understanding things Amy most needed to hear.

"I'm so ashamed." Amy sobbed.

"My dear, don't be. There is nothing shameful about true love."

After Amy had poured out her heart, the compassionate Meg Sullivan kissed her hot cheek and said, "How would you like to have your old auntie tuck you into your bed, just like when you were Linda's age?"

They climbed the stairs together and Meg gently washed Amy's tear-reddened face and helped her don her nightgown. Exhausted, Amy got into the soft, clean bed. Meg drew the lace-trimmed sheet up to Amy's waist, sat down on the bed's edge, and said, "Sleep well, my child. I'm here to watch over you." She leaned down and kissed Amy's forehead.

Amy, feeling as safe from all harm as when she had been a child visiting in this peaceful, well-run house, sighed deeply and fell into a deep, sound slumber.

Come morning, Amy woke with the sun. Disoriented for only a moment, she drew on a robe and tiptoed downstairs. She would surprise her aunt and Linda by cooking a big, hearty breakfast.

But when she reached the kitchen, she found her aunt standing before the kitchen window pouring an amber-hued liquid medicine from a large bottle into a teaspoon. A jolt of alarm slammed through Amy as she silently watched the frail woman swallow three spoonfuls.

She said nothing, but Aunt Meg sensed her presence. The older woman slowly turned and looked at Amy.

"What is it, Aunt Meg?" Amy moved toward her.

"Dr. Wise says it's a rare tropical blood disease. There's a long clinical name for it, but I can't—"

"How serious?"

Meg Sullivan inhaled deeply. "It's fatal." She gave Amy a weak smile and said, "I'm so glad I got to see you one last time."

"Dear God," Amy said, tears springing to her eyes. She hurried to her aunt, clasped her narrow shoulders, and said, "Now the first thing we will do is find another doctor!"

"Dear, specialists in the field of hematology

have been consulted. They've all come to the same conclusion. I'm afraid we just have to face it. I've only a few weeks left."

Amy swallowed back the lump in her throat. Decisively she said, "Then we will face it together. You'll come home to Orilla where you belong and we'll—"

"No," Meg said, and gently pulled away. She again stared out at her magnolia trees. "I can't do that, Amy."

"Of course you can. Don't you want to be with your family? With Linda and me?"

Tears filling her eyes, Meg Sullivan said, "Yes, but that's impossible."

"Why? I don't understand. I've never understood why you always refused to come home to Orilla. Even for a visit. I used to ask Daddy to make you come back, but he wouldn't do it. Do you hate Texas so much? Or the ranch? Is that why you left and never returned?"

"Dear lord, is that what you think?" Meg Sullivan asked.

"I don't know what to think," Amy replied truthfully.

Meg took Amy's hand, pressed it to her cheek, and said, "Amy, Amy . . . you are not the only one guilty of deception. Walter Sullivan was guilty. I am guilty."

Puzzled, Amy said, "You? I don't believe it."

Meg Sullivan looked at the dear face before her and said, "I left Texas all those years ago because I was pregnant."

Speechless, Amy stared at the pale, sick woman as Meg calmly revealed that Amy was her daughter, not her niece. She had not married Amy's father, because he already had a wife. A handsome, prominent man from San Antonio, he had spent a few weeks in Sundown while his wife toured Europe. He was suave and sophisticated and Meg had fallen hopelessly in love with him.

They had shared brief, romantic encounters in a number of secret hideaways, and a week after he had to return to San Antonio, she learned she was carrying his child.

Her brother, Walter, immediately sent her and his wife, Mary, to New Orleans. He told everyone in Sundown that Mary was pregnant and was going to New Orleans to wait for the birth of their baby.

"And so," Meg softly concluded, "when you were but a few weeks old, Mary Sullivan took you home to Texas. She and Walter raised you as their daughter. He thought it best if I never came back. He was afraid someone might see the strong resemblance between us and guess the truth."

"Dear God," Amy said with empathy, "how you have suffered, Mother."

Meg Sullivan smiled through her tears. "All my life I've longed to hear you call me that."

"Mother, Mother, Mother," crooned Amy, and wrapped her arms around the thin, sobbing woman. "Listen to me, Mother, you are coming home to Orilla, and I don't give a damn if everyone in Sundown finds out I'm your daughter!"

Meg Sullivan pulled back and smiled with maternal pride at the strong young woman before her. "I *would* like to spend my last days in my beloved Texas."

The trio arrived at Orilla the first week in October. It was still warm and dry in southwest Texas, the days sunny and perfect.

But with the approach of autumn, those golden days were already beginning to grow short. Just like the golden days left to Margaret Sullivan.

Amy was determined to make her mother's last precious days as perfect as the fall weather. The two women spent every waking minute together. They talked for hours on end, recalling happy times, sharing secrets and foolish dreams, and laughing often, like a couple of young carefree girls.

They shopped. They cooked. They took long walks. They went horseback riding. They got up early. They stayed up late. They did everything and anything they took a notion to do.

The warm, glorious autumn days stretched on and the pair began to plan a wedding celebration. Pedrico and Magdelena had set their wedding date, and Amy and Meg meant to go all out for the happy occasion. Pale-blue eyes atwinkle, the ever-romantic Meg Sullivan eagerly planned the up-coming late November affair.

She never lived to see it.

One week before the big day, Margaret Sullivan passed away. She died peacefully in the arms of her loving daughter.

Insisting that her mother would have wanted it that way, Amy persuaded Magdelena and Pedrico to go ahead with the wedding. Plans for a lavish affair were dropped. The couple married quietly and before they left for a brief honeymoon trip, Magdelena hugged Amy and said, "I do not want to go away and leave you alone."

"I am not alone. I have Linda. You're going," Amy ordered.

The newlyweds went and the next day the

warm, lovely weather abruptly changed. There
was a nip in the air in the mornings, and by dusk it
was cold enough to need a fire in the fireplace at
Orilla.

With her mother gone, Amy felt a deep loneliness, but a strange kind of peace as well. They had
shared an unforgettable few weeks. Just as she and
Tonatiuh had shared an unforgettable few weeks.
More than most people could hope for in a lifetime.

On a chill gray day toward the end of November, Amy was in a melancholy mood. She rode
alone to the Puesta del Sol where, long ago, she
and Tonatiuh first made love.

Last made love.

Beneath the heavy, dismal skies, Amy sat down
on the smooth riverbank. Arms hugging her
knees, she stared pensively out at the cold, mirror-
smooth water.

Suddenly a cold autumn wind from out of the
north disturbed the river's placid surface. It lifted
loose tendrils of blond hair about her face and
knifed through her clothes to chill her. She shivered. An eerie feeling came over her.

The wind stilled and died. The dark, heavy
clouds rolled away. A bright, warming sun appeared and cast its dazzling brilliance over everything.

Amy's breath grew short. Her heart began to
pound. Slowly she lifted hopeful eyes.

And there the Indian stood.

Naked in the sunlight.

Author's Note

There was no private railroad spur in Sundown, Texas. But, then, there was no Sundown, Texas, either.

Most readers are aware that the railroad did not reach this remote part of America until much later in the nineteenth century. A small liberty to enhance the story.

And wouldn't owning a private railroad spur be romantic?

Nan Ryan

FREE FROM DELL

with purchase plus postage and handling

Congratulations! You have just purchased one or more titles featured in Dell's Romance 1990 Promotion. Our goal is to provide you with quality reading and entertainment, so we are pleased to extend to you a limited offer to receive a selected Dell romance title(s) *free* (plus $1.00 postage and handling per title) for each romance title purchased. Please read and follow all instructions carefully to avoid delays in your order.

1) Fill in your name and address on the coupon printed below. No facsimiles or copies of the coupon allowed.

2) The Dell Romance books are the only books featured in Dell's Romance 1990 Promotion. Any other Dell titles are not eligible for this offer.

3) Enclose your original cash register receipt with the price of the book(s) circled plus $1.00 **per book** for postage and handling, payable in check or money order to: Dell Romance 1990 Offer. Please do not send cash in the mail.
   Canadian customers: Enclose your original cash register receipt with the price of the book(s) circled plus $1.00 **per book** for postage and handling in U.S. funds.

4) This offer is only in effect until March 29, 1991. Free Dell Romance requests postmarked after March 22, 1991 will not be honored, but your check for postage and handling will be returned.

5) Please allow 6-8 weeks for processing. Void where taxed or prohibited.

Mail to: Dell Romance 1990 Offer
            P.O. Box 2088
            Young America, MN 55399-2088

NAME_____

ADDRESS_____

CITY_____STATE_____ZIP_____

BOOKS PURCHASED AT _____

AGE_____

(Continued)

Book(s) purchased:_____

_____

_____

I understand I may choose one free book for each Dell Romance book purchased (plus applicable postage and handling). Please send me the following:

(Write the number of copies of each title selected next to that title.)

☐ **MY ENEMY, MY LOVE**
Elaine Coffman
From an award-winning author comes this compelling historical novel that pits a spirited beauty against a hard-nosed gunslinger hired to forcibly bring her home to her father. But the gunslinger finds himself unable to resist his captive.

☐ **AVENGING ANGEL**
Lori Copeland
Jilted by her thieving fianceé, a woman rides west seeking revenge, only to wind up in the arms of her enemy's brother.

☐ **A WOMAN'S ESTATE**
Roberta Gellis
An American woman in the early 1800s finds herself ensnared in a web of family intrigue and dangerous passions when her English nobleman husband passes away.

☐ **THE RAVEN AND THE ROSE**
Virginia Henley
A fast-paced, sexy novel of the 15th century that tells a tale of royal intrigue, spirited love, and reckless abandon.

☐ **THE WINDFLOWER**
Laura London
She longed for a pirate's kisses. . . even though she was kidnapped in error and forced to sail the seas on his pirate ship, forever a prisoner of her own reckless desire.

☐ **TO LOVE AN EAGLE**
Joanne Redd
Winner of the 1987 *Romantic Times* Reviewer's Choice Award for Best Western Romance by a New Author.

☐ **SAVAGE HEAT**
Nan Ryan
The spoiled young daughter of a U.S. Army General is kidnapped by a Sioux chieftain out of revenge and is at first terrified, then infuriated, and finally hopelessly aroused by him.

☐ **BLIND CHANCE**
Meryl Sawyer
Every woman wants to be a star, but what happens when the one nude scene she'd performed in front of the cameras haunts her, turning her into an underground sex symbol?

☐ **DIAMOND FIRE**
Helen Mittermeyer
A gorgeous and stubborn young woman mu : choose between protecting the dangerous secrets of her past or trusting and loving a mysterious millionaire who has secrets of his own.

☐ **LOVERS AND LIARS**
Brenda Joyce
She loved him for love's sake, he seduced her for the sake of sweet revenge. This is a story set in Hollywood, where there are two types of people—lovers and liars.

☐ **MY WICKED ENCHANTRESS**
Meagan McKinney
Set in 18th-century Louisiana, this is the tempestous and sensuous story of an impoverished Scottish heiress and the handsome American plantation owner who saves her life, then uses her in a dangerous game of revenge.

☐ **EVERY TIME I LOVE YOU**
Heather Graham
A bestselling romance of a rebel Colonist and a beautiful Tory loyalist who reincarnate their fiery affair 200 years later through the lives of two lovers.

Dell

**TOTAL NUMBER OF FREE BOOKS SELECTED _____ X $1.00
= $_____ (Amount Enclosed)**

Dell has other great books in print by these authors. If you enjoy them, check your local book outlets for other titles.